continued .

D0289149

Inferno's KISS

MONICA BURNS

BERKLEY SENSATION, NEW YORK

THE BERKLEY PUBLISHING GROUP
Published by the Penguin Group
Penguin Group (USA) Inc.
375 Hudson Street, New York, New York 10014, USA
Penguin Group (Canada), 90 Eglinton Avenue East, Suite 700, Toronto, Ontario M4P 2Y3, Canada
(a division of Pearson Penguin Canada Inc.)
Penguin Books Ltd., 80 Strand, London WC2R 0RL, England
Penguin Group Ireland, 25 St. Stephen's Green, Dublin 2, Ireland (a division of Penguin Books Ltd.)
Penguin Group (Australia), 250 Camberwell Road, Camberwell, Victoria 3124, Australia
(a division of Pearson Australia Group Pty. Ltd.)
Penguin Books India Pvt. Ltd., 11 Community Centre, Panchsheel Park, New Delhi—110 017, India
Penguin Group (NZ), 67 Apollo Drive, Rosedale, Auckland 0632, New Zealand
(a division of Pearson New Zealand Ltd.)
Penguin Books (South Africa) (Pty.) Ltd., 24 Sturdee Avenue, Rosebank, Johannesburg 2196,
South Africa

Penguin Books Ltd., Registered Offices: 80 Strand, London WC2R 0RL, England

This book is an original publication of The Berkley Publishing Group.

PRINTING HISTORY
Berkley Sensation trade paperback edition / October 2011

Library of Congress Cataloging-in-Publication Data

Burns, Monica.
 Inferno's kiss / Monica Burns.—Berkley Sensation trade paperback ed.
 p. cm.—(Order of the Sicari novels ; 3)
 ISBN 978-0-425-24314-5 (pbk)
 1. Female assassins—Fiction. 2. Imaginary wars and battles—Fiction. I. Title.
 PS3602.U76645I54 2011
 813'.6—dc23   2011025931

PRINTED IN THE UNITED STATES OF AMERICA

10 9 8 7 6 5 4 3 2 1

For Kati and Scott.
May your happily ever after be filled with joy,
love, laughter, and everything romance.

ACKNOWLEDGMENTS

I would like to express my thanks to Sensei Flavio Matias and Master Steve Turkington of the Action Martial Arts studio in Leamington, Ontario, Canada, for providing information on martial arts pressure point techniques, sometimes referred to as the "death touch." I would also like to thank K. T. Grant for reading and dissecting Cleo and Dante's story. You gave me insight when I had none.

Finally, for all my Facebook reader friends who encouraged me to trudge on in the creation of this book. You will never know how much your words of encouragement helped me push on to finish this book. Thank you for you support.

Chapter 1

"I don't understand why you didn't tell me."

Atia heard the angry confusion in her daughter's voice and trembled at the wave of grief and fear welling up inside her. Never in her wildest dreams had she ever envisioned being backed into a corner so bleak and inescapable twice in a matter of hours. First Gabriel and now Cleo. She didn't think she could bear losing both of her children in the same day.

Images from the Pantheon flashed through Atia's head. The vivid memory of Gabriel attacking his father and Marcus being forced to kill their son still filled her with horror. The terrible moment had played over and over in her head ever since their return to the safe house.

Then there was Phaedra and her sacrifice. First she'd saved Marcus from certain death, only to do the same for Lysander before lapsing into a coma. Atia had never seen Lysander so distraught, and with Ares's help, he'd taken Phaedra to the Order's private hospital in Genova. Outside the study window of the Rome installation, the city was starting to stir. But she wasn't ready to face the new day. Nor was she ready to face the inevitable now.

"Tell me why, Mother." Cleo's voice was soft, yet inflexible. "Why didn't you tell me I had a brother?"

"Because it was too painful." Atia knew the question was her chance to tell Cleo the truth, but her courage was wafer thin. "The Praetorians . . ."

She looked at Marcus as her voice trailed away to nothing. His features were rigid with his own grief and guilt. A guilt she wanted to tell him not to feel. He looked at her for a long moment before he turned to Cleo.

"The Collegium kidnapped Gabriel before you were born. He was two when they took him and trained him to hate the Sicari," Marcus said quietly with a grief that tugged at Atia's heart.

She could feel the anguish and sorrow vibrating off him, but she didn't know how to comfort him. Perhaps she never would. Yet despite all he'd been through tonight in the Pantheon, there was a strength flowing from him that bolstered her flagging spirits.

It reminded her why he was the reigning Sicari Lord. She wanted to reach out to him but bowed her head with grief instead. The emotion battered every inch of her as she struggled to retain her composure. The loss of Gabriel and all that might have been if she'd kept him safe consumed her with sorrow. She shuddered, and an instant later, Cleo's arms were wrapped around her.

"I'm sorry, Mother."

The simplicity of her daughter's words and the warmth of her hug reminded Atia just how big her daughter's heart was. Despite her tough exterior, Cleo had a soft side she didn't display often. Now the heartfelt sympathy of her daughter's embrace pushed tears against her eyelids, but Atia refused to cry. She needed all her wits about her for what was to come. Cleo released her and looked in Marcus's direction.

"I'm sorry for your loss, Eminence, and the manner in which you lost your son." Cleo's gentle sympathy made Marcus flinch.

Atia drew in a sharp breath at the pinched look on his face. He'd been forced to kill their son, and it was her fault. She'd not done what she should have done all those years ago. As a result, her penance might very well be the death of her relationship with Cleo. And it was more than possible Cleo wouldn't forgive her for hiding the truth.

"Cleo . . . I need . . ." *Deus*, she didn't know how to do this. Telling Cleo that her father was alive was the hardest thing Atia had ever done. "There's something else I have to tell you."

"What?" Cleo turned toward her mother, and the puzzlement on her beautiful face quickly became an expression of horror. "No. Please don't tell me my father was a Praetorian."

"No, *carissima*, no." Atia reached out and caught Cleo's hands in hers. "Your father isn't a Praetorian."

"Isn't?" Cleo frowned. Atia tried to swallow the lump of fear closing her throat.

"Your father isn't dead."

"*What?*" Cleo's voice was so soft, Atia almost wondered if her daughter had said anything at all.

"I know I should have told you, but—"

"You *knew?*"

A dark silence filled the room as Atia studied her daughter's stunned expression. With a slow movement, Cleo pulled her hands out of her mother's, and Atia drew in a sharp breath. Fear speared its way through her as the shock on Cleo's face slowly gave way to a cold, marblelike expression. Not even the sunlight streaming through the French doors eased the chill seeping its way through the study of the safe house. She'd expected outrage. Fury, even, but not this icy silence.

Cleo was never at a loss for words. Never. Even as a child, she had openly expressed her enthusiasm or dislike for anything and everything. Not even when Cleo had been hurting so badly over Michael's betrayal had she been like this. Silent and completely emotionless. Atia swallowed the bile rising in her throat and frantically tried to form a plan of action. Her daughter's silence was the one thing she'd not expected.

Desperately, she tried to think of something that would force Cleo to say something. *Deus*, how she wished she'd done things differently. No. She'd done the right thing. Cleo's safety had been the only thing she'd cared about. She would give her life for her daughter.

The mantel clock over the fireplace announced the morning hour with six melancholy chimes. The sound penetrated the room like a soft death knell. Beside her, Marcus assessed Cleo's mood with a deliberate patience that was frighteningly familiar even after all the years they'd been apart.

The tendrils of his thoughts mixed with hers for an instant before she recoiled from the gentle mental probe. He pulled his thoughts from hers with an unspoken apology. Fingers interlocked in a tight grip, Atia fought not to reach out and pull her daughter into her arms. She was certain doing so would only make things worse.

"Cleo, I wanted to tell—"

"*Don't*." The command was an angry hiss of fire on ice, and Atia flinched beneath Cleo's harsh stare. "You lied to me."

"*No!*" Atia exclaimed.

"Exactly what do you call it, *Mother*?" The sneer in Cleo's voice was a blade striking deep into Atia.

"I never said your father was dead. I simply allowed you to believe it. It was to protect you." It was a pitiful defense, and she knew it.

"Protect me from what, exactly?" Cleo said coldly. "I *have* no abilities. Not even the fucking Praetorians would know what to do with me."

"They could . . . you could have passed on your father's abilities to a child."

"Well, those *bastardi* fixed *that* problem three years ago, didn't they?"

Atia didn't look at Marcus, but her body was so attuned to his that she could tell the instant he went rigid at their daughter's words. She knew she should have explained Cleo's tragedy to him before now, but she'd been consumed with the fear of what would happen when she told Cleo the truth about her brother and father. She'd felt too fragile to deal with anything else. Now it made her look even more deceitful.

Her gaze shifted back to Cleo's face, and she caught the brief flash of despair crossing her daughter's face. Atia's stomach lurched. Her beautiful daughter would never know the joy of motherhood. That had been snatched from Cleo's hands the minute a Praetorian blade had killed Cleo's unborn child and left her barren. But Cleo wouldn't know the pain, either. The pain that came from trying to protect your child. And Atia had done everything she could to protect Cleo.

She'd lost her head more than thirty years ago, when she'd succumbed to Marcus at La Terrazza del Ninfeo. But Atia had never regretted having Cleo in her life, and everything she'd done for her daughter had been out of love. She pushed through her grief to find the strength to reach out to her daughter once more. Her son was lost to her forever, and now she had to fight to keep her daughter.

Cleo hated it when anyone lied to her, and Atia had done that, albeit through the sin of omission. She'd allowed her daughter to believe her father was dead. And it was a lie Cleo might never forgive her for. Marcus's tall, imposing presence at her side only emphasized how much Cleo had to forgive.

"I did it to protect—"

"Who is he?"

It wasn't a question. It was a command. Atia's voice died in her throat as she saw the contempt on Cleo's face. With a shake of her head, she fought to find her voice, and the seconds expanded into a long silence before Marcus cleared his throat.

"I am."

The quiet authority in Marcus's statement made Atia sag slightly as Cleo's anger and contempt gave way to shock again. Surely now she could make Cleo understand that as the daughter of a Sicari Lord, her safety had been Atia's only thought. Hands trembling, she reached out to Cleo, but her arms fell to her sides as Cleo took a step back from her. The silent move of rejection was like a poison that spread its way through her limbs, leaving pain in its wake.

"Your father and I—"

"*Don't* say that." As if suddenly remembering her place, Cleo turned and bowed her head stiffly at the Sicari Lord. "Forgive me, *il mio signore*. I mean no disrespect."

"We realize this is a shock, but I understand your mother's motives, *carissima*." Marcus's voice was soft and level, but Atia heard the note of regret in his words.

He had nothing to be remorseful for. This was all her doing. Atia briefly closed her eyes against the painful thought. If only things had been different. She looked at Cleo again, and the stubborn gleam in her daughter's violet eyes only heightened her fear. Atia didn't want to lose her. She'd already lost one child tonight. To lose another would be unbearable. Somehow she had to make Cleo understand her reasons for hiding the truth.

"I didn't tell *anyone* who your father was. Not even Ignacio. And

I didn't tell your . . ." She saw Cleo's expression harden. "I didn't even tell Marcus."

"So you *chose* to let me grow up without a father."

"I *chose* to keep you safe. And I'd do it again," Atia snapped, her fear and frustration getting the better of her.

"Safe from what? Every goddamn member of the Order is always at risk. What makes me so special?"

"You are the daughter of a Sicari Lord. The Praetorians would have stopped at nothing to take you like they did Gabriel." Atia stepped forward to reach out to her daughter again. She tried to touch her cheek, but Cleo smacked her hand away.

"I still had the right to know," Cleo said in a tight voice.

"And I had a duty to protect you," Atia replied with determination.

"Duty or not, *Madame Consul*, you lied to me. You lied to me about my brother, you lied to me about who my father is, and you allowed me to believe he was dead."

The formality of Cleo's address made Atia sway slightly. An unseen hand settled on her shoulder to steady her. She waved her hand at Marcus to dismiss the touch. His offer of comfort couldn't ease her fears.

"I was terrified of something happening to you, *carissima*. The thought of the Praetorians taking you the way they took Gabriel . . . it was unbearable." Atia's quiet statement sent a flash of understanding across Cleo's face before her expression hardened again. It was so reminiscent of her father's.

"I can understand why you'd keep me in the dark when I was a child, but when I was older?" Cleo said fiercely.

"I wanted to tell you, but with each passing day it became harder to do so. I knew you'd see my silence as having lied to you, and I was afraid."

"Afraid?" Cleo snorted with angry disbelief. "You're fearless, Mother. You take on Council members like a lioness does her prey. You chose not to tell me the truth because it was easier not to."

"It was *not* easier. From the moment you were born, I've lived in fear. If the Praetorians had known who your father was, they would have stopped at nothing to take you like they did Gabriel."

"So why now? Why not three years ago?" Cleo bit out. "You couldn't tell me the truth then? The Praetorians don't have any use for women they can't breed."

"If I had told you then, would it have changed anything?"

"*Yes.* No. I don't know. But you should have told me." Cleo's voice echoed with confusion, and Atia ached to reach out to her daughter and fold her into her arms, just as she had when Cleo was younger.

"Please, Cleo. I want us to—" She started to close the physical distance between them, but Cleo jumped back.

"*No,*" Cleo snapped. "Not another word, Mother. *Now,* unless there's some *other* dark secret you'd like to reveal, may I leave?"

Once again, Atia leaned toward her daughter, but Marcus stepped forward to intercept her. The physical touch of his fingers digging into her arm silently ordered her not to continue.

"We understand you need time to adjust to everything your mother has shared with you this morning." Marcus's voice was one of serene calm, but Atia couldn't tell if it had any effect on Cleo. His voice softened even more. "I know how difficult this must be for you, Cleopatra. It wasn't easy for me when your mother told me about you only two weeks ago. But if you'll give me the opportunity, I'd like to get to know you. All I ask is that you think about it."

Cleo acknowledged him with a sharp nod. She hesitated for a fraction of a second, and Atia thought she might say something, but Cleo simply wheeled about on one heel to stalk out of the study without a glance in Atia's direction.

The moment the door closed behind her daughter, Atia jerked away from Marcus and slowly circled the corner of the desk to sink down into the leather office chair. She'd lost her. Cleo would never forgive her for not telling her the truth. Head bowed, she closed her eyes and tried to think, but she couldn't. For the first time in a very long time, she didn't have a plan. Didn't have any sense of what direction to turn. It made her feel lost and alone.

"She'll eventually see her way to forgive you." At Marcus's quiet statement, she lifted her head up to look at him.

"No. She won't," she said bitterly. "You don't know her like I do."

"You're right. I don't." There was no accusation in his words. It was just a simple observation, but it filled her with guilt all the same.

"She hates being lied to. It started when she was a child. Her best friend fell three stories when the two of them were playing on the rampart of the east wing at the White Cloud estate. I told Cleo her friend would live. The child died. She's demanded the truth ever since. She can be very unforgiving."

"Then we'll make her see you had no other choice."

"And do *you* believe I had no other choice?" She met his gaze steadily, remembering how furious he'd been when he'd learned of Cleo's existence.

"You did what I would have done. You protected our daughter," he said quietly, but there was a flash of emotion in his vivid blue eyes that worried her. "I can't fault you for not telling her the truth."

"But?"

"You should have told *me*, Atia. I had a right to know that I had a daughter. I could have watched her grow up from a distance. You denied me even that small joy."

"If you want me to say I'm sorry, I can't." She shook her head. "I couldn't risk you taking her from me."

"And yet you risked her life in attempting to raise her alone, thinking no one would discover your secret. I could have helped protect her."

"Her life was at risk no matter what course of action I took." She bristled with resentment. "I did what I thought best for my daughter. I won't apologize for that."

"Our daughter." The fierce intensity of his words emphasized that he was still angry she'd hidden the truth from him. Like Cleo, he would have a hard time forgiving her. And the fact that she wanted his forgiveness frightened her. It showed how quickly he was becoming a part of her life again.

"Our daughter." She nodded with resignation.

Eyes closed, her fingers rubbed at her temple. Another headache. They seemed to come so often these days. A gentle, unseen touch stroked her forehead, and she sighed at the invisible caress.

"Why are you so certain Cleo won't forgive you?" At the quiet question, she raised her head to meet his puzzled gaze. "Her concern for you last night at the Pantheon demonstrated how much she loves you."

"Cleo is like you. She has a stubborn streak. When she makes up her mind about something, it's difficult to convince her otherwise."

"Then perhaps she's met her match in me."

Although his gaze was somber, there was just a hint of amusement curving his lips as he watched her. It stirred something deep inside her that helped ease some of the grief still assaulting her body. She closed her eyes at the memory of Gabriel's death and how close Marcus had come to joining their son.

A tear squeezed its way out from under her eyelid, and a harsh oath escaped Marcus. Her eyes flew open in surprise at the sound, and she saw Marcus move quickly to pull her up out of the desk chair. The moment his arms wrapped around her, she burst into tears. A shudder went through him, and she knew she was shedding tears for both of them.

The grief she'd experienced the day the Praetorians had taken Gabriel from them had been different from the pain she was feeling now. Then, she'd been filled with terror for Gabriel's life and her own. She'd killed one Praetorian before the second one had dealt her what should have been a deathblow.

Until Cleo was born, she'd wished thousands of times that the Praetorians *had* killed her that horrible day. It would be better than living with the fact that she'd failed Gabriel. Failed to do her duty. She'd not had the courage to take her son's life that day. She'd allowed herself to hold on to the hope that she could defeat the *bastardi* that had surprised her and their bodyguards.

But she hadn't. And the Praetorians had laughed at her as they'd dragged a crying Gabriel from her arms. Like her, they'd been certain she was as good as dead. They'd taunted her with departing words about how Gabriel would become one of them.

It was a memory that haunted her every day. The *bastardi* had deliberately left her to die knowing the last few minutes of her life would be spent agonizing over the fate of her child. She was the one to blame for Gabriel. And the fact that she'd survived . . . if Marcus ever learned the truth, he'd never forgive her.

She'd lied to him. She'd told him she'd been unconscious when they'd taken Gabriel. Even if she'd had the strength to do so, she could not have killed their son just to keep the Praetorians from taking him. Suddenly, she wished she were far away from Rome.

She gently pulled out of his arms, grateful he'd not attempted to probe her thoughts. Her ability to keep her mental shield in place was sorely limited at this point. If he really wanted to know what she was thinking, he would have no difficulty breaking through her thoughts. The realization terrified her.

To face his condemnation so soon after Gabriel's death heightened the deep-seated fear that had never left her since the day of their son's kidnapping. Afraid her expression might reveal more than she cared for him to see, Atia turned from Marcus and brushed away the wetness on her cheeks.

"What are you afraid of, *mea kara*?" His voice was a soft caress on her senses.

My beloved. The endearment enveloped her with warmth. It made her feel treasured. Safe. And it emphasized her vulnerability where Marcus was concerned. She had always wanted to tell him the truth, just as she had wanted to tell him about Cleo. She simply hadn't ever found the courage to do so.

Her inability to explain her mistake only emphasized the fact that she'd never stopped loving him. She trembled as his hand caught her chin, and he forced her to look at him. There was a frown of concern on his face as he studied her. She pulled away from his touch and shook her head.

"I'm not afraid, Eminence." She winced at the dark cloud of irritation that swept over his features. "With your permission, I'll take the *Tyet of Isis* back to White Cloud. It's not safe here in Italy."

"Agreed," Marcus growled. "I need to speak with Dante before we leave."

"We?" She hadn't meant to sound so sharp.

"Yes. We," he said in a firm voice. "I wish to examine the documents that are in the artifact." The minute he mentioned the artifact, she stiffened. The thought of working closely with him in studying the antiquity was alarming. She swallowed the knot in her throat.

"The Order has several researchers, including me, who are extremely knowledgeable about the *Tyet of Isis*," Atia said.

"Perhaps, but I wish to examine the parchment as well. My memories of my past life as Tevy may prove useful."

"But—"

"No arguments, Atia. I'll not be put off in this matter." His mouth thinned slightly with determination. "I intend to study the parchment with you. But that's not the only thing I plan on doing. I also intend to claim what is rightfully mine."

"And I told you that I'm not your property." A sharp hiss of air blew past her lips. "The blood bond is one of mutual agreement."

"Which you agreed to thirty-six years ago next month, if memory serves me correctly." His words made her jump with surprise. He remembered the day of their blood bond. His eyes narrowed. "Did you think I would forget? We belong to each other, Atia. And I'll go to Tartarus and back to make you see that."

The intensity in his voice made her even more apprehensive. He was acting as if everything between them was settled. It wasn't. And his arrogance in assuming so irritated her. Her gaze fell to the paperwork on her desk. Work. It had always been a sanctuary, and it would be again. She sank down into her chair and brushed several papers aside to find a pen.

"Forgive me, Eminence. I have work to catch up on." Her dispassionate comment pulled a sharp hiss of air from Marcus.

"You would try the patience of the Carpenter himself, Atia," he said harshly. "You always found it easier to hide from your problems than face them. I see nothing's changed."

"I'm not hiding from anything. As *Prima Consul* I have responsibilities I cannot avoid, and unlike you, I don't have someone waiting in the wings to help me perform those duties."

She didn't bother to look up at him as she spoke. A moment later, she felt him at her side and the instant the palm of his hand cracked loudly on the desktop in front of her, she jumped. He jerked her chair around with his other hand, and she retreated deeper into the soft leather as he bent over her.

"I'm willing to give you time, *carissima*, but nothing has changed since the other morning when we watched the sun rise over the city at La Terrazza del Ninfeo. I said you were mine, and I meant it."

"*Deus*, but you are an arrogant son of a bitch," she snapped as she violently pushed the chair and herself away from him to stand. "What makes you think you can walk back into my life and simply demand the right of blood bond? I've built a life without you, and as difficult as it might be to accept, I've been happy without you."

That wasn't exactly true. She'd learned to adapt and find happiness where she could. She didn't dare tell him how many nights she'd lain awake through the years wishing he were lying beside her. The number of sleepless nights had only increased since he'd summoned her to meet him in the Santa Maria sopra Minerva just a few short days ago when she'd arrived in Rome.

But it changed nothing. What they'd had in the past had cost her dearly. And she was too tired—too old—too scared to start over. She tightened her jaw and glared up at him. His vivid blue eyes immediately narrowed as he studied her face. It was that assessing look that always managed to see more than what she wanted to show. But over the years she'd had lots of practice hiding her thoughts from others. She'd mastered the skill as *Prima Consul*. With a vicious grunt of anger, he took a step toward her, and she immediately retreated. Something flashed in his eyes that made her want to reach out to him, but she forced herself to remain still.

"You said not too long ago that the past is always with you. It's with me as well. It would serve you well to remember that," he said harshly.

With one last hard look in her direction, he turned away and strode out of the study. Left alone, Atia stared at the closed door. He intended to have his way, and she was suddenly of a mind to let him do exactly as he wanted. She closed her eyes at the thought.

Marcus could be persuasive when he wanted to be. In the few short years of happiness they'd shared before Gabriel's kidnapping, she'd invariably given in to him when they argued. Even when he'd become leader of the *Absconditus*, he'd never forced her to do anything, despite the fact that his command was virtually law. He'd simply seduced her with words. And his touch.

The memory of those passionate moments in La Terrazza del Ninfeo caressed her thoughts. Cleo had been the result of that union. And now everything hung in the balance. Just as it had when Gabriel had been kidnapped. The heartache of that event had driven a wedge between her and Marcus. It was the only time Marcus had ever deserted her.

She'd needed him in those days and weeks after Gabriel had been taken from them. But he'd shut her out. He'd carried a burden of guilt that wasn't his to carry. Perhaps she would have been able to tell him the truth if he'd not left her. She shuddered as the memories rushed at her with the fury of a raging Praetorian. Legs weak, she sank back into her chair.

Perhaps Cleo was right. Maybe she didn't know how to tell the truth. But then the truth was never as easy to reveal as her daughter thought. Her fingers brushed across the papers on her desk. She was anything *but* fearless. She was a coward. That was the real reason she didn't want Marcus back in her life. She didn't have the courage it would take to face him and the truth. Like Cleo, it was unlikely he would forgive her sin. She closed her eyes and leaned back in her chair trying desperately not to let the tears flow. She failed.

At the soft knock on the office door, she jerked upright. Had Cleo returned? The sight of Ignacio stepping into view made her release a sigh of disappointment as she quickly wiped her eyes dry. Although the sound was barely audible, she knew Ignacio had heard it because his jaw tightened. Atia's heart sank. Their friendship had always been something she cherished. Why hadn't she realized before now that the man wanted something more than friendship from her? The answer was easy. There had never, and never would be, anyone but Marcus.

TEARS glistened in Atia's beautiful gray eyes as Ignacio closed the office door behind him. He saw her hands tremble as she hastily brushed the dampness from her cheeks. The last time he'd seen her cry was when the doctors had told them Cleo would never have any children. Ignacio's gut tightened. He'd never meant to fall in love with her. He'd known better, but he'd succumbed anyway.

Until a few nights ago, he'd actually begun to believe he could persuade her to give up the ghosts of her past. A foolish thought. He knew it was a futile hope. The fact that Vorenus had reentered Atia's life only emphasized just how unrealistic he'd been.

Just thinking about the Sicari Lord made Ignacio's blood run hot with jealousy. The *bastardo* had simply strolled back into Atia's life as if she were some prize the Sicari Lord was entitled to. Ignacio didn't care that the two were blood bonded, it didn't entitle Vorenus to lay claim to Atia again after all these years.

"You should be in bed," Ignacio said gruffly.

"I wouldn't be able to sleep." She gestured toward the paperwork in front of her. "Work will help take my mind off of everything."

"I'm sorry about Gabriel." She would never know just how sorry he was.

"Thank you." She swallowed hard.

Fingers pressing into the desk, she bent her head as if studying the papers in front of her. Ignacio knew she wasn't reading. She'd lost her son tonight, and her grief was his. The thought propelled him forward. When he reached her, Atia stared up at him in surprise as he gently pulled her into his arms.

"I'm here for you, *carissima*. I always have been." It was the truth. From the first time he'd met her, Ignacio had made it his goal to become indispensible to her. It has been expected of him. In the process he'd fallen in love. He'd fought against it and had never spoken of his feelings to her until the night he'd discovered Vorenus was Cleo's father. He almost felt sorry for the man, finding out the way he had that Cleo was his daughter. Almost.

Cleo was the child Ignacio had never had. He'd tended to her scraped knees, taught her how to fight and a dozen more things any father would teach their children. He'd allowed himself to become such a part of their lives that he wasn't sure he would be able to let go when the time came. And that time would come. It loomed in front of him like the river Styx. He crushed the thought. There had to be a way to make Atia his, no matter what the obstacles.

"I take it Cleo didn't react well to the news." His simple statement made her flinch.

"No." She gently pushed herself out of his arms in a way that said she wanted to spare his feelings. "We've fought before, but this was different. I don't think she'll forgive me for not telling her about Marcus."

Ignacio bit down on the inside of his cheek at the way Atia's voice softened when she said the Sicari Lord's name. Did she even realize she'd revealed so much in that one word? He cleared his dry throat.

"We both know Cleo is stubborn, but she'll come around," he said as he grasped her hand. "She always does. I'll talk to her."

"No. She'll think I sent you."

"I think I know our . . ." He'd almost slipped and used the word daughter. "Cleo will be more reasonable in a couple of hours. She just needs time to cool off."

"You didn't see her, Ignacio." Atia shook her head.

The sorrow in her gaze made his heart ache for her. Without thinking, his hands cupped her face and he kissed her. It was a light kiss, but she immediately stiffened beneath the touch. Ignacio pulled away from her instantly. Fuck. Her reaction was like she'd just kissed a Praetorian. He winced.

"Forgive me," he murmured.

Flustered, and her cheeks bright with pink color, Atia stepped back from him with a wave of her hand. "I . . . you know I care for you, Ignacio. You're . . . I don't know what I would have done without you over the years. I value your friendship so much, and I don't want to lose you as a friend."

Atia's words cut deeper than any wound he'd ever suffered. Bitterness with the sharpness of an asp's sting hardened his heart. Friendship. He wanted more than that from her.

"You won't lose me. I've been here for you since the beginning." He'd learned to lie so well he wasn't sure what the truth was anymore.

"I know, and that's one of the reasons you're so dear to me. Without you, life would have been so much more difficult."

Was that her way of telling him that he didn't stand a chance with her? He didn't want to know. It might make him act too hastily. He lifted her hand and pressed his mouth against her skin. So soft. So sweet smelling. *Deus*, how he loved her. But it had been a mistake to become so involved with her. He needed to leave now or he'd tell her everything.

"I'll speak with Cleo," he rasped before he turned away from the sorrowful look in her gaze and stalked from the room.

Chapter 2

CLEO grunted as she took a hit to the back of her calf. It was like someone giving her an instant charley horse. She went down on one knee and waited for the pain to subside. She couldn't remember the last time she'd allowed herself to take such a beating. That wasn't true. Just a few days after a Praetorian blade ended her pregnancy and the doctors had told her that she could never have children, she'd gone looking for trouble. She'd found three different Sicari warriors at the White Cloud estate and deliberately insulted them.

It had been her attempt at cathartic exercise. It hadn't worked then, and she doubted it was going to work now. Mario would have been just as happy listening to her rant as he was to spar with her. But she needed to do something, and she wasn't ready to talk just yet. From the confusion on his face, though, she was certain he was wishing he'd offered her a bottle of beer instead. She grimaced.

Despite the short time they'd known each other, Mario knew her pretty well. Maybe not as well as Lysander and others she'd grown up with. But she and Mario had shared almost as many secrets between them as they had shared glasses of wine. She'd met the martial arts instructor several years ago when she'd visited Rome on assignment. They'd become fast friends and drinking buddies.

She should have realized he wouldn't beat her into the hazy oblivion she was seeking. *Christus*, if she'd given it any thought, she should have gone out looking to spill Praetorian blood. She needed something to help her forget that her mother had been lying to her for years about her father. She was the daughter of a Sicari Lord. A fucking Sicari Lord.

How in Jupiter's name was that possible? She didn't have the tiniest bit of Sicari abilities. No healing powers like Phae. No sensitive abilities like other Sicari women. Okay, maybe a molecule of precognition, but that was so fleeting and unreliable, it didn't count. Hell, she didn't have a drop of telekinetic ability her mother possessed.

"Come on, Cleo. I think you've had enough."

"*No*," she exclaimed in a hoarse voice. "*I* decide when I've had enough, not you."

"Damnit, Cleo. I don't want to hurt you," Mario snapped with frustration.

"Fuck you."

She wanted to numb the pain in her heart. A workout to the point of physical exhaustion might help her accomplish that now. She forced herself to block out the physical pain and got to her feet. Limping her way back across the training mat, she met Mario's exasperated gaze. With a jerk of her head, she invited him to attack her again. This time she wasn't going to let him past her defenses. The martial arts instructor shook his head in disgust as he reluctantly stepped forward.

With several quick hand strikes, she forced Mario into a defensive position. Deliberately ignoring the pain signals shooting up her injured leg, she kicked her good leg upward and landed a hard blow to the trainer's solar plexus. He staggered back, and Cleo leaped forward to throw two more hard punches to first his chest, then his side.

Mario landed flat on the hard rubber of the training floor with a thud. It should have made her feel good to drop him to the ground. It didn't. Instead, her desire to kick someone's ass was still pounding its way through her veins. *Deus*, where was a Praetorian when you needed one? An image of her dead brother flitted through her mind, as did the sound of her mother's cry of pain. Her throat closed up at the memory. Swallowing hard, Cleo limped across the mat to stand over Mario.

"Again," she said viciously. "And don't hold back this time."

"*Christus*, what the hell is the matter with you, Cleo?" her friend exclaimed fiercely. "If I really let loose on you, you're gonna get hurt."

"Again, you son of a bitch. Just because I don't have any special abilities doesn't mean I can't beat you."

The trainer arched his back then pushed himself to his feet in one fluid motion. "This is my training room, and I say you're finished for the day."

Something exploded inside her. Splinters of anguish, fear, and anger bombarded her heart, making her chest feel like it was on fire. She wasn't ready to quit. The physical pain wasn't bad enough to mask the hurt inside. She launched herself toward the trainer, her movements hard and fast as she tried to land one blow after another on Mario.

With a loud cry, she blocked his hand, and with a twist of her body, she tried to pull his arm behind him. He blocked her attempt with a blow to her midsection, which sent her flying backward until she crashed on the mat. Stunned, she slowly rolled over and came up on all fours. Her chest was still on fire, and she struggled to quiet her ragged breathing.

"That's enough." Ignacio's deep voice made Cleo turn her head.

Her mentor stood at the edge of the training mat, a dark scowl on his face. He pointed his finger in her direction before he ordered her off the hard rubber mat with a jerk of his thumb.

"Hit the showers, Cleo." His scowl grew darker when she started to protest. "*Now.*"

Something in Ignacio's voice penetrated the turmoil she'd been engulfed in since early this morning when her mother had introduced her to a father Cleo had always believed was dead. She didn't know what hurt worse, the fact that she'd lost out having a father while she was growing up or the fact that her mother had lied to her about it. Lied to her for almost thirty-three years.

That fact alone cut deep. With a nod of her head, she acknowledged Ignacio's orders and limped her way toward the edge of the mat. When she reached Mario, the worry in his expression made her feel ashamed of the way she'd been using him as a human punching bag.

"I'm an ass. I'm sorry," she said huskily.

"You don't need to apologize to me, *carissima*. Whatever's wrong, I know you're hurting," he muttered, his gruff voice muffled by her hair as he pulled her into a tight bear hug. "You don't fight like this unless you're trying to beat off some demon inside you. If it helps you let off a little steam, fine. But locking everything up inside you isn't good, *bambina*. It'll make you sloppy when you can least afford it."

"How do you always manage to make me feel like I belong when I feel like I'm on the outside looking in?" She swallowed hard and managed to fight back her tears at the affection in her friend's voice as she hugged him back.

"Outside looking in? Jupiter's Stone, *bella*. Is that what all of this is about? You not having special abilities?" Mario exclaimed softly. "*Christus*, don't you know how powerful you are? You're the most beautiful woman in Rome. Men see you coming and their jaws drop. They can't think straight when they see you. That's one hell of a powerful ability, if you ask me."

"It's not the same thing," she murmured.

Although she'd never hesitated to use her looks to her advantage, her face was a poor substitute for a Sicari ability. Her lack of powers wasn't a secret among the Sicari. With a mother who was such a prominent figure in the Order, it was natural that people talked. And now that she was barren, she had nothing to offer a Sicari warrior looking to ensure his family lineage continued, not to mention keeping the Sicari gene pool strong.

Michael had been her last chance at happiness, and even he'd deserted her at a time when she'd needed him the most. He'd left her to deal with the pain of her loss all alone. She swallowed the knot lodged in her throat as Mario frowned at her. It wasn't something she could make her friend understand. She doubted there were any Sicari who could understand how she felt.

"Damnit, Cleo." Mario gave her a slight shake. "You've got incredible fighting skills, you're intelligent, and you're drop-dead gorgeous. If you had anything else, you'd be a goddamn Sicari Lord."

The words made her grow cold. Her expression must have revealed her pain, because Mario eyed her with puzzled concern. Not about to explain, she forced a smile to her lips.

"I'm too sweaty to be drop-dead gorgeous," she said. From the look on Mario's face, her effort to sound cheerful fell short, and she turned away. "I'll talk to you later."

"How about I take you to dinner at that little place we went to last month? The one with the ziti you liked." At his offer, she glanced over her shoulder at him. The boyish grin on his face suddenly made her want to cry.

"You're just not going to let me have a self-pity party, are you?" she asked with a watery smile.

"Nope." Mario chuckled as he jerked his head toward the locker room. "Hit the showers like Ignacio said, then meet me in the salon this evening at six."

His gaze held hers for a moment before she nodded and made her way to the showers.

The ladies' locker room was empty, and Cleo winced as she tugged off her sweatpants. Every one of her muscles ached from the brutal workout she'd put herself through since early this morning. She glanced at the clock over the entryway. Seven hours.

It had been little more than seven hours since her mother had revealed the truth about who her father was. As if it wasn't bad enough to discover she had a brother. Correction. She *had* had a brother. What would things have been like if the Praetorians hadn't taken Gabriel? Would she have been as close to him as she was to Lysander?

She felt funny not mourning Gabriel like her mother was grieving. It was hard to be sorry he was dead when he'd been a Praetorian. Maybe not by birth, but in everything he'd done, Gabriel had been one of the enemy. For her mother it was clearly different. The *Prima Consul* mask was on, but Cleo had seen her mother's sorrow underneath. And despite the way her mother had lied to her, Cleo didn't like seeing her in pain. Then there was Marcus Vorenus. He'd been grieving, too, but his grief was buried even deeper than her mother's sorrow.

The image of the man fluttered through her head as she tugged off her shirt and stuffed it viciously into her gym bag. Here she was, saddled with a father she'd thought was dead, and a dead brother she never knew. It was like she was living some twisted Shakespearean tragedy.

She grabbed soap and shampoo from her locker and limped her way into the shower. The hot spray went a long way toward easing some of the tightness in her body, but the heat only alleviated the physical pain. It did nothing to ease the ache in her heart.

Her mother had lied to her. No, she'd simply not bothered to correct Cleo's assumption that her father was dead. It was a lie of omission and a betrayal of trust. Her mother had promised to always tell her the truth, no matter how much it might hurt.

Cleo had extracted that bargain from her mother as a child. She didn't doubt it had been a childish promise to demand, but even then her mother had known her father was alive. How was she supposed to forgive something like this, let alone believe anything her mother ever said again? And what about Marcus? A Sicari Lord. *Deus*, the irony of it was almost hysterically funny. She was the daughter of a man who had the strongest abilities of any Sicari, yet she had none. Zilch. Niente.

It only emphasized her feelings that she was an outsider among her own people. Not even Mario's comment about her not needing special powers could ease the sensation that she didn't fit in and never would. That feeling was something Michael had helped cement when he'd walked away from her three years ago. It wasn't just their child that had been lost to a Praetorian sword. Her ability to have children was lost, too, and Michael hadn't wanted to adopt. He'd wanted a child to carry on his lineage. She closed her eyes and willed the heartache to ease out of her. It didn't work, so she buried it and focused her thoughts on her shower.

A little more than twenty minutes later, she walked into the changing room to see Violetta sitting on the bench centered between two sets of lockers. The first time they'd met had been when they'd both been assigned to the team searching for the *Tyet of Isis*. She liked Violetta, but she wasn't someone Cleo felt close enough to confide in. She ignored the woman and went to her locker to dress. As Cleo pulled on a clean shirt, she heard Violetta clear her throat.

"Why don't you let me take a look at that leg of yours?"

"I'm fine."

She didn't look at Violetta as she pulled on a pair of jeans. Reaching for a comb, she viciously dragged it through her hair. When she'd finished, she gathered her long hair up in one hand and secured it in a ponytail with a scrunchie.

"Mario's worried you might have some nerve damage after the blow he gave your leg."

"I don't need the *Curavi* for sore muscles."

She knew healers sometimes saw things during the healing process. And even though healers swore to hold in confidence whatever they experienced in a healing session, she didn't want to risk Violetta discovering something Cleo wasn't willing to share just yet. Some small nugget of information like her long-lost father showing up, and that he just happened to be a Sicari Lord.

"Then you'd better tell that to Mario. He's convinced your leg is going to be permanently damaged if I don't heal you." There was a prickly tone to the woman's voice, and Cleo realized she'd been too sharp with the healer.

"I'm sorry. I shouldn't have bitten your head off like that," Cleo said with regret. She turned her head to look at the healer. "Mario's a worrywart. I don't deny that my leg still hurts, but I'll be fine."

"Most people are irritable when they're in pain. No apology needed." Violetta offered her a smile. "But I'll be honest. The way you walked in here a little while ago, you sure looked like someone who could benefit from a healer's touch."

"I'll be fine, but if the pain worsens, I promise I'll come see you."

"All right, but just so you know, Mario isn't the only one worried about you," Violetta said as she stood up. "Ignacio is waiting for you outside."

"*Fuck.*" Cleo's response made the healer laugh.

"I think that was *his* response when Mario explained how you got hurt. So be prepared to have him read you the riot act. And you know where to find me if you change your mind about that leg."

Still laughing, Violetta turned and left, leaving Cleo to stew about Ignacio waiting for her outside the locker room. Damn, she didn't want to deal with Ignacio's fatherly concern at the moment. She frowned. How was he going to feel when he learned Marcus Vorenus was her real father?

He would probably be just as blown away as she was. With a sharp movement, Cleo tossed her gear into her gym bag and slammed her locker shut. As she emerged from the locker room, she saw Ignacio leaning against the wall just outside the door.

"You should have put ice on that leg right away."

"It's sore muscles, not a sprain." Her response made him mutter something under his breath.

"Come with me."

It wasn't a request, it was an order, and he didn't bother to hide his angry frustration. With a sharp movement, he pushed himself away from the wood paneling outside the locker room and headed out of the gym. She followed him in silence, certain he was going to grill her as to why she'd spent seven hours working out to the point of exhaustion. And pain.

She probably should have let Violetta heal her. No, she wasn't ready to deal with all the questions and curiosity. Keeping up with Ignacio's long stride wasn't easy, but she just clamped her jaw tight and limped after him. She wasn't going to protest. Complaining would have been pointless as far as Ignacio was concerned.

Her mentor wouldn't feel sorry for her one bit. Not that she wanted his pity. They reached the library, and Ignacio gestured toward one of the room's big, comfortable chairs.

"Sit down."

It was an order she was happy to obey, because her leg hurt like hell. She eyed her mentor carefully as he sank down into the chair opposite her. From the look on Ignacio's face, she could tell she was in for a grilling or a lecture, one or the other, and she didn't want either one. She tried to put off the inevitable.

"Is there any word about Phae?"

"Ares sent word that she's stable, but the doctors don't know when she'll come to." Ignacio leaned forward, his forearms resting on his thighs, and stared at her for a long moment. "I didn't order you in here to talk about Phaedra. Now, *talk* to me."

"There's nothing to talk about."

"Don't give me that crap. Do you really think after all this time you can fool me? I've known you since you were born," Ignacio scolded. "I know something's bugging you, and I've got a pretty good idea what it is."

"How the fuck would you know what's wrong?"

"Shall we rehash what happened last night in the Pantheon?" Ignacio eyed her with a stern look.

"What? My shock at finding out I have a Praetorian brother? No. *Had* a Praetorian brother. Something my mother never told me. Not exactly the kind of news you can swallow in just an hour or two."

"Your brother's situation is a terrible tragedy."

"Yeah, I know." She bobbed her head as she remembered her mother's frantic cry last night in the Pantheon as they fought to keep the Praetorians from taking the *Tyet of Isis*. No matter how angry Cleo might be with her mother, she still hated to see her suffering.

"But that's not what's really wrong, is it?" Ignacio's voice was firm and unflappable.

"What the hell is that supposed to mean?"

"I know you met with Atia and Marcus this morning."

"So?" she bit out fiercely.

"She told you the truth, didn't she?" His softly spoken question stunned her. He grimaced. "Don't look at me like that."

"My mother told you about Marcus? *Before* she told me?" The woman hadn't just lied to her. She'd told Ignacio who Cleo's real father was. She wasn't sure what was worse, being lied to or that the man she thought of as a father had known the truth before she did.

"She didn't tell me willingly."

"So, what, you twisted her arm? Give me a fucking break. You can do better than that."

"No one has *ever* twisted your mother's arm, *bambina*," Ignacio said with a light snort of amusement before his expression grew somber. "The truth is she was backed into a corner."

"By *him*?"

A sudden wave of anger swept over her at the thought of the Sicari Lord intimidating her mother. Cleo might be angry at being deceived, but she didn't like the idea of someone pushing her mother around. Her mentor shook his head slightly.

"I always thought he'd walked out on you and Atia. When I insulted him—" Ignacio rubbed his hand against his throat. "He wasn't happy about it. Your mother convinced him that she'd not betrayed their blood bond with me, and she told me . . . the truth."

"Right, she told *you* the truth, but not *me*, her daughter," she bit out in a sharp voice.

"You judge her too harshly, Cleopatra." He always used her full name when expressing his disapproval of something she'd done. That he continued to defend her mother irritated her and made her want to lash out at him.

"And you judge her too gently because you're in love with her." Her fierce words made Ignacio jerk upright in his chair as she released a harsh noise of disgust at her tactless observation.

"I see," he murmured. "So I'm an object of amusement in the Order for loving a woman who has never given much thought to me, other than as her *Celeris*. Her bodyguard."

"*No*." She shook her head. "I've never heard anyone say anything about the two of you. Not even that worm Cato has suggested it, and if anyone were going to say something, he'd be the one."

The man she thought of as a father frowned as he nodded and leaned back in his chair to contemplate her words. Her heart ached for him. Not once had she ever seen her mother give Ignacio any indication that there might be hope for him. In fact, she wasn't even sure her mother realized her *Celeris* was in love with her.

For as long as she could remember, Ignacio had been there for her and her mother. Ignacio was the one who'd taught her how to fight, how to stitch up a wound. He'd been there when she'd lost in the final round of the *Invitavi*, and he'd been there when the doctors had told her the baby was gone and she'd never have children. And it had been Ignacio who'd been there for her when Michael had walked away less than a month after her injury.

Ignacio had always been there when she needed him, and she loved him like a father. But he wasn't her father. Marcus Vorenus, Sicari Lord, was. No, *reigning* Sicari Lord, according to her mother.

Fuck. He couldn't just be a Sicari Lord? He had to be the goddamn commander in chief.

"*Fuck.*" She exploded out of her chair in a swift leap then collapsed back into her seat with a sharp cry of pain. Ignacio leaned forward with the obvious intent to examine her leg, but she dismissed him with a vicious wave of her hand.

"*Goddamnit to hell.* She should have told me the truth."

"It couldn't have been easy for her, Cleo. Telling you the truth three years ago or today had to be a terrifying thought for her."

"So she said, but I'm having a hard time buying it," she responded bitterly.

"When I brought her back here the morning your . . . your father found out about you, she was badly shaken up." An odd expression crossed her mentor's face. "Your father had demanded to meet you, and the thought of telling you the truth terrified her."

"My mother isn't afraid of anything."

"She's definitely afraid of losing you." Ignacio shook his head in sharp disagreement.

"*Why* do you keep defending her? *Besides* the obvious." She glared at him. Ignacio sent her a patient look.

"Because I've known your mother for a very long time, and after last night, I understand her even better than I ever have before." He leaned forward again, his hands spread in a cajoling gesture. "Atia isn't invincible. None of us are, *bambina*. Your mother has lost a great deal in the last twenty-four hours. She's pretty fragile right now, whether you want to believe it or not."

Cleo leaned back in the chair to rest her head on the soft cushions. Eyes closed, she released a harsh breath. "But she lied to me."

"Yes, but you should be asking *why* she lied to you. The Praetorians took her son when he was barely old enough to know his own name. Then you came along. Can you imagine how terrified she must have been every time you were out of her sight? I can easily understand why she'd keep the identity of your father a secret. From everyone, including you."

"Stop making it sound so goddamn logical." She opened her eyes to meet his sympathetic gaze. "Okay, so she lied to protect me, but sweet Jupiter, she could have said something three years ago when those Praetorian *bastardi* . . . she could have told me then, Nacio. She didn't have to wait until today to tell me my father is alive. And oh yeah, by the way, Cleo, he's a fucking Sicari Lord."

She saw him flinch slightly as she used her childhood nickname for him. *Christus*, was he thinking Vorenus would take his place? That she'd just forget about him and everything he'd been to her?

"Sicari Lord or not, he is your father, Cleopatra." Again with the disapproval.

Leaning forward, she grabbed his hand and squeezed it hard. The sharp edges of the ring he wore bit into her palm. She'd given him the jewelry for his birthday when she was just twelve. She'd earned money cleaning swords and other weapons over a period of several months so she could save enough to buy the ring.

When he'd read the inscription, *From your daughter, Cleo*, it had made his eyes water. That moment was as vivid now as if it had just happened. Ignacio had always been there for her. She would never desert him.

"He's not you, Nacio. He never could be," she said fiercely. He patted her hand, and there was a glitter of emotion in his eyes that sent the hair on the back of her neck dancing before she dismissed the sensation. Whatever it was she thought she'd seen, it was gone as he sent her a tender smile.

"He might not be me, but he is your father, Cleo. He deserves your respect not just because he's a Sicari Lord, but because he's your father."

Cleo didn't answer him. She simply pulled her hand from his and got to her feet. The ache in her leg deepened to a sharp pain. "*Sweet mother of Juno.*"

"That does it," Ignacio said in an authoritative tone as he came to his feet. "You're going to let Violetta perform the *Curavi* on that leg if I have to hold you down myself."

"I don't need it. All I need is some heat to loosen up the muscles, a little liniment, and I'll be good as new in a couple of days. A good soak in the tub will do wonders." She hobbled toward the door. "Besides, a healing will put me out like a light, and I have a date with Mario and a bottle of wine in a few hours."

"*Va bene*, but it will take at least two weeks for that leg to heal, so I'll send Emilio after Angotti next week instead of you." His words made her stop where she was to turn her head toward him.

"Jupiter's Stone, you mean they actually made a decision about that son of a bitch?" She stared at her mentor in surprise. Every territory in the Order had a tribunal that reviewed the cases of targets designated for execution. The three judges in Rome's tribunal were notorious for their slow review process.

"All the evidence checks out, and the tribunal issued its verdict this morning. Of course, since you'll not be up to the task for at least . . ." Ignacio cocked his head to study her leg. "What? Two or three weeks? I'll—"

"You're not giving this assignment to anyone but me."

"You realize your mother and . . . Vorenus will probably object. Rome has never been a safe place for a Sicari, but when people find out who your father is, and it *will* get out, it could be deadly for you."

"There isn't any safe place for me," she said with quiet exasperation. "As for my mother and Vorenus, you don't have to tell them anything. I'll deal with them. But Angotti's mine. I'm the one who brought him to the attention of the tribunal a year ago when I was here on assignment."

"I'm beginning to wonder if allowing you to carry out Angotti's assassination is a good idea," Ignacio said as he studied her with quiet assessment. "You sound a little too involved for my liking."

"I *know* not to make this personal," she said in a level voice, but deep inside a tiny nugget of satisfaction warmed her. It had taken several months to find out where Marta was, but she was finally going to get a shot at freeing her friend.

"Do you? I'm not so sure. In the past three years, almost every one of your assignments has involved targets connected with children who've been harmed. It's starting to look like you have a vendetta." Ignacio gave her a forbidding look. "You know the tribunal doesn't take kindly to fighters breaking the Code. If anyone even thinks your targets suffered a slow or painful death, they'll bring you up on charges. The gauntlet isn't an easy punishment to survive."

"I haven't broken the Code, Nacio, and I won't. But if I can't have kids, then the least I can do is protect other children from all the *bastardi* out there."

"Then let's get you to Violetta. It'll take at least a week to plan the assassination, but I don't want anyone questioning your fitness for duty." Ignacio gestured to the door, and she limped her way out into the hall in the direction of her rooms.

Cleo was seated on her living room couch tugging her hair out of its braid when Violetta arrived. The woman didn't comment on Cleo's change of heart but quickly performed the *Curavi*. When she finished, Violetta ordered her to rest and left. A healing was always a draining process for both the healer and the injured party, and Cleo's eyes drooped as the door closed behind Violetta.

Despite her exhaustion, she struggled with the tangled mass of images shifting randomly in her head. The memory of her mother's confession made her toss restlessly on the couch. Atia's remorseful expression fluttered through Cleo's head. She winced. Maybe Ignacio was right. Maybe she was being too hard on her mother.

A sigh parted her lips as she realized her mother had only been doing what any good mother would do. Atia had been protecting her. Would she have done any less if she were a mother? Her heart clenched painfully in her breast. She certainly hadn't been thinking about her unborn child the night she'd gone out on assignment. She could have easily asked for reserve duty until after the baby was born. She hadn't, and she'd paid the price. It was the last thought she remembered as she slipped into the darkness of sleep.

Shafts of moonlight streamed down through the girders of the abandoned bridge overhead as she quietly moved forward. A few feet away to her left, she could barely see Lysander's tall form. That was a good thing. The longer they went undetected, the easier it would be to execute their target. Assassinations weren't easy. Most of their targets had a tendency to shoot first and ask questions later.

"Just like we planned, okay?" Lysander's command echoed quietly in her earpiece.

"I'm ready if you are."

Her whisper seemed to echo all the way up to the train bridge above her head. It made her uneasy. The whole situation didn't feel right. And that was saying a lot, since she wasn't like most

Sicari females who could sense danger.

She put the sensation down to an overactive imagination and moved toward the black sedan that was parked at the opposite end of the bridge. She'd gotten halfway to the car when it roared to life and gravel sprayed everywhere as the car spun out from underneath the bridge and onto the nearby pavement.

"What the—? Cleo, we've got company."

Lysander's clipped words were followed by the sound of a sword hitting metal three times in rapid succession. Instinct made her pull her sword out of the sheath on her back and whirl around all in one fluid motion. Even as fast as she moved, she still failed to block the sword coming at her. The Praetorian's finely honed blade sliced into her raised forearm as neatly as if he were slicing a piece of steak.

"Goddamnit. Son of a bitch." A soft chuckle followed her cry, and her gaze met the menacing amusement in the man facing her.

"You're quite right, Unmentionable," the Praetorian murmured in a silky tone that was all the more unsettling because of its pleasant sound. "My mother was a bitch. A Sicari bitch who had the decency to die giving birth to me."

The callousness of the statement made Cleo's blood run cold. This guy was more malicious in his hatred than most Praetorians she'd encountered. His sword headed toward her again, and she quickly shifted her weapon into her opposite hand to block and parry. The instant her blade cut into the man's chest, she saw the surprise on his face. She managed a tight smile of satisfaction.

"Didn't expect to meet a switch-hitter with a sword, did you, you sorry ass bastardo?"

With a vicious oath, her opponent swung his sword in a furious round of strikes that had her stumbling backward. His skill was on the same level as hers, but it was the strength of his blows she couldn't match. And the option of darting out of his reach wasn't really a viable one when the guy was almost two times her size. The Praetorian's sword sparked against hers as the two weapons slid downward against each other to lock at the hilt. The gleam of triumph in the man's eye vanished as she kneed him in the groin. With a loud cry of pain, the Praetorian's sword hit

*the ground's mix of dirt and gravel as he dropped to his knees,
clutching his jewels. The tip of her sword immediately pressed
into his chest, ready to drive through the man's heart.*

*"You fought well, Praetorian. I now ask for your forgiveness,"
she said quietly. "Do you give it?"*

*"May your soul rot in hell, Unmentionable," the man snarled,
and with a flash of speed that surprised her, his forearm came up
to viciously slam into the edge of her blade.*

*The move knocked the sword away from his chest, but the
price the Praetorian paid was her blade slicing deep into his
arm until she struck the bone. With a fierce noise of anger, she
grimaced as blood spurted its way onto her hand. In the next
instant, an icy chill streaked across her skin as the Praetorian
retrieved his sword and dragged it deep through the layer of skin
beneath her belly button.*

*"Oh fuck," she whispered as her brain reacted frantically
to the injury and began to shut down everything but the most
important organs necessary for survival. "Lysander . . . I'm
sor . . ."*

*The Praetorian's vicious laugh rang in her ears as her hand
pressed against her wound. She heard the man's laughter cut
short just as she sank to her knees and tumbled to the ground.*

Gasping for air, Cleo shot upright on the couch. *Christus*, she
hadn't dreamed about that terrible night in more than a year. She
pushed her dark hair back off her face. Where the hell had that
come from? Right. Feeling empathy for her mother. Cleo raked her
fingers through her hair then shook her head and closed her eyes.
She understood *why* her mother had kept her in the dark about her
father. She just needed to process it. What she hated the most were
the cruel things she'd said to her mother. Cleo and her mother were
all each other had. Not exactly true when she thought about it.

An image of Marcus Vorenus flitted through her head. He'd said
he wanted to get to know her. And, one thing was for sure, the
Sicari Lord didn't act like he was going anywhere anytime soon. In
a way, she wasn't really surprised by it. Atia and Marcus were blood
bonded. That wasn't the sort of thing you walked away from.

Fuck, was he really trying to get back together with her mother? She winced. She wasn't going there. The first thing she needed to do was deal with her mother. She could figure out how to deal with Marcus Vorenus's return to their lives after that.

Deus, she wished Lysander was here. He was the closest thing to a brother she had, and if anyone could make her see the logic in the situation, it was him. Thinking of her friend reminded her of Angotti. The *bastardo* had been inside the convent, and he was going to tell her what she needed to know. She'd use his knowledge of the building to get Marta out of that hell hole and help Lysander at the same time.

Of course, when Lysander heard what she'd done, he'd thank her, then kick her ass, then thank her again. As for Marta—who knew what her friend would do. Cleo swallowed hard. Marta might wish she were dead. Even worse, her friend might beg Cleo for the *Nex Cassiopeia*. She shuddered. No. Marta was stronger than that. Besides, killing her friend just wasn't part of the plan.

Chapter 3

A sliver of light from a window above the alleyway made the slimy cobblestones glisten. The rank smell of the sewers made Cleo wrinkle her nose as she waited patiently in the dark. Like most old cities, Rome's current drainage system had been in place for a very long time, and the smell reflected that fact. Even despite the amount of time she'd been standing here, she still wasn't used to the stench.

The sooner she returned to the safe house for a good soak in the tub, the better. For the past week, she'd been so busy planning Angotti's execution that she'd not been able to take any time for one of her favorite activities. A bubble bath followed by a glass of Lambrusco, Italian opera, and her one guilty pleasure—a romance book. The combination had a way of easing all the tension from her body.

At least her involvement with Angotti's fate had enabled her to avoid her mother and Marcus Vorenus before they'd left for the White Cloud estate a week ago. It hadn't surprised her that the Sicari Lord had gone with her mother, although the idea that her mother might renew her relationship with Marcus Vorenus was unsettling for some reason. A small part of her was feeling jealous that she'd have to share her mother all the time. It was selfish to feel that way, but for years it had been just the two of them, and Ignacio. Now, Cleo was faced with having a father in her life when she'd gone so long without one. Concentrate. She didn't need to be thinking about her mother's confession. Angotti was her concern at the moment.

Her gaze focused on the door a short distance from where she stood. Hopefully the *bastardo* wouldn't be long now. Angotti had gone into his mistress's house a little more than two hours ago. More than enough time to fuck the woman two or three times. The *Vigilavi* police officer assigned to watch Vincente Angotti had detailed the son of a bitch's varied schedule for almost twelve months. It had taken the tribunal almost that long before reaching a judgment.

Roberto, Isabella, Giovanni, Rosa, and Lorenzo were the primary reason she'd insisted on this assignment. She remembered the pictures of five kids mixed in with the paperwork on Salvatore Conti's precinct desk in Rome. The oldest one had been eight, but it was six-month-old Isabella that locked a vise around her heart. Five lives snuffed out by Angotti's greed.

For once she was glad Rome's three-man court had taken their usual amount of time debating Angotti's fate. It had given the *Vigilavi* more time to continue their observation of Angotti. Time to turn up an unexpected present. Angotti was in bed with the Praetorians.

It was why she'd come alone tonight. She didn't want another fighter questioning her actions with Angotti. Of course, when Ignacio found out she'd come without backup, he was going to put her on the bench for at least a month. Well, it couldn't be helped. She wanted the information Angotti had, and she was going to get it before she executed the *bastardo*.

The sound of a door opening drew her up straight as her gaze narrowed on the short, stocky figure that turned around to speak to someone shielded in the darkened doorway. She heard a feminine laugh and grimaced. How in Juno's name could the woman even allow the man to touch her? Cleo gritted her teeth. This was one target she wouldn't feel any remorse over killing.

Deep in the back of her mind, she heard Ignacio's warning to make sure Angotti's death was a merciful one, as the Sicari Code forbade revenge killings. She almost snorted with derision. This wasn't revenge. It was justice. She ignored the small voice in her head that suggested maybe her motives were less than honorable. Dishonorable? There wasn't a goddamn thing wrong with executing a baby killer.

As the man stepped away from the doorway, Cleo heard the door shut, and she looked toward one end of the alley and then the other. Angotti always traveled with a small entourage, but she'd entered the alleyway after his soldiers had scouted out the dark corners from both ends of the narrow backstreet.

Sometimes Praetorian tactics were a good thing, especially when it meant rappelling off a roof to escape detection. Of course, that sort of entrance made dressing for tonight a little more challenging. Angotti loved beautiful women, and looks she had in spades.

She'd known how important it was to dress as seductively as possible. She had to silence Angotti quickly, and the only way to do that was to appeal to his baser instincts. The downside to everything had been the limits to what she could wear, since she was jumping off a building.

So she'd had to settle for a low-cut red shirt with a pair of soft black leather pants. While she had a couple of dresses, she was utilitarian by nature, and her closet was mostly filled with serviceable outfits. Although she did have a secret weakness for slutty underwear and shoes. Particularly boots like the stylish ones she was wearing tonight.

When she'd seen the flat-heeled boots with their cuffed tops and intricate pleating in a Rome storefront window, they'd appealed to both her utilitarian and feminine sides. The boots were perfect for a mission like this. Spiked boots made it virtually impossible to defend herself if she ran into any trouble.

Not to mention the noise spiked heels would have made on the side of the wall as she dropped three stories down into the alley. It was bad enough that the two long scarves around her neck kept fluttering up into her face as she'd rappelled off the roof. But she needed a gag and something to bind Angotti's hands with. She snorted a whisper of disgust at her analysis of her attire. If the son of a bitch remained true to his profile, his eyes would be on her chest and her cleavage.

She pushed herself away from the side of the building she'd been leaning against to quietly follow the man, who proved to be far more aware of his surroundings than she'd expected. She saw him turn around brandishing a weapon. The handgun had a silencer on it. Goddamnit.

"Please, *signore*. Please don't hurt me."

Lysander would have laughed at the way she feigned being a helpless female, but Angotti seemed to buy her act. He peered at her closely in the dark, relaxing his posture slightly. He didn't speak but flicked his wrist and used his gun to order her out into the small stream of light she'd been avoiding. The man's eyes widened as she came out of the shadows, and he smiled with more than a hint of lust.

Angotti's reaction didn't surprise her. His taste in beautiful women was going to be his downfall tonight. She'd dressed specifically for his benefit. A going-away present for him, of sorts. The amusing thought made her smile genuine as she stepped into the light for him to get a good look at her.

The leather pants she wore were skintight, while the short, black leather jacket she wore over her dark red shirt emphasized her waist and full hips. The snug top she wore dipped low and would have been far more revealing if not for the brooch nestled in between her breast and the scarves fluttering around her neck. The man licked his lips as if she were a dessert on his plate. His expression made her skin crawl. Suddenly the scarves around her neck were well worth the hassle they'd given her while rappelling off the roof. At least the silk covered up most of the skin her low-cut shirt revealed, along with the ornate brooch that hid her weapon of choice.

"*Bellissima*," Angotti said as he eyed her with a mixture of lust and suspicion. "How did you get past the men at the end of the alley?"

"What men?" She feigned puzzlement, although she'd seen Angotti's men earlier before she'd gone up to the roof of the building behind her. "I saw two men sitting in a car near the entrance of the alleyway. Is that who you mean?"

Angotti muttered something fierce beneath his breath. Cleo bit back a smile. The man would never get a chance to rip his bodyguards a new one. His gaze still wary, he kept the gun trained on her for another long minute before his expression changed to show he'd made a decision. With a smile in her direction, he returned his gun to the holster under his coat. A mistake on his part.

"What are you doing out here alone without a man to protect you, *carissima*?

Another mistake. Never assume a woman wasn't capable of protecting herself. She forced herself to send him a helpless look. "I didn't think I'd be out so late."

"A woman as beautiful as you should never be alone," Angotti said. "Where do you live?"

"Another street over. I was in a hurry to get home, and I thought the alley was a good shortcut." She drew abreast of him and offered him another smile.

"Dark alleys are never safe, *cara*, and you're fortunate that it was me who found you and not someone less honorable."

She almost laughed out loud at his words. The man knew nothing about honor. He'd murdered five innocents for money. He deserved a far more painful death than she was allowed to dish out. She forced a smile to her lips, barely keeping the bile in her throat from choking her.

"It was rather foolish of me, I suppose."

"A woman as beautiful as you can be forgiven such a mistake, but come. Let me see you home, *bella*. Then you can invite me in for a drink so we can get better acquainted." Angotti reached out to catch her hand in his and carried it to his wet lips. How she kept from throwing up, she'd never know.

"But we've only just met. That might be unwise of me." Cleo deliberately made her voice sound husky as she toyed with one of the silk scarves hanging loosely around her neck.

"Are you telling me you don't recognize me?"

"Forgive me, *signore*," she murmured. "I'm new to Rome."

"Then you're in need of someone who's familiar with the city to help you find where things are." Angotti bowed toward her slightly in a pitiful attempt to be gallant. His rotund body didn't accommodate his efforts well. "I'm Vincente Angotti. Businessman and entrepreneur."

"Ah, yes, I've heard of you. An apartment building of yours burned to the ground late last year, didn't it?"

He started with surprise, his gaze narrowing as if aware that he might have made a mistake in relaxing his guard. It didn't matter. Vincente Angotti was out of time. Tired of playing the helpless female, Cleo moved with blinding speed and viciously slammed the knife-edge of her hand into the man's neck. Over the years, she'd learned how to hit a certain pressure point on the side of the neck to incapacitate or possibly even kill someone.

With Angotti, his extra weight meant she had to hit hard. She grunted as his stocky body fell into her before sinking downward. He wasn't dead, but she needed him alive. At least for a few minutes. Aware that she didn't have much time, she guided Angotti down to the ground, where he sat on the wet cobblestone.

If the man had been capable of protest, he would no doubt have bemoaned the fact that his pristine, cream-colored suit was ruined. She tugged one of her scarves off her neck to bind Angotti's hands behind his back. Certain he couldn't break free of the restraint, she smacked the back of his neck and rubbed hard to stimulate the man's nervous system. As he slowly recovered from the pressure-point blow and started to mumble, she jerked the remaining scarf off her neck and gagged him.

A raw fury lashed through her as she pulled the stiletto from the scabbard nestled between her breasts. She wanted to slit the man's throat right then and there for his responsibility in the deaths of five innocent children. Her blade pushed up against the fleshy meat of Angotti's neck as she threaded her fingers through his thinning hair and jerked his head back so she could stare down into his eyes.

The man uttered a quiet cry of rage behind the scarf. Although his eyes were wide with fury, there was a glint of fear there as well. Good, the son of bitch ought to be scared. In fact, if he knew what was going to happen in a few minutes, he would be sobbing like a baby. An image of Isabella's tiny little body made her draw in a sharp hiss of air. Angotti's greed had killed Isabella and the other children.

The *bastardo* had paid Luigi Romano to torch one of his apartment buildings rather than making the upgrades necessary to meet the fire code. Worse, Angotti had known the building was a death trap, and he'd not bothered to evict the tenants before he sent Romano in to set the place on fire.

Her stomach lurched at the thought of how those five kids had died. Romano had gone to jail for his crime, but Angotti had walked away. Until tonight. A shudder whipped through her, but it wasn't one of fear. It was a desire to break every rule she'd ever sworn to obey. And it was going to take every ounce of resolve she possessed not to eviscerate the man before she slit his throat. She bent over Angotti so her mouth was close to his ear.

"I'm going to ask you some questions," she whispered. "And you're going to tell me what I want to know, *capisci*?"

The man muttered something behind the gag and jerked his head in a nod. He still hadn't lost his arrogance. It angered her, and she forced herself to draw in a deep breath. Control. She needed to remain in control. Killing this son of a bitch would give her a lot more pleasure than she should be feeling. She needed to let her anger go. She wasn't supposed to enjoy the kill. And despite her fury, she didn't want to betray the basic tenets of the Order that said every execution was one of justice. Nothing more. She drew in another sharp breath.

"I'm going to remove your gag. If you try to call for help, I'll slit your throat before you get one syllable out."

She increased the pressure of her stiletto against the man's throat. The man nodded again. Keeping the point of her blade against his jugular vein, she quickly undid the scarf. He drew in a deep breath as if about to scream, and she pressed her blade into his skin until she drew blood.

"You fucking bitch! You don't know who you're messing with," Angotti snarled.

"Oh, I know who you are. I know all about you." Perhaps it was the quiet, detached note in her voice that made the man lose some of his arrogance.

"Who are you?"

"I'd say your worst nightmare, but then I'm not into clichés."

"What do you want from me? Money? I can pay you well."

"The only thing I want from you is information."

"Information?"

"You're familiar with the Convent of the Sacred Mother on the coast at Atrani, west of Salerno?"

"The convent?" The first real sign of fear threaded its way

through Angotti's voice, an indication that some things terrified the man a lot more than the knife at his neck. She grimaced.

"I know you work for the Praetorians, you fat pig. Tell me about the convent."

"Sicari. You're Sicari." Something other than fear entered his voice. Perhaps a fascination. She hissed with frustration.

"The convent. I want to know everything about it."

"I've only been inside it once, and not for very long." Angotti's voice was hesitant, as if he was stalling for time. Why? She frowned but proceeded with her interrogation.

"Where's the security control room?"

"I don't—" He stopped as she pressed the sharp point of her blade deeper into his neck. This time fear replaced his swaggering manner. "Sweet Mother of God, they'll kill me if I tell you."

"They're not here, and I'm your biggest worry right now. Now, tell me. Where is the security control room?"

"Down the main hall." He sucked in a sharp hiss of air as she slid the tip of the stiletto across his skin in a small cut. "The first hallway on the right and a couple doors down."

"Number of Praetorians on duty."

"One, maybe—"

She pressed the stiletto harder into the man's neck. "Don't try my patience, you sorry fuck."

"Ten." Angotti whimpered. "Always ten brothers on duty."

"Is that inside or out?"

"Outside," the man choked out. "There are at least five or six more inside."

"How many others at a given time?" Her mouth tightened as she envisioned what those other Praetorians were doing when they weren't guarding the convent.

"I don't know." The man whimpered as the knife at his throat drew another drop of blood from his skin. "Ten. Fifteen. I don't know. I never counted them."

At Angotti's answer, she suppressed a groan. She was going to need a lot more help if she moved ahead with her plans. Pasquale would take some convincing, but he'd eventually come around. She'd like to wait for Lysander, but Phae was still in a coma, and Cleo

wasn't about to ask Lysander to leave Phae's side. Ares would come
the minute she mentioned Marta's name, and Violetta would join
them because her sister had died in a Praetorian breeding facility.

She could always ask Mario or Ignacio. The thought made her
grunt with wry amusement. Both men were just as likely to deck her
for even daring to suggest an assault on the convent. She bit down on
her lower lip. Maybe with a little luck she could convince a couple of
other fighters to come along. The problem was keeping the whole deal
quiet so her mother couldn't nix the idea. She smiled grimly. Maybe
keeping secrets ran in the family after all. She was wasting time and
immediately turned her attention back to the matter at hand.

"Deliveries. Who does their deliveries?"

"Sonny Mesiti."

"When?"

"I don't know," Angotti sobbed. "Please, I've told you everything. Please let me go."

Her target squirmed slightly on the cobblestones. Somewhere
nearby she heard a soft sound. She couldn't place it, but it raised the
hair on the back of her neck. She was taking too long. She tugged
Angotti's head back and exposed his neck.

"Vincente Angotti, you've been tried and found guilty of the
murder of five children."

"Whaa . . . ? No. I haven't killed anyone."

"Yes, you have, and you know it. You hired Luigi Romano to
burn down an apartment building you owned. Five children died in
that fire. Remember?"

A sickening feeling clutched at her gut as images of those happy
faces danced through her head. Her throat tightened at the thought
of Isabella. *Deus*, she'd been a tiny little thing. So small and beautiful—
no, she wasn't going to do this. Not now.

"I was acquitted," the man gasped. "I did nothing wrong."

"You were acquitted because of missing evidence."

As the precinct's chief arson investigator, Salvatore had been the
first officer called to the scene of the fire. He'd found evidence linking
Angotti to the crime, but the Praetorians weren't about to let one of
their biggest henchmen go down. They'd helped the slimy *bastardo*
wiggle his way out of a conviction by stealing evidence. As a mem-

ber of the *Vigilavi*, Salvatore had informed the Order of the man's acquittal and asked for justice. Her friend was going to get his wish.

With the tip of her blade ready to puncture Angotti's neck, she reached into the pocket of her leather jacket. Her hand gripped the plastic sleeve containing two black-and-white photographs and a slip of paper. Cleo dropped the plastic-encased evidence down on the ground in front of the man.

"See those? That's you in those pictures. You and Romano," Cleo said as a deadly calm settled over her. "The man cut a deal and pointed you out in the trial, but it was his word against yours without these pictures."

"The photos are fake. You can do anything with software these days." Panic echoed in the man's voice.

"You're right. The photos are fake. But the information on that piece of paper is the real deal."

"Re . . . receipts?"

"There are two transactions detailed on that piece of paper. One is the money in Romano's bank account that the police couldn't trace back to its source. The other transaction details are for a wire transfer from your bank account in the Cayman Islands directly into Romano's account. The monies match up exactly and are dated the day *after* the fire."

"How did you . . . ? You can't trace that sort of thing."

"But I did."

"All right, I paid Romano to burn the building. But I didn't tell him to do it when there were people inside, the stupid prick," Angotti snapped. His cockiness was back. She glanced toward one end of the alley and then the other. Nothing moved in the shadows.

"Five innocent children died in that fire." Cleo tugged the man's head back so he could look up at her. "You have children, don't you, Angotti?"

"Yes." The man's eyes widened with horror. "My God, don't hurt them. Don't hurt my *bambinos*."

"Don't insult me, you *bastardo*." Cleo released a harsh breath of disgust. *Deus*, she so didn't want to ask the *Rogare Donavi* of this sorry son of a bitch. "Now, *unfortunately*, I must ask your forgiveness."

"I don't understand." His fear was back.

"You are to be executed for the murders of five innocent children. As your executioner, I seek your forgiveness."

"You can't!" Angotti's voice grew louder as he screamed in terror.

"I didn't think you'd forgive me," Cleo said harshly.

The man's scream ended on an abrupt high note as she slit his throat. The second Angotti slumped to the ground she heard a grunt behind her. She whirled around to see first one and then another man drop from the roof of the three-story building she'd rappelled from earlier. Praetorians. Didn't these guys ever go off duty? Behind her, the sound of running feet said Angotti's bodyguards were heading toward her. Damnit, even if she'd been a coward and wanted to run, there wasn't anywhere to go.

"Do you really think we're going to let you run, Unmentionable?" one of the Praetorians sneered.

The comment infuriated her, but she quickly suppressed her anger as she remembered Mario's words of wisdom last week. She could kick these *bastardi* to Tartarus and back as long as she kept her cool. She could feel the Praetorians' thoughts pounding against the mental shield she'd erected as she watched the two of them slowly advancing toward her. At least they weren't as big as some she'd fought in the past.

Behind her, the racing footsteps slowed, and she darted a quick glance backward in time to see a burly arm reaching out to grab her shoulder. In a move that was second nature to her, she turned and caught the man's arm under hers and drove her stiletto into the back of his neck. The man went rigid and didn't make a sound. The minute she released him, he dropped to the filthy street like a large sack of flour.

One down, three to go. A laugh from one of the Praetorians behind her made her roll her eyes. Fine, let them think she couldn't take them out. She quickly deflected the second bodyguard's punch and slammed her hand into his throat, crushing his trachea. The man crashed to the ground clutching at his neck as his air supply slowly vanished. Cleo ignored him and turned to face the Praetorians.

"Okay, boys. How do you want to do this?" She glared at the two men in front of her.

"You do realize, Unmentionable, that we're not going to kill you." Just the way the Praetorian said the words made Cleo stiffen.

"Well, you'd be a fool not to, because you can't breed me." She didn't hide her bitterness.

"But think of the pleasure you'll bring the Praetorian who tries."

"No, you stupid asshole, I can't have children." Saying the words out loud made her body hurt as though she'd been sliced open again. Without realizing it, her hand reached for the spot where a Praetorian blade had skewered her three years ago. The Praetorian closest to her chuckled.

"Then I'll finish what one of my brothers failed to do the night he sliced you open."

The man's amusement made Cleo clench her teeth with fury. She'd let her mental shield slip, allowing the *bastardo* to know what she was thinking. She couldn't afford that kind of mistake or she'd wind up dead. Rolling her shoulders in an effort to loosen up her suddenly tight muscles, she sent the gloating Praetorian a cold look.

"For someone who keeps telling me what he's going to do, I don't see you doing much of anything," she drawled with more than a hint of sarcasm.

With a dark look of anger on his face, the Praetorian drew his sword in a flash of movement and lunged toward her. His friend followed close behind. Cleo visualized a defensive move to use on the Praetorian, which made him laugh.

"Your mind is easy to read, bitch." The Praetorian's confident laughter died away as Cleo used her palm to push the man's sword arm upward while driving her fist into the fighter's groin.

"It's always easy to read my mind when I want someone to, you dumb fuck." As the Praetorian sank to his knees, she jerked her own knee upward into his face. "They really need to train you assholes better. That was a rookie move."

Despite his obvious pain, the Praetorian's large hand suddenly wrapped around her calf and jerked her off her feet. She hit the ground hard, the air sailing out of her lungs as her back slammed into the cobblestone pavement. *Christus*, that move had come from out of nowhere. The sooner she dealt with this asshole, the better.

Her gaze met that of the Praetorian who was still on his knees beside her. The fighter's expression was one of cold calculation, and she saw him raise his sword upward in preparation to drive it through her. She didn't think. She simply reacted. Shooting upright, she slammed her forearm into the side of the Praetorian's face. The man's cheekbone snapped loudly beneath the blow.

Nerve endings in her forearm triggered pain sensors in her head from the blow she'd landed on the Praetorian's cheek, and as his grip on her leg eased up, she jerked free of his hold. A shadow billowed over her, and she saw the second Praetorian with his sword poised to plummet its way down into her chest.

She immediately rolled away and heard the sword clang against stone where she'd been just seconds ago. She was on her feet in a flash, and as the Praetorian rushed her, she planted a hard kick into her attacker's knee. A loud pop echoed in the alley as the man staggered to one side. The first Praetorian was coming to his feet, and in two quick steps she was standing behind him with the tip of her blade against the back of his neck.

"I ask your forgiveness, Praetorian," she said.

She wasn't really sure why she asked. The Order didn't require the *Rogare Donavi* when killing a Praetorian. The fighter growled, but she didn't hesitate before she jammed the stiletto into the man's neck. The death rattle in his throat said he'd be dead in seconds, which left only one Praetorian. She tugged her blade free and turned to face her last opponent.

The remaining fighter was limping but definitely still in the game. The Praetorian feinted to the right, and she easily countered as his sword came at her from the left. When his blade followed through and swung back again, she didn't see the fighter's foot kicking outward. The blow to her knee threw her off balance, and she stumbled. Although her recovery was quick, her slight hesitation was enough for the Praetorian to strike. As the blade sliced into the back of her calf, she fell to the ground with a sharp cry.

"*Fuck. Sweet Vesta. Mother of Juno,*" she rasped at the pain knifing through her leg.

"That, Unmentionable, was for my brother."

Fire streaked its way up Cleo's side as she struggled to her feet. She needed to be standing to fight this *bastardo*. Knuckles scraping against the rough stone alleyway, she grunted with pain as she stood upright with all of her weight on her good leg. The movement only increased the amount of nausea washing over her.

Deus, she hurt. The Praetorian's lips curled back in a feral smile of triumph as he moved toward her. The son of a bitch was already planning her demise. And if she didn't do something quick, the man would succeed. The problem was, all she wanted to do was sit down and put her head between her legs, if only to make the nausea go away. Not a good idea with a Praetorian ready to take her out.

Cleo's hand tightened on the hilt of her stiletto. All she had to do was get in close. She hopped to one side, dragging her injured leg with her in an effort to prepare herself for his attack. The Praetorian charged her, his sword straight out in front of him with the clear intent to run her through. At the last second, she twisted her hips sharply and arched her back so her upper body was parallel with the Praetorian's sword.

Despite her defensive move, the blade still managed to cut through her shirt and into the flesh of one breast. Once more, fire seared her skin, but it didn't stop her from trying to slash the man's throat. She missed, and her stiletto cut into the Praetorian's shoulder instead.

The man's snarl of pain didn't make her feel any better. He was still alive. Cleo hopped around to face her attacker only to see the Praetorian's blade flashing her way. Self-preservation forced her to launch herself backward to avoid the sword. She stumbled in the process and found herself on the ground one more time.

"I'm going to enjoy killing you, whore." A cruel smile curving his lips, the Praetorian moved forward to viciously cut into the flesh of her upper arm.

Cleo cried out in pain. Her vision blurred for a moment as the nausea she'd barely had under control renewed its harsh assault. She was out of options. Focus. If she wanted to live, she needed to focus. She forced herself to shut out everything but her determination to kill the man in front of her. He chuckled as she envisioned hitting his brachia and crushing it.

The image she projected didn't prepare him for the stiletto that whistled through the air and slammed into his throat. The Praetorian stood there for several seconds before he toppled forward in slow motion. Cleo didn't wait for him to land on top of her. She forced herself to ignore the nausea and pain as she rolled away from the spot where the Praetorian eventually landed.

She lay still for a long moment, staring up at the sky. With all the city lights illuminating the night, it was impossible to see anything but the brightest stars. Suddenly she longed to be in a lounge chair looking out at the sea at Palazzo al Mare, the Order's stronghold just south of Genova. She closed her eyes, trying hard to muster up the strength to get to her feet.

Violetta. She needed to get to Violetta. The woman's abilities weren't very strong, but Violetta could at least heal her leg wound. The cuts on her breast and arm could be stitched up. Cleo threw herself up into a sitting position with an agonized grunt. Jupiter's Stone, she hadn't hurt this bad in a long time. This is what she got for going out without a partner. She dismissed the thought.

The risk had been worth it. When she added the information Angotti had given her to the other knowledge she had about the convent, it reinforced her belief that she could rescue Marta. There were still a few pieces of the puzzle missing, but a year's worth of investigative work had just paid off in a big way. Well worth her injuries tonight. An alarm suddenly went off in her head, breaking through her self-congratulatory thoughts.

It wasn't a noise that threw her senses on alert. It was something else. A powerful frisson that scraped across her neck with unbelievable speed. Without thought, she launched herself toward the dead Praetorian in an effort to reach her stiletto. She wasn't fast enough.

The dark shadow that brushed past her tugged a cry of surprise from her lips, and she watched as the large figure knelt to pull her blade from the dead man's throat. Goddamnit. After all that effort, her life was forfeit. There wasn't anywhere to run, and she didn't have the strength to do so.

Resigned to her fate, Cleo clenched her jaw. She didn't like to admit it, but she was afraid. She particularly didn't like the way this stranger was toying with her. Praetorians were never silent. They liked to taunt their prey. This silence was making her damned uncomfortable. She watched as a gloved hand used the Praetorian's shirt to wipe the blood off the stiletto.

"Well, what the fuck are you waiting for? Just get it over with," Cleo snapped.

"I believe this is yours."

The deep richness of his voice had an immediate impact on her senses. It made her body tighten with awareness, which exacerbated the stress on her wounds, and she drew in a sharp breath as her nerve endings pounded a new message to her brain.

The stiletto clean, the shadowy figure flipped it so the hilt pointed in her direction and offered it to her. She didn't hesitate to take the weapon and kept it pointed in the stranger's direction. He didn't move from the side of the Praetorian she'd killed moments ago. Although she couldn't see his face behind the darkness of the hooded cloak he wore, she was certain he was studying her. She eyed him warily.

He was dressed in the same manner as the Sicari Lord and the Praetorian Dominus who'd fought each other in the Pantheon when Lysander had led them to the *Tyet of Isis*. The long flowing hooded cape he wore was so reminiscent of assassins from medieval times. The problem was Sicari Lords and Praetorian Dominuses looked the same to her.

And just because he'd not killed her yet wasn't necessarily something to bet on at this point. The *bastardo* hadn't *said* he was Sicari. Although the return of her stiletto was a good sign, but then again, Praetorians enjoyed their work. They'd find it amusing to make their prey think they had a chance. She waited for that odd sensation of someone probing her mind, but nothing happened.

"Who are you?" she rasped, almost afraid to hear his answer.

He didn't respond. Instead, he moved to examine the men lying dead all around her. There was a lethal, masculine elegance in his movements that sent a tingling vibration across her skin unlike anything she'd ever experienced before. She didn't want to enjoy the sensation, but she did. She liked it a lot. Fuck, what in Jupiter's name was wrong with her?

But when he reached Angotti's body, the quiet sound of fury he released made her uneasy enough to forget her nausea. He didn't move. He just stood there staring down at the dead man, and for the second time that night she experienced fear.

Chapter 4

DANTE stared down at Angotti's limp form with an anger he'd not experienced in a long time. Four months' work tracking the son of a bitch only to see it all washed away in one stroke of Cleopatra Vorenus's hand. He released an expletive of fury and immediately regretted his loss of control. What was done was done. If there was anything he'd learned in his progression through the nine levels of the *Novem Conformavi* it was that true power lay in the ability to let go of that which one couldn't control.

He closed his eyes for a brief second. It was one of the core values of the ancient philosophy and a basic lesson he'd learned early. But there were times when he still sought to master the teaching. This was one of those moments. He'd passed the second and fifth *Tabulati* of the *Novem Conformavi* years ago, but at the moment, control and tranquility seemed just out of reach.

He stared down at the dead man. If he'd gotten here fifteen minutes sooner, he would have gotten the information for developing a reasonable plan to rescue Beatrice. He suppressed a sigh. Pointless to dwell on what might have been. Angotti was dead, and with him the key to the Convent of the Sacred Mother. It wasn't Vorenus's fault he'd gotten here too late. She'd just been doing her job. And she'd gotten hurt in the process. He'd just have to find another information source, despite the fact that it meant more delays.

Dante clenched his jaw then grew still as his gaze swept the scene. Where was her partner? Jupiter's Stone. The woman had come here alone. Why? Rome was one of the most dangerous places in the world for a Sicari. It was why the Order had a strict rule that Sicari were to travel in pairs while in the city. Cleopatra had deliberately broken that edict. In the distance, he heard the sound of a siren. It might not be headed this way, but it was best not to wait and find out.

"Cornelia, there's a mess here," he murmured into the surveillance mike he wore. "Our guest ran into more than just Angotti's bodyguards. Have Vincenzo and Lucius clean it up before company arrives."

"Yes, Tribune." Despite the quiet respect in the woman's voice, he could still hear the question.

"Our guest executed him before I arrived." He could almost see his *Praefect*'s expression of disappointment at his words. Frustration swept through him. "We'll find a way to get her out, Cornelia. I gave you my word."

"What is meant to be, will be, Tribune. But I appreciate your efforts."

Cornelia's quiet, serene response was typical. The woman had completed the *Novem Conformavi* at the age of twenty and was able to control her emotions unlike any Sicari Lord he'd ever met. Not even Marcus possessed her mastery of emotions. It was why Dante had always questioned Marcus's decision to make him Tribune.

Cornelia's steely control would have made her the better choice to lead the Sicari Lord's guild. Although she would have been the *Absconditus*'s first female leader in the recorded history of the Sicari Lords. Her decisions would be logical because of her superior ability to set aside personal sentiment. He, on the other hand, struggled on a daily basis to keep his emotions in check. Like the frustration he was experiencing now.

"Our guest is injured. Bring the car around."

"Vincenzo and Lucius are on their way. I'll meet you at the Via Pomi alleyway entrance."

He didn't reply, knowing Cornelia would do as she said. Instead, he turned back to the woman who'd unknowingly cost him more time and trouble. Cleopatra was no longer on the ground, and it took him a moment to find her. She'd tried to hide herself in the darkest section of the building's shadows, where she stood watching him.

Even from where he was standing, he could see it was an effort for her to remain on her feet. Just the way she pressed her body into the building's wall for support said her legs could give way at any moment. She had the look of a cornered animal, and from the tension rolling off of her, she was ready to go down fighting. A blistering onslaught of jumbled thoughts and emotions slammed into him as he studied her.

He stiffened as he fought not to put her thoughts into some form of coherency. It was forbidden to read the minds of other Sicari without permission, but at the moment, he was finding it damned difficult to close himself off to her. The powerful way her tension wrapped itself around him to burrow deep into his body startled him.

He'd never experienced anything like it. Even more surprising was how difficult the sensation was to ignore. With great concentration, he pushed it aside until it was just a small vibration against his skin, but the effort it took to bury the tactile pressure of her emotions unsettled him.

Slowly approaching where she stood pressed against the wall of the alley, Dante frowned at his inability to see her shadowed features. It would help if he could at least read her expression. He didn't have to read her thoughts, because her feelings were strong enough to give him an idea of what she might be thinking. With each step that closed the distance between them, her emotional state was a razor scraping along his senses.

She was afraid, and he didn't like it that she was scared of him. He dismissed the thought. There were only about two feet between them when he saw her slide downward an inch or two. Without a second thought, he stretched out his hand to help keep her upright against the wall. In the next instant, her blade was digging its way across the back of his gloved hand.

"Goddamnit," he bit out.

"Don't come any closer or I'll gut you like a fish."

Her blade had sliced straight through the leather glove and into his skin. He glanced down at the opening of his cloak where her stiletto pressed into his stomach. He couldn't remember the last time someone had gotten past his guard so easily—not only to cut him, but to threaten him as well.

Again, her emotions and thoughts barreled into him. He'd never encountered a Sicari with the ability to plow right through his natural ability to block another individual's thoughts and emotions. It wasn't just disturbing. It was damned uncomfortable. He grimaced as he painstakingly reinforced his mental shield to keep from ordering her thoughts in a rational order. It didn't help matters that if he simply dropped his shield, he would know exactly what she was planning for her next move.

Despite his annoyance, his admiration for her went up another notch. Marcus clearly had no idea how skilled his daughter was in hand-to-hand combat. No wonder she'd managed to survive two bodyguards and two Praetorians without a partner. Still, she'd broken the rules, and he wanted to know why.

Without touching the weapon, he visualized the blade twisting out of her hand and landing in his. She didn't quite gasp, but the tension in her body spiked in a way that was almost a tactile sensation. He braced his good hand on the wall behind her and leaned forward, determined to intimidate her into answering his questions, but froze. Every thought of interrogating her went out the window as he stared at her face. Until now, he'd not been close enough to really see her, and the air left his lungs.

She wasn't just beautiful. She was timeless. He doubted there was an artistic master past or present who could do her justice, no matter the medium chosen. With her oval-shaped face and flawless complexion, she was stunning. Knowing of Angotti's love of beautiful women, the son of a bitch must have been completely disarmed by her. The nostrils of her slender nose flared slightly, a sign of her agitation, while her violet eyes were wide in her face.

And sweet Vesta, her mouth. It was temptation in its most powerful form. Plump and lush, her mouth invited a man to sin with her. What would it be like to kiss her? Just thinking about it was like taking a punch to his midsection. Jupiter's Stone, his oath. Had he lost his mind? She drew in a deep breath as she glared at him.

"Well, finish it," she rasped.

"Finish it?" He shook his head as he tried to collect his wits and concentrate on the matter at hand.

"Just slit my fucking throat and get it over with. That's what a Praetorian Dominus does, isn't it?"

Despite the bravado of her words, the fear vibrating off her had found its way into her voice. *Christus*, he didn't like being compared to a Praetorian, but what else was she supposed to think? He should have explained who he was from the beginning. Instead, he'd allowed her imagination to run wild. Still, it didn't make her insult any more palatable.

His only excuse was that he wasn't used to meddling in the Order's affairs. His conscience laughed loudly. He'd been so riveted by her face that he'd forgotten all about the *Absconditus* and the Order. He blew out a harsh breath and shoved the hood of his cloak off his head so she could see his features.

Every Tribune and Sicari Lord of the *Absconditus* wore the cape to honor Maximus Caecilius Atellus, the first Sicari Lord, and it was a way to protect their identity in instances like this. But reassuring Cleopatra that she was safe was more important than protecting his identity. As the hood fell backward to expose his face, an emotion flared in her eyes, but it vanished too quickly to identify it.

"I'm not the enemy," he ground out. "Although it's clear *you* think I am."

He tugged the glove off his injured hand and showed her the wound. It wasn't a deep cut, but it stung. With an effortless thought, he mentally reached out to remove the stiletto's leather sheath from between her breasts. The sound of her gasp made his mouth go dry.

Suddenly, he found himself wishing his invisible touch had been a physical one and her gasp had been one of pleasure. The moment her eyes widened, his throat tightened at the possibility that his reaction to her had been physical and not an impulsive thought. Alarm zigzagged its way through him. With an abrupt move that made her jump, he jammed the stiletto into its sheath and squatted in front of her. It amazed him that she was still standing, considering what little he could see of the cut on her leg.

"Let me see your injury," he demanded. Her back still against the wall, she shifted her body slightly to prevent him from examining her leg.

"*Not* until you tell me who you are."

He sighed and looked up to meet her suspicious gaze. "My name is Dante. I'm Sicari like you."

"The only Sicari I've ever seen dressed like you was—" He saw her eyes widen then narrow all in the space of two seconds. "Fuck, another Sicari Lord."

He didn't bother to correct her or explain the difference between a Sicari Lord and a Tribune. The existence and hierarchy of the *Absconditus* wasn't common knowledge among the Order, and he was fairly sure Cleopatra knew next to nothing about the Sicari Lord's guild. And *now* certainly wasn't the time for a lesson. He narrowed his eyes as he looked up to see her mouth tighten with anger before her beautiful features became a cold mask. Puzzled, he resisted the urge to reach out and touch her mind to find out what she was thinking.

"We're wasting time. Show me your leg," he said, but she didn't move.

"*He* sent you, didn't he?" The words had a brittle quality to them that made him narrow his gaze at her. For a moment, her face revealed a look of anguish that tugged at him. It was gone as quickly as it had come, but it was enough to tell him that she was struggling with the recent revelation of who her father was.

"Do you mean Marcus?" he asked quietly as he got to his feet. It was obvious she wouldn't let him look at her leg until she was certain he wasn't a threat.

"Yes." The response could have punctured a tin can, it was so sharp.

"No, Marcus didn't—"

"Don't you fucking lie to me."

"I'm not in the habit of lying," he said stiffly, his gaze steady as he looked into her angry eyes. "Did I know you were Marcus's daughter? Yes. Did he send me? No. I came because of Angotti."

Deus, since when had he ever twisted the truth to suit his own ends? While it was true Marcus hadn't instructed him to keep an eye on Cleopatra, there had been a silent request in the Sicari Lord's voice when he'd mentioned his daughter had remained in Rome. Dante would have come whether her target had been Angotti or someone else.

"That sounds pretty damn convenient," she snapped.

"Jupiter's Stone," he said in disgust. "It wasn't convenient at all. I got here *after* you killed Angotti. Trust me—I'm not happy about it."

"Sorry about that." Her cavalier response made him grit his teeth, but he reined in his temper. Her tough exterior was a façade. There was a wild tumult of emotions running beneath the surface that she was fighting hard to hide.

"You broke the rules tonight. You decided to carry out Angotti's execution without a partner. Why?" he asked softly. He frowned at the flash of vulnerability that crossed her beautiful face.

"What I do is my business," she said with a quiet defiance.

"No. It's my business, because Angotti was valuable to me," he said in a hard and inflexible voice. "Now, I won't ask you again. Why did you come here without a partner?"

Cleopatra turned her head away from him, clearly debating how much to tell him. He growled with irritation, and the sound made her jerk her head back toward him.

"The *bastardo* had information I wanted. I knew having someone with me might make it more difficult getting Angotti to talk."

"What kind of information?" Dante's muscles hardened as tension wrapped its claw around him. Maybe the last four months monitoring Angotti might bear fruit after all.

"I wanted to know what he knew about the Convent of the Sacred Mother." Cleopatra's words made him suck in a sharp breath.

"What did he tell you?"

Dante watched as her mouth tightened in a stubborn line so like her father. Leaning into her once more, he steeled himself not to let her mental impact on his senses or her beautiful face distract him. He succeeded. Her curves caught his attention instead. Suddenly, his senses ignited in a different way, his body on full alert as his muscles drew up taut. He'd been so busy studying her face he'd not noticed the gash on her arm and breast. Her shirt was splayed open to reveal a lace-edged bra. The sight of it made his mouth go dry, while his fingers itched to tug the lingerie downward to see the stiff nipples pushing the material outward.

Heat streaked across his skin, stirring something deep inside him. He'd been attracted to women before, but his training had always enabled him to put aside his lust. This was different. The strength of his reaction to this woman was a powerful, fiery force that spread its way through his body until he was hard *everywhere*.

His primal response created a knot in his throat that was hard to swallow, and for the first time in his life, Dante was sorry he'd taken his oath. The traitorous thought made his muscles twist even tighter. Hands braced on the wall behind her just to keep from touching her, he leaned into her. Her tension level and something else he didn't want to identify rocketed off the charts, but all he cared about was getting the information he wanted without doing something stupid.

"I asked you a question," he said in a strained voice. "What did Angotti tell you?"

When she didn't answer him immediately, his hand caught her chin and forced her to look at him. It was a mistake to touch her. Fire singed his fingertips, and he jerked away from her. The knot in his throat was back, but larger this time. *Deus*, what was wrong with him? The thoughts of Vincenzo and Lucius brushed against his senses. Grateful for the interruption, he turned toward the two dark shapes emerging from the shadows. Behind him, Cleopatra gasped.

"Oh fuck, please tell me they're with you."

"They're with me," he said without turning his head. With a gesture toward Angotti and his bodyguards, he lightly touched the minds of the two warriors.

"Leave Angotti's men where they are. The police will assume it was a hit the guards tried to stop."

"Yes, Tribune."

"Make sure you search the Praetorians before you dispose of them in the catacombs."

Both men gave him a quick bow of respect before they picked

up the bodies of the dead Praetorians and disappeared back into the shadows. Satisfied that the cleanup was well in hand, he glanced over his shoulder toward the end of the alley. A car rolled to a stop and doused its lights. As always, Cornelia was prompt.

The sound of leather scraping softly against stone caught his attention, and he turned to see Cleopatra sinking down toward the cobblestones. Her head resting on the wall behind her, there was an air of defeat about her. The sudden urge to pick her up and comfort her made Dante suppress a groan. He needed to get her to a healer, and then *he'd* get as far away from the woman as he could. He returned to her side and squatted beside her.

"A friend of mine has a sister in that convent," he said quietly. "If Angotti told you something about it, whatever he told you might help me save her."

"You're planning a rescue, aren't you?" Her violet eyes widened slightly before they closed and she breathed a heavy sigh. "If I tell you, I want in on the plan."

"Out of the question," he snapped. Marcus would have his head if he agreed to her demand.

"Then I can't help you."

Despite her obvious exhaustion and pain, there was a determination in her that he recognized. She was more her father's daughter than she knew. The shrill wail of a police car echoed, closer this time, and he blew out a harsh breath. Someone had called the police, and he wasn't in the mood for questions. They needed to leave now.

"By the gods, I must be out of my mind," he said grimly. "The first thing we do is get you to a healer. Then we talk. Agreed?"

"Yes." It was more a sigh than an answer. It made him frown.

"Can you walk?"

"Ye . . . no."

It was obvious she didn't like admitting to any weaknesses. He studied her drawn features with a sense of doom. He couldn't explain it, but he was certain refusing her demands wasn't going to be easy. It was bad enough Marcus would want to flay the backs of everyone involved in an assault on the convent.

But if Dante agreed to Cleopatra's participation in the rescue, it was anyone's guess what the Sicari Lord would do to him. He sighed as he envisioned the potential ramifications of his actions then closed his eyes. The fifth *Tabulati* taught one to seek tranquility in all one did. He could use a little of that right now. With a soft oath, he carefully lifted Cleopatra into his arms and stood up.

"Oh, *that* was a compliment," she muttered wearily.

"What?" Startled, he stared down at her in surprise.

"You didn't have to make it sound as though you were picking up a tub of lard."

"That's *not* what I was thinking," he growled with embarrassment. He wasn't even using his telekinetic ability to help carry her. If anything, she felt just right in his arms, and it scared the hell out of him.

"Uh huh." Her skeptical response tugged another growl out of him, but he didn't respond.

All he cared about at the moment was getting her to the car so he could put some distance between them. The woman was wreaking havoc with his senses. And holding her in his arms like this wasn't helping matters. The way she was nestled against his chest placed her head just below his nose, and the sweet smell of soap floated upward from her dark hair.

He had to fight hard not to lower his head and breathe in more of the delicious scent. Even harder to fight was the blazing heat streaking through his blood until his body was taut with something he could only describe as expectation. His jaw locked with tension as he quickened his stride to get to the Via Pomi where Cornelia was waiting with the car.

"Thank you." Her soft words wrapped a vise around his heart. "If you hadn't come along, I would have had a tough time getting out of this alley on my own."

"Breaking the rules has consequences, but you're welcome," he said gruffly.

"So, what, *you* don't break the rules?"

"I try not to." He winced. He'd done an excellent job breaking some rules tonight.

"I break the rules all the time," she said. There was almost a note of pride in her voice, and it made him smile.

"Is it worth it?"

"Sometimes, but at others . . ."

The way her voice died off into nothing made him frown. He didn't know how he knew it, but he was certain that at some point she'd broken a rule and gotten hurt because of it. It aroused the protective instinct he'd experienced a few minutes ago. He pushed it aside, trying to reassure himself that he'd feel the same thing for anyone who was in trouble. Another breach in the teachings of the first *Tabulati*. He was learning how to lie well, even to himself.

Chapter 5

BEYOND the glass of the living room window, Dante could see nothing but the black night. It engulfed the *peristylium* centered inside the *Absconditus*'s stronghold like a shroud. During the day, the inner courtyard was a pleasant combination of open spaces and flower beds, but at the moment, darkness cloaked its beauty.

Dante turned his head away from the window to pour a splash of Hennessy into his snifter. He lifted the glass to study the amber liquid inside and breathed in the liquor's aroma. The cognac's familiar scent of vanilla and oak tickled his nose. It washed away the memory of the rank smell in the alleyway where he'd found Cleopatra.

Her image flashed in front of his face, and his fingers tightened around the glass in his hand. The woman was an unexpected development. *Unexpected* really wasn't a good description of Cleopatra. The woman was more like a ticking time bomb. She'd made an impact on him that still had him reeling.

It had taken every bit of mental acuity he possessed to keep the woman's thoughts and emotions out of his head. The result had been his inability to suppress his physical reaction to the woman. No, not just a physical reaction. He'd experienced a connection between them that he'd never had with anyone before. It ran deep, and the knowledge made his stomach bunch into knots.

Dante took a drink of the expensive liquor and turned back toward the window. The smooth, almost nutty flavor of the cognac on his tongue was a good first step in easing the tension holding his body hostage at the moment. The pane of glass in front of him mirrored the interior of the massive complex's smallest living room.

Of the three salons in the house, this one was his favorite. He'd always found this room to be the most comfortable of the *Absconditus*'s location in Rome. Over a hundred and fifty years ago, a wealthy Rome merchant had built the house using an ancient Roman floor plan. The guild had purchased the house at the turn of the century in order to establish an observation post to monitor Praetorian activities.

Situated in the heart of their enemy's territory, the property had grown over the years to become one of the *Absconditus*'s major strongholds. The guild had surrounded and fortified the complex with a high wall of stone including limited access points. When combined with the continuous updates of new security features, the compound was a virtual fortress.

The main building was capable of housing twenty to thirty guild members, but the *Absconditus* had purchased adjoining properties over the last sixty years to expand the complex. The installation now encompassed three city blocks of fortified living quarters. More than a hundred members of the guild lived in the stronghold, along with more than fifty direct descendants of the first Sicari Lord's *Vigilavi*.

Of all the properties the Sicari Lord's guild owned, Dante liked this one the best. He wasn't sure why. There were other *Absconditus* compounds that were far more beautiful. Perhaps it was because this was where he'd grown up, and it was the only real home he'd ever really known. There was little he remembered of his life prior to the day his mother had left him here in Marcus's care. Even that memory consisted of nothing but bits and pieces.

His jaw tightened at the thought of the mother he barely remembered and the father he'd never known. If his father had lived, would things have been different? Would his mother still have given him up so easily to the *Absconditus*? Without thinking twice, he blocked out all thoughts of his mother and the past. He couldn't change it, and he wasn't ever going to learn his mother's reasons for leaving him with Marcus.

Dante finished his cognac then set the empty snifter on the cabinet. He didn't drink on a regular basis, but after the last three hours, he'd needed something to help ease the tightness in his muscles. It had been a long time since he'd felt this uneasy. Cleopatra Vorenus had probably set his work back several months. He ignored the fact that she'd managed to test his knowledge of every level of the *Novem Conformavi* he'd ever completed.

The minute the Praetorians had taken Cornelia's daughter almost a year ago, he'd started working on a way to rescue Beatrice from the Convent of the Sacred Mother. Cleopatra had thrown a major monkey wrench into those plans.

Angotti had been a key element to Beatrice's rescue. The crime lord *had* to have known quite a bit about the convent's operations, considering how many times the son of a bitch had visited the breeding facility. There was no doubt in Dante's mind that the *bastardo* had enjoyed himself at the expense of the Sicari women held prisoner there.

Dante released a sound of disgust and rubbed the back of his neck with his hand. He could only hope that Cleopatra had gotten some useful information before she'd killed the son of a bitch. Once more, a vivid image of Cleopatra's face filled his head. Not only had her emotions and thoughts stormed the gates of his mental faculties, but he'd responded to her presence on a base level as well. There was something about her vulnerability that had aroused his protective instincts.

What really concerned him was the way he'd questioned his vow to the guild the second he got close to her. *Concerned him?* It scared the hell out of him. She'd managed to upset not only his plans, but his senses as well. Cleopatra was the first woman to ever appeal to his base emotions so strongly. Not even the test he'd undergone years ago had aroused such primitive, territorial sensations. His primal reaction to her presence had thrown him off balance.

Even if he hadn't dedicated his life to the *Absconditus*, she'd be off limits simply because she was Marcus's daughter. A quiet sound made him turn his head, and he saw Cornelia standing in one of the room's two entrances. His *Praefect* crossed the oak parquet flooring and sank into the overstuffed couch a short distance from where he stood.

The neutral color of the soft leather furniture was a stark contrast to the standard outfit Sicari wore when out on a mission. The black turtleneck and pants emphasized Cornelia's lithe body while the color of the couch highlighted her olive-toned complexion. With short, dark curls framing her face, his second-in-command appeared much younger than she was.

"How is she?" he asked. The depth of his concern for Cleopatra's welfare made his gut tighten into knots again, but he dismissed the emotion. She was Marcus's daughter, and it was natural to worry about the woman's well-being.

"She'll be fine. She's asleep now, but Noemi was able to heal her leg wound completely, as well as her other cuts. By tomorrow morning, she'll be up and about without any problem."

"Good." He nodded his head sharply.

He didn't like the strong surge of relief that sped through him. It was one thing to be thankful to the gods that Cleopatra was safe and well, but what he was feeling was beyond simple gratitude. The level of his response meant his awareness of her was even stronger than he'd feared.

The woman was beautiful enough to be one of Armani's runway models in Milan, but it wasn't her beauty that had sent that jolt of electricity through him. There had been something beneath the surface that had twisted his insides up in knots. The memory of how he'd wanted to kiss her made every muscle in his body grow taut.

And he sure as hell didn't like the memory of how her shirt had been splayed open so he could see a lot more than the top of her breast. An image of dark red lace swam in front of his vision. Immediately, he tried to swallow the lump swelling his throat closed.

"Are you all right?" Cornelia narrowed her eyes at him. "You look worried."

Worried? He was way beyond that point. He was shaken to the core. Cleopatra was the first woman to make him lose sight of his vow to the *Absconditus*. Not once since taking his oath at the age of fifteen had he ever regretted giving his vow to the guild. Not until tonight.

"No. I'm just angry that I didn't reach Angotti before Cleopatra slit his throat," he lied.

Deus, tonight he was recanting everything he'd learned in the first *Tabulati* of the *Novem Conformavi*. One of the tenets of the first level of the ancient philosophical teachings was honesty, and he'd been breaking that discipline left and right this evening. He clenched his teeth with frustration at his inability to remain true to his beliefs.

He looked away from his friend's astute gaze. Cornelia was older than him by only sixteen years, but in many ways, she was like a mother to him. While he was growing up, her strong intuitive abilities had always told her when he needed to talk. That was something his mentors, Placido and Marcus, had never been able to do where he was concerned.

"It wasn't your fault," she said quietly, but he heard the unspoken disappointment in her voice. "I'm sure the Order won't be pleased to learn she performed the assassination alone. Did she say why she didn't have a partner with her?"

"She said Angotti had some information she wanted."

"She questioned him?" Cornelia's surprise made him look back at her as she shook her head in puzzlement. "What for?"

"She asked him about the convent. I think she's planning an assault on the facility."

"By *herself*?" The amazement in his friend's voice made him grimace. "Why would she do that?"

"I don't know. She wasn't very forthcoming about her motives. All she said was that Angotti had information about the convent she wanted."

"And she didn't tell you what he said?"

"She *wouldn't* tell me," he said through clenched teeth as he remembered Cleopatra's stubborn refusal to talk. "She tried to blackmail me into letting her join the rescue team before she'd tell me anything."

"You didn't *agree* to that, did you?" The appalled note in Cornelia's voice made him send her a look of annoyance.

"You know me better than that," he said with disgust. Regret flashed across his *Praefect*'s features as her gaze met his.

"I'm sorry. It's just that even if she is a Sicari, she's still a stranger. The fact that she's even here in the complex makes it dangerous for her *and* us. We should have taken her back to the Order's safe house."

"She's not quite the stranger you think she is," Dante said quietly as Cornelia eyed him with a questioning look.

"Of course she is. We know nothing about her."

"She's the daughter of Marcus and the *Prima Consul*."

"*Daughter?*" Cornelia gasped and shook her head in disbelief. "I knew Marcus had blood bonded with the *Prima Consul* and their son was taken by the Praetorians years ago, but I didn't know he had a daughter."

"Neither did he until a few weeks ago. He didn't fill me in on all the details, but I don't think Cleopatra has adjusted to the news quite as well as Marcus has."

"What do you mean?"

"She thought Marcus had sent me to keep tabs on her, and she wasn't happy about it."

"Marcus? I thought you'd found out about Angotti from the tribunal records. I didn't realize it was Marcus who told . . ." Cornelia's eyes widened with horror. "Sweet Vesta. He's found out what we're planning."

"No. He's monitored the Order's tribunals for years." Dante shook his head in a reassuring manner. "But Angotti's sentencing was the first time he's ever cited a specific case to me."

"Then he doesn't know what we've been planning?" His *Praefect*'s expression of panic dissolved into one of relief.

"If he does, it wasn't because I told him anything. I had a hard enough time convincing *you* that my plan to rescue Beatrice had merit," he said in a dry voice. "Do you really think Marcus would be any easier to convince?"

"I doubt it." Cornelia made a face as she acknowledged that Dante was right. "So how do we explain her presence here?"

"Aside from Placido and me, you're the only other person in the *Absconditus* who knows about her relationship to Marcus. So for the time being, we simply state what's common knowledge. She's the *Prima Consul*'s daughter. We'll let Marcus decide when or if he tells the rest of the *Absconditus* of his relationship to Cleopatra."

"And how do you propose getting her to tell you what she knows about the convent?"

"I don't know," he grumbled with frustration. "In the span of just a few minutes, I learned she's as stubborn as Marcus."

"Well, you'd better figure something out, because he's not going to be very happy if you take her with us."

"An understatement, don't you think?" He arched his eyebrow at Cornelia, who nodded unhappily.

His jaw tightened with determination. He'd get Cleopatra to talk. He didn't have much choice. He'd raised Cornelia's hopes where her daughter was concerned, and while she might not admit it to him or herself, she was counting on him to succeed. He studied his friend's gloomy look as she turned her head to stare at one of the paintings on the wall. There was an air of hopelessness about her that illustrated just how upset his *Praefect* was.

Cornelia had always hidden her feelings well, but when Beatrice had been taken, she'd withdrawn even more. His friend had lost her husband to a heart attack two years ago, and her daughter was all Cornelia had left. Dante didn't like seeing her this way. She'd never admit it, but she was terrified for Beatrice. She'd obviously sensed his concern, and she turned her head back to him.

"You're doing the best you can, Dante. Even if we do get Beatrice out, you know as well as I do that most women either request the *Nex Cassiopeia* or find some other way to end their lives." Cornelia's eyes darkened with pain as she shook her head. "Living through that hell would challenge even the strongest Sicari woman."

His friend averted her gaze once more, and Dante experienced a sense of helplessness. It was a sensation he didn't like. He'd made a promise to himself that he'd get Beatrice out of that Praetorian hell-hole, but Cornelia was right. Her daughter might actually ask her rescuer to end her life under the Order's *Nex Cassiopeia* rite.

The thought of assisted suicide wasn't an idea he relished, but Beatrice had a right to choose her own destiny. The Order's law on that matter was clear. A swift, honorable death was the right of every Sicari. But the gods would be cruel to make Cornelia her daughter's executioner. His stomach clenched at the thought.

While the *Absconditus* did its best to protect its members, there were times when it wasn't possible. That had been the case with Beatrice. No one could have anticipated that an innocent visit to a small art gallery in Venice would result in her kidnapping. The Praetorian presence was almost nonexistent in the legendary city, and the gallery's connection to their sworn enemy had gone unnoticed until Beatrice was taken.

Even then it had taken precious man-hours to link the gallery to Beatrice's abduction. It was the only time Dante had ever seen his *Praefect* lose control. Cornelia had come close to torturing the gallery owner during the interrogation, and she'd assassinated him without Marcus's approval. Fortunately, the reigning Sicari Lord had understood better than most the pain Cornelia was experiencing.

Dante's second-in-command coughed, and he jerked his gaze up from the wood floor he'd been studying.

"I asked if you'd contacted Marcus to tell him that his daughter was here."

"Yes," he said with a quick nod. "I sent him a text message while you and Noemi were with her."

"Did you tell him she'd been hurt?"

"There wasn't any point. She was safe, and I knew Noemi would see to her wounds."

"The name Cleopatra suits her. She's quite beautiful."

Cornelia's statement brought to mind the first time he'd seen Cleopatra's face in full detail. His brain had shut down to the point where he'd not been able to think straight. She'd affected every one of his senses, and a lightning strike couldn't have knocked him off his feet any harder. Not even her namesake could have been more beautiful. He suddenly empathized with Julius Caesar and Mark Antony.

"And Jupiter's Stone, she has a mouth like Placido," Cornelia said with amusement, but he didn't respond. A long moment passed before his *Praefect* released a soft snort of laughter. "You didn't hear a word I said."

"What?" He shook his head slightly in an attempt to clear the images of Cleopatra's lovely face from his head. "No, I heard you. Cleopatra has Placido's colorful way with words."

Now that his *Praefect* mentioned it, Cleopatra's language was definitely saltier than even some of his most hardened fighters. It was distinctly at odds with her beautiful face, but he could see where she might believe it would make her fit in better with other fighters in her guild. It couldn't be easy being the *Prima Consul*'s daughter. And now that she'd discovered her relationship to Marcus, it wouldn't get any easier.

"If you keep frowning like that, your eyebrows are going to fall off." Cornelia's voice pierced his thoughts, and he jerked his gaze toward her. She'd often used the expression when he was younger to make him laugh.

"I didn't realize I was frowning," he said with a slight smile.

"Quite fiercely, I might add." Cornelia cocked her head to one side as she studied him with a look of affection. "When you were a boy, I always knew something was troubling you deeply when you frowned like that."

The observation immediately set him on edge. It had been a long time since his *Praefect* had been able to read him so easily. He shrugged and smiled with forced amusement.

"I'm concentrating on how to make Cleopatra share whatever information she has."

"I know you better than that," Cornelia said quietly. "You always were a serious child, never letting others see how badly you were hurting."

"Hurting?" Suddenly uncomfortable with the direction in which the conversation was headed, he returned to the liquor cabinet and poured himself another drink. "You make it sound like I was miserable as a child. I had a happy childhood here in the *Absconditus*."

"Did you? I sometimes wonder." Cornelia sighed. "Marcus always pushed you so hard, and Placido . . . you worshipped him to the point that you would have cut off your right arm if he'd asked you to."

"I wasn't as bad as that." Dante scoffed with a small laugh at Cornelia's dramatic statement, and when she frowned with skepticism, he shrugged again and smiled. "Maybe a finger, though."

His *Praefect* rolled her eyes at him, and he laughed. His earliest memories were of Placido teaching him how to hone his telekinetic abilities. They were happy memories. Placido's love of life had always made lessons fun, and while Marcus had been the most demanding of mentors, the Sicari Lord had never withheld his praise.

Still, as a child, he knew his great respect for both men had bordered on the edge of hero worship. Perhaps it still did. He held up his glass to her, silently asking if she wanted a drink. When she shook her head no, he took a sip of the cognac he'd poured.

"All right, maybe you were willing to give up just one finger. But I always thought everything you did was done with the singular goal of pleasing Marcus and Placido, instead of what you really wanted."

"I don't think it's a bad thing to admire one's teachers or even to aspire to be like them," he scolded gently.

"Of course it isn't," she snapped in a manner that was unlike her. "But it's not healthy to give up everything for a cause."

"What are you really trying to say, Cornelia?" He narrowed his gaze at her.

"What I'm saying is that I saw the way you looked at Cleopatra tonight. And something tells me you're regretting a decision you made when you were too young to know any better."

Cornelia's soft words made him stiffen, and he quickly assumed an unreadable expression on his face. *Christus*, had he been that enthralled with Cleopatra? Of course he had. Otherwise, his *Praefect* wouldn't be subtly reminding him that she'd never approved of his vow.

Although Cornelia had eventually come to respect his choice, she'd done everything possible to persuade him not to take the oath. She'd warned him that he'd come to regret it. The fact that Cornelia's prediction had come true earlier this evening was bad enough, but for his friend to have witnessed it was humiliating.

"You're mistaken," he said in an icy tone of voice. One more lie and he would completely undo his entire first level of training in the *Novem Conformavi.*

"Lie to yourself if you like," his *Praefect* said stoically. "But what I saw tonight was a man ready to stake his claim after only a few minutes in the woman's presence."

"If you're suggesting I've forgotten my duty—"

"I'm suggesting nothing of the sort. I'm saying that tonight I saw a man meet an unmovable force. You can deny it all you want, but I know what I saw."

"Then get your eyes checked," he snarled. "My duty has always been, and always will be, to the *Absconditus*. I've not forgotten that any more than I've forgotten what it meant when Marcus made me Tribune."

"Marcus made you Tribune because no one had ever seen a boy with such powerful abilities before. Even as a child you displayed signs of being a great leader."

"And yet you're still of the opinion I made a mistake in dedicating my life to the *Absconditus*."

"Yes. You were fifteen years old when you made your vow. A vow, I might add, that you *know* isn't binding because you made it *before* you came of age. And, despite your maturity even then, I think you made that vow because it's what you thought Placido and Marcus wanted," Cornelia said in a quiet, firm voice.

"No," he growled, his patience thinning. "I knew I could have only one mistress, and that was the *Absconditus*."

"*Jupiter's Stone*." Cornelia's composure slipped dramatically as she stared at him in openmouthed horror. "Are you telling me you think being the reigning Sicari Lord means the *Absconditus* always has to come first, even at the cost of your own happiness?"

"I'm telling you that I *chose* to put the *Absconditus* first, because it's what *I* wanted."

Dante turned away from her and walked to the window to stare at his reflection. In the glass, he saw Cornelia lean forward with one hand resting on her hip and a dark frown of worry on her face. How in the hell had he allowed the conversation to get this far? Not once in all the years since he'd taken his oath had he ever shared with anyone his real reasons for committing himself to the *Absconditus*.

Marcus and Placido had grilled him about his decision. They'd carefully kept their own opinions out of their discussions, but even if they'd told him not to take the oath, he wasn't sure he would have obeyed. He'd seen how intense emotional ties could make it difficult to lead the Sicari Lord's guild. Marcus was a prime example of what having two mistresses could do to a man. As the reigning Sicari Lord, Marcus had been separated from his wife for years. But Dante was certain it was Marcus's duty to the *Absconditus* that forced the Sicari Lord to stay away from Atia.

Over the years, Dante had seen his mentor struggle to hide his feelings whenever someone mentioned the *Prima Consul*. But it wasn't just his love for Atia the man had lost. Marcus had lost a son and the joy of watching his daughter grow up. In leading the *Absconditus*, Marcus had paid a dear price for his service to the guild.

Even Placido, despite his robust love for life, had lost a great deal when he'd been the reigning Sicari Lord. Placido's determination to remain impartial during his leadership had cost the ancient warrior his wife when he'd unknowingly sent her on a mission that ended in her death. It was just one more reason why Dante believed committing himself to the *Absconditus* had been the right choice for him. He would never have to make the kind of choice Placido had or lose as much as Marcus had.

"I'm worried about you, Dante." He met his *Praefect*'s troubled gaze in the glass reflection.

"Why?" he asked as he turned to face her. "Because I chose to lead a solitary life? It doesn't mean I'm unhappy."

"I wonder if you know what real happiness is," Cornelia said as if she were musing out loud rather than talking directly to him.

"Real happiness?" He chuckled with amusement and a fair share of relief that she was no longer probing into his reasons behind his chosen state of celibacy. "What's real happiness?"

"It's when you come home to someone who's there to welcome you with a hug. It's that warm feeling you get when you go to sleep at night knowing you're loved."

Now he was certain Cornelia was just musing out loud. Her words sounded husky, as if she was on the verge of tears, and he cleared his throat. His second-in-command obviously missed her husband, and she'd been living a hellish existence since Beatrice's kidnapping. It was understandable that after all these months she was close to reaching her breaking point. The kind of pressure she was under eventually wore a person down.

"I think we both need some sleep," he said in a matter-of-fact tone.

As if suddenly aware that she'd been thinking out loud, she jerked her head up and met his gaze with a flash of embarrassment flickering in her eyes. He deliberately turned away to give her time to compose herself, and he tossed back the remainder of his drink.

"I think you're right," Cornelia said a short moment later. He turned to watch her uncurl her slender frame out of the couch in a fluidly graceful move. "It's been a long day, and I'm teaching class in the morning."

"Which level of the *Novem Conformavi*?" he asked as he remembered several of the classes she'd led when he'd been a student. Her gaze met his, and she arched her eyebrow.

"The fourth *Tabulati*," she said.

"Temperance and awareness," he murmured as they started walking toward the hallway that connected all the rooms facing the inner courtyard.

"Why don't you stop by? I don't think any of my students are ready for the rank of Tribune, but you might find a Patrician worthy of the line of succession." Cornelia came to a halt, forcing him to do the same. She cocked her head to one side as she studied him. "That is, unless you already have someone in mind."

"I've not thought about it."

"It might be a good idea for you to start, because I think you're going to need to make a decision sometime in the very near future."

Dante didn't answer her for a minute. Cornelia was right. Marcus was clearly thinking about retirement, which meant Dante, as the future reigning Sicari Lord, needed to select two fighters to succeed him. *Absconditus* law clearly stated that if the reigning Sicari Lord chose to abdicate the position, a Tribune and a Patrician had to be selected before the leadership reins were passed.

The royal houses of Europe had always referred to their leadership succession as an heir and a spare. The role of Tribune and Patrician served a similar purpose within the *Absconditus*, but the guild's leadership wasn't rooted in blood or name. The selection was based on the strength of the guild member's telepathic and telekinetic abilities as well as temperament.

The ideal candidates were *Absconditus* warriors whose abilities and personalities were as close a match to the same qualities Maximus, the first Sicari Lord, had possessed. Generally, the Tribune chosen was a warrior who'd passed the sixth *Tabulati*. In Dante's case, there had been no other guild members with powers as strong as his, which is why he'd become Tribune at so young an age.

"I never did understand why Marcus didn't choose you to be Tribune, or at the very least, Patrician," he said.

"Because when it comes to making decisions, I'm a better follower than a leader. I see only black and white. You see all the shades in between."

"That doesn't make me a leader."

"But it does. If I were a true leader, I wouldn't have simply accepted Beatrice's fate. As the Sicari Lord, I would never have tried to find a way to rescue her," she whispered. Her gaze shifted away from his to stare at the window that stood between them and the night. "I would have complacently accepted the inevitable. You were the one who saw possibilities where I believed they didn't exist. And that's what a leader does. They forge trails where others see only the wilderness."

Almost as if she regretted letting him see her vulnerability, Cornelia jerked her head toward him and forced a smile to her lips.

"You'll make a wonderful Sicari Lord, and I shall be as proud to serve under your leadership as I have been to serve under Marcus's," she said in a quiet voice. "Now, if I don't get some sleep, I'm going to have trouble controlling my class in the morning."

"Let me guess. Giuseppe and Santino?"

"Yes," his *Praefect* said with a sigh. "Those two would die for each other, but Santino knows precisely which one of Giuseppe's buttons to push."

"They'll eventually settle down. Remember Tony and Alfredo? They used to fight like mad dogs when I was growing up."

"I'd forgotten about their sibling rivalry," Cornelia said with a nod. "Let's hope that happens with Giuseppe and Santino, because both of them are demonstrating remarkable abilities. Not as powerful as you at that age, but close. In fact, either one of them would be an excellent choice for Patrician."

Without giving him a chance to reply, she walked out of the room, leaving Dante to ponder her last statement. He'd put off even contemplating the selection of a Tribune or a Patrician. A part of him had been hoping Marcus wasn't really ready to retire. But deep inside, he'd known his time to take on the role of Sicari Lord would come a lot sooner than he was prepared for.

Maybe he should stop by Cornelia's classroom before his work-out tomorrow morning. He'd need to make a decision quickly if Marcus were to suddenly announce his retirement. Slowly, he followed in his *Praefect*'s footsteps down the long, continuous hallway that wrapped its way around the inner courtyard of the house. The thought of selecting a Tribune and a Patrician as his heirs to the Sicari Lord title was a sobering one.

Both Marcus and Placido would offer counsel, but the ultimate decision was his. Whomever he chose would lead the *Absconditus* after he retired or in the event of his death. He sucked in a deep breath and quickly released it. This was something he'd trained for since he'd turned fifteen. It wasn't unexpected, and yet for the first time he was beginning to understand how completely alone he was.

Chapter 6

"WHAT do you mean *he's dead*?" Nicostratus snarled. Dead. One of his most lucrative financial resources had been disposed of as neatly as a deck of cards.

"Angotti's body was found early this morning, along with his bodyguards and two men assigned by Dominus Russo to monitor Angotti's activities." Prior Draco Verdi's voice was quiet, almost detached, as he made his report. "The man's mistress described a sole female as the assassin. The executioner was trained in Sicari techniques."

"You've identified this Sicari bitch?" he asked harshly as he absorbed the knowledge that his adopted son had placed Angotti under surveillance before his death at the hands of Marcus Vorenus. Had Gabriel been plotting against him? What did it matter, the boy was dead and any plot was dead with him. Still, the thought only added to his anger.

"Her name is Cleopatra Vorenus."

The Prior's statement shot a blast of fury through Nicostratus, and he expressed it with the back of his hand against Verdi's cheek. The loud crack of the blow echoed sharply in the Patriarch's library despite its high ceiling and massive size. For a split second, he acknowledged the fact that the Prior barely flinched under the vicious slap, even though Nicostratus's ring had sliced into the man's cheek.

"Do you mean to tell me that fucking whore is still in *my* city?" He spoke quietly as he sent the Prior a cold look.

"We didn't know until this morning that she hadn't left with the *Prima Consul*. We still wouldn't have known if Angotti's mistress hadn't identified her," the Prior replied.

"I want her found and executed."

Nicostratus glanced down at his ring and saw blood on the Chi-Rho symbol carved into the gold crest. With a grunt of disgust, he quickly circled his desk and retrieved a tissue with which to rub the ring clean.

Rome was his. Even though the *Absconditus* had a strong presence here, Marcus Vorenus knew the Praetorians outnumbered them at least five to one, and possibly by more. But Vorenus had crossed the line when he'd led that motley group of Sicari into the Pantheon and taken the one thing Nicostratus wanted more than anything else. The *Tyet of Isis*.

It was a sign that God was making him pay a penance for past sins. What those sins were, he didn't know. Everything he'd done throughout his life was for the good of the Collegium and the Church. Then there was Gabriel's death. A small part of him would miss the boy. The poor Sicari *bastardo* had always been so eager to please him.

That kind of devotion was hard to come by and required a great deal of energy to cultivate. He pressed his palms against the dark mahogany wood of his desk and leaned forward to pin Prior Verdi under his gaze. Nicostratus didn't like the man's composed expression. It said he wasn't intimidated being in the Patriarch's presence.

Any other warrior for the Collegium would be showing fear now in the face of the Patriarch's anger. And yet, a small part of him couldn't help but admire the Prior for it. Surely underneath that calm, relaxed appearance, the man was feeling some trepidation. Even Gabriel, who could have easily killed Nicostratus, had been afraid of the Patriarch.

"What else is there?" he asked, his tone advising the man to take care.

"Our informant with the local police allowed us to question Angotti's mistress. She saw the whole thing happen from her bedroom window. The mistress said Vorenus took out all four men in a matter of minutes."

"Surely she had a partner," Nicostratus said with disgust at the thought of a single woman killing five men. He slowly sank down into the chair behind his desk.

"No, sir, she was alone."

"Then perhaps you're mistaken. My sources tell me the Sicari are under strict orders to always travel in pairs while in Rome," he snapped. "Not even Marcus Vorenus's daughter would be so stupid as to defy the Order's edict and venture out into the city on her own."

"It doesn't make sense to me either, Excellency. But it *was* Cleopatra Vorenus. One of my men pulled up pictures of possible Sicari assassins on his phone, and Angotti's mistress picked Vorenus out of the lot."

Faced with such irrefutable truth, his anger grew in strength. First Marcus Vorenus had stolen the *Tyet of Isis* from him, and now the *bastardo* had left his daughter here to assassinate Angotti. The crime lord had been an invaluable commodity to him. Angotti's reputation for ferreting out information had made him exceptionally good at keeping Nicostratus up-to-date with Sicari movements.

The fat Italian's informative reports had also circumvented several threats that would have exposed the Praetorian presence within the Church—something that hadn't happened in almost two thousand years of the Church's history. On top of all that, Angotti had offered Nicostratus multiple opportunities to expand and hide his personal finances as well as those of the Collegium's.

Nicostratus steepled his fingers and rested them against his mouth as he contemplated what Angotti's death would mean for him and the Collegium. Since the time of Octavian, the first Monsignor, during the reign of Constantine I, the Collegium had operated secretly inside the Church. Financial resources had never been a problem until recently. Thirty years ago, he could have easily shifted funds from one account to the other without detection.

These days it was becoming more and more difficult to siphon off monies from the Church's coffers to fund the Praetorian cause.

The technology that made it easier for him to invest monies he'd acquired for the Collegium and his personal use was a double-edged sword. Lately the internal audits from the Church's accounting office were becoming more frequent and even more annoying.

It was almost as if someone were trying to expose the Collegium's presence in the Church. He tightened his jaw at the thought. What if Gabriel had been trying to do that? No. Gabriel might have been difficult at times, but the boy had been fanatically loyal to the Collegium. He would never have done anything to harm his family. His reason for living. Nicostratus's gaze focused on Prior Verdi again.

"What else does Angotti's woman know?"

"About the assassination or Angotti's connection to the Collegium . . . or you, Excellency?"

Verdi's unflappable manner registered with the Patriarch again, and he narrowed his eyes at the Prior. Intelligent and shrewd. The man had figured out that Angotti was of immense importance not only to the Collegium, but to Nicostratus as well. For the first time since the man had told him about Angotti's death, the Patriarch's anger abated somewhat, and he allowed his mouth to curl slightly in approval.

"You're quite astute, Prior." He arched his eyebrows at the man. "Exactly how did you know Angotti was important to me?"

"The man had your contact information in his BlackBerry."

"Easily explained by his connection to the Collegium." Nicostratus shrugged. He wondered if the Prior played chess. No, the man was clearly a poker player, because he was bluffing.

"Yes, Excellency, but Angotti also had your birthday, the name of your favorite wine label, a notation of your tastes in music and art, plus a recent note to inform you of two transactions to a Swiss bank account. Information that indicates a close connection as opposed to a superficial one."

"Who else saw the information?" he asked as he held his body rigid to keep from leaping out of his chair.

"Only me." Verdi reached into his pants pocket, withdrew a small phone, and handed it to Nicostratus. "One of my men is a computer expert. He was able to hack the lockout code on the phone without much trouble. He gave it to me as soon as it was unlocked."

Nicostratus accepted the phone and stared at it for a moment before he laid it on the desk in front of him. He refused to let the Prior see how disturbed he was by Angotti's carelessness. His jaw hard with tension, he studied Verdi carefully. The man intrigued him. There were few Praetorians in the Collegium who were so skilled at hiding their thoughts.

"Obviously this wasn't a simple murder. What does Angotti's mistress think happened? Did she say anything that might put the Collegium in jeopardy?"

"The woman believes her lover was murdered in some bizarre cult ritual. She gave no indication that she has any knowledge about the Collegium or anything else about our brotherhood."

"I see. But you're not sure that she knows nothing." He watched the Prior hesitate before he shook his head.

"She admitted to knowing Angotti was involved in illegal activities but said that he told her nothing about his business." Verdi shrugged. "There are no guarantees, but my gut says she knows nothing."

"Since your *gut* says she's not a threat, what do you suggest we do about her?" He studied the man closely as he waited for a response. Nicostratus narrowed his eyes as he saw a brief flicker of hesitation break through the man's stoic expression. "Come now, Prior. What do you think we should do with the woman?"

"She needs to disappear. Quietly," Verdi replied.

Although the man's tone was matter-of-fact, Nicostratus thought he heard regret in the Prior's voice. The Patriarch eyed him closely, but Verdi's expression revealed nothing but indifference as to the woman's fate. Nicostratus's gaze took note of the fresh cut on Verdi's face. There weren't many Praetorians in the Collegium who didn't act like whimpering cowards in front of him when he lost his temper.

This man was clearly different. Nicostratus leaned back in his chair, folded one arm across his chest to support his elbow while he stroked his chin with his fingers, and studied the Prior intently. With Gabriel dead, he needed someone to act on his behalf in routine administrative matters. The fact that Verdi was coldly calculating was evident in his swift decision about Angotti's mistress. He liked that about the man.

"You seem quite sure of your decision, Prior Verdi."

"One can never be too careful in shielding the Collegium from our enemy, Excellency." He spoke like the most stalwart of Praetorians.

"True," Nicostratus said with a nod of sage agreement. "But in this case, I think we can err on the side of generosity and allow the woman to live. There's another female who shall not be so lucky."

"As you wish, Excellency." The man's gaze flickered with puzzlement, and Nicostratus smiled at him. Yes, the man was the perfect choice to replace Gabriel.

"Despite my initial reaction to your news about Angotti, you've impressed me, Prior."

"You honor me, Excellency," Verdi said with a slight bow.

"I think your talents might be wasted in your role as Prior. What would you think about working here in the main office of the brotherhood?"

"Here, Excellency?" There was a hint of surprise in the man's voice, revealing a crack in his stoic composure.

"Yes," Nicostratus said with a smile. "With Dominus Russo dead, I require someone to take his place to help me manage the daily administrative needs of the Collegium. The Monsignor can't be bothered with such trivialities. As the Patriarch, that's my role, and I'd like your help." Nicostratus laughed at the stunned expression on Verdi's face. For the first time since the man had entered the library, the Prior had actually displayed an emotion.

"I don't know what to say, Excellency." The man seemed completely taken aback, which pleased Nicostratus immensely.

"A simple yes will do." He gestured toward one of the chairs that faced his desk. "Sit down."

Verdi hesitated for several seconds before he seated himself in the chair. What Nicostratus had just offered was a high honor— something that many Praetorians would give their right hand for— and yet this man seemed almost reluctant about taking the position.

"Is there something wrong, Prior?" His question made the man shake his head as he met Nicostratus's gaze.

"No, Excellency. I'm simply surprised . . . and humbled by your offer."

"Honesty. I like that." The Patriarch nodded his approval. "May I call you Draco?"

"Certainly, Excellency."

"Tell me, Draco, are you aware of what happened several days ago at the Pantheon?"

"Yes, Excellency. The Sicari stole the *Tyet of Isis* and killed His Grace."

"Precisely, and now you bring me the unfortunate news that Angotti, a trusted business associate of the Collegium's, has been murdered by the daughter of our greatest enemy, Marcus Vorenus."

Just the sound of his arch nemesis's name made the Patriarch's body knot up with a tension born of fury. Marcus Vorenus had been a thorn in his side for years, and now his sworn enemy had left his daughter behind while the Sicari Lord had followed his *Prima Consul* bitch back to Chicago like the dog he was. The sudden image of Cleopatra Vorenus charging at him in the Pantheon flashed through his head.

It had been easy to thwart her attack, but what hadn't been so easy was dealing with how he'd hurt his son. The moment his sword had pierced Lysander's body, he'd actually experienced a painful remorse. Lysander could have been what Gabriel had never been. A true son. He didn't like admitting it, but he was grateful the boy was still alive.

Nicostratus focused on Draco Verdi again. The man's face was an emotionless mask. That could be a good thing or a bad thing. The fact that it was difficult to figure out what the man was thinking was annoying. He immediately stretched out his thoughts to probe his newly promoted assistant's mind. He met strong resistance, as Draco sent him a cold look.

"If you wish to know something, Excellency, you have but to ask." There was the faintest hint of defiant censure in the man's voice, and Nicostratus noted it with a grudging respect.

Not only did Draco Verdi have the ability to protect his thoughts, but he had the courage to defy the Patriarch of the Collegium. Nicostratus found himself liking the man even more. And for him, that said a great deal, because there were very few people he liked or even respected.

"Agreed." Nicostratus nodded. "Now then, tell me how much you know about the *Tyet of Isis*, Draco."

"Not much, other than that the artifact has the potential to make the Sicari and Praetorians stronger."

"Precisely, so the balance of power rests with whoever holds the secret of the artifact."

As he considered the statement, Nicostratus grimaced. Up until a few days ago, he'd been certain the balance between the Praetorians and Sicari would soon fall to the Collegium. All of that had changed when the Sicari swine had taken the *Tyet of Isis* right out from under him in the Pantheon.

Making matters worse was the fact that he'd had assurances from his mole deep within the Order that the *Tyet of Isis* was to have been his the moment it was found. His spy would pay the price for that broken promise. All this time it had been on Church property. The irony of the artifact's hiding place wasn't lost on him. He met Verdi's unreadable gaze.

"You don't seem the least bit curious as to what the artifact's secret is, Draco."

"I would imagine the box contains a recipe or a map."

The man's response made Nicostratus go rigid. Was Verdi guessing, or did he know more than he should? Only the Monsignor and the Patriarch knew the contents of the *Tyet of Isis*. Since the first Monsignor, the Collegium's leaders had been told the artifact carried a map that would strengthen the Praetorian brotherhood.

"How do you know that?" He eyed Verdi closely.

"We've been searching for the *Tyet of Isis* for as long as the Sicari, and it's well known that the artifact is believed to make the holder more powerful." Verdi eyed him with a look that said the man was even more astute than Nicostratus had thought. "I don't believe in magic, so it seems logical to assume that the artifact holds either a recipe for something to ingest that will make the owner more powerful or at the very least a map showing where the recipe can be found."

"I see." Nicostratus steepled his fingers again to study Verdi over the top of them. "So you think there's a recipe for a magical elixir in the *Tyet of Isis*?"

"A magical potion?" Verdi shook his head. "No, Excellency. If it's a recipe for anything, it's a matter of biology."

"*Biology?* What does biology have to do with the artifact?" he scoffed.

"It's strictly a hypothesis of mine, Excellency, but I believe the artifact contains a recipe, a blueprint if you like, for changing an individual's DNA to give the person telepathic *and* telekinetic abilities."

Nicostratus slowly took in the man's words. He'd always believed the *Tyet of Isis* contained a map leading to some important treasure. He'd been a fool never to have considered the possibility that it might be something that would physically transform a person. If the artifact *did* contain a recipe for a potion that changed a person's DNA, it made the situation that much more dire. The Order of the Sicari had a research-level medical facility that could easily test any potion made from a recipe such as Verdi had suggested.

"Interesting, Draco. I suppose you've some research to back up your theory?"

"I gave one of the brothers who practices medicine some DNA samples to study. His conclusion was that Praetorian and Sicari DNA have markers that point toward different abilities. It's a mutation that might possibly be replicated."

An icy chill swept over Nicostratus as he stared at the man opposite him. It was critical that they reclaim the *Tyet of Isis* from the Sicari. He rose from his chair and began to pace the floor. There was no telling how long it would take Vorenus and his people to solve the mystery of the artifact.

"We must get it back. And quickly," Nicostratus said.

He stopped at his chair and dug his fingers into the soft leather padding of the headrest. If his mole in the Order failed to retrieve the *Tyet of Isis*, he wasn't sure what else—

He slowly released his grip on the chair. Oh, it couldn't be that easy. Could it? The idea bouncing around in his head made him smile. Hands clasped behind his back, he resumed his pacing. He saw Draco's quizzical look and chuckled.

"We shall kill two birds with one stone, my dear Draco."

"Excellency?"

"I want every resource we have scouring Rome for Cleopatra Vorenus. The moment they find her, I want her brought to me."

He waved his fingers in a cavalier fashion. "Alive, of course. *And* unmarked. The privilege of marring that pretty face of hers is mine. Once we have her, I'll offer her to Vorenus in exchange for the artifact."

"Will the Sicari Lord *agree* to such a trade?" Draco asked in a skeptical tone, and Nicostratus smiled.

"I'm certain he will. Even if he doesn't, the *Prima Consul* herself will trade the artifact for their daughter."

"How can you be so sure, Excellency?" Draco eyed the Patriarch with more than a hint of foreboding.

"How can I be so sure?" Nicostratus chuckled softly. It was a sinister, menacing sound. "Because I stole their son years ago and gave him my name."

"Gabriel Russo?" the Prior said with obvious surprise.

"Exactly. Gabriel was my creation and my enemy's torment. So you can see why both Vorenus and that *Prima Consul* bitch of his will be more than willing to give up the *Tyet of Isis* to me. Although, if my man inside the Order does his job right, I shall have the artifact *and* Signorina Vorenus without any bargaining at all."

"I knew we had spies inside the Order, but one deep enough to get close to the artifact, Excellency?"

"You sound surprised, Draco."

"I confess I am."

"I've been the Patriarch for almost thirty years, and in that time I've cultivated many . . . relationships. I even have two resources in the upper echelons of the Order itself," Nicostratus said. "The *Prima Consul* could be assassinated if I so decreed."

"I am honored that you've entrusted that knowledge to me, Excellency." Draco bowed his head in a slight nod of deference.

"And now you know something that can get you killed," Nicostratus said with malicious glee as the man started at the subtle threat. "As my right hand, you'll be privy to many things. But if you betray my trust, your life is forfeit."

"Yes, Excellency." At Draco's response, Nicostratus nodded his approval.

"Now then, there are some things we need to accomplish right away if we're to retrieve the *Tyet of Isis*." Nicostratus sat down in his chair and pulled stationery from his desk along with a stick of wax and a small box. "This is an authorization for you to have limited access to the Collegium's banking account. Give this note to Signor Maida. He'll see to it that you're able to withdraw and deposit funds. All investments and transfers are at my discretion and that of the Monsignor."

He quickly folded the handwritten letter and sealed it in an envelope then lit the wick at the end of the short stick of wax. The melted wax splashed onto the flap of the envelope and began to set. As the wax was cooling, Nicostratus pulled a seal from the desk drawer and removed his ring to slide it into a notch on the seal. The moment it snapped into place, he used it to make an impression on the wax. He offered the sealed envelope to Draco. The expression on the man's face amused him.

"The seal is a remnant from years past when sealed documents meant they were genuine. A bit dramatic, but it appeals to the romantic in me," he murmured with a smile, knowing full well that there wasn't a romantic bone in his body. The seal represented his complete authority. "When you give this to Signor Maida, he'll know it's an official authorization from me."

With a wave of his hand, he dismissed Draco then immediately turned his attention to the paperwork in front of him. The Prior quickly got to his feet and bowed slightly before heading toward the door. The man had just reached the door when Nicostratus came to a decision.

"As an afterthought," he said without looking up from his paperwork. "I think your initial assumptions about Angotti's mistress were correct. Make her disappear. Quietly."

No sooner had he spoken than something malevolent scraped across his mind, and he jerked his head up to look at the Prior's back. Almost at the same moment, Draco wheeled around, his expression still stoic, but his posture that of a warrior prepared for the unexpected.

"Is everything all right, Excellency?"

"Of course, why wouldn't it be?" Nicostratus lied as he studied the Prior closely.

"There for a moment, I thought . . . forgive me. I'm mistaken."

Nicostratus frowned as the man bowed again then left the study. Clearly the Prior had felt something as well. If it weren't for the man's reaction, he'd be inclined to think the sensation he'd experienced had come from Draco himself.

His fingers drummed a soft rhythm on the desktop as he wondered if he'd made a mistake where the Prior was concerned. Normally he would have researched a potential successor to Gabriel quite extensively, and yet he'd chosen Draco without any forethought at all. Nicostratus grunted.

He lifted the lid of his laptop and clicked the e-mail icon. He'd have James run a full profile on Draco starting tomorrow. If anything out of the ordinary showed up, then Draco Verdi and he would have a discussion that would end nice and neat.

Chapter 7

CLEO stood in the salon staring up at the portrait hung on the wall over a half-moon table. From his manner of dress, she wondered if the man in the painting was a Sicari Lord. He wore the same type of attire she'd seen her fa— She'd seen Marcus and Dante wear. She ignored the Freudian slip.

As she studied the portrait more closely, she drew in a quick breath of surprise. She wasn't well versed in Italian artwork, but there was one artist she knew well. Sofonisba Anguissola. As far as she could tell, the portrait on the wall was an original. Her gaze focused on the man's face.

She wondered if he might have been the leader of the Sicari Lords in his time period. Just like her father—Marcus was today. Another Freudian slip. She frowned and released a harsh sigh. Eventually, she would have to face the man. It wasn't something she really wanted on her bucket list, but in all fairness to Marcus, it wasn't like he was a deadbeat dad.

Her mother had lied about his existence to Cleo and had kept Marcus in the dark as well. The thought made her tighten her mouth with anger. If there was anything her mother should never have lied to her about, it was who her father was. She understood the reasons for her mother's actions, but it was the past three years of silence that she was having trouble accepting.

Atia should have told her the truth after Cleo had lost the baby and the doctors had confirmed she'd never be able to have children. Her hand automatically went to her stomach. She'd always wanted kids, and now . . . she closed her eyes for a brief moment. It was over and done with. Dwelling on it wasn't going to change anything. But it should have changed her mother's decision about keeping her father a secret.

Cleo's gaze returned to the portrait on the wall. It was bad enough learning that her real father was alive, but the fact that he was a Sicari Lord only raised the bar for her. The Sicari Lords had always been an elusive part of the Order's long history. Until that night in the Pantheon, she'd not really believed they existed. Now, she was knee-deep in Sicari Lords.

Her lack of skills had always made her feel like she was standing on the outside looking in when it came to the Order. It was why she pushed herself so hard to be one of the best-trained fighters the Order had. But the *Absconditus* . . . this was something altogether different. She'd never felt so completely out of her depth in her entire life. So far this morning she'd seen more than a dozen people during her quiet exploration, and she had no idea who was a Sicari Lord and who was *Vigilavi*. And she sure as hell didn't want to ask.

Just being here made her nervous, and she didn't like the feeling, especially when her host had deserted her last night. The man had disappeared moments after their arrival, leaving the stoic Cornelia to arrange for Cleo's *Curavi* and a room for the night. On some inexplicable level, the way Dante had abandoned her ticked her off.

On the other hand, she wasn't sure she was quite ready to face the man just yet. Particularly when there was something about him that made her body tighten with pleasurable tension. When he'd pushed back his hood last night, her heart had skipped a beat. She'd always appreciated the beauty of the human face, and Dante's was no exception.

Despite the darkness, he'd been close enough for her to see his sharp, angular features. It had been impossible to tell the color of his eyes, but his dark hair had a slight curl to it, and *Deus*, that mouth. He could easily pleasure a woman in so many ways with that beautiful mouth of his. Her stomach did a slight flip-flop at that last thought. What would he be like in bed?

She frowned. Somehow Dante didn't seem like the type who'd easily fall into bed with just any woman who crossed his path. If anything, he seemed a little uptight. Although she had to give him major points for having the kind of voice that could give a woman an orgasm without even touching her.

She drew in a quick breath then blew it out just as quickly. *Christus*, the man wasn't just a Sicari—he was a Sicari Lord. And ever since Michael, she'd made it a point to only get involved with *Vigilavi*. They understood the Order, and like her, they didn't have any special powers. They wouldn't reject her because she was a freak.

"*Signorina.*"

She jumped as someone tapped her on the shoulder, and she whirled around to assume a defensive posture. The young man facing her eyed her with amusement until she scowled at him. In an instant, his expression became one of polite respect. He couldn't have been more than fourteen or fifteen, but he had the air of someone much older.

"*Signorina*, I am here to take you to the Tribune Condellaire."

"Tribune?" She narrowed her gaze at him in puzzlement as a small, indefinable thought fluttered around in the back of her mind like a mad butterfly. "You mean Dante?"

"Yes, *signorina*. The Tribune would like you to join him in the garden."

Now the man wanted to see her. He'd left her hanging all morning feeling lost and out of place, and he'd finally decided he was ready to see her. Instead of coming for her, Dante had sent someone else to fetch her. And it *was* a summons, which was like adding insult to injury. *He* needed *her*, not the other way around.

She had the information from Angotti, and she wasn't about to let Dante off the hook when it came to her involvement. She was going into that convent whether he liked it or not. She jerked her head at him.

"Lead the way," she said.

The boy's manner changed immediately at her authoritative tone of voice. It was as if he'd suddenly realized she wasn't just another pretty face and he'd underestimated her. It didn't surprise her. A lot of people, mostly Praetorians, did that. It was the downside to being pretty. First impressions often resulted in others thinking she was a helpless, brainless female. The truth was she'd easily give up her looks if she could have a Sicari ability. The young man bowed slightly in her direction then gestured for her to follow him.

He led the way out of the salon and down a corridor she'd not explored yet. It brought them into another salon like the one they'd just left. This room was similar to all the others she'd visited this morning. It was elegantly furnished, and artwork filled the walls, tables, and anywhere there was space available. Despite her limited experience, she was certain most, if not all, of the artworks were priceless pieces. The house was a virtual living museum.

No. The word *house* was a misnomer. It was actually a palace. Small, but a palace nonetheless. Surrounded by a tall, unassuming stone wall, the Sicari Lord installation didn't look like much from the street. But once you were past the gates and inside, it was breathtaking. She'd spent all morning walking through at least six different rooms and studying the opulent decor and each room's artwork.

They moved from one room to the next via the corridor that connected them until they reached a stained glass door. The young man opened the door without touching the handle. He stepped aside and waved his hand toward the open doorway.

The late-morning air was pleasantly warm despite the fact that it wasn't quite April yet. A lattice walkway covered in grapevines provided shade from the sun beaming down on a large ornamental garden situated in the middle of the house. She'd gotten glimpses of the sizable courtyard from one of the windows earlier, but as she stepped out from under the covered walkway, she took her first good look at the garden.

As she studied her surroundings, she realized the house was designed like an ancient Roman residence, centered around a *peristylium*. The stone columns she'd seen lining the hallway had to be the remains of a colonnade walkway. The breezeway had since been closed off, making it one long hallway that wrapped its way around the garden.

She stepped out from under the covered walkway and welcomed the warmth of the sun on her face before a movement she saw out of the corner of her eye diverted her attention. Across the expanse of the stone-paved courtyard, she saw Dante going through the slow movements of a martial arts exercise. Immediately, she experienced a quiet tranquility that relaxed her. It was an unfamiliar sensation, almost as if she was experiencing his calm state of mind. Fuck, what was she thinking? She couldn't sense emotions. But physical chemistry? That, the man had in spades, and she loved looking at him.

The only thing he wore was a pair of black, loose-fitting trousers. Entranced, she watched his leg come up in a slow high kick, his foot flexing inward with his toned arms extended in perfect position. The muscles of his back rippled as he slowly descended from the high kick and sank down toward the ground.

In a controlled movement, his leg slid out to one side, while his entire body dropped into a low crouch until she couldn't see any space between his extended leg and the ground. As he moved, his hand followed the line of his inner thigh, gliding toward his foot then up into the air. The slowly defined movements of his exercise displayed the power of his muscular arms and emphasized the strength of his legs.

She didn't budge an inch as she watched him move fluidly from one position to the next. It was like watching a large tiger in a confined area. Raw, lethal power hidden beneath the skin, and the promise of blazing speed. Even if she'd wanted to, she couldn't have turned away, because he was beautiful to watch.

Her gaze followed the path his arms made through the air, and she couldn't help remembering how he'd carried her to the car last night. She'd liked it. Maybe a little too much. And now, seeing him like this . . . Her mind shifted gears as she imagined running her hands over his delicious-looking chest, shoulders, and back. From there her thoughts went a little wild as she pictured what else she'd like to do to the man.

The way he suddenly stiffened then jerked out of his exercise to whirl around and face her made her frown as she walked toward him. *Christus*, was the guy blushing? No, he couldn't be. Exertion. That's what it had to be. Of course, if he'd been reading her mind—

Okay, that thought didn't make her happy.

Telepathy was an intimacy that required permission among the Sicari, and she'd not given it. She didn't care *how* glorious his body was. On second thought, she might be able to give a little for that reason. And *Deus*, he did have a body.

The color in his face seemed to deepen, and she eyed him suspiciously as she came to a halt in front of him. Hell, he looked like she'd caught him with his hand in a cookie jar. Then again, maybe it was because she was still drooling over him like a woman who hadn't had sex in a while.

She ignored the voice that emphasized precisely how long it had been. Instead, she reminded herself that he'd abandoned her last night and taken his sweet time summoning her this morning. Not to mention how he'd sent junior for her rather than coming himself.

"You wanted to see me?" Her irritation at the way he'd left her hanging for the entire morning came through loud and clear in her voice.

"Yes, we need to talk about what Angotti told you." Dante turned away from her and picked up a black martial arts jacket off the grassy area where he'd been exercising.

"Not until I have some assurances from you about including me in the rescue mission," she said as she watched him shrug on the jacket then tie it closed.

As he knotted the sash around his waist, she noted his strong hands and long fingers. In the next breath she envisioned his hands caressing her breasts, his thumbs rubbing across her nipples until they ached for him to suckle her. The image made her wet, and she drew in a deep breath then released it in exasperation. *Merda*, she needed to stop thinking about the man's body and focus on the topic at hand. But damn, the man really was delicious eye candy. He was a red-hot waiting to dissolve on her tongue. An odd expression crossed his face as he met her gaze. For a second time, she got the impression he was embarrassed.

"I have some concerns about letting you go to the convent."

"Like what?" Cleo narrowed her gaze at him. If he even mentioned her lack of special abilities, she'd deck him.

"You carried out an execution without a partner, despite knowing what the standing rule is in Rome." There was a sharp edge to his voice that said he wasn't going to give way easily.

"I told you why I didn't take a partner," she snapped. "I would have needed to explain my reasons for grilling Angotti, not to mention my methods."

"It was reckless."

"Reckless implies that I rushed into the assassination without a plan, which isn't true. I planned Angotti's assassination carefully, and while the Praetorians were a bit of a surprise, I knew it was more than possible they might turn up," she said in a matter-of-fact voice. "I weighed all the options, and my plan was a risk I was willing to take. Angotti had the information I wanted. If there had been another way to get what I wanted, I would have taken that route. There wasn't."

She worked hard to keep from appearing defensive as he studied her with a careful look she was already starting to recognize despite having known him less than a day. His expression of assessment and calculation reminded her of Lysander when he was evaluating a decision he had to make. He even tilted his head in the same way Lysander did when considering something.

Now that she could see Dante in the full light of day, the resemblance between the two men was pretty remarkable. She scoffed at the notion. She was going off the memory of what Lysander used to look like. It had been more than a year since that night in a Chicago warehouse when they'd found Lysander with half his face peeled off.

Still, there was something similar about the man who was like a big brother to her and the Tribune standing in front of her. The two men looked enough alike to be brothers. She brushed off the thought as her imagination was running wild this morning. As she studied his face, she could tell he was thinking long and hard about how to respond to her. Did he know she had no special Sicari abilities? It was common knowledge in the Order that she was different. She flinched at the thought.

Dante folded his arms across his chest and eyed her carefully. He knew. Cleo was certain of it. It was why he was looking at her like that. Lysander always had that look when he was about to tell her something she didn't want to hear. Now Dante was going to tell her she couldn't go with him on the mission because she wasn't a true Sicari.

"An assault on the convent is far too dangerous—"

"*Don't*. Don't even *think* of going there," she snapped fiercely. "Just because I don't have any Sicari abilities doesn't mean I can't fight. Like *this*."

With a quick move, she kicked her foot out to hook it around the back of Dante's leg and tugged hard. He easily thwarted her attempt to drop him to the ground by twisting his body in midair as he fell backward. In less than a second he landed in a push-up position, and his foot lashed out at her leg. She drew in a sharp breath as she quickly jumped to one side. She was crazy. She'd just attacked a Sicari Lord.

Instinctively, she danced backward as he sprang upright. The expression on his face said he wasn't happy. No big surprise there. Invisible fingers wrapped around both her arms as he slowly used his telekinetic ability to draw her toward him. She knew better than to resist, and instead, she deliberately threw herself forward.

The move surprised him, and as she slammed into him, her momentum threw him off balance. An instant later, he was on his back and she was on top of him. With her face inches from his, she was able to see the color of his eyes for the first time. They were the shade of an angry sea at night. Dark blue and mysterious. *Christus*, his voice wasn't the only thing about him that would easily make a woman forget who she came to the party with.

As their gazes locked, she breathed in the tangy aroma of spice. The potent male scent of him stirred up an image of a warm night, hot skin, and tousled silk sheets. Beneath the palm of her hand, she could feel the racing beat of his heart. The sound of ragged breathing caught her attention. Was that sound coming from her?

No, not only her. His breathing was just as harsh and shallow. The tension in him was palpable, and her own heartbeat quickened as the sudden pressure of his erection swelled against her inner thigh. Her gaze drifted downward to his mouth, and an impish desire to break through that restrained manner of his swept through her.

She didn't think. She simply acted on the impulse of the moment and bent her head to brush her lips across his in a tentative kiss. She'd only meant it to be a quick touch, but the taste of fresh mint made her mouth linger against his. His body went rigid beneath her.

Desire coiled through her belly to spread its heat through her limbs. His arousal hardened further, and she shifted her hips until his hard length was pressing into the apex of her thighs. His mouth moved against hers, and she nipped at his lower lip with her teeth. *Deus*, even without trying the man had her so turned on she was willing to forget he was a Sicari Lord.

She stiffened against him. He was right. She *was* reckless. First she'd hit a Sicari Lord, and now she was attempting to seduce one. Embarrassment slid its painful net around her as she broke the kiss and lifted her head. The world suddenly shifted, and Dante rolled her over until he was the one on top.

His expression was harsh as he stared down at her. If she hadn't been so humiliated by her seduction attempt, she might have thought him embarrassed as well. She swallowed hard at the way he quickly got to his feet and stepped back from her. The stiff way he moved gave her the impression that he felt soiled being so close to her.

Not that it would surprise her. There were a lot of Sicari men who'd found her lack of abilities unattractive. Except Michael. He'd not cared until the day she'd lost the baby and her ability to have children. But that had made his rejection all the more painful. Without any order from Dante, she scrambled to her feet. Head bowed, she breathed in a sharp breath.

"I'm sorry, *il mio signore*, you were right. I'm reckless and deserve whatever sentence you hand out."

Humiliation held her rigid in front of him, and she jumped as he uttered a violent oath beneath his breath. Her gaze jerked upward at the sound. Desire, anger, and confusion hardened his expression into an icy façade as he turned away from her.

"It's not your fighting skills I'm concerned about," he ground out.

"I don't understand." Puzzled, she shook her head in bemusement.

"It's *who* you are that's the problem."

"Who I—"

Cleo stiffened as the full impact of his statement slammed into her. Marcus Vorenus. Suddenly, now that people knew she was the daughter of a Sicari Lord, she needed to be handled with care. Well, she refused to let anyone treat her like some precious object.

"I want to talk to him," she said with a quiet hiss of air breaking past her lips. "*Now.*"

His features expressionless, Dante turned his head toward her. Those dark, stormy eyes of his studied her for a brief moment before he nodded sharply.

"Come."

Without waiting for her response, he turned and headed toward the corner of the garden. Cleo followed him with a rigid stride that matched his. She was going on this mission whether Dante Condellaire or Marcus Vorenus liked it or not. In the far reaches of her brain a trigger went off, but she didn't pay any attention. All she cared about at the moment was making sure she was included in the rescue mission.

She'd put too much effort into researching, analyzing, and planning the assault on the convent not to be included on the mission team. There was no way of knowing what her information might bring to the table in terms of a rescue plan, but it was clear Dante didn't have enough information to move forward with his own plan.

If he did, he wouldn't have tried to pressure her into telling him what Angotti had revealed. It would explain why he was so angry last night. He'd been furious that he'd not arrived before Angotti's execution.

As she followed Dante into the house, she fought to gain control of her anger. If she were going to convince Marcus to let her participate in Marta's rescue, she needed to sound logical and rational when she spoke to him. They passed through several rooms via the corridor that surrounded the courtyard until they turned into a smaller hallway that led to a monitoring room.

It took her a moment to adjust to the low lighting, and when she did, she saw almost twenty different video screens that surveilled the perimeter of the mansion. The young man and woman watching the video feeds immediately jumped to attention as Dante entered the room. He waved them to stand down and turned to the woman.

"Mary, contact White Cloud and get His Eminence on screen."

"*Si, il mio signore,*" the woman said as she spun her chair around to face the console.

Cleo winced. Eminence. The word made Marcus sound even more important. While the woman at the console worked quickly to connect them, Dante stood beside her with his arms folded across his chest like a silent guardian waiting to be summoned back to duty. She was certain he expected Marcus to override her protests. Ironically, so did she. The silence in the room was almost suffocating as they waited, but she refused to let her anxiety show.

She was about to go head-to-head with a powerful Sicari Lord, and even if he was her birth father, it was still an intimidating thought. One of the monitors flickered with movement, and her throat closed tight with fear. Hell, facing those two Praetorians last night hadn't scared her like this. The realization made her angry.

She didn't have anything to fear. This was her life, and she was entitled to live it as she pleased. As Marcus's face appeared on the screen, Dante gestured toward the headset the young woman at the console offered her. Cleo hesitated for only a second before she stepped forward to take the mike and sit down in front of the video screen. She wasn't quite sure how to begin, and Marcus cleared his throat.

"I'm glad to see you're safe and well, Cleopatra," the Sicari Lord said quietly. "I understand you ran into a slight bit of trouble."

Cleo glanced over her shoulder at Dante, whose expression hadn't changed. She looked back at the monitor and nodded. "Nothing I couldn't handle, but the Tribune's assistance made it easier for me to get to a healer."

"Healer?"

She saw Marcus frown darkly, and Dante growled with displeasure directly behind her. So the Tribune hadn't told Marcus everything about last night. Was it possible Dante hadn't mentioned his plan to rescue the women in the Convent of the Sacred Mother either? She was suddenly certain he hadn't. She liked that. It gave her leverage. She shook her head.

"Just a cut on the leg. I was fine."

"Good." Although a hint of suspicion still remained on his features, Marcus seemed reasonably satisfied with her answer.

"We do have a slight problem, though," she said in a firm voice. "I have some personal business here in Rome that I'd like to wrap up before I return stateside."

"Personal business?" The questioning note in his voice matched the wariness of his expression.

"A friend of mine I want to spend time with," she said smoothly. It was true. She did want to see Marta again. "While I was here, I thought I could offer up my skills to the Rome guild, but the Tribune here seems to think my bloodline should limit me to duties that involve less . . . risk."

"I see," Marcus murmured.

Cleo locked her jaw as she watched the monitor screen closely. For the first time, she could see a resemblance between herself and the man who was her father. He was clearly calculating a response designed to keep her in check without appearing to be manipulative. She wasn't about to give him time to back her into a corner.

"I'm glad you understand, because I'm certain my mother will have informed you by now that I do not like to be treated any differently than anyone else."

"I wasn't suggesting you should be, Cleopatra."

The Sicari Lord's use of her formal name grated on her nerves. She really didn't like it when people called her by her full name. It always made her feel like she was a kid again, about to be scolded by her mother. Although, come to think of it, she didn't really mind when Dante used her full name. It sounded soft and lovely when he said it. She focused her attention back on the conversation at hand.

"Good. The Tribune here had me worried that I was suddenly on lockdown just because we happen to . . . *know* each other." She stared hard at the screen in front of her and saw a flash of frustration darken her father's face.

"No. You're free to carry out your duties," Marcus replied with a growl. "All I ask is that you keep in mind that the *Prima Consul* will blame me if anything happens to you."

At the mention of her mother, Cleo grimaced. The man wasn't playing fair. Just because Cleo was still angry about being lied to didn't mean she didn't love her mother. And she knew her mother loved her. But she still wasn't ready to deal with the issue yet. It remained a raw wound that needed a little more time to heal. She tilted her chin slightly in defiance before nodding sharply.

"Understood," she bit out. "Although, we both know the *Prima Consul* has no one to blame but herself."

"You judge her too harshly, Cleopatra," Marcus said quietly.

The observation was the exact same one Ignacio had made when she'd first learned the truth about her father. *Merda*, was Marcus still in love with her mother? She drew in a deep breath. She sure as hell didn't want to face that question at the moment. It was hard enough coming to grips with the fact that she had a Sicari Lord for a father, let alone the possibility that he might become a permanent presence in her life.

"I judge her no less than I would myself. I just need time." Her quiet response pulled a reluctant nod from Marcus.

"As you wish. When you're ready, come home to White Cloud. I know your mother misses you."

Cleo nodded then tugged the headset off and tossed it at the woman manning the console before she hurried out of the control room toward the courtyard. *Deus*, why in Jupiter's Stone was she suddenly feeling lousy about this whole situation with her mother? It wasn't as if *she'd* done anything wrong.

The moment she stepped out into the sunlight, she closed her eyes and lifted her face up to the sun. Something damp hit her cheek, and she blinked trying to see the blue sky that was nothing but a blur. Fuck, she was crying. Viciously wiping tears off her face, she dragged in a deep sobbing breath and paced the stones leading into the center of the *peristylium*.

She hated it when she cried. It was bad enough that she did it watching sad movies, but over her own troubles? Hands on her hips, she closed her eyes and willed the tears to vanish. She didn't want anyone feeling sorry for her, least of all Dante. She didn't need or want anyone's pity no matter the reason.

The back of her neck suddenly started to tingle before the sensation spread. Dante. What was it about this guy that made her whole body go off like a metal detector? She quickly brushed aside the remnants of her tears and turned to face him. He stopped in front of her and studied her for a long moment.

"Are you all right?"

"Yes," she said as she bobbed her head in the affirmative.

"Good."

She couldn't remember the last time she felt this awkward. Not only had she dropped him to the ground, but she'd kissed him. *Deus*, she'd reacted like a third grader on the playground, while Sir Galahad here had done the gentlemanly thing and just brushed it off. She owed him an apology. Hesitating, she nibbled at her lower lip. Did she really want to open up that can of worms again? She tightened her jaw. Yes, she really did.

"I'm sorry about what happened earlier."

"I don't need an apology."

"Maybe not, but you've got one anyway," she said in a voice tight with embarrassment. "I shouldn't have dropped you to the floor like that . . . and I . . . well, the kiss just seemed like the thing to do at the time."

"Are you finished?" His question made her jerk her head up to see an odd look on his face. So help her, if he were laughing at her, she'd drop him to the ground again. Sicari Lord or not.

"Yes, I'm finished."

"Then let's move on," he said quietly. "I might not want to take you with me to the convent, but something tells me I don't have much choice."

"You mean the fact that you haven't mentioned your little project to Marcus?"

"Correct." His mouth tightened as he scowled at her. "The minute you skirted that issue with Marcus, I knew you'd hold my feet to the fire."

"And you were right." She offered him a small smile of triumph. "So how do we proceed?"

Chapter 8

CLEOPATRA'S question made him grimace. She had the same instincts her father did. She'd not missed the fact that he'd avoided telling Marcus of his plans. Just as she'd known last night a partner would have hindered her ability to get information from Angotti, she knew Marcus would not condone Beatrice's rescue from the convent. Cleopatra wouldn't hesitate to use that knowledge to her benefit. Resigned to her participation, he eyed her satisfied expression with more than a hint of irritation.

"After we compare notes on what we both know, we'll formulate a plan of attack," he said as he glanced down at his clothing. "Right now, I need to change clothes and give Cornelia a message from Marcus."

Dante sucked in a sharp breath of air as her gaze slid over him, and his chest tightened at the way his body immediately responded to her. He'd been fighting to keep himself out of her thoughts since she first entered the garden this morning. But his control had slipped drastically the minute the images from her head found their way into his.

Now, from that suggestive look on her face, he had a good idea what she was imagining. He immediately strengthened his mental shield, but it was impossible to remain unmoved by her. She had an innate sensuality that gave those beautiful violet eyes of hers a sultry, sleepy look. A part of him wondered if this was what she looked like when she woke up in the morning—ready and willing to be kissed.

His mind reeled at the image taking root in his head, and his mouth went dry as he fought to keep his senses from overriding his self-control. The expression on her face became one of confident amusement as she smiled at him. He suddenly realized she'd said something to him, although he was at a loss for what it was.

"What?"

"I asked if you needed help," she said with an impish grin.

"Help?" The erotic image of her undressing him hit him with the force of a Praetorian kick to his solar plexus.

"Yes, I asked if you wanted me to find Cornelia while you changed. But if you need help with something else . . ."

Her voice trailed off into nothing and left little to the imagination. *Christus*, the woman was trying to seduce him. And doing it well, given the strength of his erection. A knot developed in his throat at his sudden urge to read her thoughts. He viciously suppressed the desire.

It was bad enough he'd accidentally entered her thoughts earlier. That had been enough of an education for one day. A fiery heat filled his face, and he knew he was blushing like a teenager. Irritated by his inability to practice the control he'd learned in the *Novem Conformavi*'s second *Tabulati*, he scowled at her.

"*No*, I'll find Cornelia when I've finished changing." He could hear the growl of annoyance in his voice, and apparently so could Cleopatra, because a small laugh escaped her full lips. He suppressed an oath of frustration, and he wasn't sure if his irritation was the result of her laugh or the fact that he'd been focused on her mouth. "I'll meet you in the library after lunch so we can discuss our next steps."

"Okay," she said with a slight shrug as she slid her gaze over him once more. "But if you need me to—"

"*No*," he snapped. "Excuse me."

He stalked away from her, all too aware that it wasn't the type of exit he would like to have made. By the gods, he was in trouble. Cleopatra was different from any woman he'd ever met. There was something about her that sent every one of his senses spiraling out of control whenever he got close to her.

It took him only a couple of minutes to reach his rooms, and the way the door slammed shut behind him only emphasized the impact the woman had on him. The serenity and self-control he'd regained from last night's interaction with Cleopatra had disappeared the instant she'd entered the courtyard.

His ability had always been strong when it came to sensing the presence of others, even when he couldn't see them. But his sensory perception had gone off the scale the second Cleopatra had gotten close to the *peristylium*. With a noise of frustration, he strode into the bathroom. A shower always had a way of helping him think through his problems. And Cleopatra was one of the biggest problems he'd come up against in a very long time.

By the time he was naked, the water was hot, and he quickly stepped under the showerhead. Hands braced against the tile, he welcomed the pulsating spray beating down on his neck. The steady rhythm was usually a soothing one for him, but not today. *Christus*, when had he lost his ability to control his emotions? Every level of the *Novem Conformavi* built on the previous foundation, and by the age of eleven he'd excelled at controlling his reactions to whatever he encountered. Now, after all his years of training, he'd suddenly discovered his control had limits.

When he'd first sensed Cleopatra's presence in the garden, he'd been determined to complete his exercise and remain indifferent to the feelings she aroused in him. His resolve to control his emotions and finish his workout had interfered with his ability to keep himself from penetrating the peripheral edge of her thoughts. And sweet Juno, what thoughts.

As the woman had watched him exercise, she'd been imagining the two of them entwined in acts of pleasure he'd not even dreamed about. Hot, incredible images that had jerked him out of his exercise routine. And he'd not been able to purge those pictures from his head since. His cock grew hard as the visions he'd seen in her mind kept playing over and over again in his own thoughts.

How could he work with her when his body had ideas of its own where she was concerned? The shower water pounding against his back, he looked down at his growing erection. It was a test. The gods were testing him and his loyalty to the *Absconditus*. They'd sent her to tempt him. And Juno knew she was a temptation unlike any other he'd faced.

Closing his eyes, he tried to shut out the memory of her openly displayed attraction to him. He might be inexperienced, but that smile of hers had been a clear invitation to sin. He was certain of it because of what he'd seen in her head. Desperately, he tried to ignore the images in his thoughts but failed.

Even more damning was the way his body throbbed for something he understood but had never experienced. He swallowed hard. Despite his desire to maintain his control, he knew there was only one way to ease the need pulsing through him.

With a ruthless grip, he grabbed his erection in one hand and stroked himself. The immediate effect was one of intense pleasure despite his intent to make it otherwise. An image of Cleopatra in an erotic position drifted through his head, and his cock jumped hard in his hand. Another picture of her filled his mind, and he released a low, harsh groan as his body demanded satisfaction.

The water splashing down over him, he gulped in deep breaths as he pumped hard and fast on his erection. More erotic images of Cleopatra flew through his head, each one more potent than the next. With every arousing vision, the friction against his cock grew more intense as he worked his hand faster and faster.

White-hot heat surged through his veins, spreading its way into every muscle in his body until it drew his sacs up tight. With a shout, he threw his head back and milked his cock until it had spent the last of its white fluid. Deep, harsh breaths rolled out of him as he leaned back against the cool tile, the shower splashing over the lower half of his body. *Deus*, he'd masturbated before, but never like this.

In the past, the images in his head had been of faceless, unknown women to help him satisfy his body's physical ache, nothing more.

But just now—this had been something altogether different. As he'd pumped his hand over his cock, he'd envisioned more than just Cleopatra's face and body.

He'd imagined what it would be like to experience her for the first time. His first time with a woman. He ducked his head and allowed the water to wash over the back of his neck. Somehow he was certain his hand on his cock was nowhere near as satisfying as being inside Cleopatra would have been.

Masturbating had merely been his desperate attempt to satisfy his stark longing for a woman that his vow of abstinence said he couldn't have. He'd failed. A shudder lanced through him. He was on the edge of a precipice, and if he didn't tread lightly, he'd tumble into an abyss. The thought scared the hell out of him. With a snarl of frustration, he slapped his palms against the tile wall behind him and pushed himself back under the spray of water.

A short while later, he'd just finished rolling the sleeves of his shirt up over his arms when he sensed an old presence that he knew well. Placido. Centering his thoughts, he concentrated on filling his consciousness with the tranquility he'd learned in the fifth level of the *Novem Conformavi*.

As a sense of calm swept over him, he offered up a brief prayer to Jupiter that he'd recaptured some of the peace he'd lost in the last twenty-four hours. It would help him match wits with the old Sicari Lord, whose intellect was rivaled only by his legendary abilities as an intuitive and seer.

With an invisible touch, Dante closed the folding doors of his closet and the drawer of his clothes chest. When he entered his living room, he mentally opened the door for the oldest living Sicari Lord before the man could knock. More than eighty years old, the ancient warrior stood in the doorway of Dante's apartment with a smile of satisfaction on his face.

"The strength of your abilities continues to grow, my boy. One day you will be even more powerful than Marcus or myself."

"You honor me with your presence and your words," Dante said as he invited the man into his home with a bow of respect.

Placido had once been the reigning leader of the *Absconditus*, but he'd surrendered those duties to Marcus years ago. Although he still retained the honorary title of Sicari Lord, his role was that of advisor and teacher of the younger students enrolled in the *Novem Conformavi.*

The elderly Sicari Lord still possessed a proud bearing and strong stride, but he seemed to move slower with each passing year. Eventually the old man's time would come to join other Sicari Lords in the Elysium Fields. It was then that the *Absconditus* would lose a wise counsel and mentor, while Dante would lose a good friend. As his gaze met Placido's, the elderly man sent him a look of disgust.

"From the expression on your face, you think me not long for the *Rogalis,*" the ancient warrior snapped. As Dante grimaced, the old man sighed heavily. "You are not wrong to think it so."

"I'm certain there are many years yet before we plan your funeral."

"Many?" Placido snorted with cynical amusement as he arched an eyebrow at Dante. "I didn't come here to discuss my future. I wish to discuss yours."

"Mine?"

Dante frowned in puzzlement. What was there to discuss? He was Tribune, heir apparent to the reigning Sicari Lord. When Marcus stepped down from his position, Dante would take his place. It had been decided long ago.

"I understand we have a guest." It was a statement, but Dante heard the question in his friend's voice.

"Yes, Marcus's daughter," he said with a nod. "When he checked in yesterday, he mentioned Cleopatra was still in Rome. I decided to keep an eye on her for him."

"I see." Placido moved toward the doors of the balcony that overlooked the *peristylium* below. He opened them and breathed in a deep breath of fresh air. "I saw Signorina Vorenus from the library window. She is quite beautiful."

The statement caught Dante off guard, but he managed to maintain the calm center he'd found despite his friend's observations. He wasn't sure why Cleopatra would interest Placido.

"She is." He kept his response simple. He'd learned a long time ago the elderly warrior enjoyed testing him.

"I sense a disturbance in you." Placido turned away from the open doorway and narrowed his gaze at him. "You're troubled."

"I am *disconcerted*."

Technically, it wasn't a lie. The first level of the *Novem Conformavi* was taught early, and he'd been five when he'd learned the principles of the first *Tabulati*. Honesty, loyalty, and generosity were the foundations for the other eight levels of training. Not that he'd practiced them last night. His jaw locked with tension. His reply had simply avoided *speaking* the obvious, because he was most definitely in trouble.

"Disconcerted," Placido murmured with a sage nod of his head.

It was clear Dante's choice of words had not fooled the old man. The Sicari Lord studied him for a long moment before turning back toward the garden view. The silence in the room edged its way across his skin like a sharp blade. For a brief moment, his thoughts raced back to the images he'd seen in Cleopatra's head and how his release in the shower had been a temporary reprieve from the desire she aroused in him.

He was beginning to realize he was in far deeper than he'd originally thought. It explained why Placido's intuitive nature had brought him here. Dante was in a desperate struggle with his attraction to Cleopatra, and the ancient Sicari Lord knew it. But Dante wasn't ready or willing to discuss the matter with his friend. This was something he needed to resolve on his own. He cleared his throat.

"Marcus asked me to watch over her until she returned to Chicago, so she'll be staying here for a while." He was pleased his voice displayed none of the chaotic emotions from earlier.

"I sense Signorina Vorenus is the reason you're . . . disconcerted," Placido said with a hint of what sounded like amused satisfaction as he turned to look at him.

"Her presence has been somewhat disruptive, but it's temporary."

"What is? Her presence or your disconcerted state?" This time the old warrior's slight smile made it obvious he was entertained by Dante's current condition.

"Both." He forced himself to remain silent in the face of the other man's gentle mockery.

"Good. At least you admit that she affects you."

"As I said. It's temporary," Dante said firmly. "She's simply a test."

"Ah yes, your oath." Placido bowed his head to rub his gnarled hand over his jawline. "Do you remember when you finished the third *Tabulati*? Your fifteenth birthday, I think."

"Yes. As I recall, my final test involved hunger and a chocolate fudge cake."

"A test to see if you understood the concept of temperance," the ancient warrior muttered in a voice riddled with something Dante couldn't identify.

"I remember I didn't pass the test the first time. I thought it was a test of my self-control."

"Did you know that Marcus and I wagered as to how long you would go hungry before you succumbed to eating that dessert?"

"No," Dante said with surprise, grateful his friend had stopped talking about Cleopatra.

"Marcus said you wouldn't last more than forty-eight hours. I said you would go at least seventy-two." Placido looked up at him, his smile one of pride. "You went almost five days without food. It was an amazing feat of self-control."

"I'm surprised I lasted that long," Dante muttered as he remembered how hard it had been to sit in that small cell.

He'd been given all the water he wanted, but no food except for his favorite dessert—a single slice of double fudge chocolate cake on the table in front of him. The dessert had been replaced almost hourly to ensure it was fresh and moist looking. It was present the entire time he was in that room—silently tempting him to eat as his hunger grew.

"The story of your ability to abstain is still whispered among the students, but your endurance grows with each retelling," Placido said with a deep chuckle.

"But I still failed the test," Dante muttered. It was the only test he'd failed throughout his training in the *Novem Conformavi*. "It took me another try to realize that it wasn't the length of time I went hungry that mattered, but my ability to eat only part of the cake, no matter how hungry I was."

"You've never had any trouble denying yourself pleasure." The sober expression on Placido's face made Dante frown. Was his mentor disappointed in him? The old man grimaced. "Do you remember what happened after you took your vow and rose to the fourth *Tabulati* a few weeks later?"

"I was made Tribune."

"Tribune." The elderly warrior nodded. "Marcus thought I was foolish for suggesting someone so young to be the heir apparent to his title. But Giovanni's death left us without an heir, and despite your difficulty with the third *Tabulati*'s concept of temperance in all things pleasurable, your misguided feat of abstinence displayed a strength of control that impressed Marcus, so he agreed."

"I didn't know Marcus had opposed my becoming Tribune." Dante frowned. Once more the old Sicari Lord had mentioned the word temperance. Did his mentor think him unfit to take over leadership of the *Absconditus*?

"He didn't object to you becoming Tribune, only to the fact that you were so young when we gave you the title." Placido folded his arms across his chest. "I think he might have been correct. We should have given you more time to mature. For a boy of fifteen, the burden we laid on your shoulders was a heavy one."

"I don't understand. Have I disappointed you in some way?"

"Not at all. I am as proud of you as I would be of any son I might have had if my wife had lived. But I'm concerned we pushed you too hard, too fast."

"I don't think you did anything of the kind. I have no regrets about my life in the *Absconditus*." Dante suppressed the memory of how he'd wished last night that he'd not taken an oath to remain celibate.

"And your vow?" Placido eyed him carefully with a quiet expectancy.

"My vow?"

He struggled to ignore the chaotic emotions the question stirred inside him. The last thing he wanted was to disappoint the Sicari Lord. If Placido were ever to guess that Dante had experienced a slight lapse in resolve, it would cause the elderly warrior concern. He didn't want to let either Placido or Marcus down. Other than

Cornelia, they were the only family he had. Disappointing them was unacceptable.

"You took your oath of celibacy *before* you came of age, Dante. You know full well you have the right to free yourself from that obligation."

"I can't do that."

"No, you *won't* do that," Placido sighed heavily. "Which makes it that much more difficult for me, because I can't help but think that your choice was based in part on the expectations Marcus and I placed on you, my boy."

"You've been talking to Cornelia."

"Yes, and I think she was right all along. I see now that you took your vow too soon."

"Fifteen isn't that young," he said with a dismissive twist of his lips.

"You were half the age of the few who choose to express their beliefs with an oath. And there are even fewer who take a vow such as you did," Placido growled. "I wanted to lash Tito for even putting the idea in your head."

"I don't know why," Dante said stiffly. "Tito simply answered my question. I wanted to know if he regretted not taking a wife."

"He *did* have a wife, but like many Patricians before and after him, his wife died young. Tito's oath was more about his grief and fears than a statement of his dedication to the guild."

Placido crossed the carpet to sit down in a straight back chair pressed against the wall. His movements were weary, and Dante stepped forward to offer his assistance. The old man glared at him and waved him away. Confused, Dante shrugged slightly as he met the ancient Sicari Lord's gaze.

"Tito's reason for his vow might have been different than mine, but I fail to see how his choice affects me."

"*By the gods*, it was supposed to be a vow of *temperance*, not one of abstinence," Placido snapped as he rested his hand on his thigh and shook his head vehemently. "Temperance means *avoiding excess*, not the complete absence of all pleasure."

Dante frowned at the frustration the old man was showing. The display of emotion was unlike the Sicari Lord. And it didn't help matters that they were discussing a topic settled long ago, despite his fleeting wish last night and this morning. He winced inwardly as he admitted the desire he'd felt just within the past few hours. It was a temporary situation. A short-term lapse in control. A small voice in the back of his head laughed mockingly.

"If you felt this strongly about it, why didn't you say something then?" Dante asked quietly, uncertain of what to make of his friend's observations.

"*Fotte*. Do you think I didn't consider it? But I knew that if I or Marcus even hinted at our doubts, you would have found something else to swear to in hopes of pleasing us." At the Sicari Lord's sharp words, Dante started to protest, but Placido raised his hand in an imperious gesture. "Don't deny it, boy. We both know you would have gone to Hades and back if Marcus or I had asked it of you. Sometimes I think you still would. But we wanted you to make up your own mind. It's one of the reasons we invited those young women to visit the compound a few days before you took your oath."

There was a sheepish note in the man's voice as his mouth twisted in a frown of embarrassed regret. Dante studied his friend in confusion and watched as Placido shifted in his seat, looking exceedingly uncomfortable. He shook his head at the Sicari Lord.

"Are you saying it wasn't a test?" Dante rasped.

"Vesta preserve us, of course it wasn't!" Placido exclaimed with disgust. "Marcus and I thought that once you got a taste of what a woman was like you'd change your mind about the vow. We had no idea you'd think we were testing you. If we had, we would have told you it was a secret ritual all Tribunes went through before the title was conveyed to them."

Dante cringed inwardly at the memory of that day. He'd been studying in the library when Placido had summoned Dante to his quarters. The ancient Sicari Lord had been in his early sixties and was known for his bawdy appetites when it came to women. Dante had always believed it was in response to Placido's need to fill the hole in his life left by the loss of his wife.

The women in the Sicari Lord's apartments had been beautiful and voluptuous. Thinking back, he realized they'd not been anywhere near as enticing as Cleopatra. But to a boy of fifteen, they'd been goddesses. He'd had a hard-on the minute he'd walked in the door. It had only gotten worse when Placido had suggested Dante take one particularly beautiful young woman into the bedroom. Certain it was a test, he had done as the Sicari Lord had instructed.

He'd followed her with his heart in his mouth. *Christus*, the things he'd imagined that woman doing to him. How he managed to keep from coming as she'd undressed in front of him was beyond his comprehension even now. All he remembered of that agonizingly long half hour was that the test Placido had thrown at him was the hardest one he'd endured since.

It had been a lot harder to resist that woman than the thick slab of chocolate cake he'd stared at for more than four days. If he'd known it wasn't a test, would he have given in to temptation with that young woman instead of walking away from her? It was a question he thought he knew the answer to, and yet how could he be sure when so many years separated him from the event. His gaze met Placido's, and anger surged through his veins.

"Why come to me with your confession now? What purpose does it serve except to offer you the opportunity to clear your conscience after all these years?" His sharp tone made Placido grow pale, and Dante immediately regretted his brutal outburst. But the ancient warrior recovered quickly and shrugged.

"I think we both know that in the last twenty-four hours you've been questioning the decision you made so long ago."

"You're wrong."

"You dare to lie to me, boy?" It was the Placido of old glaring at him. "I know your heart better than anyone, Dante. I know you're questioning everything where this woman is concerned. I've sensed it ever since you returned to the *Absconditus* with her."

Dante's jaw tightened at Placido's words. The man was right. He'd been suppressing his attraction to Cleopatra from that first emotional connection he'd felt last night. When Placido had brought up the past, Dante had immediately wondered whether he could have resisted Cleopatra if she'd been the woman that day almost twenty years ago. She was just as sensuous as that woman had been. No, Cleopatra was much more potent to the senses than the woman Placido had introduced him to that day so long ago. His muscles hardened as his head was flooded with erotic images of Cleopatra.

If she'd been the one testing him all those years ago, he would have failed the test of his virtue miserably. But he was stronger now, more than capable of withstanding the temptation she presented. Faint laughter echoed deep in his mind. He met Placido's gaze as his mentor eyed him with deep regret.

"Marcus and I thought that if we showed you how beautiful women are, it would make you realize that you were choosing to give up something you knew nothing about." Placido shook his head ruefully. "We'd hoped you'd see that a woman has much to offer a man. The right woman can be a lover, partner, and friend. Women soften our rough edges."

"It was an admirable goal, but it's in the past, Placido. I made my choice, and it was the right one. I did what was best for the guild," Dante said in a firm voice.

"You've always done what's best for the *Absconditus*. What about what's best for you?" the Sicari Lord muttered with a grunt of fierce exasperation.

"You're beginning to sound like Cornelia. Isn't this conversation coming a bit late?"

"It's never too late to change the mistakes of the past. And I've made many. But allowing you to take that vow was the worst. I let you put others in front of your own needs—me, Marcus, everyone, and even the *Absconditus* itself."

"That's an exaggeration."

"Is it?" Placido's expression was fierce as he challenged Dante.

He studied the older man's features with a frown. Was it possible the ancient warrior was right? Dante had always strived to make his mentors proud of him, but he couldn't believe he always put the needs of others in front of his own. It simply appeared that way because his needs were the same as those of the *Absconditus*. He shook his head in disagreement.

"It's my duty to care for those in guild. It's what the reigning Sicari Lord does, and as Tribune it's what I've been training for most of my life. I knew that when I made my vow."

"*Jupiter's Stone.* Becoming Sicari Lord is a commitment, *not* a bloody sacrifice." Placido exploded with anger and glared at him with a savage look on his face. His mentor's reaction surprised Dante once again.

"And Marcus?" He arched his eyebrows at the elderly man. "What of the sacrifices he's made?"

"His situation is different."

"I don't see how. He's sacrificed everything for the sake of the guild."

"*No.*" The ancient warrior spat out the word in violent protest. "Marcus didn't sacrifice himself willingly. But you—you gave your heart and soul to the *Absconditus* before you had a chance to discover what else life had to offer. And now . . . now . . ."

"Now *what*?" he asked gently.

Dante stepped forward and squatted in front of the old man. Despite his age, Placido's blue-eyed gaze was vividly bright. The penetrating look the Sicari Lord sent Dante made him feel as though the man had pinned him like a butterfly to a display board.

"You will have to make a choice."

"A choice?" Dante shook his head with concern. As one of the few Sicari Lords blessed with the gift of sight, Placido's predictions were legendary for their accuracy. "What kind of choice?"

"A choice that involves our guest," Placido said with a weary sigh of frustration.

"That's pretty damn vague. First you come in saying you sense Cleopatra's presence here upsets me, then you start questioning me about my—"

Dante sprang to his feet and stepped back from his friend as he battled the anger threatening to swallow him whole. It took him at least a minute to harness the fury tightening his limbs as he stared down at the old warrior. Placido didn't avoid his gaze. Instead, the elderly man's eyes were narrowed with assessment. It was almost as if the Sicari Lord were looking for something. Dante schooled his features into a dispassionate expression.

"If you're suggesting I'd choose a woman over my commitment to the *Absconditus*, you're wrong."

"The only thing I'm suggesting is that no one would judge you if you were to break your oath," Placido said quietly. "I'm saying you will have to make a choice, and it will involve Signorina Vorenus."

"This choice, who else does it affect?"

"Every choice is a ripple in a pond. It affects everyone in its path directly or indirectly."

"*That* is really helpful," Dante bit out with a ferocity that declared his temper was getting the best of him, but he'd suddenly stopped caring. "If you can't tell me who, then tell me *what* the choice is I have to make."

"Do not confuse an ordinary choice with one of destiny, Dante."

"*Deus*, I hate it when you do this." Dante scowled at the man. "The least you could do is give me some guidance here. Is she in danger?"

"You already know the answer. The future remains unwritten until it happens."

"That's the answer you always give when you want me to figure something out on my own," he snarled as he began to prowl the room. "And here you were just a few minutes ago lamenting the fact that you and Marcus hadn't stopped me from taking my oath."

"And I already regret telling you what I've told you," Placido said with a weary sigh. "But it was a choice I made, and as I said, a choice is a ripple that can have far-reaching consequences."

"Remind me to thank you later for that thought-provoking wisdom," Dante said with more than a hint of sarcasm. The inner peace and control he'd barely managed to salvage while showering had disappeared again. Was there such a thing as an ordinary choice?

The ninth *Tabulati* of the *Novem Conformavi* taught that everything in the universe was interconnected. That teaching alone meant that every choice one made was tied to one's destiny. He suppressed a groan. Cleopatra Vorenus was becoming a major problem. He wanted to put her on the first plane back to Chicago where she belonged. He rejected the notion. He wanted her where he could keep an eye on her. Keep her out of trouble. The realization made his stomach lurch.

Was that the choice? Was he supposed to send her back? Was that his destiny? Sending her away before he lost control? Even if he tried that, she wasn't likely to go willingly and would probably find a way to return. Then he'd be right back where he started. This time he couldn't contain his groan. Things had been bad enough already, but now Placido had managed to muddy the Tiber River that much more.

Chapter 9

MARCUS clicked on the END CALL button, and Dante's visage dissolved into the background of the flat-screen monitor. Jupiter's Stone. How was he supposed to explain to Atia that he'd agreed to let their daughter remain in the heart of Praetorian territory? The woman was going to rip his heart out when she learned he'd not ordered Cleo to come back to the States.

The fact that Cleo was unwilling to leave Rome showed how much of a rift existed between mother and daughter. Worse, she'd convinced Ignacio Firmani to give her the Angotti assignment. If he'd known that ahead of time, he would have tried to stop her. *Tried* being the operative word. Cleo got just as much of her stubbornness from him as she did from Atia.

But even if he'd known ahead of time, it was doubtful he would have been able to convince her to do nothing, short of ordering her not to assassinate Angotti. And that would only have put more distance between them, something he was trying to avoid. As much as he might want to use his authority to keep her safe, he was certain his efforts in that direction would only alienate her. *That* he didn't want. He'd missed too many years with her as it was.

He wanted to get to know his daughter. Although how in Juno's name he could do that if she remained in Rome, he didn't know. It didn't please him that Firmani had allowed her to go after Angotti. The decision made him question the man's judgment. Atia put great faith in her *Celeris*, but there was something about him Marcus didn't trust, even if Firmani had been guarding Atia for years. Marcus snorted softly.

He was jealous. Clear and simple. He was jealous of Firmani. The man was in love with Atia, even if she didn't realize it. Marcus shoved the chair away from his desk and glanced at the mantel clock over the fireplace. Almost six fifteen. Atia might already be in the research lab.

The woman still liked to rise at the crack of dawn, while he preferred a more reasonable hour. He rose from his chair and crossed the bedroom floor to where a small fire blazed in the fireplace. White Cloud had all the modern conveniences, but he'd always preferred to sleep and wake to a wood fire. Probably a habit left over from his past life as the ancient Roman soldier Tevy.

He pressed the heels of his palms against the mantelpiece and stared down at the fire. Images from the distant past danced in the flames. One of these visions was of the Milvian Bridge and the fireballs raining down from the sky to kill his friends and many of his men. Octavian was to blame for that day of carnage. Even in his present incarnation as the Nicostratus, Patriarch of the Collegium, the man hadn't changed in almost two thousand years. Whether he was Octavian or Nicostratus, he was still a murderous *bastardo*.

Marcus violently pushed himself away from the mantel with a dark sound of fury. Whatever it took, he would see the man dead. As Octavian, the man had betrayed his brothers in the Guard. But as Nicostratus, the *bastardo* had done something much worse. The man had taken an innocent boy and turned him into a monster. Marcus closed his eyes as the pain of that terrible moment in the Pantheon washed over him again.

Marcus had killed Gabriel—his own son.

The memory sliced into him as viciously as Gabriel's sword had pierced his side. Marcus parted his robe and bent his head to see the spot on his thigh where his son's weapon had nicked a major artery. There was still a small scar. He'd not allowed anyone to touch him after Phaedra's healing ritual. He would have died if not for her. And now she lay unconscious in the Sicari medical facility in Genova. She'd given everything to save Lysander. It was the same type of sacrifice he would willingly make for Atia.

With a grimace, he moved quickly back to the desk and opened up the webcam software to contact the Genova hospital. It took several minutes for the doctor to reach the computer, and when a woman finally appeared in front of the camera, Marcus knew from the doctor's expression that Phaedra's condition hadn't changed.

After a brief update, he ended the conversation and sat staring at the blank monitor screen for several moments. Surely, Vesta wouldn't be so cruel as to keep Lysander and Phaedra apart a second time. Shouts of panic and anger in the corridor abruptly interrupted his train of thought, and he immediately called for his clothes with the mere whisper of a thought.

In less than sixty seconds he was completely dressed. As he strode toward the door of his suite, he summoned his sword, and the weapon flew through the air into his hand almost at the same moment he flung his door wide open. The sound of chaos was louder in the hall. A young boy raced by, and Marcus reached out with his thoughts to drag the youngster to a halt. Terror filled the boy's face as he cried out in fear.

"It's all right, boy, I'm not going to hurt you," Marcus said in a calm, quiet voice as he slid his sword into the sheath hanging at his side. "Tell me what's happened."

"It's one of the researchers, *il mio signore*. They've been murdered."

Murder. The boy had to be mistaken. Sicari resolved their differences in open combat before members of the Order. Murder was virtually unheard of among the Sicari. Atia's face flashed before his eyes, and his heart sank into the pit of his stomach.

"Have you seen the *Prima Consul*, boy?"

"No, *il mio signore*."

Fear churning in his stomach, he released his mental grip on the boy then raced down the hall toward the research lab. Juno help him if something had happened to her. *Deus*, he'd not been this frightened since the day the Praetorians had taken Gabriel. The closer he got to the lab, the more crowded the hall became.

Desperate to find Atia, he commanded people to stand aside. Some people moved the minute he ordered them to do so, while he had to shove others out of his way. Just outside the research lab, a short, rotund man with a balding head stood arguing with a fighter he recognized from Lysander's temporary guild in Rome.

He frowned as he tried to remember the fighter's name. Pasquale. That was his name. Luciano Pasquale. He didn't know the other man. The minute the fighter looked up, Marcus caught his attention.

"The *Prima Consul*, is she—"

"She's fine, *il mio signore*," Pasquale said with a reassuring nod of his head. "She's in the lab with the *Celeris*."

Relief crashed through him before irritation took its place. *Firmani again*. Of course he'd be with Atia. It was the man's job. He clenched his jaw. The sooner he put the *Celeris* out of work the better. But the only way that was going to happen was if he convinced Atia they were meant to be together.

As he pushed past the man Pasquale had been arguing with, pudgy fingers bit into his arm. He stiffened at the touch and turned his head to direct a cold look at the short, stocky man delaying him. The man immediately jerked his hand away but wilted only slightly under Marcus's glare.

"Who in Juno's name are you? If Pasquale won't let me in the lab, what makes you think *you* can go in?" the man snapped in anger.

Suddenly, Marcus was sorry he'd given orders that no one was to divulge who he really was. Although Pasquale had been in Rome, the fighter didn't know anything more about Marcus than anyone else here at White Cloud. Only a select few knew he was a Sicari Lord. To everyone else on the estate he was a *Legatus* from the Rome guild who was an expert authority on the *Tyet of Isis*.

The expert part was true, but the rest was merely to keep the Order from exploding with more tension than there already was in the organization. The revelation that Lysander was half-Praetorian with the skills of a Sicari Lord had created enough of a stir in the Order already. The only thing that made people's eyebrows raise when they met him was his last name. He knew they were wondering about the connection between him and Atia, but no one had dared mention the obvious.

"Marcus Vorenus. Who are *you*?"

"Cato, member of the Sicari Council." The man's gaze narrowed as he looked at Marcus. "Where do I know you from?"

"You don't," he said in an icy voice before he brushed past the two men and entered the lab.

The lab's temperature was intentionally cool in order to preserve the delicate documents stored in the room. White Cloud's library of research books was extensive, and its lab was one of the best in the States. Atia sat bowed over in a chair, while the body of a man lay sprawled on the floor behind her. Bent over Atia, the *Celeris* was rubbing her back in a comforting manner.

The sight sent fury streaking through Marcus. Firmani might be Atia's bodyguard, but the man was taking liberties Marcus didn't like. Food, milk, and a tray lay on the floor where someone had dropped them, and he stepped around the mess. As he moved forward, Atia's head jerked up. The moment her gaze met his, she was on her feet and running toward him.

It was a moment of intense jubilation and relief. He was the one she needed and wanted, not Firmani.

He pulled her into a tight embrace as she buried her face in his shoulder. Over her head, he met the gaze of the *Celeris*. The devastation on the man's face made Marcus feel sorry for him. It was obvious he loved Atia, and Marcus understood what losing her would feel like.

The pain on Firmani's face quickly vanished, and Marcus didn't have to read the man's mind to know the bodyguard hated him. Burrowed deep into his chest, Atia was trembling hard, and he was certain it wasn't from the chilly temperature. It was most likely shock.

"It's all right, *mea kara*. I'm here now," he murmured as he stroked her hair. Despite the whitish silver color, it was as silky as the day they first met. "Are you all right?"

"Yes." Her answer was muffled in his shirt.

"Tell me what happened."

Although her tremors had eased somewhat, she remained pressed against his chest, and he waited patiently. When she didn't respond to his command, an uneasy sensation slid through him. It wasn't like her to act so frightened.

Even when the Praetorians had taken Gabriel, she'd exhibited a steely strength in her determination to find their son. If the death of their son had stripped her of that fortitude, Nicostratus had one more crime to pay for. After a long moment, she lifted her head, and the expression of fear on her face made his gut tighten.

"I couldn't sleep, so I came down to the lab to study the document we found in the *Tyet of Isis*. When I arrived, the lights were out. Sandro always comes to the lab early, and I sensed something was wrong." She shuddered and closed her eyes for a brief moment. "I almost called for help then, but I told myself Sandro had simply taken the morning off. When I turned on the lights, that's when I saw him."

"Did you see anyone? Hear anything?" The thought that the murderer might have been anywhere near her made his gut twist viciously with fear.

"No. At first I thought Sandro had just collapsed, but then I saw the blood on the floor." She blanched at the statement, and he knew she was reliving that moment. "I knew there was only one reason why someone would kill him, so I immediately checked the lockbox to make sure the *Tyet of Isis* document wasn't missing. It was still where I'd left it yesterday."

"What about Pasquale? Where did he come from?"

"Luciano was on duty in the security control room. It was the *Vigilavi* girl who always brings Sandro breakfast who sounded the alarm. I didn't know she'd come into the room until she dropped the tray and screamed." Atia pulled away from him and pressed her fingertips into her temple. It seemed natural for Marcus to automatically reach out with his thoughts to caress the spot. Her hand fell downward until it came to rest on his arm. "Before I could stop her, the girl panicked and went screaming for help. Pasquale arrived a couple of minutes later. That's when I went to Sandro and . . ."

As her voice trailed off into nothing, she breathed in a deep, shuddering breath. It was a sound that made his heart ache for the harrowing emotions he sensed in her. It wasn't just that she was in shock or upset at the death of a man he knew had been her friend. There was something else underlying the fragile control she was clinging to by a thread.

"There's something you're not telling me," he said quietly.

"It's . . . I can't tell you . . . I have to show you."

She pulled away from him then led him toward Sandro's body. The moment he saw the researcher, he went rigid at the sight of a familiar backward C over a diagonal line carved into the man's cheek. The incomplete Chi-Rho mark Gabriel had used on all his murder victims was one he'd never expected to see again.

"*Fotte*," he rasped.

For a brief second he wondered if perhaps he'd dreamt killing his own son as he stared down at the mark. He knew better. He and Atia had quietly held a *Rogalis* for Gabriel at Palazzo al Mare the day after the battle in the Pantheon. This was someone else's work. Someone who either didn't know Gabriel was dead or was sending a message. Either way, Sandro's death told him that Nicostratus's reach was far greater than he'd feared.

"I don't understand . . . The murderer didn't even try to take the document." Atia's voice wavered as she looked up at him.

"You, or something else, startled the intruder. The Praetorians know that document might shift the balance of power if we decipher it," he said grimly as he looked around the lab. "Is there another way out of here?"

"Yes, through the dark lab." She shook her head. "But there wasn't anyone here when I arrived. I'm sure of it."

"Can you think of any other reason why someone would want to kill the man?"

"No," she said with a shake of her head. "He was well liked by everyone."

"Then we can only assume that whoever killed Sandro was working for the Praetorians, which means we have a traitor among us." His dark words made Atia draw in a sharp breath.

"That's not possible."

"Then how else do you explain the man's death, *carissima*?"

"I can't," Atia said in a whisper.

He watched her as she struggled with the knowledge that there was a viper in her house and they didn't know where. She rubbed at her temple again, and he longed to help ease her pain, but instinct said she'd only resent his touch at the moment. He looked down at the dead man again.

"Who else has seen the mutilation?"

"Just Ignacio, Pasquale, myself, and now you," Atia replied.

"The *Vigilavi*?" His abrupt question made her shake her head.

"She didn't get any farther than where she dropped Sandro's breakfast tray." Atia's gaze shifted toward the mess on the floor just inside the research lab's doorway. Marcus looked at Atia's bodyguard.

"We need to have the man prepared for the *Rogalis* with as few people seeing his body as possible. Murder is one thing, but this mark will create widespread panic," he said grimly. "We have no choice but to trust Pasquale, since he's already seen the body. Do you have one or two men you can rely on to keep their mouths shut?"

"Yes." Firmani nodded abruptly then looked at Atia. "Benedict? Fabrizio's only been with us a little more than a year."

"Yes, Benedict is completely loyal to me." Atia nodded her head as she looked at Marcus. Color had returned to her face, and she looked far more composed now. With his thoughts, he lightly brushed his fingers across her cheek. She frowned slightly but didn't say anything as he turned back to Firmani.

"You need to move the man's body quickly. In the meantime, Atia will address the residents and call a special meeting of the Council." Marcus turned his head as Atia uttered a small gasp.

"A special meeting . . . ? But I don't—"

"You don't have much choice," he growled. "There's a belligerent little worm outside who I've no doubt will cause trouble otherwise."

"Cato." Atia and her *Celeris* said the name simultaneously and with equal disgust.

"That's the one," he said in a sharp tone as he remembered the Council member's self-importance. If the man had had any idea who he was talking to, Marcus was certain the obnoxious toad's attitude would have been completely different.

"Marcus is right, Ignacio. I need to meet with the Council and reassure the rest of the estate's residents. If you'll see to Sandro and his *Rogalis*, I'll deal with Cato." Her voice was strong and commanding as she turned toward Marcus. "Do you think we should find a safer storage place for the document?"

It was a good question, and he frowned. If the document were less fragile, he would have been inclined to say yes, but the research lab had been designed to protect ancient artifacts. It was still the best place to keep the document. He shook his head.

"This is the safest option available to us. Once Firmani has seen to the body, I'll work on making improvements to the security system in the room."

"His name was Sandro," she bit out in a tight voice. He flinched as he realized his pragmatism had made him seem uncaring. Marcus bowed slightly toward her.

"Forgive me, *mea kara*. I meant no disrespect to Sandro." His jaw tightened as she nodded sharply at him before turning back to her *Celeris*.

"Ignacio, take care with him."

Her voice softened as she glanced down at the dead man then turned and left the room. As she walked away, his senses picked up on Firmani's malicious satisfaction. Slowly, he turned his head toward the man. The small smile on the *Celeris*'s face disappeared as Marcus eyed him with a cold calculation.

"You heard the *Prima Consul*. See to the man's body." His command made Firmani stiffen, but the *Celeris* nodded sharply then pulled a cell phone from his pants pocket and tapped on the screen. Marcus didn't bother waiting to ensure the man followed Atia's instructions. He was certain Firmani would do as he was told, and not just because the *Prima Consul* had ordered him to.

Firmani was too much in love with Atia to refuse her. What if she cared for the *Celeris*, too? The thought made Marcus's entire body grow rigid with jealous tension. Little more than two weeks ago when he'd found Atia at La Terrazza del Ninfeo in Rome, she'd defended Firmani. She'd pleaded for the man's life. Had that been because she was in love with her *Celeris*?

She'd mentioned breaking their blood bond that morning before Firmani had even showed up. His gut knotted at the possibility. No. He couldn't believe that. Just a few minutes ago, when Marcus entered the lab, he'd been the one she'd run to, not Firmani. He was the one she'd clung to. It had been his arms Atia had sought solace in, not those of her *Celeris*.

A grim smile twisted his lips as he crossed the room toward the locked cabinet that held the *Tyet of Isis* document. He would win her back. He wouldn't fail in that task. He'd spent too many years dreaming about her and how he would regain her love after Dante became the new Sicari Lord. He would not lose her now.

For the moment, he would do as she asked, just as Firmani would. He had no doubt the *Celeris* would do what he could to steal Atia from him, but he wasn't going to let that happen. His thoughts were still on Atia as he examined the high-tech security lock on the steel lockbox that held the parchment he knew the Praetorians wanted desperately. As he looked around the room, he began to itemize the extra precautions that could be taken to protect the valuable document.

Several hours later, all of Marcus's ideas were close to completion as the *Vigilavi* security expert on staff directed the placement of the last security camera that would give the control room a continuous view of the research lab. Sometime in the next week, new steel doors would be installed that could be locked remotely to prevent anyone trying to steal the *Tyet of Isis* document from escaping.

Satisfied the artifact was far more secure than it had been before the murder, he left the lab and headed to Atia's suite. Pasquale had returned to the lab a short time ago and informed him that the *Prima Consul* had spent more than three hours fielding questions from the Council, or more specifically, Cato.

That the Council member had named Marcus as a possible suspect didn't surprise him. He was a new arrival and not above suspicion. And while the worm's audacious suggestion that Atia might also be the murderer wasn't surprising, it infuriated him. Pasquale's report had simply made him hunger for the chance to reduce the Council member to a quivering mass of fear.

It would be a mistake to do anything, though. Atia wouldn't tolerate any interference in her affairs, even if it was to her benefit. As he came to a halt in front of Atia's rooms, he started to knock then changed his mind. She was his wife, and he had every right to enter.

The door opened quietly, and as he entered the main living area, it was as if he'd stepped back in time.

The room was almost a replica of the living room they'd had at Rennes-le-Château when they were first blood bonded. He moved deeper into the space, absently using his ability to close the door behind him.

Pictures on an end table caught his eye, and one of the framed photographs floated up off the table into his hand. It was a picture of him and Gabriel, taken shortly before the kidnapping. His throat swelled shut as grief welled up inside him. If only he'd taken Atia and Gabriel with him to the *Absconditus* that week.

"What are you doing here, Marcus?" Atia's voice was like a cool breeze on the back of his neck.

Her tone said his presence had caught her by surprise and she wasn't happy about it. He slowly turned to face her. Her rumpled clothing and tousled hair made him think she'd just gotten up from a nap. She looked as though the weight of the world rested upon her shoulders. But it was the bleak sadness in her gray eyes that tugged at him.

The force of her grief hammered away at his mind, the intensity of it as sharp as a finely honed blade. It made him want to pull her into his arms for the second time today.

"I came to check on you," he said quietly. "Pasquale said the Council meeting was rather contentious this afternoon."

"Perhaps a little more than usual, but nothing I couldn't handle." She pinched the bridge of her nose. "Cato is a *bastardo*. He enjoys making things difficult."

"When was the last time you ate?" His question made her frown.

"I don't remember," she said with a slight shrug. "Last night, I suppose."

"*Christus*," he muttered. "You never did know how to take care of yourself."

Without asking her permission, he strode down a short hallway to the small kitchen that was in every one of the larger suites on the estate. If he was going to succeed in winning her back, he needed to woo her. He'd start with a little wine and some home cooking. She'd always enjoyed the meals he used to fix for them.

The refrigerator wasn't bare, but the contents left a lot to be desired. He pulled out a brick of Fontina cheese, along with fresh salad ingredients. As he searched the cabinet for some pasta, Atia came into the kitchen.

"What are you doing?"

"Fixing you something to eat." He pulled a box of fettuccine from the cabinet and placed it on the counter next to the stove.

"That's not necessary. I can easily order something from the main kitchen."

"And pass up the opportunity to mock my cooking?" His attempt at brevity was rewarded with a slight smile from her.

"I never made fun of your cooking," she said with a shake of her head.

"Yes, you did." He quickly filled a pot with water and set it on the burner to boil.

"No, what I poked fun at was your singing."

"Singing and cooking are part of being Sicari," he grumbled.

"Yes, but only when you can actually sing," she said with a laugh.

Her laughter was a beautiful sound, and he grinned at her while unwrapping the block of Fontina cheese. With a knife he'd found in one of the drawers, he started to shave pieces off the solid white block. As the slivers of cheese piled up on the cutting board, he began to hum "La Donna è Mobile."

"If you insist on singing, I'm going to have a drink."

"So now I'm driving you to drink?" he said with a raised eyebrow.

"No, your singing is."

"I was humming." He eyed her with amusement at the way she shook her head.

"The problem is you never just hum," she said in a wry voice as she pulled a bottle of Galluccio wine from the rack sitting at one end of the counter.

She neatly pulled the cork from the bottle with a corkscrew as Marcus continued to shave the cheese. The water had started to boil, and she moved around him to drop the fettuccine into the hot water.

His body grew tight at her close proximity, and his cock was hard in an instant. What little concentration he had remaining van-

ished as the soft scent of her perfume feathered its way into his nose
when she accidentally bumped into him. A second later, the knife
slipped and nicked his finger.

"*Fotte.*"

"*Deus*, Marcus, I'm so sorry," she gasped in dismay.

Moving quickly, she grabbed a nearby towel and ran it under
cold water before she returned to his side. Gently, she took his hand
in hers and dabbed at the cut. All thought of the annoying injury
to his finger fled him as he drank in the sweet essence of her. Jupiter's Stone. He'd always remembered her scent, but the memory had
never been this sharp and enticing. This was like being drunk on a
heady wine. Even after all these years, she had the ability to make
him ready to rut like a bull. He bit down on the inside of his cheek
as he dragged in a ragged breath.

"It's a scrape. Just leave it be, Atia," he growled as he pulled his
hand away from her. She glared up at him and grasped his hand
more firmly.

"Let me look at it. You might need a healer."

"It's a small cut. I don't need a healer." He needed her. Every
part of him was on fire, and if she wouldn't let him put some distance between them, he wasn't going to be held responsible for what
happened.

"Damn it, Marcus. Why do you have to be so hardheaded?" she
snapped and pulled his hand back toward her.

"And why don't you ever listen?"

His voice was tight with need as he swept the counter clean with
one simple thought then lifted her up onto the flat surface with
another mental command. The lovely curve of her mouth formed a
small O as she gasped with astonishment.

"What are you doing?"

"What do you think I'm doing?" he rasped and leaned into her.
"I'm showing my wife that I find her as beautiful and sexy today as
I did the first time we met."

"This is ridiculous," she said as her fingers splayed across his
chest. "We're too old to be acting like teenagers."

"Old?" he growled. "Does this feel like an old man?"

His hands moved her legs apart and jerked her forward until she was pressed into his hard erection. Her eyes widened with surprise, and he was certain there was a hint of desire flashing there as well.

"Marcus, please." She sucked in a sharp breath as he pulled her closer so she was snug against his cock.

"I'm more than ready to please you, *carissima*." His suggestive comment made her blush, and she shook her head with a hint of shocked surprise.

"We aren't young anymore, Marcus. And here on the counter . . . it's . . . it's hedonistic and unlike you." The scandalized note in her voice faded into obvious confusion. He liked seeing her off balance, but he didn't like her implied observation that he was incapable of doing something spontaneous.

"I'm fifty-six, Atia. I'd hardly call that ready for the funeral pyre," he growled. "As for unconventional, what are you afraid of?"

"I'm not afraid of anything. It's just—"

"Then forget you're the *Prima Consul* and let me pleasure you, because right now, all I can think about is sliding in and out of you until we're both satisfied."

She gasped softly, the pink color in her cheeks darkening. He stared at her for a long moment, expecting her to say something, but she appeared too disconcerted. *Christus*, she was beautiful. When they'd first met, she'd been lovely, but then the sharply defined curves of her face had reflected an innocence they'd both lost over the years. Now, there was a soft roundness to her visage that hadn't been there more than thirty years ago.

It only heightened her beauty, making him wish he'd not missed all those years that had changed her. Changed him. He reached out with one finger to lightly trace the line of her throat down to the vee of her blouse. The way her breathing quickened made him smile. If there was one thing that hadn't changed between them, it was the sex.

They'd always been good together in bed, and if he could use that to make her see how much he loved her, had always loved her, then he would. He'd do anything to get her back. Her throat bobbed nervously beneath his finger. His gaze met hers, and this time he could plainly see the desire in her eyes.

The instant he mentally reached out to undo the top button of her shirt she inhaled a sharp breath. The sound made his body tighten with excitement. His gaze never left her face as he slowly used his ability to undo one button after another all the way down the front of her blouse. As her shirt flared open, he stared at the sculpted bra holding her breasts.

He'd always loved her breasts. He ached to remove the barrier between his mouth and the stiff nipple he could see through the material covering her. No, not yet. That could wait. He needed to let her know it wasn't just her body he wanted. He wanted much more than that.

Slowly, he leaned forward and breathed in her perfume. It was different than what he remembered in their youth. This scent was more subtle. Richer. Mature. He recognized it as the fragrance of a woman, not the girl he'd blood bonded with. Mixed in with the soft scent was something else. Desire. The slight hint of musk that said she wanted him.

He swallowed hard. She might want him, but did she still love him? He pushed the thought aside. He refused to believe she had ever stopped. Love had never been the problem. It had been Gabriel's kidnapping and the way she'd retreated from him afterward that had broken them apart. The hunt for their son and his duties as the reigning Sicari Lord had only widened the gap between them. He trailed his fingers down to the valley between her breasts, his breathing almost as erratic as hers.

"I've missed you, *mea kara*. For years, night after night, I've dreamed of lying beside you. Holding you. Loving you," he said softly. "And every morning I'd awake alone."

Cupping her cheek with his hand, he rubbed his thumb over her mouth. A breathless sigh brushed past her lips as her gray eyes darkened.

"I've missed you, too," she whispered. It was a small concession, but at the moment, he'd take whatever she would give him. His hands slipped inside her open shirt to caress the smooth skin of her waist as he leaned forward and brushed his mouth across hers.

As if a dam had broken inside her, she suddenly cradled his face in her hands and kissed him with an intensity that was enough to drive him mad. The taste of her reminded him of the peaches she loved to eat. Her lips parted beneath his, and his tongue swept into the inner warmth of her mouth to taste the sweet fire of her. A shudder shook him as her tongue danced with his.

Jupiter's Stone. He'd forgotten the power her kiss had always held over him. A mindless craving for her made him blindly pull her deeper into his chest. The result was her wiggling against him in a way that made his blood burn through his veins.

Heat streaked over his skin and found its way to his groin, where his erection hardened to a painful ache. *Christus*, he wasn't going to be able to take this slowly like he'd intended. The woman had always pushed him over the edge, and now wasn't any different. Another shudder wracked his body as her hand rubbed over his cock through his trousers.

At the touch, he lost his self-control. His hands left her waist to skim the waistband of her slacks. With blinding speed, he lifted her up off the counter and her pants slipped past her bare feet to hit the floor. She murmured a slight protest, but he easily silenced her as he returned her to a sitting position and sought the white-hot silk of her mouth.

Her response was passionate and intense. It aroused him to a frenzied state as her fingers freed his erection from his pants. Pleasure exploded through him as she gripped him then slid her thumb over the tip of him, smearing the first drops of his cum over his skin. He growled with need as he craved something more around his cock than her hand.

Roughly, he ripped her panties at the sides. The fragile material easily gave way beneath his strength, and his mouth swallowed her small cry of pleasure as he slipped two fingers inside her. Hot cream coated his fingers, and he almost spilled his seed at how tight she was. *Christus*, the minute he embedded himself inside her, he might not be able to keep from coming right then and there.

He lifted his head to stare down at her, and triumph surged through him at the desire on her face. She murmured a protest and thrust her hips forward in a silent demand for him to continue stroking her. He had no doubt she wanted him, but he wanted to hear her say it. He wanted to know that even after all these years, she still cared for him.

"Tell me what I want to hear, *carissima*," he rasped. A small mewl of need broke past her lips, and she shook her head.

"Marcus, please," she begged as he retreated from her slightly, her hands clutching at his shirt.

"Tell me you love me, Atia. Say it." He met her gaze, and the second he saw her hesitate, a vise wrapped painfully around his chest. Sweet mother of Juno. What if he was wrong about her? Worse, what would he do if she no longer loved him?

Chapter 10

ATIA froze at Marcus's command to confess her soul. It had been a long time since he'd demanded such a sacrifice. Did she have the strength to risk her heart a second time with him?

"Tell me, Atia. I want to hear you say it," he growled.

He widened the space between them a bit more, and her body, as well as her heart, cried out a protest. Even though she knew deep down there was little hope for them, it was useless to lie about her feelings. If she denied them, he'd know she was lying

"I love you," she whispered. "I've always loved you."

The sharp intake of his breath betrayed how uncertain he'd been of her answer. It was a startling revelation, but she forgot it the instant he closed the space between them and kissed her. As his tongue tangled with hers in a passionate frenzy, her heart skipped a beat and then another.

She'd forgotten how wonderful his touch could make her feel. He tasted like hot spice and everything deliciously male. The harsh, masculine heat of his mouth slid from her lips to blaze a path down to the base of her throat. The sharp scent of men's soap brushed across her senses.

Despite this impetuous moment, there were some things about him that had remained unchanged over the years. She experienced a sudden longing to feel the hard muscles of his chest between her fingers, and she tugged his shirt out of his pants to push it upward.

He briefly broke off their kiss to pull the long-sleeved turtleneck over his head. As he tossed it aside, she reached out to touch him. Against her fingers, his muscles were as hard now as they'd been the first time she'd touched him. The only difference was the fine dusting of silvery hair diving downward toward his trousers.

Her mouth went dry at the way she longed to see every part of him bared to her. Slowly, she explored his chest, her gaze drinking in the majestic sight. Her touch extracted a dark growl from him as he bent his head to kiss the side of her neck.

As her fingers spiked through the silky roughness of his hair and cupped the back of his neck, his invisible touch caressed her skin and unsnapped her bra. A fraction of a second later his mouth encircled the tip of her breast. Sweet Juno, how was it possible his touch could affect her so easily after all these years? She moaned as his tongue circled her nipple before his teeth abraded the stiff peak. Every inch of her was on fire, and the time they'd been apart faded away.

The intensity of his caresses stirred something deep inside. Not since that bittersweet night at La Terrazza del Ninfeo had she felt so alive. It wasn't until this moment that she realized she'd been doing little more than existing. She'd never stopped longing for him. Never stopped hungering for his touch.

The warmth of his hands slid under her bottom and pulled her closer to the edge of the counter. In the next breath, he thrust deep into her, and her head fell backward as she uttered a cry of pleasure. The heat of his mouth brushed over her throat, leaving her breathless as wave after wave of pleasure rolled over her. *Deus*, it was as good between them now as it had been the first time.

Her body clenched around him with every stroke, and she loved the way his strong arm cradled her as he rocked his hips against hers. Every inch of her was alive with sensation. She wasn't a girl anymore, but her body was responding to his touch as if she were thirty years younger.

Eyes closed, she reveled in the sinewy feel of his body as the friction of his hard length sent first one and then another tremor rocking its way through her. His body hardened against hers as he lifted his head to stare down at her.

"You're mine, Atia," he rasped. "You belong to me and no one else."

The raw, possessive nature of his words sent a thrill through her as she stared into blue eyes blazing with desire. The passion in his gaze was for her and her alone, and his look made her heart beat faster. She barely had time to breathe before his body was furiously pumping into hers. Hard and fast, he pulled her with him along a wave of pleasure.

Blind to everything but the way her body responded to his, she cried out his name as the wave crested. A dark roar echoed out of him, and he throbbed violently inside her, while her body clutched at his with equal strength. Time seemed to stand still until the world slowly righted itself as Marcus rested his forehead against hers. His breathing ragged, he shuddered as she reached up to touch his cheek.

"Thank you, *mea amor*," he whispered.

"I enjoyed it, too," she said as she sought his mouth to kiss him gently. "Although I still say we're too old to be acting this way."

"Sweet Juno, *carissima*." He choked out a laugh. "I think we just proved less than a minute ago that we're far from old," he teased as his gaze scanned the kitchen before dropping down to where they were still joined. Heat filled her cheeks.

"You didn't give me much choice, did you?" Despite her attempt to scold him, the breathless note in her voice destroyed the effect.

"Where we're concerned, I don't plan to give you much of a choice at all."

The relentless tone to his statement sent a shiver down her spine. As he pulled away from her, the sensation of loss only heightened the dismay winding its way through her. Time and events had placed a barrier between them, and she wasn't sure they could overcome it. Worried he would sense her sudden tension, she hopped off the counter to pick up her pants. Strong hands caressed her bottom as she bent over.

"I'd forgotten how beautiful your bottom is, *mea amor*."

Startled by his touch, she jumped away from him with a small cry of surprise. She whirled around to face him, holding her pants in front of her while clutching her shirt closed. The instant she saw him frown she knew her ridiculous attempt at modesty had alerted him that something was wrong. She swallowed hard as she focused every bit of her skill into keeping her thoughts hidden. Forcing a smile to her lips, she managed to meet his gaze without flinching.

"I'm going to change," she said breathlessly. "Are you still going to fix me something to eat?"

"Yes." He eyed her warily for a long moment before he smiled. "And when we're done eating, I intend to make you hungry again."

There was no mistaking the significance of his suggestive words, and she struggled with the mixed emotions skimming their way through her. When she didn't answer him, his frown returned. She immediately drew upon every bit of her *Prima Consul* experience to disguise her real feelings behind an amused expression.

"Arrogance, like pride, goeth before the fall, *caro*."

"Go change, or I'm going to show you just how arrogant I can be," he growled with a playful smile, but she could still see the suspicious glint in his eye.

Not about to argue with him, she kept a smile on her lips as she left the kitchen. When she was certain he couldn't see her, she hurried across the living room floor to her bedroom. Behind her, she heard Marcus's slightly off-key singing. The sound made her release a half laugh, half sob as she raced into her bedroom and shut the door. Her back pressed into the wood, she closed her eyes and started to shake violently.

Deus, what had she been thinking? How could she have been so stupid? Making love with Marcus was the worst thing she could have ever done. And Juno help her, she'd confessed she still loved him. While he'd not said he loved her, his behavior had left her with little doubt. He wouldn't be so adamant about resuming their relationship if he didn't. If there was one thing about Marcus she could depend on, it was his loyalty and faithfulness.

But it annoyed her that he'd demanded she share her feelings without verbally expressing his love for her as well. His confidence was one of the things she loved best and least about him. It emphasized his decisive nature as well as his determination to protect those he loved, but it was exasperating all the same.

His silent assumption that they would continue as if the past thirty years hadn't happened was more than irritating. It was disturbing. Her stomach lurched. It didn't matter how either one of them felt. It was pointless to even consider resuming their relationship. It was impossible to recapture the past, and that's what they'd tried to do moments ago.

And no matter how wonderful it had felt, it was an illusion. They could never go back. She swallowed the tears she so desperately wanted to shed. Making love with Marcus just now had left her feeling far more vulnerable than she'd felt in a very long time. The sensation wasn't an unfamiliar one.

Marcus had always had an unsettling effect on her, and he knew it. There was no doubt in her mind that he would use that knowledge to keep her off balance until he got his way. He would use every emotional weapon he possessed to override her objections as to why they shouldn't resume their relationship. Her confession that she still loved him would be the first thing he'd use.

Still trembling, she quickly discarded her clothes and moved toward the bathroom. She needed a shower. If she was going to succeed in convincing Marcus that what had just happened could never happen again, she needed to wash his scent off her skin. Otherwise it would linger as a subtle reminder of how wonderful their lovemaking had been.

The flash of movement out of the corner of her eye made her turn her head toward the mirror. The woman staring back at her winced. When had she become so old? It seemed like yesterday that she and Marcus had blood bonded. She leaned forward to examine her face carefully. There were a few lines around her eyes, but the rest of her skin was smooth and youthful looking.

With a critical eye, she stared at her naked body. She wasn't a girl of twenty anymore, and her figure had begun to sag in different places, the skin less supple than years ago. She turned away from the mirror. It wasn't just time that stood between her and Marcus.

She could never forget what had happened to Gabriel. In Rome, when Marcus had summoned her to the Santa Maria sopra Minerva, she'd said she blamed him for Gabriel's kidnapping. Even though she'd quickly denied it, she understood why she'd tried to lay the blame at his feet. It was easier to fault Marcus for the past than to admit the truth.

If he ever found out she'd not taken their son's life when she'd known she could no longer keep him safe . . . she swallowed the bile rising in her throat. She'd not had the courage to save Gabriel from his fate, and she loathed herself for it. Afterward, her guilt had only been magnified when Marcus had left her alone to hunt for their son.

She'd wanted to go with him, but he'd been adamant in his refusal. For the longest time she'd hated him for that. It had made her believe Marcus blamed her for Gabriel's kidnapping, even though he'd denied it. But he had every right to blame her. A sob escaped her as she twisted the hot and cold faucet handles in the shower.

Even now the memories of those final moments before losing Gabriel were as vivid as when they'd happened. Right down to her blood spattering his small face and the stabbing pain that had ripped through her body the moment the Praetorian had struck her from behind.

She stepped into the spray of water that was still warming up and immediately shuddered. It was impossible to know whether it was from the water's cool temperature or the memories. For years she'd wondered if she could have fought harder that day or done something different to keep Gabriel safe.

Steam filled the shower as the spray grew hotter and warmed her chilled body. For four years, she and Marcus had lived, loved, and celebrated Gabriel's birth at the Rennes-le-Château estate. They'd been so happy. Atia had known Marcus would eventually take her and Gabriel to Rome to live in the *Absconditus*, but she hadn't wanted to leave their happy sanctuary. Instead, she'd pleaded with him to stay at the château until he took on the role of reigning Sicari Lord.

That had been a mistake. Gabriel would still be with them if she'd not convinced Marcus to stay at Rennes-le-Château. One more reason it was her fault that they'd lost Gabriel. Another sob escaped her as she wrapped her arms around her waist and allowed the hot water to wash away her tears.

She wasn't sure how long she'd stood in the heat of the shower, but the sound of Marcus calling her name made her jerk up her head. Through the steam covering the frosted glass of the shower door, she could make out his tall, dark shape as he entered the bathroom.

"Dinner's ready, *carissima*."

"I'll be out in a moment," she called with more than a hint of panic at the possibility of his entering the shower.

"I can keep it warm if you like." The teasing note in his voice made her heart slam into her chest. *Deus*, even when she knew things between them were hopeless, the man still held sway over her.

"No, I'm almost done."

"Hurry up then."

She watched his dark shadow disappear from the bathroom and expelled a deep breath. Tonight. She needed to end this tonight. Things had gone far enough, and she couldn't let them go any further. It would only lead to disaster.

Moving as quickly as she could, she finished bathing then left the bathroom to dress. The entire time she was pulling on her clothes she kept expecting Marcus to burst in on her. When she was finally dressed, her nerves were as taut as piano wire and her chest was tight with tension. She quickly ran a comb through her short curling hair and ignored the feeling of panic streaking through her.

The moment she left the bedroom, she knew she was in trouble. All the lights had been dimmed in the apartment, and she heard the melodic voice of a popular Italian singer in the background. Soft candlelight flickered in the small dining area that was a part of the living room. The table had been set for two with a vase in the middle holding a single rosebud.

Where had he gotten a rose at this time of day? She trembled as she remembered the day they first met. He'd showered her in rose petals that night. Deep inside she longed to recapture those wonderful moments, but she was a realist. She knew it wasn't possible. Marcus emerged from the kitchen and set a bowl of salad on the table. As he turned toward her, he stretched out his hand.

"Come eat, *mea kara*," he said.

There was nothing seductive, teasing, or wicked in his voice, only a tenderness that made her throat close against the emotion welling up inside her. Sweet Juno, sending him away was going to be far more difficult than she'd ever imagined. Her heart was racing as she moved forward.

She deftly avoided accepting his hand and seated herself at the table. A quick glance up at his face said he wasn't happy she'd evaded his touch. Averting her eyes, she undid her napkin and spread it out in her lap while Marcus sat down opposite her. Tension skimmed its way through her, drawing every one of her muscles taut and rigid.

As she served herself some salad, she could feel Marcus's gaze on her, and she steeled herself to look at him. The calculating expression on his face was unnerving, and she slowly put the salad tongs back in the bowl. He handed her the bowl of fettuccine Alfredo before helping himself to the salad.

"Do you remember the first time we met?" he asked quietly. The question caught her by surprise, and some of her tension eased. At least he hadn't probed her as to her less than relaxed manner.

"Yes, I remember."

"You weren't happy with me at all."

"Can you blame me?" she muttered with a small amount of irritation. "You were so damned arrogant. One minute Seneca is introducing me to you, and the next you literally drag me away from my best friend's bonding festivities and my date for the evening, Carlo Giaccone."

"He wasn't for you, and I didn't have much time. I was supposed to return to Rome the next day. I wanted to make sure you knew I'd be back for you." An invisible finger caressed her cheek for a brief instant before it was gone.

"A point you made quite clear throughout the first few moments of our conversation."

"And what changed your mind about me?"

There was a note of curiosity in his voice, and she met his gaze steadily. It was the first time he'd ever asked her the question. He'd seldom questioned anything in those early years. He'd simply accepted it as though it were his due. His had been the manner of a Tribune about to become the reigning Sicari Lord.

"The rose petals all over my bedroom."

"The roses," he repeated with a small nod. "They weren't easy to acquire at that time of year."

"You must have wiped out half a dozen florists in Couiza, Espéraza, and Montazels."

"Not to mention the misappropriation of the Order's helicopter."

"So that's how you got them to Rennes-le-Château so quickly," she exclaimed with a small laugh. "I always wondered how you'd arranged it. And it explains why Seneca was so furious with you the next day before you left."

"He didn't stay angry for long when I told him I intended to blood bond with you." His words made her jaw sag as she stared at him in astonishment.

"I didn't know you'd told him that. He never said anything."

"I told him I'd not spoken to you about it."

"But we barely knew each other." She could feel the blush rising in her cheeks as he sent her a look of amused disbelief.

"I knew every beautiful inch of you by morning."

"You know what I mean. One night in bed together doesn't constitute the strongest foundation for a blood bonding ceremony."

"It wasn't the sex that made me want to bond with you, Atia. Although what happened in the kitchen a little while ago was an excellent reminder of how good it's always been between us." He eyed her intently as he spoke, and it was a look she knew well. He was about to lay down a boundary. "I bonded with you because I loved you from the first moment I saw you, and I wasn't going to let anyone or anything stand in my way until you were mine, then *or now*."

It was a firm, inflexible boundary. An emphatic statement that said he intended to have his way in the present, just as he had in the past. She flinched. How was she supposed to fight such determination, especially when he'd made it clear that he still loved her? That above anything else was enough reason to surrender. She dropped her gaze and picked at her salad with her fork.

"You've not lost your touch for fixing a meal with the least amount of ingredients. It looks delicious," she said quietly.

When he didn't answer her, she forced a smile to her lips and looked up at him. The frown on his face puzzled her. She'd expected to arouse his anger by deliberately changing the subject, but he seemed more worried than angry. Even more troubling was the flash of fear she saw in his cerulean blue eyes. He picked up his fork and took a bite of salad.

"And you've improved the art of changing the subject."

His eyes met hers across the flickering candlelight. It brought back memories of other times when he'd surprised her with a romantic candlelight meal. She averted her gaze and twirled several strands of fettuccine around her fork.

"Did Luciano finish making all the arrangements for Sandro?"

"Yes, and with the improvements that have been made to the research lab's security, I believe the document from the *Tyet of Isis* is as safe as we can make it."

"The Council is frightened," she murmured. "And I can't blame them. There have always been spies in the Order, but this was a Sicari murdered on our own ground. The last time anything like this happened . . ."

She stared down at her plate as the memories threatened to overtake her. A strong hand grasped hers, and she clung to it as though it were a life vest. She lifted her gaze to meet his. There wasn't any need to speak, because his eyes told her that everything she was feeling, he was feeling, too. They sat like that for a long moment, before Marcus released her hand and leaned back in his chair.

"I suppose the Council's instructed you to find the killer."

"Yes, although they know it's unlikely I'll be able to do so."

"Other than those of us who were in Rome, have there been any new arrivals to the estate?"

"Not that I'm aware of. There aren't even any outside guild members here on vacation." She shook her head. "And we've not had anyone new transferred here in more than a year."

"Then that means whoever killed Sandro has been on the estate for a while." Marcus grimaced, and she saw his jaw clench. "We need to find a way to flush the traitor out."

"We can use the document to do that." She saw resistance cross his features, and she leaned forward. "We both know it's what they're after, so we taunt them with it. We keep working at deciphering it. And whether we're close to unraveling what the damn thing says or not, we let everyone, including the *bastardo* who killed Sandro, think we're on the verge of solving the puzzle."

"No. Doing that puts you in harm's way," he ground out in a tight voice.

"What about you? You're not invincible."

"I never said I was, but your abilities are limited, despite our blood bond. I refuse to put you at risk like that."

"To paraphrase my . . . our daughter, every Sicari is at risk all the time. I'm no different. The *Prima Consul* can be replaced."

"But *I* can't replace *you*." His words echoed harshly in the room. "If you think I'm just going to let you offer yourself up as bait, you can think again."

"You don't really have any say in the matter, do you?" she said calmly as she took another bite of fettuccine.

When he didn't answer, she looked across the table at him. *Thunderstruck*. It was the only word that came to mind as she stared at the expression on his face. She quickly ducked her head to hide her smile. She couldn't remember ever seeing him speechless before.

"What in Jupiter's Stone does that mean?" he snapped.

"This is *my world*, Eminence. And unless you're going to announce yourself to the Council as the reigning Sicari Lord, I'm afraid you'll have to control your tendency to order others about. Particularly me."

She raised her head and met his glare with one of her own. This was her guild. She was the leader of the Order, and unless he was willing to step forward and acknowledge that the *Absconditus* existed, he had no real power here. For once she was in charge. And he knew it. His eyes narrowed as he fixed his harsh gaze on her.

"By the gods, you're a stubborn woman, Atia Vorenus."

His flatware rattled loudly against his plate as he shoved his chair away from the table and stood up. Hands braced on the table, his face was dark with frustration as he glared at her. Not about to let him intimidate her, she continued eating her meal. After a long moment, he released a violent sound and stalked away.

He was every inch the Sicari Lord as he paced the carpet. Tall, regal, and proud. He was far from happy with her at the moment. And he'd be even less happy when she told him that she didn't want things to go back to the way they'd been all those years ago. She quietly laid her fork on her plate and turned in her chair.

"Marcus, I think we need to come to an understanding. I've made a new life for myself since we were blood bonded." She watched him draw up short, his mouth open in protest. *Deus*, if only she had the fortitude to let him overrule her, but she didn't. She shook her head. "Loving you is easy. It always was. But neither one of us can erase the past—no matter how hard we try."

"I'm not trying to erase the fucking past," he snarled.

"I didn't say you were. I'm saying we can't go back to that time before Gabriel was taken from us," she bit out with frustration as she sprang to her feet.

"I'm not trying to relive the past, Atia. I'm just trying to enjoy what's left of my life with the woman I love. I want to grow old with you."

"It's not possible." The words were hard and inflexible even to her ears.

"I don't believe that."

"It doesn't matter what you believe, Marcus. What matters is that I'm saying no."

"Then explain it to me. Tell me why it's not possible."

"Because we blame each other for what happened, and that won't ever go away," she cried out in a bitter voice.

The blood drained from his face as his eyes darkened with an emotion she couldn't identify. She thought it might be fury, but it could just as easily have been pain. It was impossible to tell. The silence in the room stretched thin as an ancient parchment about to crumble under the strain.

"I never said I blamed you," he said in a wooden voice.

"You didn't have to say it," she said with resignation as she rubbed her temples. The beginnings of a headache had set in, and she wanted to go to bed. It had been a long, emotional day.

"Don't put words in my mouth, Atia." His expression was hard and icy. "I never blamed you, but that's the second time in less than a month you've blamed *me* for Gabriel's kidnapping."

"I don't blame you."

"Then exactly what is it you find me guilty of?"

"*Deus*, I refuse to do this now," she snapped. "I'm tired and too much has happened today."

He took a step toward her, and the violent anger radiating off of

him was like a raging bonfire. Hot and fierce. The way he was leaning into her made her swallow hard, and the sudden chime of the
apartment's doorbell caused her to close her eyes with relief. When
the chime sounded again, she started toward the suite's front door.
As she passed Marcus, he caught her arm.

"Don't."

It was more a plea than a command, but she didn't have the
courage to do as he asked. Instead, she tugged free of his grasp and
walked toward the door. She understood him well enough to know
that even this brief interruption wouldn't stop him from trying to
wear down her resistance.

Chapter 11

ATIA opened the door to see Ignacio standing in the corridor, his expression grim. A tremor shot through her, as her first thought was of Cleo.

"What is it? What's wrong?"

"Cleo's still in Rome," he snapped as he brushed his way past her into the room.

"What do you mean she's still in Rome?" she gasped in horror.

Cleo should have been back in Chicago by now. The temporary guild she'd established to find the *Tyet of Isis* had been disbanded over a week ago, and all its members had returned to their respective guilds. Her *Celeris* moved deeper into the suite then jerked to a halt at the sight of Marcus standing in the center of the living room. She saw Ignacio glance toward the remains of the candlelight meal in the dining area before he turned back to her.

"What the fuck is he doing here?" Ignacio asked. The fury in his voice shouldn't have shocked her, but it did. She knew Ignacio cared for her, but she was slowly beginning to realize his feelings were even stronger than she'd suspected.

"You don't have the right to ask that question," she said in a stilted voice.

"You're right. I don't," Ignacio said bitterly. "But as someone who cares for Cleo as if she were my own child, I want to know why you allowed *him* to approve her staying on in Rome when she'd finished her assignment."

The *Celeris* jerked his head in Marcus's direction as his accusation sounded like a bomb going off in the room. Stunned, Atia stood frozen in place. Her gaze flew to Marcus's impassive expression, and she saw a flicker of emotion in his blue eyes. It was true. He'd given Cleo permission to remain in Rome.

"Why would you do such a thing?" she said fiercely. "Why would you allow her to stay in that viper's nest?"

"She didn't leave me much choice." Marcus's response drew a snort of disbelief from Ignacio, but Marcus still hadn't even acknowledged the man's presence.

"Choice?" she asked in disbelief. "One word from you and she would have done as you ordered. Haven't we lost enough already? Did you have to put the only child we have left in harm's way?"

"And if I'd ordered her home?" Marcus growled with a ferocity that startled her. "I would have lost all hope of ever being a part of her life, and you would have found it difficult to convince her that *you* didn't have a part in my summoning her home."

The reality of his words sank in as she struggled to understand why her daughter would have chosen to remain in Rome. What had possessed Cleo to stay behind? Her identity wouldn't be a secret to the Praetorians, which meant she was courting danger wherever she went in the city. Atia closed her eyes at the horrible possibilities taking shape in her head. Suddenly, she drew in a quick breath. Cleo had had an assignment. She sensed Ignacio's acute discomfort, and she jerked her head toward him.

"You gave her *an assignment*?" Atia gasped in outrage.

"Yes," he said with a grimace. "I agreed to it months ago when she passed some important information to the tribunal. I would never have given her the assignment if I'd known she was planning on staying in the city afterward."

"Who in the name of Jupiter could be so important a target that she'd ask for an assignment so far away from home?"

"His name is Angotti. He's a small-time crime boss in the Rome syndicate that works for the Praetorians."

"If he's so unimportant, why would Cleo feel the need to perform the task herself?"

"Because over the past three years she's been manipulating all her assignments. With the exception of two or three people, all of her targets have committed crimes involving children."

"What?" Atia gasped in horror.

"Are you certain of this?" Marcus snapped as he took a step toward the *Celeris*.

"Yes." Ignacio darted a glance first at Marcus and then at Atia as he nodded with a grave expression. "I asked her about it before she went after Angotti. She said it wasn't a vendetta, and I believed her. Now I'm not so sure."

"What do you mean you're not so sure?" Atia glared at her bodyguard. If anyone suspected Cleo of performing her assignments outside the Sicari Code, they'd have her brought up on charges before the Council. And she had no intention of sentencing her own daughter to run the gauntlet if she could help it.

"She didn't have a partner with her when she assassinated Angotti. She went alone," Ignacio said with a dark frown.

"*She went alone?*" Her stomach lurched unpleasantly at the thought of her daughter's reckless behavior. She swayed on her feet, and both men stepped toward her. With a hiss of anger and fear, she waved them aside as she looked at Marcus. "Did you know about this?"

"That she went alone? No," Marcus said as he shot Ignacio a hard look then shoved a hand through his silver-tinted hair. "But I'm glad I told Dante she was still in the city. I knew he'd watch out for her without my asking him to. And I wouldn't have agreed to her staying in Rome if she hadn't been with Dante."

"Sweet Juno, I should never have let Lysander convince me to send her to Rome with him. None of this would have happened if she'd stayed here."

She rubbed her temple as the throbbing in her head increased.

Invisible fingers pushed hers aside as Marcus took over the task of massaging her forehead. It felt wonderful. She closed her eyes for a brief moment and welcomed the swift relief brought by his unseen touch.

"I want her brought home, Marcus. I want her safe," she whispered.

"Dante will keep her safe, and she's a skilled fighter. She held her own in the Pantheon despite her lack of abilities." Marcus's voice indicated he wasn't about to change his mind. "If we send for her now, *carissima*, you'll only widen the gulf between the two of you, and I'll lose all hope of knowing my daughter."

He was right. She knew that. But the logic warred with her maternal instinct to protect her child. She'd failed Gabriel, and she couldn't bear to do the same with Cleo. An image of Marcus and Gabriel in the Pantheon fluttered through her head. It took her breath away as she remembered those terrible moments.

Gabriel and Marcus fighting each other so viciously. Then Gabriel striking his father down. Her own plea for Marcus's life only to see Gabriel sink to the stone floor from the fatal blow of Marcus's sword. The pain of that moment pressed its way into every inch of her until it felt as though someone were ripping her heart out all over again.

She'd already lost her son. She couldn't lose her daughter, too. First one tremor and then another rippled through her. Instantly, Marcus enveloped her in his warmth, and she pressed her face into his shoulder.

"It will be all right, mea kara. I have great faith in Dante and in our daughter. She will be fine."

The soothing caress of his thoughts mingling with hers eased Atia's trembling. Slowly, she pushed herself free of Marcus's embrace. As her gaze met his, she recognized the sorrow in his blue eyes. She was certain he was remembering Gabriel's kidnapping. The loss of their son had cost both of them so much.

Losing Cleo would be no less painful, and as agonizing as it was to admit, Marcus was right. If she had any hopes of mending her quarrel with Cleo, she couldn't demand her daughter's return without just cause. *Deus*, Ignacio should never have let Cleo take on her most recent mission. She turned to her bodyguard.

"How could you have been so shortsighted as to give Cleo that assignment just after we'd fought Nicostratus in the Pantheon?" she asked with a growing sense of outrage.

"I'm not a mind reader, Madame Consul. As I said, I had no reason to believe she wouldn't leave the city once the mission was complete. I made a mistake."

"A mistake I could expect of someone less experienced, but you, Ignacio? You know better."

"Are you implying I deliberately put Cleo in harm's way?" The cold anger in Ignacio's voice emphasized how much her comment had insulted him. She frowned. It didn't surprise her that he was offended, but he displayed no remorse either. It wasn't like him. She shook her head as she tried to reassure him that she was merely disappointed in his actions.

"Of course not," she responded with regret. "I know you wouldn't do anything of the sort. Sandro's murder has me on edge. I'm sorry."

"I'm sorry, too, because it tells me that you no longer trust my judgment," Ignacio said. "Therefore you shall have my resignation on your desk by tomorrow morning."

Stunned by his declaration, Atia shook her head in protest as her *Celeris* bowed sharply then turned and walked toward the door. She took a quick step forward.

"Ignacio, please. I don't want you to resign. You know how much I rely on you. I need you."

His hand holding the door open, Ignacio turned slightly in her direction. Bitterness had hardened his features into a cold mask as he looked at Atia then to the man behind her and back to her again.

"No, Madame Consul," he said in an icy voice as he flashed a look in Marcus's direction. "You already have my replacement. I can only hope he will serve you as faithfully as I have and that he doesn't put his own needs ahead of yours."

The moment the door closed behind the man, Atia moved to go after him. An invisible hand grasped her arm to hold her back.

"Let him go, Atia. His pride is wounded, and he's in love with you."

"I know," she said softly as she faced Marcus. "I always knew he cared for me, I just didn't realize how deeply."

"That morning at La Terrazza del Ninfeo." His lips twisted in a grim smile. "I thought I'd lost you to him."

There was a look on his face that said he was waiting for her to reaffirm her feelings for him, but she remained silent. She'd already confessed her soul to him once this evening. To do it a second time would only give him more power over her. Power she wasn't willing to give. When she didn't speak, Marcus sighed heavily.

"I don't think I've ever met a more stubborn woman than you, Atia," he said with quiet exasperation. His frustration was suddenly amusing, because he looked just like Cleo did whenever she was annoyed about something. She smiled slightly, which made him scowl darkly.

"Cleo looks just like you when she's irritated." Her words made Marcus's expression lighten.

"Then you must aggravate her as much as you do me." Although his voice still held a note of exasperation, there was humor there as well. Her smile widened.

"We've had more than our fair share of battles. Cleo can be incredibly stubborn."

"Like her mother." Marcus's blue eyes studied her with an intensity that suddenly made her uncomfortable. "I know you're worried about her, Atia. I am, too. But you can't keep her locked up because of what happened to Gabriel."

She closed her eyes against the truth in his words. It was true. No matter how much she wanted to lock Cleo up to keep her safe from harm, she couldn't. Losing Gabriel had left a wound that would never heal, even though she'd only known him a short time. She'd never known the man he might have become. She'd only known the monster Nicostratus had created.

But losing Cleo would be like losing not just another piece of her heart but a part of herself as well. She didn't really see Marcus move. She only realized the space between them had disappeared. As he cupped her face in his hands, his touch ignited a familiar fire inside her. She trembled and opened her eyes to look at him, struggling not to let him see how disturbing the simple caress was to her.

"Why do you think I blame you for Gabriel, *carissima*?" His question doused her skin with a frigid chill. She swallowed hard and shook her head.

"Not now, Marcus. I don't want to do this now."

"Then when?" he said through clenched teeth. "Tomorrow? Next week? If I let you, you'll avoid discussing it altogether."

"*Deus*, and you call me stubborn," she said as she jerked away from his touch. Frustrated, she blew out a harsh sigh. "You push too hard. You always did."

"I push because I refuse to let the past come between us."

"You can't just wipe it out with a wave of your hand, Marcus." She made a gesture in midair as if she were waving a wand. "It doesn't work that way."

"Then tell me what will work, Atia. Tell me how I'm supposed to get my beautiful, stubborn wife to accept the fact that we belong together?"

"You can't," she snapped, angry that he refused to drop the matter. A knot swelled in her throat as she put more space between them. "I'm not the girl you married, Marcus. Losing Gabriel changed me. Changed us."

"Tell me how it changed? When I came back from Rome that last time, you wouldn't even talk to me."

"Because you left me," she cried out. "You went looking for Gabriel's kidnappers and left me alone. I needed you."

"Are you saying you wanted me to stay at the château and do nothing?" The ferocity of his question made her wince.

"No. But you wouldn't take me with you. You shut me out. You took on a burden that wasn't—that wasn't yours to carry."

"I didn't shut you out. You weren't in any condition to go with me."

"You *did* shut me out. You went racing off to Rome in search of Gabriel, and you didn't call me for almost two weeks, Marcus. *Two weeks*," she hissed angrily as she remembered those terrible dark days. "Is it any wonder I didn't want to talk to you when you came back? I felt like you'd deserted me. You left me alone to deal with the fact that it was my fault Gabriel was gone."

"*Christus*, it wasn't your fault, *carissima*," Marcus exclaimed as he stepped toward her, but she avoided his grasp. "Is that what you've believed all these years? Those Praetorian *bastardi* almost killed you. It wasn't your fault, Atia."

"It *was* my fault," she shouted. "I lied to you. To everyone. I was a coward. I could have taken Gabriel's life before those *bastardi* took him out of my arms and I didn't."

The minute the words were out of her mouth she regretted them, as the color drained from Marcus's face. Stunned, he stared at her as if she'd taken a sword and plunged it into him. Her entire body was as tight as a piece of elastic stretched to its breaking point. Slowly, Marcus's disbelief faded and his fury rolled over her senses like a tidal wave. If she had been feeling less drained, she might have been able to keep from drowning under his harsh emotions. She couldn't. Her headache had weakened her ability to protect herself, and it was impossible not to feel the impact of his anger.

"Sweet mother of Juno," he snarled. "What kind of a man do you think I am, Atia? Do you really think I would have judged you for not following the old ways?"

"Yes," she whispered. "You practiced the ways of the first Sicari Lords. You still do. What was I supposed to think?"

"That I would have understood," he said fiercely. "That I would have told you it was all right."

"Would you have?" She shook her head. "I don't think so."

"All this time you've believed me to be that much of a *bastardo*." The disgust in his voice cut deep like a razor.

"No. I believed your loyalty to the *Absconditus* was, and still is, absolute. The minute the Praetorians took Gabriel, he became a serious threat to the Order as well as the *Absconditus*. I was certain you would despise me for choosing our son's life over the Order. So I lied."

She bowed her head, unable to bear looking at his angry features. The confrontation was every bit as painful as she'd imagined it would be. Exhausted, the pain inside her was a raw wound. The ache made her feel like she'd aged twenty years in the last half hour. The throbbing in her head only added to the mental anguish tearing her apart inside. She wanted to end this. Be done with it. The tension between them thickened as she opened her eyes to look at him. The fury blazing in his eyes made her hesitate for a moment before she drew in a deep breath.

"I think you should go, Marcus."

"Fuck."

The violent response made her nerve endings scream with tension, and fear propelled her backward as he took a quick step in her direction. She wasn't sure if it was anger or anguish that made his features darken that much more as he came to a halt. They stared at each other for a long moment before Atia turned her head away, unable to bear the censure in his gaze any longer.

"Please go, Marcus."

The quiet command drew a dark noise from him, and she jerked her head in his direction to look at him again. His face was a sharply defined mask that hid everything he was feeling. He'd even regained control of his emotions, as she realized they were no longer bombarding her senses. With a low growl of frustration, he started to move toward the door then hesitated.

He didn't say anything, and the invisible stroke of his hand against her cheek startled her. Emotion flashed in his blue eyes, making them darken, and she could have sworn he was in some great torment. As they stared at each other, somewhere in the depths of her mind she heard the whisper of his thoughts touching hers. The instant her mind recoiled from the mental touch, it was gone.

Marcus drew in a sharp breath, and with another guttural sound, he left the suite. As the door closed behind him, Atia stumbled forward to collapse into the soft cushions of the sofa. Tears rolled down her cheeks as she huddled against the arm of the couch and cried until she couldn't cry anymore.

Chapter 12

THE sound of the library door opening made Cleo look up from the building plans she'd spread out on the table in front of her. Instantly, her senses were on fire as Dante walked into the room. Her entire body might as well have been a magnet, the way she was drawn to him. As he crossed the room toward her, she enjoyed watching the way he moved.

He was dressed in black again, but this time it was a neatly pressed black cotton shirt rolled up at the sleeves to reveal his forearms while the shirt flared open at the neck. The black pants he wore were just as crisp looking as the shirt, with a sharp crease running down the front of his trousers to brush the top of his Italian-made shoes. And they had to be Italian-made. She didn't know how she knew. She just did. Maybe it was that careless yet flawless look of a man who'd just stepped out of the best men's shop in Rome.

As he drew closer, her heart rate quickened to twice its normal pace. *Deus*, he was without a doubt the sexiest, most confident man she'd seen in a very long time. Her gaze drifted over his tanned arms with their dusting of black hair. She'd always loved a man's arms.

They emphasized male strength and beauty in one fell swoop. Well, short of the rest of a man's body.

And she was willing to bet that Dante Condellaire—

Cleo stiffened as her thoughts slammed to a halt. Condellaire. That's what had really been bugging her every time she heard his name. It hadn't registered with her this morning, and she'd forgotten it until now. It was an old Sicari name, but it was rare to hear it.

Lysander was the only one off the top of her head she could think of with the same last name. Perhaps they had a connection somewhere in the past. It wasn't impossible, since the Sicari population numbered less than three thousand all over the world. Then again, Dante was a Sicari Lord and Lysander wasn't. Well, her friend did have *some* Sicari Lord talents, considering he had a Praetorian father. Dante came to a stop in front of the table, and she forgot all about his possible relationship to Lysander.

It was clear the gods had taken their time creating Dante, right down to those dark blue eyes of his that reminded her of the sea during a storm. Eyes that were studying her carefully at the moment. A shiver skimmed its way across her skin as she met his gaze. Something had changed. In the garden when she'd teased him, she'd had the advantage. Not now.

He was in complete control, and she was the one who was suddenly feeling discombobulated. She wasn't sure she liked the feeling. Her gaze flew to his sensuous mouth, and she saw it tip upward slightly. Her heart skipped a beat. Now she was certain she didn't like the way she was feeling. Suddenly, she was glad there was a table between them.

Folding her arms across her chest, she narrowed her gaze at him and waited for him to say something. Hands clasped behind his back, Dante studied her. The appraisal in his dark eyes made her edgy, and she forced herself not to squirm beneath his observation.

"Why are you so eager to get into the convent?" His quiet question made it clear he expected an honest answer.

"I have a friend in there, and I want to get her out."

"How do you know she's in the convent?" Again, his tone indicated he wanted a straightforward answer.

"Marta was taken more than a year ago when one of the Chicago guild's missions went south. I tracked her back to the convent a few months later."

She didn't bother to go into detail about Lysander's torture or her desire to help not only Marta, but her best friend as well. Lysander was like a brother to her, and she knew he still felt the sting of that failed mission.

"And you're sure she's there?" he asked quietly.

"Would it matter if she wasn't? It's a breeding facility, and that means there are Sicari women . . . and children there," Cleo said grimly. Dante's gaze narrowed for a moment before he nodded.

"All right," he said with a somber expression. "Why don't we make a pact? You tell me everything you know about the convent, and I'll give you my word you'll be part of the team."

"You mean the *assault* team that enters the convent when you authorize the rescue."

He frowned, and she instinctively knew he'd been trying to keep his promise vague. Now that she'd narrowed the definition, he wasn't so keen on the terms. With a cheerful smile, she waited for his answer. Irritation flared in his blue eyes. She'd backed him into a corner, and he wasn't happy about it.

"Done," he bit out in a fierce tone. "But you're to do as I say. No questions asked. *Capisci*?"

"Understood."

"All right then. Show me what you have."

"Take a look," she said with a smile as she nodded toward the blueprints she'd been studying when he'd entered the room.

With a fluid move that reminded her of the power she'd seen him exhibit in his martial arts exercise, Dante's invisible touch flattened the floor plans on the table. One hand pressed into the tabletop, he examined the architectural drawings of the convent for a moment before he raised his head to look at her.

"Where did you get these?" he asked with amazement.

"I had them sent over from the safe house along with the rest of my things." She stressed the last few words in her reply. Best to let him know she had no intention of going anywhere. "I have a source who does odd jobs for me when I need something."

She didn't bother to mention that Antonio had been her lover over a year ago and, despite going their separate ways, he was always willing to help her whenever she asked. Something told her the man was still in love with her. It was the reason she'd left him. Love wasn't in the cards for her. Not even with a man outside of the Order.

"I've been trying for almost a year to get my hands on these floor plans."

"Maybe you just didn't ask nice enough," she said in a husky voice.

Her hands caressed the table as she extended her arms out to the side and leaned toward him until her face was inches from his. She knew she was being deliberately provocative, but she didn't like the way the balance of power had shifted between them. It made her feel vulnerable, and she didn't enjoy the sensation one bit. Being provocative was a way to balance things out.

Although he didn't move, she could see the way his entire body went rigid as he looked up to meet her gaze. Something flashed in his blue eyes, and she suddenly wished she'd worn something a little more feminine instead of her black knit shirt and slacks. Suggestive words and body language would only get her so far where this guy was concerned. And the thought of breaking through that steely exterior of his filled her with more excitement than she knew she should be feeling.

That impetuous kiss she'd given him this morning had been hotter than anything she'd experienced in a long time. She knew it had affected him, too. His hard-on had announced that fact loud and clear. A tremor rocked through her as she remembered the way her body had responded when she'd pressed against his erection. As suddenly as the memory assaulted her body, she recoiled from the thought.

What the fuck was she thinking? He was a Sicari Lord. She knew better than to get involved with one of her own kind. No, not her kind. This man was way out of her league. Still, what would it be like to tempt him? And she was certain temptation was something he was trying to avoid where she was concerned. She jerked away from the table, suddenly uncomfortable in his presence.

Distance. She needed to put some mental distance between the two of them. That was the best way to handle things. More importantly, she had to stop letting her attraction to the man interfere with her goal of freeing Marta from that hellhole the Praetorians had her in. An odd expression crossed Dante's face, and once again, she wondered if he was reading her thoughts. The notion made her edgy.

"Reading my thoughts is forbidden, *il mio signore*."

"I wasn't reading your mind, Cleopatra," he murmured. "Your face is expressive enough that it's unnecessary."

"Oh really?" she snapped. "What am I thinking now?"

"You're feeling vulnerable, and you're worried I'll find a way to keep you from going with me to the convent."

"Well, you're right about me thinking you'll find a way to lock me out of the rescue," she said with a grim smile. "But vulnerable? That's a bit of a reach."

Deus, she was a liar. The man had every one of her senses on full alert. He had no idea how much she wanted to see him completely naked and aroused. Her stomach did a flip-flop at the image filling her head. She'd lost her mind. Her gaze met his, and although he gave the appearance of being in control, she was certain it was a façade. He straightened upright as if aware he'd revealed more than he cared to.

"Tell me what else you know." His terse words were an order, and she quickly pointed to the drawing on the table.

"The convent is heavily guarded. Angotti said there are always ten guards on duty outside the convent and at least five or six more inside. That doesn't count the Praetorians who're inside for . . . other reasons." Her words made Dante draw in a sharp hiss of air.

"That's at least twenty or more Praetorians on-site with more on the way if they get an alarm out," he said grimly as he ran his hand over the back of his neck. "Not only do we have to fight Praetorians, but we need time to get the women out, and some of them might not be in good shape."

"Angotti told me where the control room is. If we take out their communications links, that will buy us enough time to get in and out before they know what hit them."

"And exactly how do you think you can get to the control room before they realize they're under attack?" The dark, skeptical tone of his voice made her smile. Dante Condellaire, like most people, underestimated her.

"Because we're going to get inside without them knowing it." Her confident words made him snort with disgust. Her smile widened as she pointed to the western side of the convent's exterior wall. "We go in here. They won't be expecting us if we enter this way."

"That's because that side of the building is situated on a cliff that drops straight down to the Tyrrhenian Sea," Dante said in an irritable tone of voice. A long, tapered finger traced the edge of the convent's west wall. "Are you actually proposing we scale the cliff?"

"Actually, we don't have too far to climb," she said as she reached for a stack of photos and spread them out in front of him. "I shot these last year. Notice the caverns here and here? These are the remains of an old tunnel system that used to lead up to the convent several hundred years ago."

"How do you know that?" Dante arched his eyebrow at her with a healthy dose of skepticism.

"When I learned Marta had been taken to the convent, I did some detailed research on the place in hopes of finding a way in. It took me a while to find anything useful, but I eventually located a journal written over a hundred years ago by a *Vigilavi* who worked at the convent doing odd jobs. He talked about a tunnel system the sisters had used to get down to the sea for fishing. The cliff face collapsed at the top while the guy was working for the nuns, and they stopped using the tunnel. In his journal, the *Vigilavi* wrote about building a balustrade on the balcony that connected with the tunnel."

"And you think these two caverns are part of that tunnel system?"

"I know they are. I explored them shortly after I took these pictures."

"*Sweet Virgins of Vesta*, are you out of your mind? How in Juno's name did you even get in there? A boat couldn't get that close to the rock face without the risk of being damaged."

He grabbed one of the photos and stared down at it before he lifted his angry gaze to glare at her. She sent him a disgusted look. It wasn't like she'd just gone exploring at the drop of a hat. She'd had a *Vigilavi* fisherman observe the cliff for more than five months, not to mention the two weeks she spent in the sun watching the rock face, before she'd ventured into the tunnels.

"I used scuba gear and an underwater scooter to get from the boat to the cliff wall. The cavern at the base of the cliff was easy to get in to. It leads upward to this opening, which is where the tunnel ends." She circled the desk to look over his shoulder and pointed to the yawning cavern high up on the cliff. "The balcony just above is actually part of the rock, and the portion of the tunnel that led from the cavern to the balcony fell into the sea a long time ago."

"And what makes you think the Praetorians don't know about the tunnel system?"

"The Praetorians took possession of the convent about twenty years ago when the order of nuns became too small to maintain the place." She breathed in the musky cologne he was wearing and wondered if he wore it often or if today was different. "I'm certain from the amount of cobwebs and debris I had to go through that no one's been in that tunnel in more than a century. Parts of it have caved in some, but there's enough room to get through those areas. Even if the Praetorians know about the tunnel, they don't think it's a threat. And my hunch is that they don't have a clue that it's even there or they would have blocked off the balcony a lot more securely. There aren't any cameras or motion sensors either, otherwise they would have caught me."

"I thought you said you weren't reckless."

"I'm not, but I was willing to take a risk. Two different things."

He released a guttural sound of disgust as he studied the photographs and the building plans. Standing this close to him made her senses go haywire again as she breathed in his essence. Damn, the man smelled unbelievably delicious. He was spicy heat and raw male. Her gaze drifted over his profile, and she suppressed the urge to brush her fingertips along his strong jawline.

"It's going to take some time to get all the details into place," he murmured as he braced his hands on the table to peer at the blueprints.

"We can be ready in three weeks."

At her confident statement, he turned his head to look at her before he straightened to his full height. She swallowed hard at the way he towered over her. He arched his eyebrows in a silent demand for an explanation.

"I've already got most of the equipment on order or in place. But most importantly, I've got a distraction to help us breach the inside a little easier."

"A distraction?"

"Sonny Mesiti," she said in a tight voice as Angotti's sniveling echoed in her head. "He delivers weekly food supplies to the convent. We steal one of Sonny's delivery vans and make a special delivery the night we go in. Attacking them from the front once we've taken charge of the control room will make things easier *and* we'll have transport for the hostages."

"All right." He looked down at the photographs again and sifted through them with his long fingers. "I want to do some more reconnaissance, but on the surface, I think your plan is a good one."

"I'm glad you approve," she said in a wry tone.

"Why wouldn't I approve?" Dante turned away from the table, an expression of puzzlement on his face.

"I don't know." She shrugged with a small amount of resentment. "I think it was the *on the surface* piece that rubbed me the wrong way."

"I was merely reserving the right to abandon your plan if the reconnaissance doesn't verify your data."

Cleo bobbed her head at his explanation, suddenly feeling like an idiot for taking his thorough assessment of the situation personally. The man was doing the same thing Lysander, Ares, or Ignacio would do if she went to them with a plan. Still, it stung a little.

"It's a good plan, Cleopatra. I just want to be sure we don't have any surprises." *Deus*, she loved the way he said her name. It was a low, husky stroke of syllables rolling off his lips.

"I understand," she said quietly as she tried to focus on something other than his mouth. "So who's in the convent that you want to rescue?"

"Cornelia's daughter. I gave my word to her that I'd find a way to rescue Beatrice." There was a warmth to his voice when he said Cornelia's name that told her his relationship with the woman was special.

"I see," she muttered. "I'm sure you'll keep your word to her."

Wonderful, no wonder she'd embarrassed the hell out of the guy earlier. He was already involved with someone. *Christus*, what did it matter that he was seeing someone else? Whether he was or wasn't, he was the last man she needed to have an affair with. She almost groaned at the idea. She was a fucking idiot.

"*No*, Cornelia and I . . ." His rushed response trailed off as a sheepish expression swept across his face only to be replaced with a stoic look. "What I meant is that she's my friend. My mother left me in the care of the *Absconditus* when I was four, and Cornelia took me under her wing. She became my *Praefect* when I was named Tribune."

Cleo tried to ignore the relief surging through her at the way he'd quickly corrected her initial impression. To hide her reaction, she moved swiftly from the table to plop down in a nearby wing back chair. He turned his head as she walked away, but she avoided looking at him. With a quick twist of her hips, she turned her body so her legs dangled over one arm of the chair with her back pressed into the corner of the smooth leather seat cushion.

"*Praefect*?" She deliberately kept her voice devoid of anything other than curiosity as Dante turned toward her.

"It's a rank equivalent to a *Primus Pilus* in one of the Order's guilds. Although the *Absconditus* is a guild like others in the Order, it operates somewhat differently than what you're used to."

"Differently how?"

"For one thing, we're not all Sicari Lords. Marcus and Placido are the only Sicari Lords left at the moment." The strength in his voice emphasized he was once again in control, and it made her want to squirm in her seat.

"I don't understand." She shook her head and could feel her brow furrow as she stared at him. "There are only *two* Sicari Lords?"

"Marcus is the current reigning Sicari Lord. His decisions are the ultimate law of the Sicari," Dante explained quietly. "Even the Order is subject to the Sicari Lord's decrees, although it's rare that any Sicari Lord uses that authority in such a manner."

Dante leaned back against the table behind him. Long legs stretched out in front of him, he looked relaxed, but there was an air of power about him that said he was always on guard. Raw, lethal, and in a strange way, almost untouchable. He represented a challenge to her, despite the fact that she didn't need his kind of stimulation. An expression of amusement crossed his features.

"What?" She scowled at him.

"I can see the wheels in your head churning like mad. The idea of taking an order from the Sicari Lord doesn't sit well with you. But then you don't like taking orders all that much, do you?" His intuitive observation made her edgy.

"I've been known to disobey an order or two," she admitted in a begrudging tone of voice.

"And when you're *not* under orders?" Again, amusement. The man could be downright annoying when he wanted to. Fine. She'd end this dance right now.

"Under the covers? I guess that depends," she said in a soft, silky tone of voice.

It was hard not to smile with satisfaction as a dark red color flushed his face while his body went rigid. He didn't move, and for a brief instant she could have sworn he had the look of a man ready to bolt from the room like a panicked stallion. She saw his throat bob as he swallowed hard, which made her certain the suggestive comment had thrown him into a tailspin.

Even though she couldn't tell what he was thinking, she knew what she *wanted* him to be thinking. Damnit, this fixation of hers was beginning to rub her the wrong way. Even worse was how she was suddenly wishing she hadn't made him uncomfortable. And he was very uncomfortable. She could feel it. The realization surprised her, which made the awkward moment even more strained because she was to blame for it.

"I said under *orders*," he said stiffly.

"Right. Sorry," she said in a contrite tone and looked away from him. "So this other Sicari Lord you mentioned, what does he do?"

"Placido used to hold Marcus's position in the *Absconditus*. But he still retains the title as an honorary one." His voice was still stiff, and her conscience tapped her again, pulling a soft sigh from her as she continued to avoid his gaze.

"So what does that make you and all the others in the—what did you call it, the *Absconditus*? Are you saying no one else here is a Sicari Lord?"

She frowned. If Marcus and an old man were the only Sicari Lords left, then they were the last ones unless they had heirs. And while Marcus was her birth father, she wasn't a candidate to carry on the bloodline. The painful thought wrenched at her midsection as she caught a glimpse of motion out of the corner of her eye. Once again the fluid beauty of Dante's movements fascinated her as he unfolded his arms and wrapped his fingers around the edge of the desk he was leaning against.

"Just as with the Order's guilds, the *Absconditus* has a hierarchy to avoid complete chaos."

"And you don't like chaos." It was an observation, not a question, and she turned her head to shoot him a tentative look. Relief dashed through her when she saw his embarrassment had vanished. He shrugged.

"Balance requires opposing forces. Without chaos, there would not be order."

She nodded. "Chaos" she understood a little too well at the moment. Her entire world had been turned upside down in the last couple of weeks, and if chaos wasn't a word for it, then she didn't know what else to call it. She looked away from him.

"How long have you known my . . . Marcus?"

"I was four when my mother left me on his doorstep and walked away without looking back. Marcus took responsibility for me." The flat statement made her jerk her head back in his direction.

Despite the stoic look on his face, she sensed the raw pain he was feeling. It surprised her how powerful the sensation was, because she rarely experienced a knowing with such strength or accuracy. And she was dead certain her senses weren't playing tricks on her. The thought of him growing up without a mother to love him made her sad. It was probably why he seemed so distant and untouchable.

"What about your father?" she probed gently. He hesitated before he looked away from her.

"I never knew my father. Marcus told me he died fighting Prae-torians." Dante straightened and, with his hands behind his back, strode across the floor to stare out the window.

"I'm sorry." She meant it.

"It was a long time ago," he said quietly without turning to look at her.

"Maybe, but it couldn't have been easy. I know what it's like to grow up without a father. You didn't have anyone."

"I had Marcus, Placido, and Cornelia."

It was an abrupt, emphatic declaration that he didn't care that he'd grown up an orphan. She would have believed him if it weren't for the soft note of sorrow threading through his words. That and the odd twinge that grabbed at her heart as he stood in front of the window. Although she wanted to probe deeper, instinct told her not to ask him any more questions. There was something about his stiff posture that said he'd already shared more than he'd intended to. The silence expanded between them before Dante cleared his throat and turned to face her.

"You'll like Marcus if you give him a chance."

"Not if he insists on playing the overprotective father, I won't," she said as she uncurled herself from the wing back chair and moved away from him to the far wall lined with bookcases.

"I think you both probably need time to adjust to each other." Despite his almost silent tread, her senses were on fire as he crossed the room. "I know I'd need time if I were in your shoes."

"But you're not," she muttered.

"You're right. I'm not."

The soft tone of understanding in his voice made her turn to face him. There were still several feet between them, and the empathy in his expression made her heart skip a beat. The man was too damn good-looking. Irritated he could distract her so easily, she turned back to the books on the shelf. Her fingers ran across the spines of the texts lining the bookshelf as she quickly changed the subject.

"So are you close with . . . Marcus?" She wasn't sure why she asked the question when she wanted to stop talking about the man.

"He and Placido are like fathers to me. They both conducted my lessons in the *Novem Conformavi*."

"The what?"

"It's a nine-level training program all members of the *Absconditus* must complete." His words made her thoughts automatically jump to the medieval epic poem *The Divine Comedy*.

"Are we talking Dante's Inferno?" she quipped as she glanced at him over her shoulder.

"Far from it," he replied with a wolfish grin.

It was a smile that made her heart jump before it skidded out of control. Heat filled her cheeks, and she quickly returned her attention to the shelves of books in front of her. When was the last time she'd been disconcerted by a man's smile? She couldn't remember, which was almost as unsettling as the way Dante made her feel. She tipped her head to one side as she read a familiar title, and she pulled a copy of Shakespeare's *Henry V* off the shelf. She automatically flipped through the pages until she reached Harry the king's Saint Crispin's Day speech. It was one of her favorite parts of the play.

"You like Shakespeare?" The curiosity in his voice made her smile, and she briefly glanced at him as she displayed the title of the book to him.

"Not all of his plays, but *Henry V* has everything I like."

"Such as?" His question made her face him.

"Intrigue, fighting, heroes overcoming impossible odds, romance, a rousing cry to arms, a great battle—"

"Romance?" At the amusement in his voice, she glared at him.

"Yes, *romance*. Got a problem with that?"

"Show me."

He folded his arms across his chest and smiled at her again. It wasn't just a command, it was a dare. She immediately turned the pages to the end of the play and Harry's efforts to woo Katherine, the daughter of the French king. Her finger quickly traced its way down first one page and then another until she tapped the section she'd been searching for.

"The second scene of the last act is very romantic," she said fiercely as she studied the text to find one of her favorite phrases. "Here—this is one of my favorite lines."

Cleo knew the words by heart, and with her eyes closed, she visualized the actors from the DVD she owned. "You have witchcraft in your lips, Kate. There is more eloquence in a sugar touch of them than in the tongues of the French council, and they should sooner persuade Harry of England than a general petition of monarchs."

She released a soft sigh after the last words and opened her eyes, intent on challenging Dante to disagree with her. But the moment she looked into the stormy intensity of his dark blue gaze, she forgot what she was going to say. Instead she found herself measuring the distance between them with her senses.

The man was so close it was impossible not to breathe in the deliciously rough, spicy scent of him. Had he moved closer while she was reciting the Bard's poetry? Not that it mattered, because she sure as hell wasn't going to protest. Nervously, her tongue darted out to lick her dry lips.

A primal sound echoed out of his chest, and the tension in the room skyrocketed until it was a palpable caress of heat on her skin. His firm lips were inches away, and she waited with bated breath for him to lower his head and kiss her.

In the next instant, the library door burst open, and Dante had put more than three feet between them in the blink of an eye. Startled, she turned to see a little boy panting from exertion dart into the room.

"Tribune," he gasped. "It's Giuseppe and Santino. They're fighting again."

Dante muttered something under his breath, and for some reason she didn't think it was due to the interruption. In fact, he seemed almost relieved.

"Where are they, Pietro?"

"In the big training room."

"I need to take care of this," Dante said as he looked at her with an odd glint in his eyes. "I'll have someone do reconnaissance to back up your data, and we'll go from there."

With that, he strode out of the library followed by the small boy. Cleo stared after them with frustration.

"*Fuck.*"

The word echoed fiercely in the large room. The man had been about to kiss her. She knew it. She blew out a harsh puff of air. In less than twenty-four hours, Dante had managed to turn her life upside down almost as easily as her mother had more than a week ago. She wasn't sure she was ready for another upheaval. No, not an upheaval. It would be an inferno, and Dante Condellaire would consume her. But then a little bit of fire could be a good thing. The erotic image the thought brought to mind made her smile, and she ran after him. The man wasn't going to walk away from her that easily.

Chapter 13

DANTE hurried down the hall with Pietro running to keep up. As they reached the stairs to the second floor, he heard footsteps pounding behind him. Cleopatra. He muttered a fierce imprecation. *Christus*, he'd almost kissed her a moment ago. Was he insane? The fact that his body was on full alert the minute he came within five feet of her made him tighten his mouth with irritation.

What in Juno's name was wrong with him? Why did the woman affect him like this? She was like a hot wind blasting at his senses whenever he got near her. With a grunt of frustration at the thought, he took the stairs two at a time.

At the top of the stairwell, he could hear the sound of steel crashing against steel echoing nearby. Goddamnit, he was going to teach Giuseppe and Santino a lesson today they wouldn't forget. He strode down the glass-enclosed corridor overlooking the inner courtyard toward the largest training room in the *Absconditus* complex.

Padded from floor to ceiling, the room was devoid of any kind of equipment other than the swords his two troublemakers were wielding. He barely had time to wonder where the instructor was when an unseen force sent Santino flying backward until he hit the padded wall behind him and slid to the floor. As Giuseppe leaped forward with his sword high over his head, Dante envisioned jerking the weapon from the boy's hand and dropping it to the floor.

"That's enough," he said in an authoritative tone.

In seconds, both boys were scrambling to go down on one knee in a bow of respect. The children who'd been watching the fight immediately came to attention. Pietro had joined the other children, and Dante caught the look of fear on the child's face. Mentally, he squeezed the boy's shoulder. As their gazes met, a look of relief swept over the six-year-old's face.

No sooner had he silently reassured Pietro than his senses went into overdrive as Cleopatra entered the room. He didn't have to see her to know exactly where she was. It was as if he had a homing beacon inside him fine-tuned to her frequency. He drew in a quick, angry hiss of air as he realized he wasn't focusing on the issue at hand.

Turning his attention back to the troublemakers, he moved to stand in front of them. He didn't speak for a long moment, deliberately letting the silence in the room stretch out the tension radiating off the boys.

"Why are you in here without an instructor?" The quiet question made the two boys look at each other for a moment before they ducked their heads.

"Well?" This time he didn't bother to hide his displeasure.

"We wanted to settle our argument by ourselves." Giuseppe sounded as if he was trying to give the answer Dante wanted to hear as opposed to the real reason.

"So you invited the others to come watch?" Dante growled as he glanced at the younger children in the room. "Do you realize one of them could have gotten hurt while viewing this stunt of yours?"

The two teenagers paled significantly at his words. They looked at each other before bowing their heads again. The fact that they recognized the danger they'd put the other children in pleased Dante, but it didn't make him any less angry. They'd disobeyed orders by fighting unsupervised.

"Who started this?" he asked.

"I did, Tribune." Santino lifted his head to meet Dante's gaze with a look of regret. Somehow Dante didn't think the boy's regret was so much for having started the fight as it was for being caught.

"Explain."

"Giuseppe said I would never pass the third *Tabulati*." There was a belligerent note to the teenager's voice despite the look of trepidation on his face. Dante arched his eyebrow.

"Since the third lesson of the *Novem Conformavi* is that of temperance and restraint, do you think Giuseppe is correct in his assessment, Santino?"

The boy's facial expression didn't change, but Dante could see the rigid tension in him. Suddenly a smile brightened Santino's face. "No, Tribune. I believe Giuseppe is wrong. He was about to beat me, and I demonstrated great restraint by letting him do so."

It was a clever response, and Dante immediately bit down on the inside of his cheek to keep from laughing outright at Santino's answer. Behind him, Cleopatra made a choked sound. Like him, she was obviously trying not to laugh. Somewhere in the deep recesses of his brain he acknowledged that he liked that she had a good sense of humor. Standing next to his brother, Giuseppe uttered a vocal disagreement. Dante sent the boy a silent admonishment before he turned his head back to Santino.

"Humor is a good thing, Santino. One can only hope you will be equally amused by your punishment," Dante said quietly. "I hope during your *Castigatio* you *both* show the same equal restraint with me."

The brothers both paled at his words, and the sound of Cleopatra's sharp breath of dismay made his mouth tighten with irritation. Did the woman actually think he'd beat Santino and Giuseppe? He intended to teach the boys a lesson, not hurt them. He'd never liked seeing the *Castigatio* used on men. While discipline meant the difference between life and death, he found the ancient punishment less than effective.

A senior officer using a staff to punish those who'd disobeyed was more likely to breed anger and rebellion, not respect. Like the Order, the *Absconditus* rarely used the punishment, as there were other discipline methods available for a seasoned fighter. Where younger members of the *Absconditus* were concerned, the *Indictio* was generally a strong enough consequence to emphasize the need for discipline in all things.

The hard labor of scrubbing a bathroom with a toothbrush, painting a wall over and over again, or some other repetitive menial task seemed to work wonders for most children. For Santino and Giuseppe, the *Indictio* hadn't worked, so he was left with little choice but to scare the daylights out of the two. The brothers were well aware that Dante's version of the *Castigatio* meant they had to fight him, and their chances of winning were nonexistent.

The two teenagers slowly got to their feet. The look on their faces indicated they dreaded what was to come. Both boys readied their swords, but with a small flick of his fingers, he envisioned their weapons tugged violently out of their hands. With another thought, he sent the swords whistling upward through the air until the blades slammed into the ceiling.

He didn't have to look at Cleopatra or the other children to sense their surprise. His attention focused on Giuseppe and Santino, he narrowed his eyes at the two brothers staring up at the swords embedded in the roof. Their fear was almost a tangible force, and he folded his arms across his chest with a sense of grim satisfaction.

"Since you think fighting is the best way to solve your problems, you shouldn't have any problem expending your anger on me." His thoughts brushed against the minds of the two boys who stood motionless in front of him. *"Begin."*

For a moment, he wasn't sure either one of them was going to obey his silent command. Suddenly, Giuseppe did a quick tuck and roll in an effort to get past Dante. Effortlessly, he sidestepped the boy and visualized his hand cracking against the boy's rear. Giuseppe yelped at the invisible blow, rubbing his backside as he got to his feet. Dante turned to face the boy. A snicker from one of the smallest children watching the match made Giuseppe glare at the offender, and Dante mentally pictured his leg sweeping Giuseppe's feet out from under him.

"Pay attention, Giuseppe. Distractions can get you killed." His thoughts were harsh inside the boy's head.

Santino's thoughts filtered their way into Dante's mind, and without turning around, he saw the boy launch himself into the air a full second before Santino actually moved. The blow the teenager had planned to land on Dante's head never materialized. Without moving, Dante visualized grabbing the boy's feet the minute Santino threw himself up into the air. A moment later the boy was hanging upside down where Dante left him for several seconds. Slowly, he walked around the boy dangling in front of him. When he released his mental grip on the teenager, Santino collapsed to the training mat with a cry of surprise.

"Praetorians can read your mind easily if you allow them. You told me what you planned to do, Santino, even though I couldn't see you."

As Santino scrambled to his feet, Giuseppe launched himself forward in an attempt to surprise Dante, who immediately threw up an invisible wall that Giuseppe crashed into. The boy grunted then reeled backward to crash down onto the mat and stare up at the ceiling with an expression of surprise that made Dante frown.

"Don't just lay there, Giuseppe. A Praetorian would have his sword deep in your chest at this point."

Behind him, he sensed Santino closing off his thoughts. The boy was a quick learner. A good trait for a Patrician. Santino rushed forward, his plan of attack almost completely obscured. But with a gentle probe of the boy's mind, he saw what the teenager had planned. Neatly, he sidestepped Santino's swiftly thrown punch intended for Dante's jaw and the foot meant for his side. It was easy to envision his hands on the boy's shoulders before he whirled Santino around to face the opposite direction and gave the boy a swift kick in the rear with an invisible boot.

"If I can read your mind, a Praetorian can, too. Don't ever forget that."

For more than fifteen minutes, he forced the boys to attack him until they were clearly exhausted. With each successive defeat, the teenagers got to their feet more slowly, and their expressions showed how demoralized they were. Yet despite their punishment, they both refused to surrender. It was a characteristic that might save them in the future, but he still wasn't sure they'd learned their lesson.

Time would tell. With an oath of irritation, he jerked his head in a quick, sharp movement. A second later, his thoughts lifted both teenagers off their feet, causing them to shout with surprise and fear. His mental ability carried the brothers across the mat to where he dumped them in front of him.

"Get up." His command was a vicious growl, and the boys scrambled to their feet to stand at attention. Dante leaned down so his face was level with theirs. "Fighting amongst ourselves makes us weak. Something the Praetorians want us to be. Neither *one* of you is ready to move up to the next *Tabulati* of the *Novem Conformavi*. If I'd been a Praetorian, both of you would have been dead in less than a minute. The next time I catch you fighting, I'll see to it that Placido administers your *Castigatio*. He won't be as forgiving as me. *Capisci?*"

White as ghosts, the boys bobbed their heads vigorously in silent acknowledgment of the warning. Whenever Dante had done something wrong as a kid, Placido had always managed to put the fear of Jupiter in him. From the looks on Giuseppe's and Santino's faces, it was clear the old Sicari Lord's name still inspired fear and awe. With a deep, low sound rumbling in his chest, Dante sent the boys a harsh stare.

"The two of you will remain here until *both* of those swords have been retrieved using nothing but your abilities." Dante straightened upright to look at the other children in room. "As for the rest of you, the show is over."

His words sent all the children racing toward the door. He saw Cleopatra quickly step out of the way of the stampede, and without another look at the brothers, he crossed the gym's floor toward her. Heat assaulted his body the minute he reached her side, and he suppressed a groan. Disciplining Giuseppe and Santino had drained his mental abilities substantially, which would make it difficult to block out the sensations Cleopatra aroused in him. To avoid touching her, he gestured for her to precede him through the doorway. Just outside the door, Pietro stood waiting for him.

"I didn't mean to get them in trouble, Tribune." There was a note of trepidation in the child's voice, and he saw Cleopatra wince. The discomfort he noticed in her expression snagged its way into his consciousness before it eased. Dante squatted so he was at eye level with the child and shook his head.

"You didn't get them in trouble, Pietro. All you did was come tell me what was happening," Dante said quietly. "You did the right thing. Someone could have gotten hurt if you hadn't come to find me."

"You don't think Giuseppe and Santino will be mad at me, do you?"

"Not after I talk to them," Dante said with a smile. He playfully rubbed the child's head. "Go on now. You're all going to be in trouble the minute Cornelia hears what happened."

The boy's eyes widened at the revelation, and then he nodded his head and raced off down the hall without having to be told twice. Dante watched him go as he straightened upright.

"You're really good with kids," Cleopatra said in a warm voice, and he turned his head to look at her in surprise. Her praise was just as unexpected as the pleasure her words gave him. "Do fights like that happen often?"

"Santino and Giuseppe are brothers. They're always fighting about something," Dante said with a slight smile as he met her curious gaze. "But they know well enough not to fight without supervision. One of the younger children could have been hurt."

As they started walking back toward the stairs, Dante's hand accidentally brushed against Cleopatra's. His throat immediately closed up at the sensations barreling through him, and his walk became rigid as they proceeded down the hallway.

"Several of the children in the room were pretty young," Cleopatra murmured. "At what age does a child start the *Novem Conformavi*?"

"Somewhere between the ages of five and six." At his statement, she came to an abrupt halt and stared at him in horror.

"You can't be serious."

"I was five when I started the *Novem Conformavi*. To complete all nine levels usually takes anywhere from twenty to twenty-five years." At his words, she gasped.

"*Five*. That's so young. Not even the Order trains anyone before the age of nine."

"The *Novem Conformavi* is more than a training program. It teaches the art of self-defense and how to use our abilities. It's a way of life. A commitment," he said in a harsh tone as he remembered his oath.

"But five?" She shook her head in dismay. "It's so young. Don't their parents object?"

"With the exception of two, all of the children in that room today were orphans."

"All of them?" she whispered as she looked up at him.

The color drained from Cleopatra's beautiful face, and a haunted expression swept across her features. The heartache in her violet eyes was intense, and it tugged at his heart. A sharp pang stabbed at his thoughts, and in the next instant, her emotions engulfed his senses in a way he'd never experienced with anyone before.

It was as if their thoughts had merged to become one. The connection he'd experienced with her before had been nothing compared to this. This was a tangible and real force barreling through him. He wasn't simply aware of her pain—he experienced it. The image of a Praetorian blade biting into her stomach, killing her unborn child, made his body burn with excruciating agony. *Christus*, how long had she been living with this anguish? He dragged her into his arms in a hopeless attempt to absorb all her pain into his body and ease her suffering. Her torment was his, and it was a raw wound that dug as deep into his soul as hers.

"The *bastardi*," he rasped softly as images from her past continued to flash through his head.

Gently stroking her hair, he held her tight as she trembled in his arms. The violence of her tremors made his heart ache for her. It was bad enough she'd lost her baby, but to lose her ability to have another child made it even more tragic and heartbreaking. Images flowed fast between them, and the image of a man walking away from her made him tighten his embrace. Someone had deserted her. His jaw hardened with anger at the thought as he waited for her shudders to end.

After several minutes, her trembling subsided, and like an outgoing tide, her emotions receded from him as well. When she retreated from his arms, it was as if his lungs had been deprived of precious air. His reaction set off an alarm in the deep recesses of his mind, but he ignored it. All he cared about at the moment was easing her suffering if he could. He framed her lovely face with his hands and stared down at her.

This wasn't the same woman he'd met in a dark alleyway who'd defeated two Praetorians single-handedly. Violet eyes wide with anguish revealed a fragile, vulnerable woman. It stirred something to life deep inside him. The fierce protective emotion swelling inside him set off more alarms that he paid no heed to. He could deal with the aftermath later. All he could think of at the moment was to do everything in his power to keep her safe from anything and anyone who might hurt her.

She pulled free of his grasp and turned her head away from him. He watched her swallow hard as she fought to collect herself. The fact that she hadn't cried troubled him. It wasn't healthy to keep so much pain and suffering locked up inside her. As she looked at him, a shuttered expression crossed her features in her attempt to hide her pain from him. It was too late for that.

"How . . . ? You know what happened."

There was a self-conscious note of resignation in her voice that made him clench his jaw. What sort of an explanation could he give her for what had just happened? He'd not probed her thoughts, but the strength of the connection between them had made him cognizant of not just her thoughts, but the physical pain of her past.

"Yes. I saw everything," he said with a nod. He swallowed hard, uncertain what else to say to her. Saying he was sorry seemed completely inadequate for what she'd lost.

"But you didn't . . . you didn't probe my thoughts," she said in obvious confusion.

"No." He shook his head, knowing he had no solid explanation for what had happened. "I think yours connected with mine."

"That's impossible," she rasped. "I don't have any Sicari abilities."

"Anything is possible, Cleopatra, and it's the only explanation I can come up with. It could be your abilities were latent until now." He didn't mention that it wasn't the first time he'd been able to see her thoughts.

She turned her face away from him, clearly struggling to make sense of what had just happened between them. He reached out to touch her shoulder, and she jerked her head around to meet his gaze.

Pain had darkened her lovely features once more, and he fought the urge to pull her back into his arms. As if suddenly realizing she was revealing more than she wanted to, her expression went blank.

"Pietro? What about his parents?" she choked out in a clear effort to turn the conversation away from her. Again he was consumed with the need to hold her until her pain was gone. The dangerous waters he'd been treading sent a wave crashing over him until he was certain he was close to drowning. In a desperate bid to maintain his self-control, he immediately closed himself off to everything except answering her question.

"I rescued Pietro from a breeding facility more than six years ago in the nursery. He was only a few hours old, and his mother and sister were dead in the room next door."

"The *bastardi*," she bit out fiercely.

Her eyes flashed with fury, but even if he hadn't seen the outrage in her expression, he could sense it—experience it. It was clear they were still closely connected in some way. Worried he might show her something terrible, he suppressed images of the last Praetorian breeding facility he'd entered. The slaughter of innocent babes simply because they were female wasn't something he wanted her to experience if their connection was still strong enough for her to see what was in his thoughts.

Cleopatra met his gaze for a moment before she turned and headed down the corridor. Dante caught up with her in two strides. His instincts said she didn't want to talk, so he simply walked alongside her in silence. Slowly, the tension in Cleopatra ebbed away.

As they wound their way silently through the hallways of the complex toward her apartments, their unhurried walk enabled both of them to regain a calm frame of mind. The connection he'd felt between them was still present, but it was little more than a whisper brushing against his senses.

That they were still connected didn't surprise him. It would explain why he'd been able to read her thoughts so easily even when he'd tried to block them out. It wasn't until they were outside her apartment that he realized he should have gone in the opposite direction five minutes ago. As they came to a halt in front of her door, he cleared his throat as uncertainty twisted its way through his body.

She seemed in complete control, but beneath the surface he sensed a stark emotion that troubled him. It made him reluctant to leave her alone, and he didn't like how awkward he felt. His desire to protect her hadn't faded. If anything, it was stronger than when he'd experienced all her pain. He cleared his throat as he tried to think of a way to exit gracefully. Fortunately, she solved the problem for him.

"Cornelia said there was a workout room where I could exercise?"

Her voice was devoid of emotion, but an image of a training room flashed in his head. He flinched at the vision of her grueling workout. She punished herself for something that wasn't her fault. Instinct guided him to reach out and cup her chin. The moment he realized what he was doing, he dropped his hand and clenched his fist at his side. She studied him in silence, waiting for his reply, and his body was suddenly on fire with an emotion he didn't understand.

"It's in the northeast part of the complex," he rasped. "The way the buildings are connected over the city blocks can make it confusing if you've not been there before. I'll have someone come show you the way."

"All right," she said with a nod. Her mouth parted slightly as if she were going to say something else, but then she just gave a slight shake of her head. "I'll see you at supper, then."

As she started to close her door, he remembered that he should tell her the evening meal was always formal. Placido had begun the tradition. The ancient Sicari Lord had said that one's appreciation for civility and the arts was the difference between a civilized culture and a barbaric one. His palm smacked against the door to keep it open, and he caught her by the elbow. It was a mistake to touch her.

The instant he did so, a shock of electricity streaked up his arm into his chest. As powerful as a lightning bolt, the sensation made him freeze. His hand still wrapped around Cleopatra's arm, he stared down at her. The startled look on her face gave way to an expression that made his blood run hot with desire. It was an emotion he knew he should suppress, but he wasn't sure how to control it.

Need blazed in her violet eyes, holding him rapt and unable to retreat as she leaned into him. Impulsively, he lowered his head slightly to breathe in the scent of her hair. Last night she'd smelled of sweet soap, but today it was a citrus-based aroma. Not that it mattered. Everything about her was delicious.

Worse, her sweet scent was making his body respond on a base level, and he was already hard inside his trousers. Mere inches separated them as she tipped her head back to look up at him. *Christus*, he had to put distance between them. Now. But something strange, unrecognizable, was quickly taking control of his body. She brushed her fingertips over his mouth. The touch ignited a new barrage of emotions inside him until a base sensation drove every clear thought from his head.

"Has any woman ever told you what a beautiful mouth you have?" she murmured in a voice soft with what sounded like a sense of wonder.

The husky tone in her voice echoed with sweet seduction as her words caressed his senses until fire streaked through his veins, warming every part of him. Stark hunger warred with his conscience as he stared down at her. He wasn't being honest with her. He already had one mistress. As her fingers traced the outline of his lips, her violet eyes studied him intently. It was almost as if she could see straight into his heart and the battle he was fighting inside.

"Cleopatra—"

"Sweet Vesta, don't you know when a woman wants you to kiss her?" she whispered.

Her hands cupped his face to gently pull his head downward. Panic and confusion surged through him as he tried to maintain his sanity, but in the next instant her mouth was against his. She tasted like cool spring water against his parched mouth. Fresh and ever so sweet.

A shudder swept through him as his hands gently grasped her waist. Somewhere off in the distance he heard the sound of a door shutting before he was caught up in the taste, scent, and feel of her. From the honeyed taste of her lips to the way her pulse fluttered beneath his hand when he caressed the smooth softness of her throat, she filled every one of his senses like a potent drug.

A soft mewl whispered out of her, and his cock jumped at the sound. By the gods, not even Jupiter himself would be able to resist her. Fear lanced through him at the thought. If the most powerful of the gods wouldn't have the strength to withstand her, how could he? It wasn't a question of how.

It was a question of *whether* he wanted to resist. Sanity seemed on the verge of returning when she gently nipped at his lower lip. He immediately drew in a sharp breath then stiffened as her tongue darted into his mouth. The heated intimacy of the kiss startled him for only an instant before his senses exploded with pleasure.

Tentatively, his tongue mated with hers in a gentle exploration of her mouth, making him hungry for more. Her tongue swirled around his as she teased and tempted him to respond until she was pulling him into a whirlpool of sensation that threatened to undo him completely.

As she pressed her body into his, she nestled herself against the hard thickness of his cock. He jerked at the sensations slamming into every one of his muscles when she rubbed her body across his erection. The emotions vibrating off her were hot and fiery. Need pulled at him, and he shuddered as images began to flow through his head.

He wasn't sure where her thoughts ended and his began, but all of them sent him reeling. Images of his mouth exploring every inch of her, his hands caressing a firm, supple thigh. Something unknown tugged at him, and he trembled with a hunger he didn't understand as her mouth left his and slid across his cheek then down the side of his neck.

Along the way, she nipped at him with her teeth, which pulled a low groan out of him. His heart thundered in his ears as his fingers found her silky skin beneath her sweater. The moment he touched her, she leaned back and quickly removed her shirt. The sight of her full breasts encased in lace made him suck in a sharp breath. A second later, the lace disappeared, and he stopped breathing altogether.

He swallowed hard and stretched out his hand to trace his fingers along the tops of her breasts before he cupped one to stare in wonder at the beautiful, lush curve of her resting in his palm. The pebbled surface of her mauve-colored areola surrounded a stiff peak, silently enticing him to touch her.

Fascinated, he brushed his thumb over her nipple. The low moan that echoed out of her throat made his cock grow so tight and hard it ached. But it was a pleasurable sensation. The pad of his thumb rubbed over her again, causing her to whimper. She arched her back so her breast thrust higher. If he bent his head, he could take her in his mouth.

Warning shouts echoed in the back of his mind, but he barely heard them as he lowered his head and kissed the top of her breast. She moaned again. The sound made him relax slightly. Even if he didn't know what he was doing, he was obviously doing something right. The thought was like a stumbling block, and he stiffened. He shouldn't be here. His internal protests went the way of the wind as the tip of her breast brushed across his lips.

"*Deus*, suck on me," she pleaded in a rough whisper.

Operating strictly on instinct, he tentatively took her into his mouth and suckled her. Soft and fragrant, her scent filled his nostrils. Somehow it made her taste even better. Savoring her sweetness, he circled her nipple with a hesitant stroke of his tongue.

The gentle sigh that passed her lips made him bolder, and he sucked a little harder on her. She encouraged him by placing his free hand on her other breast. While his fingers explored one breast, his mouth caressed the other. When his teeth accidentally abraded her stiff peak, he stiffened in fear that he'd hurt her.

Instead, she gasped sharply in a small cry of what he was certain was delight. Heat, confusion, pleasure, and insanity closed around him like Praetorians ready to destroy him. He was hovering on the brink when an intoxicating image flooded his head. He didn't know if the erotic vision was his or hers, but it was raw and visceral.

The mental image of his body pinning her to the wall, her long legs wrapped around his waist as he pounded his body into hers, flooded his head. It was like hitting a brick wall. He jerked free of her in a vicious, sharp move. The bewilderment on her face made him draw in a deep breath then release it.

Jupiter's Stone. What the fuck was he doing? The moment of panic he'd experienced seconds before became a full-blown attack as he struggled to breathe. How could he have lost control of his senses so easily? He ran a shaky hand through his hair and struggled to regain his voice. Hands on her hips, Cleopatra eyed him with confusion. Naked from the waist up, her stance epitomized the essence of her. Confident and bold. It made her all the more beautiful, and Dante's body protested viciously as he took a step backward.

"What's wrong?" she said in a quiet voice filled with puzzlement.

"Forgive me, I shouldn't have . . . I lost my head." Dante stumbled over his words as he looked away from her and took another stumbling step backward. What the hell was he supposed to say to her? That he wanted her but couldn't have her?

That he wanted her so much he was willing to break his oath?

The thought made his midsection ache as if he'd taken a kick to the stomach. In the back of his mind, he heard Placido's voice telling him he would have to make a choice where Cleopatra was concerned. Was this the choice? The second his gaze locked with hers, another wave of panic crested over him. He couldn't make a decision. Didn't *want* to choose. He wanted his cake and he wanted to eat it, too. The realization scared the hell out of him.

"*Lost your head?*" she snapped. "What the *hell* is that supposed to mean?"

"It means . . . I just meant to tell you . . . we dress formally for the evening meal," he choked out with a cough. "I . . . Forgive me. There are matters I need to attend to."

Her slack-jawed expression made his gut twist with regret and embarrassment as he whirled around and bolted from the room as fast as he could. *What in the name of Jupiter had gotten into him?* He'd put his oath to the *Absconditus* in jeopardy. He'd never done that before in his life. Actually, his oath had been in jeopardy the moment he'd carried her to the car last night.

His mistake just now was hiding the truth from her simply because he wanted her. He was a *bastardo*. He knew being with her was impossible, but it didn't stop the need she stirred inside him. It didn't stop him from wondering what it would feel like to experience firsthand the images he'd seen in his head just moments ago.

Images so erotic that he wished to Jupiter he'd never made his damned oath. Shamed by his thoughts, he released a harsh breath. He'd made his bed, and he had little choice but to lie in it without her. Once more he remembered Placido's words about a choice he would have to make. He'd made his decision a long time ago, and the only way to ensure he didn't break his oath to the *Absconditus* was to tell Cleopatra the truth. In the short time he'd known her, he'd come to realize that she valued truth, honor, and loyalty above everything else.

Her determination to rescue her friend from the Convent of the Sacred Mother showed she was willing to put her own life at risk for the sake of friendship. It was just one more reason to like her. And he liked her far more than he should. If he'd not taken his oath, they might have . . . He grunted. That was a road he had no business traveling. The problem was, a very strong part of him wanted to follow her down that path. That more than anything else made him realize how close he was to falling into an abyss that held just as much promise of heaven as it did hell.

Chapter 14

DANTE sensed Cleopatra before she even reached the archway leading into the salon. Her presence was like a tsunami headed straight for him. He wasn't looking forward to this evening at all. The way he'd left Cleopatra earlier hadn't been one of his better moments. Deliberately, he kept his gaze focused on the day's edition of *Il Messaggero*. Not that he could even focus on the newspaper article he'd been reading, but it would at least give him time to acclimate himself to being in the same room with her. Across from him, he heard Placido inhale a sharp breath.

"Jupiter's Stone," the old Sicari Lord said in a ragged voice.

Startled, Dante dropped the newspaper to look in his friend's direction, expecting to see the ancient Sicari Lord bent over in pain. Instead, the old man had gotten to his feet to stare at the living room entrance with a dazed expression on his face. Dante followed Placido's gaze, and the air left his lungs as he slowly came up out of his chair.

"Sweet mother of Juno," Dante rasped as he struggled to breathe.

Cleopatra hadn't just dressed for dinner. She'd dressed for dessert.

Her dark, wavy hair was the perfect frame for her flawless features, and it flowed downward to caress the beautiful curve of her shoulder. The strapless black dress she wore pushed up her full breasts, making them look like plump melons ripe for the picking. The thought made his head spin as he watched her sashay forward in a pair of stiletto heels that made her look—*Christus*, he didn't know what they made her look like. That wasn't true. They made her look good enough to eat, and he didn't need her kind of temptation.

Unable to help himself, he stood spellbound as she moved toward him and Placido. Her gaze met his, and his throat tightened at the flash of anger he saw in her violet eyes. He didn't blame her for being angry. He'd humiliated her. He deserved whatever punishment she inflicted on him. And he was certain she intended to extract her pound of flesh tonight. She'd taken his words to heart and dressed for dinner in such a way as to make certain he knew exactly *what* he'd passed up earlier this afternoon.

Every step she took in his direction highlighted the way the dress's pleated material fit snug against each one of her curves. He'd never seen a woman's body outlined so deliciously before in his life. Even more disturbing was how the dress ended about two inches below her bottom, where it clung to her thighs like silk against wet glass.

The black stiletto heels she wore made her bare legs look even longer than they already were. He suddenly envisioned his hand gliding over a sleek calf up to a lush thigh. Surprise swept across her face before she arched her eyebrow at him with a sardonic look that made him realize he'd unintentionally touched her with his thoughts.

Heat flushed his face as he struggled to accept the fact that he'd lost control. Sweet Juno, what was happening to him? Whenever the woman came near him, it was almost impossible to stay out of her thoughts, and now he'd touched her with his telekinetic ability. Praise Jupiter he'd not lost complete command of his faculties this afternoon when they'd kissed. Particularly when he remembered how easily her thoughts had flooded his. What he'd seen had sent him reeling. If he hadn't retreated when he had, the images he'd seen might well have come true.

Now as he watched her cross the floor in his direction, the memory of those visions sent a powerful surge of lust pounding through his veins. *Christus*, what would it be like to peel that dress off of those beautiful hips, that gorgeous body. The thought shot an icy chill through him. He needed to find a way to control this attraction he was feeling for her. If he didn't, everything he held dear would be in jeopardy. And he couldn't let that happen.

"Bellissima." Placido's voice was gruff and full of appreciation as Cleopatra stopped in front of them. "Dante, introduce me to this exquisite creature."

"Cleopatra, this is *il mio signore*, Placido Castillo," he said quietly, avoiding Cleopatra's gaze.

"Cleopatra." The ancient Sicari Lord said her name as if it were a prayer. Placido's obvious infatuation shot an unfamiliar emotion streaking through Dante as he watched his mentor take his time kissing Cleopatra's hand. "Your beauty rivals that of your namesake, *carissima*. You will sit next to me at supper."

"I would be honored." The husky sound of her voice made Placido beam at her, and Dante bit down on the inside of his cheek. The old man was acting half his age at the moment.

"*Excellent*," the ancient warrior exclaimed with delight. "I understand you're going to be staying with us for a while. We'll have to have Dante find an assignment for you."

"I don't think the Tribune knows quite *what* to do with me, *il mio signore*."

Amusement filled Cleopatra's voice, but her violet eyes still glittered with anger as she looked at him. It didn't matter whether she was referring to earlier this afternoon or his invisible touch from a moment ago. She was absolutely right. He didn't have a clue as to how to handle the woman. His collar grew tight around his neck, and he struggled not to tug at the shirt. Placido arched an eyebrow at him and grinned.

"Well, I'm not so old as to have forgotten what to do with a beautiful woman, *carissima*," Placido said with a smirk.

The sexual innuendo in the Sicari Lord's words made Dante stiffen as he glared at the old warrior. The man had always loved women, but he was far too old for Cleopatra. Amused by Placido's comment, Cleopatra laughed. It was a low, sultry sound that sent another hot surge of lust barreling through Dante.

"Perhaps the Tribune simply needs to learn how to relax," Cleopatra said in a stage whisper as she smiled haughtily in Dante's direction. "He *does* seem a bit stiff, doesn't he?"

For a fleeting instant, she glanced downward at his crotch, and his cock stirred in his trousers. As her gaze locked with his again, he clenched his jaw at the laughter dancing in her beautiful violet eyes. The woman knew she'd thrown him off balance, and she was enjoying the fact. Placido eyed him with a gleam of wicked amusement in his eyes as well.

"Don't underestimate Tribune Condellaire, *carissima*. Once you get to know him better, I think you'll find him to be quite charming."

"Not to mention meticulous, thorough, and an organizational freak." Cornelia's voice was quietly neutral, but as Dante turned toward her, there was a twinkle in her eyes. He was about to retort, but his *Praefect* shifted her attention to Cleopatra and nodded. "*Molto bene*, the dress fits you perfectly."

"I appreciate you letting me borrow it for the evening," Cleopatra said with a dazzling smile. "When the Tribune said everyone dressed formally for supper, I was at a loss as to what to wear. I only own a couple of dresses, and they aren't really formal."

Dante felt the wind go out of his sails. So she hadn't deliberately dressed like this to remind him what he'd lost this afternoon. His gaze shifted back to Cornelia, who was wearing a sedate-looking black dress. It was a flattering look, but it had none of the sex appeal of Cleopatra's dress. Disappointment struck hard at the core of him. *Fotte*, he'd been insane to think she might have dressed to entice him. Punish him.

"Why haven't we seen you wearing it before, Cornelia?" he asked.

Regret blistered through him as he heard Placido hide a snort of laughter behind a cough. The sound said the Sicari Lord had heard the annoyance in his voice and knew precisely why he was irritated. The old man was becoming a thorn in his side. Cornelia eyed him carefully, her expression closed off.

"I bought it on a whim. It's fortunate that Signorina Vorenus and I are the same size." Cornelia looked at Cleopatra with a genuine smile of satisfaction. It had been a long time since he'd seen his *Praefect* smile, and he could only assume it was because Cleopatra had brought them information that would help free Beatrice.

He watched with fascination as Cleopatra shook her head, her hair brushing across her bare shoulders. It was the first time he'd seen her hair free of the braid she'd worn since last night, and his fingers itched to slide through the silky darkness. She smiled at Cornelia.

"Please, call me Cleo. I've never been one to stand on formalities." She looked down at her dress and ran one hand over her hip in a way that made him draw in a quick breath. A second later she offered Cornelia an impish grin. "Besides, good friends always borrow each other's clothes."

Cornelia laughed quietly, and it surprised him. Cleopatra had charmed his *Praefect*, and even Placido was enchanted with her. The sound of excited voices floated in their direction, and he looked past Cleopatra toward the small group of fighters entering the room.

The minute he heard the long, low whistle, he knew it was for Cleopatra, and a fierce territorial emotion slashed through him. She immediately turned her head and laughed. Even though she'd accepted the wolf whistle as a compliment, he directed a hard stare of displeasure at the newcomers. One of the younger fighters went crimson under Dante's look, while a couple of his companions chuckled and nudged him in the side.

Before Dante could say anything, Cornelia took Cleopatra by the arm and guided her over to the small crowd. As his *Praefect* introduced her to the fighters, he noted how the men jostled one another to get close to her. Placido leaned toward him with a confiding air.

"The woman is enough to arouse even this old man." Mischief filled the Sicari Lord's voice, and Dante flashed him a glare.

"Is she?" He was pleased with his reserved, detached response.

"Lie to yourself, Tribune, but don't lie to me," Placido said with a snort of laughter. "I might be old, but my eyesight is still good. You can't keep your eyes off the woman."

"I'm more than capable of appreciating a beautiful woman without lusting after her," he growled as he watched Cleopatra flirting

with two of his best fighters. "Cleopatra is simply a test of my dedication."

"Bah," Placido snorted with disgust. "If you expect me to believe
that, then you really think me a fool."

"You're not a fool," he said with quiet sincerity. "But you are a
meddlesome old man."

"No," the Sicari Lord said in an affectionate tone as he grasped
Dante's shoulder with his bony fingers. "I'm someone who cares
about you and your future."

He glanced in Placido's direction to see a fatherly expression on
the Sicari Lord's face. With a brusque nod, he silently acknowledged
the old man's words. The ancient warrior squeezed his shoulder
before he sent Dante a cheeky grin.

"Now then, I think I should go rescue our young lady from the
attentions of all these hot-blooded males. Unless you care to do the
honors?"

He shook his head despite his desire to do just as Placido suggested.
With a shrug, the old man walked away. As he watched his friend reach
the small crowd of Sicari males surrounding Cleopatra, Dante struggled with the violent need to drag her out of the room and away from
them. A low groan rumbled in his chest. *Deus*, he was in deep waters.

The realization continued to plague him throughout the evening
meal as he watched Cleopatra flirting with Placido and another of
his fighters. Disgusted by his inability to ignore the way the Sicari
Lord and Tony were making fools of themselves over her, Dante's
mood deteriorated throughout the meal.

When several people rose from the table, he almost sighed with
relief. He couldn't remember the last time he'd ever been so grateful
for a meal to be finished. Rising from his chair, he overheard Tony
offering to show Cleopatra the garden. Before he realized what he
was doing, he moved to stand at the fighter's side.

"Don't you have a mission tonight, Tony? If Cleopatra wants to
see the garden, then I'm sure *il mio signore* Placido would be happy
to serve as her escort," he said quietly as he nodded toward the
ancient Sicari Lord.

The fighter started to protest, and Dante stared him down. Tony sent him an odd look before he shrugged and turned back to Cleopatra. Capturing her hand, Tony kissed her fingers as he bid her good night. Dante watched in silence and fought the sudden urge to pound the other man into the ground. Placido rose slowly to his feet and winked at Cleopatra.

"Would you like to see the garden under the few stars the city lights allow, *carissima*?"

"In your company, *il mio signore*, I would find it most enjoyable."

"Careful, you mustn't get my hopes up, *bella*. I'm not a young man anymore." Placido shook his finger at her. "In all honesty, I'm feeling a bit tired, so I'll have Dante escort you for a stroll in the night air."

Dante stiffened at Placido's words and glared at his friend. What in Juno's name was the man thinking? Being alone with Cleopatra had proven challenging enough over the last twenty-four hours, but in the dark? *Christus*, Placido was testing him again. But was it a test of his commitment to the *Absconditus* or was it something else his old friend was trying to teach him? Either way, it didn't matter. Being alone with Cleopatra wasn't a good idea at all.

"Perhaps Cleopatra might like to wait until another time—"

"Nonsense, my boy," Placido scoffed. "The night air is warm enough for a pleasant stroll, and you can always talk business. Although I'll think you mad if you do."

"I'm perfectly capable of walking in the garden by myself," Cleopatra said with a laugh. "There's no need for Dante to join me."

There was just a hint of bitterness in her voice, but there was a challenge there as well. She was essentially saying he was afraid to be alone with her. She was right, but he was damn well not going to admit it to her or anyone else.

"There may be no need, but *il mio signore*'s orders are never questioned," Dante replied.

The sharp note in his voice was reserved for Placido, but he saw the way Cleopatra stiffened before she sent him a cold look. The old Sicari Lord shook his head with disapproval as he reached out to carry Cleopatra's hand to his mouth.

"Forgive him, *carissima*. It's past his bedtime, which explains why he's so cranky."

"Why doesn't *that* surprise me?"

Although she answered Placido with a laugh, the sarcastic note threading its way through her response didn't escape him. Tension locked his jaw as he realized he'd managed to insult Cleopatra while letting Placido know he didn't like being pushed into a corner. He glared at the old man before he gestured for Cleopatra to precede him out of the dining room.

He would have offered her an arm, but the thought of her being so close wasn't something he was ready for. Not to mention he was certain she'd refuse. As they moved through the hallway to one of the doorways leading into the garden, he tried to comprehend what he was doing.

Why in Jupiter's name hadn't he just let Tony show her the garden? He didn't like the answer. He'd wanted to keep Tony from being alone with her. *Fotte*, he would have done the same thing even if her escort had been Placido. As they moved out into the night air, he was at a loss for what to say.

It didn't help matters that she seemed quite content with the awkward silence stretching between them. At least it was awkward to him. She appeared to be completely indifferent to his company. It was a change from this afternoon when he'd come close to losing control of his sanity. With the grace of a well-trained fighter, she moved toward the small stone temple situated in one corner of the garden.

The secluded spot made his gut tighten as he followed her. He stood at the entrance to the gazebolike structure. Two stone benches faced each other, while a small altar was opposite the temple entrance. Unable to help himself, he watched with fascination as she crossed the marble floor to one of the benches.

With her back to him, she braced a hand against the arm of the bench then bent over to remove first one shoe and then another. The movement exposed the edges of a softly curved bottom, and his cock was hard in seconds. Still ignoring him, she sat down, her fingers wrapped around the edges of the bench's seat as she looked up at the ocular opening in the temple's ceiling. Moonlight danced across her face, and he couldn't remember the last time he'd seen anything more beautiful.

"I like Placido," she said with a smile. "He must have been a real charmer in his prime."

"In his prime? If he heard you say that, he'd be insulted," Dante said with an overwhelming sense of relief. Praise Juno. She wasn't going to mention this afternoon.

"Tony's just as charming." She looked at him with an expression that immediately made him uncomfortable. "Is that why you kept him from showing me the garden? Protecting my virtue like you did earlier today?"

There was a sharp edge to her voice that illustrated once again her humiliation at the way he'd rejected her. *Christus.* He should have known better. She had no intention of letting him off the hook about this afternoon. Not that he deserved to be let off so easily. Dante cleared his throat as he desperately tried to come up with an explanation for his behavior. He didn't have one. Just the truth. Something a part of him wanted to ignore.

"He had a job to do. I simply reminded him of the fact." Dante knew he was skirting the truth, but he wasn't about to admit that something else had made him interfere. He'd moved deeper into the temple before he realized that might be a mistake.

"I see." Her obvious skepticism made him grimace.

"He's taking one of the older students out for his first execution." He saw her go rigid for a moment before she nodded.

"The first time is always the hardest."

Her barely audible statement made Dante frown. He'd done some checking on Cleopatra's recent missions, and over the past three years there had been a pattern to her assignments. Almost every one of the criminals she'd executed had hurt or killed children.

She had been involved in just enough executions for other crimes to make it appear a coincidence, but something told him the events weren't happenstance at all. Even Angotti had indirectly been responsible for the deaths of five children when he'd ordered Luigi Romano to burn one of his apartment buildings to the ground.

"I remember my first execution," he said quietly. "It was a young man who'd murdered an entire family in their beds as part of a mob initiation."

"You sound as if you regret carrying out his judgment." There was a hard note in her voice that troubled him.

"No. His sentence was a just one. I simply wonder what he might have done with his life if he'd chosen a different path." He met her gaze steadily until she averted her eyes. "And you?"

In the moonlight, she paled slightly, and her throat moved as she swallowed hard. She suddenly seemed fragile and vulnerable again— far removed from the confident, self-assured woman he believed her to be. The urge to pick her up and hold her as she fought with unseen demons made him stiffen.

"Yes, I remember," she whispered. "He was a forty-three-year-old man who'd raped a three-year-old boy. I remember how hard it was to perform the *Rogare Donavi* with the *bastardo*. I didn't want to ask his forgiveness. I wanted to carve him up into little pieces while he was still alive."

Fury and rage pulsated off of her, and he remained silent. For some Sicari, the first execution of judgment was a burden that never fully disappeared. It was always there under the surface. The event was life changing, and the impact it had made on Cleopatra was evident. But the loss of her baby and the end result could only have magnified her anger for those who harmed children.

Although there was no reason to believe she'd broken the Sicari Code when executing her targets, anyone holding a grudge against her could make trouble for her if she continued to manipulate her assignments. He frowned as he considered how to answer her.

"Your feelings are justifiable, Cleopatra. I don't know many Sicari who wouldn't have felt the same way you did." His words seemed to have little effect, as she nodded sharply then looked up at the moon through the gazebo's open ceiling.

"It's a beautiful night. A bit warmer than usual for this time of year." The abrupt change in topic said she'd closed herself off to further retrospection.

"You're not cold, then?" His gaze swept over her bare shoulders.

"Not at all," she said as she looked up at him with a wry amusement that hinted she'd either forgiven him or was on the verge of doing so. "I suppose you'd have gallantly offered me your jacket if I was."

"Yes."

"You're a challenge, Dante Condellaire." The vulnerable woman he'd seen seconds ago was gone, but the change was no less potent. She leaned back against the bench and folded her arms, which pushed her breasts up higher. His mouth went dry as he remembered touching and suckling her. He forced himself to meet her amused gaze.

"Am I?" He wanted to groan at the cryptic reply. It was almost a blatant invitation for her to probe deeper.

"Oh, most definitely," she said in a voice that had suddenly become a soft, sultry caress. Her confidence was alarming. "And I do love a challenge."

"Then I think you're about to be disappointed, as I'm anything but."

"Really?" She arched her eyebrow at him in the moonlight. "Then explain to me why you keep dancing around the elephant in the room?"

The question made his muscles go taut with tension. *Fotte*. That direct, to-the-point mannerism of hers had a way of making him squirm under the microscope—not a pleasant feeling. Irritated by the amused expression on her face, he glared at her. He was a Tribune, heir to the Sicari Lord title. He'd faced down more Praetorians than he could count, and he'd be damned if he was going to let this woman intimidate him. He shrugged with an indifference he didn't feel.

"Are you referring to what happened in your room?" He breathed easier at the disconcerted look on her face. Good. He'd thrown her off balance. She hesitated, but from her scowl of irritation, he was far from out of the woods in terms of explaining himself.

"Yes, I'm referring to what happened," she said fiercely. What he'd thought was forgiveness might have simply been the eye of the storm. "One minute it was . . . it was incredible, and the next minute you were running for cover."

He didn't know how to answer her. What he'd experienced had

been a hell of a lot more than incredible. It had been mind-blowing and scary as hell. She'd been hot and sweet on his tongue, and even now he could still breathe in the soft freshness of her skin.

And sweet mother of Juno, the memory of suckling her was enough to make his cock stir in his trousers. The direct look she sent him didn't surprise him. But he tensed at the determination in her gaze. Somehow he was certain he wasn't going to like what was coming.

"Did you read my mind earlier? Just when things were getting hot?"

How in Jupiter's name was he supposed to answer that? He flinched. The connection he'd had with her from the moment they'd met was something he had no way of explaining. As for earlier today, he wasn't sure if he'd read her mind or if the images he'd seen were his. It didn't matter; she'd obviously been thinking about it at the same time he was. He flinched as he considered telling her the truth. Why was it so hard for him to tell her? The immediate answer that came to him wasn't the one he wanted to admit to.

"You know it's forbidden for a Sicari to read the minds of other Sicari without permission."

"Forbidden. Right," she mused as she studied him with a look of puzzlement. "What I don't get is just when we were about to have some incredible sex, you ran for cover."

He coughed at her blunt honesty. That hadn't been just direct—that had been a blow to the gut. His throat tightened, making it difficult to get air into his lungs. There was a hint of triumph in the way she leaned forward and wrapped her fingers around the edge of the bench once more. Jupiter help the Praetorian who came up against her in a fight. The woman was relentless.

"You're mistaken." Jaw tight with tension, he stared at her for a long moment before he turned his back on her and moved toward the altar, putting several feet between them. "I was not running for—"

"You know, I really hate it when people lie to me, and you're lying to me right now," she bit out in a fierce voice behind him. "If I made you uncomfortable because I made the first move instead of waiting for you to do it, fine. Just say so. Don't lie about it."

"No," he growled as he whirled around to face her. "I . . ."

His voice died in his throat as she left the bench and closed the distance between them until mere inches separated them. The air left his lungs as the scent of her soft, exotic perfume filled his nostrils. Sweet mother of Juno. The woman was temptation personified. Desperately, he struggled to hang on to his presence of mind.

"You're trembling," she whispered, a puzzled frown furrowing her lovely brow.

Unable to speak, he didn't move as she ran her fingertips along his cheek. He knew he should be grabbing her hand and pushing her away, but he was powerless to move. The minute she went up on her tiptoes and kissed him softly, he knew he'd lost his resolve. Another shudder wracked his frame at the sweetness of her touch.

It was like a warm breeze off the ocean, and his mind reeled at the desire rising inside him like a tidal wave that he couldn't control or run from. With a groan, his hands gripped her waist and tugged her against him. As his mouth captured hers, he heard her gasp with surprise before she wrapped her arms around his neck.

The warmth of her forced its way through his clothes until he was hot with need. It was as if someone had dropped him into the desert and she was the only water for miles around. Tentatively, his tongue probed against her lips, and she opened her mouth to give him access to its sweet fire. A second later, her tongue was dancing with his.

Somewhere in the back of his mind a battle raged between the dark and light of his soul as he pulled Cleopatra snug into his body. It was as if the gods had made her just for him. She retreated slightly from him, her mouth blazing a trail of searing pleasure down the side of his neck. Her arms were no longer around his neck, and he heard a soft rustle just before her hand guided his toward her bare bottom.

He drew in a sharp breath and shuddered as his fingers stroked the soft curve of pure flesh. His senses reeled. Was she naked underneath her dress? He slid a hand upward to her waist but found not even a wisp of silk or satin. *Fotte*. She wasn't wearing a thing. A second later, he heard the soft sound of a zipper just before her mouth was sliding over his again.

Christus, she tasted good enough to eat. Even sweeter than the chocolate cake served at supper. His hands slid downward along the soft curve of her bottom as her tongue swirled around his. The image of his mouth exploring every inch of her made him groan as she pressed her body closer to his until they were as one.

In the next breath, he went rigid with shock as her fingers slipped into his trousers and found his cock. Stunned by the intense pleasure her touch gave him, he didn't move as his brain tried to comprehend the sensations pounding their way through his body. *Deus*, he loved what she was doing to him.

He growled quietly and thrust his hips forward as her thumb circled around the tip of him then rubbed over the sensitive spot just below the mushroom cap of his erection. Her mouth grazed his cheek as her lips tugged at his ear.

"I want you, Dante," she whispered.

Numbed and reeling from her caresses, Dante heard the words but didn't comprehend them at first. His body was a slave to her every touch. She caught his other hand in hers then guided his fingers to her hot center. Alarm bells went off in his head as his fingers acted of their own accord and slipped between her wet folds.

The sweet cry she uttered at what he was certain was an awkward caress sent a shock wave through him. She liked what he was doing. The thought made him even hotter than he already was. A moment later, her hand tightened around him and stroked his cock harder. He jerked against her touch. *Fotte*, if she kept this up, he was going to make love to her right here and now.

He froze as an icy cold engulfed him. The sensation was no different than if he'd stepped out into the Arctic air without wearing any clothes. Jupiter's Stone, what was he doing? How in the name of the gods had he forgotten his oath so easily? Shame blasted its way through him. He quickly retreated from her, his body protesting viciously as he put several feet between them. The look of surprise and humiliation on her face made him flinch. He turned away from her, and with a grimace, he awkwardly adjusted his erection in his trousers and tugged clumsily at his zipper.

He'd rejected her again, and there was no excuse for it. He could have pushed her away the moment her mouth had brushed lightly across his, but he hadn't. This time it had been him escalating their kiss. He was a *bastardo*, and the fact that he was the cause of her dismay lashed at his conscience with a relentless fury. What was he supposed to say to her?

The truth.

"Do you mind telling me what the hell just happened?" she said with a restrained fury that didn't surprise him. He swallowed hard as he faced her. She'd already straightened her dress, and the disappointment it stirred in him made him wince.

"I made a mistake—"

"You bet your ass you did. This is the second time now that you've run hot and cold on me, and I want to know why. If this is about me always making the first move then say so, goddamnit," she said in a fierce tone as she closed the distance between them in a flash and jabbed at his chest. "You're attracted to me, and *don't* say you're not, because you were *so* into that amazing foreplay just now. So what's the problem? Are you worried about me being the boss's daughter?"

"Your relationship to Marcus has nothing to do with us," he snapped with a shake of his head.

"Then what's the problem? Is it something I said? Did?" She glared at him in frustration before her expression became a cold mask of marble. "Oh, I get it. It's not something I did—it's what I am."

She shot him an icy look of contempt then stalked over to the bench and retrieved her shoes. The abrupt change in her demeanor left him staring at her back in stunned silence. Despite his confusion, he couldn't help but notice the way her dress bared the edge of her bottom once more as she bent over to pick up her shoes. His hands immediately tingled at the memory of caressing her bare skin. In a split second, he was hard again and was forced to suppress a groan.

Fotte, the woman was twisting him into knots. Still confused at the way his body continuously betrayed him where she was concerned, he struggled to grasp the full meaning behind her comment. Not about to let her leave without an explanation, he almost reached out with his hand to hold her back, then thought better of it. Instead, he mentally grasped her arm and spun her around.

"What you *are*? What the hell are you talking about?"

"You're attracted to me, but you hate yourself for wanting to fuck me," she said in a bitter tone. "You just can't stomach the thought of sleeping with a freak. Fine by me. Now let me go."

Beneath the bitterness in her voice was the stark sound of humiliation and a deeper pain. It surprised him that the connection he'd felt with her had hidden this particular emotion from him. As her emotions mingled with his, he realized this pain was something that ran deep beneath the layers of everything else that had shaped her life in recent years. It was a dull ache that he'd only just now experienced.

The idea of her hurting filled him with an urge to pull her close and ease the suffering he sensed in her. He didn't have a clue as to what she was talking about, but rejecting her was one of the hardest things he'd ever done in his entire life. Even now he wanted to drag her off to his bedroom and spend the night kissing every inch of her. Exploring every delicate curve of her body while she taught him exactly how he could please her.

"I don't know where you got that idea, but I don't think you're a freak."

"Sure you do. You're like a lot of the Sicari men I know. The minute they find out I don't have any abilities, they run away as fast as they can. I'm not really Sicari. I'm one of nature's mistakes. And you know what's really funny? My real father is a fucking Sicari Lord. How's that for irony?

The pain in her voice was poignant. It was an emotion he understood well. His mother had given him up to the *Absconditus*, and it was always there in the back of his mind. Without thinking clearly, he used his ability to drag her into his arms. It probably wasn't the smartest thing to do, but all he cared about at the moment was making her realize she wasn't the problem.

He was.

She struggled fiercely, but he easily overpowered her. The logical side of his brain assumed command and effectively shut down most of his sensory receptors, but he knew it was only temporary. He needed to make her understand as quickly as possible, but she was obviously not in the mood to listen.

"Let me go, you son of a bitch."

"Stop struggling, Cleopatra, and listen to me."

"I don't want to hear you ease your conscience."

"Jupiter's Stone, woman, shut up and listen to me," he said harshly. She froze in his arms as he glared down at her. "I don't give a damn whether you have Sicari abilities or not."

"Right," she sneered. "I've had too many men walk away from me for just that reason. So you'll forgive me if I don't believe you."

"Believe what you will, but I know for a fact that every man who's ever walked away from you was a fool," Dante said quietly. Surprise flashed across her face as he swallowed hard. "Who or what you are has nothing to do with me pushing you away. I'm the problem. *Not* you. When I was fifteen, I swore allegiance to the *Absconditus*."

"I'm listening," she said. Her tone said he had a short time frame to convince her.

"I took an oath to dedicate my life to the *Absconditus*."

She didn't say anything. She just looked at him with an expression of exasperated puzzlement. He frowned, realizing it would be difficult making her understand what he was trying to say. Already he was feeling like that fifteen-year-old boy he'd been the day Placido had sent him into that bedroom for what he'd thought was another test.

"You mean like one of the Carpenter's priests?" she asked softly, her eyes narrowing at him.

"Yes." He drew in a deep breath then released it slowly.

"As in a *celibate* priest?" Her voice was just a little bit louder.

"Yes."

"You've got to be fucking kidding me," she exclaimed. "You're a *virgin*?"

He winced at the way the word rolled off her lips. Guilt slashed at him as she broke free of his hold for a second time. Embarrassment, shock, and dismay darkened her face as she took two steps back from him.

"I should have—" He didn't get a chance to finish.

"And all this time you allowed me—and you *kissed me. Touched me.* Hell, you almost made love to me. And this whole time you didn't say a goddamn word to me? Not *one fucking word*!"

"I should never have let it get as far as it did." He bit down on the inside of his cheek at the humiliation and anger he heard in her voice.

"You think?" she said tightly. "What kind of a man are you? Was it some sort of game? To test yourself?"

"*No*." He shook his head. "It wasn't like that. You're a beautiful woman. I couldn't—"

"Don't say another fucking word. I've heard more than enough. Just do me a favor. Stay the hell away from me. *Period*." With a final glare of contempt in his direction, she whirled around and stalked away from him and out of the gazebo. In seconds she disappeared from view. This time he didn't try to stop her.

"*Fotte*."

His fist slammed into the side of a gazebo column. He should have just told her the truth the first time she'd kissed him. And tonight— tonight had been one of the worst mistakes he'd ever made. Guilt and shame hit him hard. He should have just let Tony show her the damn garden. Why in the name of Tartarus had he been so hell-bent on preventing the fighter from being alone with her?

The answer wasn't one he liked. Admitting he was physically attracted to Cleopatra was one thing. But the possessive feeling he'd experienced when Tony was flirting with her was a new sensation and something altogether different. What he liked even less was his loss of control where she was concerned. The minute she came anywhere near him, his entire body reacted as if he was on fire.

He understood the physical nature of the attraction, but there was something stronger, more compelling, beneath his fascination for her that troubled him deeply. Cornelia's observation from last night reared its ugly head. His friend had been right; he did want to stake a claim where Cleopatra was concerned, and he had no right to do so.

Christus, in twenty-four hours he'd gone from being a rational man to one ready to break every tenet he believed in, threatening everything he'd trained for over the past fifteen years. Marcus was ready to retire. Atia's arrival in Rome weeks ago had accelerated the Sicari Lord's restless manner. Dante had known his time to lead the *Absconditus* was drawing near the minute Marcus had followed Atia back to the White Cloud estate.

The Sicari Lord's actions made it clear he was determined to get his wife back. That meant Dante's life was about to change drastically. Up until now, all his decisions within the guild had been of the administrative type. Now they'd be decisions of life and death both within the *Absconditus* as well as the Sicari Order.

For centuries, the *Absconditus* had been a hidden guild within the Order. Over the years the number of children born with both telekinetic and telepathic abilities had declined drastically. Some of it was simple genetics, but the Praetorians had been a major factor as well with their ruthless persecution of the Sicari.

The Order, determined to protect their kind, had created the *Absconditus* to preserve the strongest of their race from extinction. The *Prima Consul* and a few trusted members of the Order were the only ones privy to the existence of the *Absconditus*. While the Order and the *Absconditus* were separate from each other, as the reigning Sicari Lord, his decisions would overrule the *Prima Consul* in matters that concerned both entities.

He might have been young when he'd taken his oath, but he'd known even then that with the exception of the Sicari Lords still alive he was the strongest of all in the *Absconditus*. It had been not just his duty, but his desire, to protect his family. The family that had always been there and not deserted him. That had been the reason he'd taken his vow.

Placido had struck a nerve by accusing him of always putting the interests of others first. It wasn't far from the truth when he'd made his decision all those years ago. His affection for Placido and Marcus *had* played a large part in his decision to focus all his resources on the guild. He couldn't deny that. They'd raised him. They'd been his father *and* his mother.

But growing up he'd overheard and seen things that told him how much Marcus had sacrificed for the sake of the *Absconditus*. Even Placido had paid a price. Both men had loved and lost. It was something Dante had no intention of experiencing firsthand, even if Cleopatra did tie him into knots.

What he'd told Placido was true. It was a temporary state of affairs. His confession tonight had ensured that. When they'd completed the rescue at the convent, Cleopatra would go back to Chicago, and when Marcus retired, Dante would be in charge of the *Absconditus*. Everything was falling into place as planned, except for one thing. He'd never expected to find himself longing for a woman he couldn't have.

Chapter 15

"THAT'S fabulous news. When? How is she? Are they still in Genova?" Cleo rattled off her questions in rapid succession into her cell phone as Ares's voice echoed in her ear.

"*Christus,* one at a time, Cleo." Ares chuckled. "Phae came out of the coma day before yesterday. We almost lost her until Lysander blood bonded with her. She's tired, but is doing great."

"He blood bonded with her?" Cleo gasped in amazement. She closed her eyes and offered up a brief prayer to Juno for the good news. Her two friends had finally gotten their act together. "So where are they now?"

"They left for the States this morning. Lysander and the doctors wanted her to stay another week, but she insisted on going home. She said she can rest at home just as easily as she can in the hospital."

"Have they said anything about an official ceremony or celebration?"

"Lysander mentioned doing something in another month or so when Phae's fully recovered. In the meantime, the two of them are going to honeymoon at the White Cloud estate." Static in the cell phone made Ares's voice crackle slightly, and she couldn't hear what he was saying. She turned slightly to keep the connection clear.

"What?"

"I asked why are you still in Rome? When I talked to Atia yesterday, it was obvious she wasn't happy about it." The sudden shift of direction in their conversation made her tense.

"I know she's not, but I'm not ready to go back to Chicago or White Cloud," she said quietly, unwilling to reveal *any* of her reasons for staying in Rome.

"So where the hell are you?" Ares asked pointedly. "I checked the Rome guild, and they said you hadn't reported in."

She turned her head at the sound of footsteps and saw Dante enter the library. Her senses were immediately humming with electricity. Damnit, what the fuck was wrong with her? The man had dedicated himself to the *Absconditus*. He was untouchable. Irritated by her physical response to the man, she turned sharply away from him to finish up her conversation with Ares.

"I'm in a safe place, okay? Marcus knows where I am, so you don't need to worry about me," she said in the best reassuring voice she could muster. "I need to go. Tell Lysander and Phae I can't wait to see them."

"Damnit, Cleo, I know you're up to something. You didn't stay behind just—"

"Look, there's someone here. I'll talk to you later."

Heedless of her friend's curse-filled protest, she pressed the END button on her cell phone. Ares would probably read her the riot act for that the next time they saw each other. The man hated it when she hung up on him. The sound of Bonnie Tyler's "Holding Out for a Hero" echoed from her phone, and she glanced downward. Ares. She pressed the IGNORE button and turned the phone off before shoving it back into her pants pocket.

Stiffening her shoulders, she turned to face Dante. Awkward. That was the only way she could have described it if someone had asked. Damned awkward. She wanted to believe he was as uncomfortable as she felt, but he looked completely at ease. It was irritating. It was even more irritating that she was feeling self-conscious.

She rarely cared what others thought of her, and certainly not what this man thought. A snort of laughter echoed in the back of her head. She ignored it. It had been this way for three weeks now. Ever since that night in the garden, the two of them had been dancing around each other as if they were sparring partners. They'd done everything they could to avoid each other.

Actually, she was pretty sure she was the one doing all the avoiding. A couple of times, Dante had tried to talk to her, but she'd dodged him completely except when others were present. It wasn't like he was the first Sicari male to reject her. But his *reason* was definitely a first. She'd been pissed as hell when she'd left the garden after he told her the truth about his oath. Partly because she'd never been that sexually frustrated before, and partly because the man hadn't bothered to tell her up front that he'd committed his body, mind, and soul to the *Absconditus*.

It didn't help that she had to take some of the blame herself. She'd been hell-bent on seducing the guy and hadn't really given him a chance to say much of anything.

And if she were really honest with herself, the real reason she'd been avoiding him like the plague was because she was embarrassed. Dante was different from the other Sicari males who'd passed her over. She didn't know how, but he'd touched something deep inside her. It made his rejection hurt worse than she cared to admit. If possible, it made her feel even more inadequate than ever before.

She'd made it a rule to stay away from Sicari men after Michael, and Dante was as Sicari as they came. So for the life of her, she couldn't figure out why she'd made a play for him. It wasn't like she didn't know better. She bit the inside of her cheek. It didn't help matters that his dedication was a complete waste in her opinion.

The man was beautiful. What in Jupiter's name had convinced him that he couldn't lead his guild *and* have a healthy, loving relationship at the same time? She sucked in a sharp breath. Loving relationship? Had she lost her mind? Even if his oath wasn't an obstacle, a relationship was the last thing she wanted.

It indicated permanency. Something she knew was out of her grasp. Despite that knowledge, her heartbeat still reverberated in her ears like a freight train as he crossed the floor toward her. Fight or flight? The instinct of survival at work.

Only problem was, she couldn't dart off so easily this time. The entire rescue team was due in the library in a short while for last-minute instructions regarding tonight's raid on the convent. She'd just happened to show up early. Then there was the possibility that her subconscious had arranged for her to get here before everyone else.

Was it possible she'd secretly hoped to find a moment alone with him? She swallowed the ball of fear wedged in her throat. It didn't matter whether her subconscious had finagled her early arrival or not. Flight was no longer an option. She didn't have much choice but to stick it out until someone else showed up.

Leaving the room right now would make her look like a coward. Something she wasn't, even if she'd been acting like one for the past few weeks. She tensed as he stopped a couple of feet away from her, and despite the reasonable distance between them, a heat wave of sensation rolled over her skin. Her stomach lurched as she realized his ability to set her on edge hadn't weakened.

It wasn't just a physical attraction. And there was plenty of that on her part. Her body was an explosion of awareness whenever she got near him. If anything, his presence was stronger than before, and something else had slipped into her heart as well. She sneered inwardly at the fanciful thought.

They barely knew each other. How was it possible to have any feelings other than lust for a man she didn't know very well? And yet she did know him. Watching him with Pietro the day of Giuseppe and Santino's fight had only emphasized the little things she'd been picking up on since he'd carried her out of that dark alley.

He was compassionate, kind, and loyal. Sure, he was a little uptight, but that could be from dealing with her none-too-subtle come-ons. He had a caring nature and reminded her a lot of Ares and Lysander. In the back of her mind, the resemblance she'd drawn between Dante and Lysander stirred to life before her thoughts returned to Dante's qualities. It was that caring nature of his that made her realize she had feelings for him she shouldn't have. Feelings she didn't want to examine because their only possible outcome was heartbreak.

"Can we talk, or are you going to run away again?" That dark, sexy voice of his was like a warm, lazy finger trailing its way down her back. She flinched before she stiffened her shoulders.

"Run away? I don't know what you're talking about," she lied. He arched his eyebrows at her, and she gritted her teeth. She didn't like it that he could see right through her.

"I want to explain the night in the garden," he said quietly.

"What's there to explain?" She shrugged in an open display of sarcasm. "You took a vow of celibacy and didn't bother to tell me until *after* I made a fool of myself trying to seduce you."

There. She'd said it. It was out in the open now. She thought saying it would make her feel better, but it didn't. In fact, the disappointment winding its way through her body was alarming. She dealt it a crushing blow. He was off-limits.

"You are *not* a fool," he said with a quiet intensity that surprised her. "But I was a fool for not telling you the truth right away."

"And why didn't you?" she bit out fiercely. "Why let me think you were interested in me if you knew you couldn't . . . that there would never be anything between us?"

"Because I wanted you." A tortured look flashed across his face as she stared at him in disbelief. "I've wanted you from those first few moments I found you in that alley the night you assassinated Angotti."

"And this is supposed to make me feel better how?" she snapped. She ignored the heat skimming through her that made her nipples hard and tingly.

"Damnit, Cleopatra. This isn't easy for me." He shoved a hand through his hair. "I took an oath. It's not something I can just toss aside."

"Fine, you can't break your vow of celibacy." Hands resting on her hips, she tilted her head in an open display of irritated disgust. "But just because you're attracted to me doesn't mean you had to keep me in the dark. You should have just told me the truth. I would have understood."

"It's not that simple."

"*Yes*, it *is*." She puffed out a breath of exasperation. "I respect the decision you made, and I just don't see the problem."

"It's a problem because every time I get near you, I *want* to break my oath," he said in a raw whisper that scraped across her senses like fire, and she saw a flash of torment in his dark blue eyes. "Not once in all these years have I ever regretted dedicating myself to the *Absconditus*. That is, not until I met you."

Stunned, she didn't have the slightest idea how to react to his confession. In a strange way, he'd just paid her the highest compliment a man could ever pay a woman. He found her desirable enough to consider betraying something he believed in deeply. She'd obviously not made it easy for him. In fact, after that mind-blowing moment in her apartment and then that incredible encounter in the garden, she'd have to say he'd reacted like any normal, hot-blooded male would.

It didn't matter that he'd given off enough signs that he wasn't experienced with women. She should have known something was off when he was so tentative in his kisses and even his caresses. But she refused to take all the blame for the situation, and she sure as hell didn't like the idea that he might be thinking of her as forbidden fruit.

"Are you blaming me for being a temptation you're having trouble resisting?" she asked in a frigid tone. "Because if you are, I'm not buying it."

"*No*, that's *not* what I'm saying," he growled as he turned away to cross the floor and stare out the window. "*Christus*, I don't know *what* the hell I'm saying."

Hands clasped behind his back, he stared out at the inner courtyard. The reddish orange light of the setting sun streamed through the window to throw his tall figure into shadowy relief. As she studied his solitary stance, her heart suddenly ached for him. He seemed so alone, and it made her long to go to him. Instead, she didn't move. She was feeling edgy enough about tonight. She didn't need something else weighing down on her—like seeing him get hurt or worse.

"Look, tonight we're getting those women out of that Praetorian hellhole. I'll be gone in less than two days, and our lives can go back to normal." The idea that she could fall back into her daily routine without thinking about him again struck her as hopeless. "I'll be gone and you won't feel *tempted* to label me Lilith in your fall from grace."

"You are *not* some Lilith tempting me to sin. I'm telling you that all of this is *my* fault," Dante snarled as he turned sharply to face her, his features harsh with turbulent emotion. "It's a hell of a lot more than the need to possess your body, and Juno knows how much I want to explore every inch of you with my hands and mouth."

"Would it be so bad if you made love to me?" she asked, deliberately avoiding the implication that he had feelings for her.

She saw him pale and immediately realized how unfair her question had been. His oath wasn't just something he paid lip service to. He'd taken his vow because he cared about the people he'd sworn to protect and lead. Even if he did have feelings for her—no, she wasn't going there.

"It's a question I ask myself every day, and—"

Whatever he was about to say never passed his lips, because at that precise moment, Cornelia entered the library. There was a curious look on the woman's face as she turned first to Dante and then to Cleo. Although Dante's expression had become indecipherable, Cleo knew her own emotions were easily readable, so she moved away toward the maps laid out on the table. Cornelia joined her and stood at her side in silence for a moment.

"He's worried about you."

"What?" She jerked her head up to look at her new friend.

"Dante. He's worried you'll get hurt."

"That's a risk everyone takes tonight."

"True, but you're special."

"Because I'm Marcus's daughter, I know," she murmured. A shiver went down her back as she remembered Dante saying his desire for her was more than the need to make love to her.

"No, because he likes you. Cares about you," Cornelia said with a quick glance behind her in Dante's direction. He was talking with one of the team members who'd just walked in the door. "He cares about you a great deal more than he believes he has a right to."

"Yeah, the oath. He's told me all about it. No need to warn me off," she said with a shrug of feigned indifference.

The last thing she wanted to reveal was how much it bothered her that Dante's oath stood between them and the possibility of happiness. Deep inside she heard the sound of mocking laughter.

"You misunderstand me, Cleo. I never wanted Dante to take that ridiculous oath to begin with. I think he was entirely too young when Marcus and Placido agreed to let him swear his allegiance to the *Absconditus* in such a way." The woman sighed softly. "I don't know about Marcus, but I know Placido has finally realized it was a mistake to let Dante take the oath so young."

"It doesn't matter," Cleo said with a sudden bitterness she knew she shouldn't feel. What the fuck had Marcus and Placido been thinking to let a fifteen-year-old make a vow like that? "I'm not going to try and seduce him into betraying his vow. I refuse to be the bad guy in that scenario."

"I know you won't," Cornelia said as she met Cleo's gaze. "Which is why I'm praying Dante will see the light."

"See the light?" What the fuck was Cornelia trying to say? Was she suggesting that Dante had deeper feelings for her than simple desire?

"I hope he comes to realize that he cares enough about you to do something about it. He knows his vow isn't binding. He took it before he came of age."

"But it's binding to him," she said quietly as she realized how well she'd come to understand him in the short time they'd known each other. Astonishment crossed Cornelia's features as she nodded her head.

"Exactly. You know him better than I thought."

"I don't know how, but I can read him a lot more clearly than I can myself, I think. So what does that say about me?" It was a rhetorical question, and she didn't expect an answer.

Cornelia didn't give her one. She just reached for Cleo's hand and squeezed it in a reassuring manner. The idea that the woman felt sorry for her made Cleo gently tug her hand free and turn her attention to the maps on the table. She knew them by heart, but it was easier to pretend interest in them than to see pity in the woman's gaze.

She was certain Cornelia wanted to say more, but the arrival of two additional fighters drew the *Praefect*'s attention away from her. The room continued to fill with Sicari warriors until there were at least fifteen people present. The assault tonight was going to be a two-pronged attack. One team would use Sonny Mesiti's service van to make an unexpected delivery, while the second group would enter the convent from the cliffside.

A sudden tingle on the back of her neck announced that Dante was directly behind her. She drew in a sharp breath at the way her body reacted whenever he got near her. The heat of him warmed her back for a fraction of a second before he continued past her to circle the table.

The team had already gone over all the final arrangements the day before, and after a brief review they were loaded up for the four-hour drive south to the Amalfi Coast. At a pre-determined point along the way, the two teams split to head in different directions.

As a member of the seaside assault team, Cleo knew how risky this operation was, and for the first time she experienced trepidation. Had she been wrong to think up this crazy plan? No. It couldn't be too crazy if Dante had gone along with it. She'd seen how thorough he was in the team meetings when planning this assault. The man was far too logical and careful to have implemented her plan if he thought it had even the slightest possibility of failure.

It was almost ten o'clock when they arrived at the dock rented specifically for the mission. Isolated and remote, the landing was perfect for their use. The team moved swiftly to carry the scuba gear and propulsion units onto the sleek yacht tied to the dock.

As she carried her own gear toward the gangplank leading up to the boat, a strong hand grasped her elbow and held her back. Immediately the heat flowed up and over her entire body as she turned to look at Dante.

"When we enter that convent, you're to stay with me. Understood?"

It was a harsh command that told her not to think about arguing with him. She met his hard gaze, and the flash of emotion she saw cross his handsome face made her heart skip a beat. Cornelia was right. He was worried about her, and it wasn't just because of her father. A small jolt of surprise blasted through her. It was the first time she'd thought of Marcus as her father. And there was something about Dante's overprotective manner she found both irritating and pleasurable.

"I'm a good fighter," she said in a firm tone. "I can take care of myself."

"I know that, but if you run into trouble, I want to be there. I don't want anything to happen to you."

"Fine, I'm sure my father will appreciate your attention to my safety." It was her way of putting distance between them, but he didn't let her get away with it.

"Marcus doesn't have a fucking thing to do with it. I care about your safety. If something happened to you . . ." His voice trailed off into silence.

Amazement mixed with pleasure sped through her veins at his words. He did care about her. Probably more than he wanted to admit based on his expression. He had feelings he couldn't or wouldn't act on. There was a harsh bite to that thought that hurt, and worse than she wanted to admit.

"I can take care of myself," she said with small bit of rebellion. "But if it'll make you feel better, I'll stick to you like glue."

"It will make me feel better," he growled with obvious exasperation at her cavalier response. Without another word, he ushered her forward and onto the boat. As he left her on the deck and disappeared below, she scowled at his back. He was acting like this was her first mission. The thing was, a part of her liked the way he was acting.

She enjoyed the way his manner made her feel as though she was a treasured object to be protected. In fact, not even Michael had ever made her feel that way. It was a sensation she enjoyed far more than she should. She shook her head at her fanciful thoughts.

"This is so fucked up," she muttered to herself and sank down onto one of the seats lining the port side of the boat.

The usual state of edgy nervousness assaulted her as she stared out over the Tyrrhenian Sea, and the yacht slipped quietly away from the dock. It wasn't a new sensation. She always felt like this just before she went out on mission. But tonight was different. She was confused, too. It was an unfamiliar feeling, and she didn't like it. It only added to her jangled nerves.

She took in a deep breath of fresh sea air then released it slowly in an effort to relax. Overhead the night sky was brilliant with stars.

Normally Rome's city lights obscured the night sky, but out here on the yacht, which was running with the minimum of lights to avoid detection, the night was as crystal clear as she'd seen it in weeks. Out of the corner of her eye, she caught a flash of movement and jumped as Cornelia sat down beside her.

"I apologize," the *Praefect* said in a soft voice. "I didn't mean to startle you."

"It's okay. I'm just a bit on edge. Happens before every mission. How are you doing?" She studied the woman's shadowed features.

"I'll be fine."

There was something in the woman's voice that said she didn't want to talk, so Cleo remained silent. She couldn't even begin to imagine what Cornelia was feeling at the moment. Did the woman regret having children? Was the joy of having a child overshadowed by the pain she had to be experiencing now? Somehow she was certain the answer Cornelia would give her was yes.

Cleo turned her head into the wind, and a couple of strands of hair pulled loose from her braid to brush her cheeks. She pushed them aside as she stared out at the dark water. Although she didn't envy Cornelia the pain she was enduring now, Cleo envied her for having a child. It was the one thing she could never have.

No, not the only thing she could never have. She couldn't have Dante either. The thought ripped through her with an emotional force similar to taking a kick upside the head. She sucked in a sharp breath. *Deus*, she hardly knew the man. What did it matter that she couldn't be with him? She swallowed hard. It mattered, and that was the scariest thought of all.

Chapter 16

MARCUS stood in front of the wall screen that displayed a digitally enhanced image of the *Tyet of Isis* document. It amazed him how remarkably well preserved the parchment was after almost two thousand years of storage in the small box. Still, it had taken Atia and another researcher three weeks just to unroll the fragile paper so it could be photographed yesterday.

Today was the first time he'd seen the details of the document up close. The centuries had destroyed portions of the artifact and created a jagged border that ate into the text and symbols on the parchment. Some of the material had crumbled as it had been unrolled, leaving several holes in the document.

Despite the lost text, he'd been able to glean quite a bit of information from the manuscript, and even from the drawings interspersed in the text, including icons he recognized from his past life when he'd lived and fought at the side of the first Sicari Lord in ancient Rome. Even through the centuries, some of his memories as Tevy were as real and vivid as his current life.

The fluttering of Atia's thoughts brushed his mind. The door of the research room opened quietly, but he didn't turn around. As

usual, she was early. It was something he'd counted on this morning.
There had been little opportunity for him to be alone with her for
the past several days. He was certain it had been a deliberate move
on her part.

Although he couldn't see her, it was easy to tell she was hesitating to enter the room. She'd always been good at shielding her mind,
but their bonding years ago had created a connection between them
that allowed him to feel her emotions even when he couldn't read
her thoughts. The bond between them had grown stronger with age.
He only wished the connection had been this strong after Gabriel's
kidnapping. He drew in a harsh breath.

It had been three weeks since Atia's confession, and he'd not
attempted to confront her about it. He'd needed time to take in her
revelation about the day of Gabriel's kidnapping. Her declaration
had stunned him, but knowing she'd kept her secret all these years
because she'd been afraid of him had been a painfully bitter pill to
swallow. It only emphasized the chasm between them because he
understood now why she'd been afraid to tell him the truth.

When she'd shared the full story of that day, he'd argued that
he would have understood. But perhaps she was right. In all likelihood, his anger, fear, grief, and inflexibility would have made him
condemn her for failing to keep their son out of Praetorian hands.
He was glad she hadn't told him the truth for that very reason. His
condemnation of her would have been undeserved. He understood
now how difficult it would have been to take their son's life that day.

The stark memory of Gabriel in the Pantheon rocked through
him. Logically, Marcus had accepted that Gabriel was no longer
his son, but it had not made it any easier to fight him. It was how
Gabriel had been able to gain the upper hand in their battle. Deep
down, Marcus knew there had been several moments when he could
have easily finished off his son.

He'd known from the first clash of their swords that he was a
better fighter than Gabriel. But he'd not pushed his advantage, and
over the last week he'd come to realize it was because he hadn't
wanted to kill his son. He flinched as his body remembered the slicing pain his son's sword had inflicted on his thigh.

It had been a mortal wound. But Gabriel hadn't been happy with that. He'd wanted to destroy Marcus completely. As Gabriel had hovered over him, ready to land the final blow, Atia's plea for mercy had made their son hesitate. It had been long enough for Marcus to do what was necessary.

His muscles tightened into hard knots at the memory. Thrusting his sword deep into Gabriel's heart had been the most gut-wrenching thing he'd ever done in his entire life. The pain of that moment had surpassed the agony he'd experienced when the Praetorians had taken his son.

It made him understand all too well why Atia couldn't have taken Gabriel's life the day the Praetorians kidnapped their son. He'd found it hard enough for him to kill his son despite knowing what Gabriel had become. But sweet Vesta, he couldn't imagine how difficult it would have been to take Gabriel's life when he was nothing more than a toddler. Now he understood the sorrow she'd been living with all these years.

The door to the research room closed, but the warmth of her presence remained. He knew she'd wanted to run, but her pride wouldn't let her. Again there was the flutter of her thoughts against his, and he turned to face her. The small frown on her face was one he recognized. She was planning. Most likely strategizing how to get rid of him. He wasn't willing to let her come up with a way to do that.

"Have you had time to try and read this?" He gestured toward the screen with a slight jerk of his head. The question startled her, but she recovered quickly.

"Yes, I looked at the images last night before locking up. It was late, and I wasn't really able to make heads or tails of it. The drawings of the standards from the different legions of the Roman army didn't make sense to me. They're obviously part of the message, but without knowing what the different positions mean, I couldn't decipher it," she said with disappointment.

Her frustration was something he understood. She'd been searching for the *Tyet of Isis* for most of her life, and now that she'd found it, she was faced with yet another puzzle. The fact that he probably wouldn't be of much help to her in solving the riddle didn't sit well with him. It irritated the hell out of him that he could remember horrific scenes of men dying in battle, and yet recalling a simple tilt or twist of the Roman standard was beyond his capability.

"Actually, the drawings of the standards would make perfect sense if you were a member of the Praetorian Guard two thousand years ago," he said wryly, knowing they didn't make much sense to him now, even though he had been a part of the Guard in his past life as Tevy.

"Then you know what it says?" she asked with restrained excitement.

"No. I said it would made sense if you were a member of the Praetorian Guard two thousand *years ago*." He shook his head. "I only remember bits and pieces of my life as Tevy. The different positions of the standards here aren't the common ones used by the Roman army. These are specific to the first Sicari Lord's legion and refer to specific actions."

"What kinds of actions? Are you saying it's a map?" Disappointment flashed across her lovely features. It made him want to wrap her in his arms.

"Based on what I've translated so far and the varied angles of the standards, I believe so. You see the drawings of the *signa* here, here, and here?" He pointed to several standards drawn on the document. "Do you notice anything different about them?"

"All of them are drawn at various angles and positions," she said.

"Precisely," he said. "In battle, the standard was a rallying point. The *signa* could be seen above all the fighting, and it was used to give commands to the troops. A trumpet would sound over the noise of the fighting, which told the men to look for the standard. Using different tilts and angle positions of the standard, a general could give commands to his men."

"So you're saying that the different positions of the standards in this document are telling us where we should look for whatever it is we're supposed to be looking for?"

"Yes, even the coins are a clue." He pointed to the images drawn front and back in all four corners of the document. "Do you recognize them?"

"They're drawings of a Sicari Lord coin except for the one in the lower right-hand corner," she said in a cautious tone.

Avoiding his gaze, she slowly moved to stand a little nearer to him. So close and yet as far away as the years they'd been apart. The thought was no less painful than a dagger thrust between his shoulder blades. He had his work cut out for him where she was concerned. His thoughts reached out toward hers and encountered chaos.

Beneath that serene façade of hers she was far more apprehensive than she wanted him to believe. He retreated before she had the chance to realize he was attempting to probe her thoughts. Without taking his eyes off the enlarged image of the document on the screen, he dared to take a step toward her and pointed to the lower right-hand portion of the screen.

Even with the corner of the document destroyed, the one image remaining was easy to identify. The head of Ptolemy I Soter was quite prominent. Little remained of the image next to Ptolemy's, but Marcus recognized the remaining fragment.

"This one is a Sicari Lord coin, too."

"What on earth makes you think that?" she scoffed as she dismissed his statement with a wave of her hand. "It's nothing like the other three, which are almost identical to the Sicari Lord coins we have in the vault. This one has Ptolemy Soter's image on it, and what's left of the image beside it certainly doesn't boast any Latin text like the other three coins."

"It's Macedonian," he said quietly.

"*Macedonian?*" She looked at him in surprise, her outwardly serene composure giving way to the woman he knew in his youth. Curiosity and excitement sent color cresting over her cheeks as she stepped closer to the screen to study the small portion of text that time had failed to erode. Bending slightly to examine the image, she shook her head and tilted it in his direction. "All right, it looks like Macedonian writing, but that makes it even *less* likely it's a Sicari Lord coin."

"He lives twice who dies well," he said quietly.

"What?" Her brow furrowed as she straightened upright to study him in puzzlement.

"The Sicari battle cry. It's the text on the back of the coin."

"How could you possibly know that?" She stared at him in disbelief. "There's barely enough text on the image to even make out what it says."

"I know because I own a coin just like it." He watched her lips part in a silent gasp, and a knot twisted his gut as the desire to kiss her rose up inside him. He crushed the need. "It's been handed down to every reigning Sicari Lord since the time of Maximus."

Atia turned her head to look at the document on the screen once more. Her surprise had given way to contemplation as she studied the writings in front of her.

"Why would a coin with Ptolemy's image on it bear the Sicari motto?" she mused.

"Ptolemy gave a coin to only the most trustworthy of his personal bodyguards, as a proxy that declared the soldier was acting on Ptolemy's behalf. Most of the men who received a coin were with him and Alexander when they invaded India." Marcus folded his arms across his chest as he studied the document for a moment before looking back at his wife. "Although I'm sure the story has lost pertinent details over the centuries, it's said they came back from their campaign changed men."

"Changed how?" she asked. When he arched his eyebrows at her, she shook her head with skepticism. "Are you suggesting they had the same abilities as a Sicari Lord or a Praetorian Dominus?"

"Yes." Marcus nodded. "I think whatever transformed them in India they brought back with them."

Atia drew in a deep breath and released it as she silently considered his theory. Although her thoughts were still blocked off to him, he could sense her growing excitement as she bit down on her lower lip. Her gray eyes grew warm with exhilaration as she met his gaze. He was immediately reminded of the first time they'd met. Her eyes had glowed with the same intensity he saw lighting her expression now. He'd captured her heart then, and he suddenly believed it was possible to do so again. Somehow they'd find a way to put the past behind them.

"If they brought something back with them, it would have had to be a potion or possibly even a plant," Atia murmured.

"Since it probably had to be something they ingested, a potion is the most likely explanation. Whatever it was, it must have changed their molecular structure . . . modified their DNA to account for the Sicari abilities. Our abilities."

"Then you think whatever we're looking for has the ability to transform our genetic makeup?'

"Yes. It would explain the stories that the *Tyet of Isis* could lead to our destruction." With a nod he looked at the document on the screen. "If the Praetorians found a way to enhance their abilities, they would have an advantage that the Order might never recover from."

Out of the corner of his eye, he watched her nibble at her lower lip, her attention clearly focused on his words. Unfortunately, the only thing he could focus on at the moment was what a lovely mouth she had. He bit down on the inside of his cheek, using the pain to keep him from doing anything that would break this tenuous peace between them. He needed to be patient.

"Is it possible you drank or ate something that changed you when you lived in ancient Rome?" Atia asked quietly as if thinking out loud.

"Probably, but I doubt I knew it at the time. My guess is that only one or two people had access to the secret, and they surreptitiously gave it to the soldiers, who in turn would see themselves as blessed by the gods." The back of his knuckles rubbed the line of his jaw as he sensed a swell of amusement in her. He cocked his head in her direction. "You find something funny in this?"

"I'm just wondering if Tevy believed himself blessed by the gods or that he *was* a god when he acquired *his* special abilities." Was she teasing him or taunting him? Ridiculing, most likely. She'd always said he was too arrogant. He grimaced.

"You really do have a low opinion of me, don't you?" Somehow he managed to keep his voice even, despite the sting her words inflicted.

"What?" Confusion made her frown as she shook her head.

"You've always said I was arrogant. I imagine you think I was equally so when I was Tevy."

"No," she exclaimed as her hand stretched out to him. "I didn't mean it that way at all. I was teasing you. I have no doubt your integrity as Tevy was the same as it is today. You're a good man, Marcus. You always have been."

"Am I? I wonder." He bowed his head to study the floor beneath him. The marbleized white stone looked as fractured as his thoughts. "I managed to fail you at a time when you needed me the most. Hardly the markings of a *good* man."

And he had failed her. *Christus*, she'd nearly died. He'd lost his son that terrible day. Losing Atia as well would have pushed him over the edge, but then he'd wound up losing her anyway. Gabriel's kidnapping had driven a wedge between them, and it had illustrated how little they'd understood each other then. Perhaps even now. Atia's hand touched his arm.

"We both failed. I should have trusted you. I should have told you everything when Gabriel was taken."

"I'm no longer certain you made a mistake in not telling me what happened when Gabriel was taken," he rasped as his throat tightened with emotion. She jerked with surprise, and he swallowed hard in order to speak. "I'd like to think otherwise, but my perspective has changed in recent weeks. I now understand what it's like to face the prospect of killing your own child."

He wanted to believe he wouldn't have judged Atia for not following the old code, but they'd known even then that Gabriel would be a powerful Sicari Lord. If she had told him how she'd failed to sacrifice their son to save him from the Praetorians, he doubted he would have forgiven her. He didn't like admitting it, but he knew it was true. He couldn't blame her for being afraid to tell him the truth or for hiding Cleo from him.

"We were both faced with a terrible choice, but you were stronger—braver than me." Her face grew pale, and her voice cracked for a moment before she continued. "You did what a Sicari Lord is trained to do. You chose to put aside your personal feelings and protect others. It was the right thing to do."

"And you did the right thing not telling me about Cleopatra." He saw her jerk with surprise as he met her gaze with a steady look. "If you believed me incapable of forgiving you for Gabriel, why wouldn't you think I'd take her from you? I can't fault you for that. I only wish things had been different."

She turned away, and her sorrow swept through him like a raging storm. It matched his own torment. Uncertain as to whether she would reject his physical touch or not, he reached out with his thoughts and gently forced her to face him.

They stared at each other for a long moment before she came to him of her own accord. She didn't cry. She simply clung to him with a strength that surprised him. After several long moments, she pulled away from him and put some space between them. He didn't want to let her go, but instinct told him not to protest.

Patience was the only way to win her back. The thought made him suppress a grunt of frustration, but she must have sensed his disappointment. Her gray eyes darkened with emotion as she met his gaze. For an instant, he thought she was about to open up to him, but she didn't. With a shake of her head, she looked away and moved to resume her study of the document on the screen.

It took every bit of willpower he possessed not to break the silence and drive the conversation in the direction he wanted. Arms folded across his chest, he dug his fingers into his biceps, hoping the discomfort would keep him silent. Several drawn-out moments later she shot him a quick look before returning her attention to the screen.

"Lysander might have some memory of what the different positions of the standards mean," she said quietly. "I think we should ask him to take a look at the document."

"I thought he was still in Italy?" Marcus frowned in surprise as Atia shook her head.

"No. He arrived last night with Phaedra. She insisted on coming home, and the only way Lysander would agree to let her leave the Genova hospital was if she came to White Cloud to rest."

"All right. Then we should get him to take a look at the document as soon as we can." He paused for a brief moment. "I also think it's time he knows the truth. Dante as well."

She whirled to face him in surprise. "You're going against Aurelia's wishes? She didn't want them to know about each other. It was for their safety."

"They're no longer children. Dante will soon be the reigning Sicari Lord, while Lysander is the first Sicari Lord reincarnated. It stands to reason they'll eventually meet. In truth, I'm surprised they haven't already." He frowned slightly as he considered what would happen when the half brothers met. The resemblance between the two was remarkable, even in spite of Lysander's disfigurement.

"Neither one of them will be happy that we've kept this from them. Lysander will understand why, but will Dante?"

Atia's question made Marcus wince. She was right. He wasn't sure how his protégé would react to the news. He shook his head and rolled his shoulders slightly.

"Like Lysander, he'll be angry, but I think he'll understand the reasoning for keeping them separated. I imagine his reaction will be similar to Cleopatra's when you told her about Gabriel and me." The instant she paled, he regretted his choice of words. He quickly reached out with his thoughts and touched her cheek. "Her reaction was a normal one, Atia. She will forgive you. I'm certain of it. Her anger had already begun to fade the day I gave her permission to remain at the *Absconditus*."

"Something you shouldn't have done," she said tightly. He stiffened at the rebuke in her voice, and she sighed. "I'm sorry. You were right to let her stay, but I don't like her being in Rome. I didn't like it when Lysander chose her for his team, and I don't like it now. It's not safe for her. Have you not heard anything at all from Dante?"

"Nothing." He rubbed the edge of his jaw with his knuckles. "His *Praefect* called the other day to discuss a minor business issue. When I asked about Cleopatra, all Cornelia said was that she was proving a challenge for Dante."

"That doesn't surprise me," Atia said with a small smile. "Cleo follows orders, but she doesn't hesitate to question them."

"Then she's her mother's daughter." He laughed softly. "I can remember a number of times you balked at doing something I told you to do."

"That was because you weren't used to someone questioning you." Her smile widened. "Do you remember the day I found that Sicari dagger in the dig near Rennes-le-Château?"

"It wasn't Sicari in origin," he growled with irritation. She laughed.

"Yes it was, but you couldn't admit that I was right. You still can't." Her gentle chiding made him release a disgusted grunt as he rubbed the back of his neck.

"Will it make you feel better if I admit that I'm not always right?" The question made her gape at him in surprise. He felt a flush of heat rise in his face. "It's not easy to say that, but I've made plenty of mistakes. One of them was letting you leave me that night at La Terrazza del Ninfeo."

"As I recall, I didn't give you a choice," she said quietly. "I had to return here for a Council meeting."

"Would you have stayed if I'd told you I loved you?" The question made her eyes darken with an emotion that gave him a small sliver of hope.

"I . . . I don't know." She averted her gaze and shook her head. "That whole night was . . . it was like a dream. None of it seemed real."

"You said once it was a mistake," he rasped as he remembered her words they day he'd found out about Cleopatra.

"*No*," she exclaimed as she quickly faced him. "It gave me Cleo, and it . . . it . . ."

"It what, *mea amor*?"

It was easy to define the emotions emanating from her. Confusion, sadness, and fear. The fear startled him. She had nothing to fear from him, and he gently reached out with his thoughts to touch her mind. She didn't retreat from the mental caress. If anything, she opened up herself to his thoughts, welcoming him. Still, the vibration of her fear drifted into his mind until he realized what she was frightened of. She was afraid to trust him.

His mouth went dry at the hope taking root in his heart. He immediately pulled back, aching to probe deeper and reassure her but knowing he couldn't force her to come to him. And he didn't want her like that anyway. He wanted her to come to him with a willing heart because she trusted him and loved him.

The moment she took a hesitant step toward him, his heart slammed into his chest. Fear wasn't a foreign concept to him. He'd experienced it more than once, but he'd always been in control and able to defend himself. This was completely different.

For the first time in his life, he was afraid he might actually lose everything that he held dear. He tried to swallow the knot squeezing his throat shut, but he failed. Barely able to breathe, he watched her take another step toward him. Her fingers lightly touched his cheek, and a shudder ripped through him.

Christus, he'd never been so uncertain of her as he was at this moment. After all they'd been through, would she risk loving him again? Slowly, he bent his head, allowing her all the time she needed to pull away from him. When she didn't move, his lips caressed hers in a featherlight kiss.

"Tell me what that night meant to you, *carissima*," he whispered as he breathed in the sweet floral scent of her.

"Everything," she choked out. "It's the only thing that's comforted me when I've been alone in the dark, wanting you beside me."

"Does this mean you're willing to grow old with me?" He remained still as he waited for her answer.

"Yes."

Her reply rocked him to the core, causing his hands to tremble as he grasped her shoulders and pulled her into his arms. Every part of him was shouting with a jubilation that was almost painful in its intensity. He'd won.

She was his once more, and this time he wouldn't give her up. Not for anyone or anything. Hunger etched its way through him, hammering away at him as he crushed her mouth beneath his. The sultry taste of her on his tongue made him hard in a second.

Jupiter's Stone, he needed—wanted to show her how much he loved her. Her mouth moved heatedly against his, and a harsh rumble rose in his chest as her hand brushed across his stiff cock. Instantly, his hands grasped her buttocks and nestled her tight against his erection. Her mind touched his with an erotic image of her kneeling at his feet, sucking and licking him until he wasn't able to hold his seed anymore. He groaned at the titillating picture in his head, while his tongue tangled with hers in a hot, fiery dance that made him ache for release. She rubbed against him with her hips, the friction of the material between them making him ready to take her here and now, and to hell with the possibility of someone discovering them. With a quick twist, she was out of his arms.

"*No.* Not here," she said in an achy whisper that betrayed how aroused she was.

"Then where?" He glanced pointedly down at his cock then smiled at the flush filling her cheeks. "You're beautiful, *mea amor*."

"And you're blind as a bat," she whispered as her cheeks grew even darker with color.

"I've always been blind where you were concerned, *carissima*." His chest tightened as he cleared his throat. "And if we don't get somewhere private, I'm likely to be blind to everything except making love to my wife."

The corners of her pink mouth tilted upward as she took his hand. It was a tantalizing smile, and the desire shimmering in her gray eyes dragged the last bit of air from his lungs. He watched in silence as she quickly shut down the computers and secured the *Tyet of Isis*. In less than a minute she was in front of him again, and with a gentle tug on his hand, she pulled him out of the research lab. He went willingly. Content to follow her wherever she went.

Chapter 17

ATIA trailed her fingers down the middle of Marcus's chest as she stared into his blue eyes. The love she saw there made her heart skip a beat with the joy that had enveloped her since earlier in the morning. Over the course of the last few hours they'd talked and made love as they rediscovered each other. In the shower a few short minutes ago, they'd bathed each other with a tenderness she couldn't remember ever sharing with him.

There was a new awareness in the way they touched, as well. Every touch echoed with a silent understanding that they'd lost so much and their time together now was that much more precious. *Deus*, she'd never thought it possible to ever be this happy again. And then there was the passion. The memory of how his mouth had nibbled, suckled, and teased her sex made her want to do the same for him.

Straddled across his thighs, she smiled as his body flexed with tension the instant her thumb slid casually over the tip of his erection. Blue eyes darkening with desire, he released a harsh breath when she dragged her forefinger down the hard, thick length of him.

Leaning forward, Atia pressed her mouth to the thin line of hair that dove downward to his erection. A wet droplet from the tip of him dampened her nipple as her breast brushed against him. Slowly, she slid her lips down to the small indentation just above his thick length. Every inch of him was beautiful.

Her movements unhurried and deliberate, she blew a small breath over his erection before her mouth trailed across his skin to the spot where his hips joined his waist. The sharp breath he drew in made her lift her head to look at him. Need hardened his features as he reached for her. She easily evaded his grasp and quickly turned her head to take him into her mouth.

The swiftness with which she did so pulled a low cry from him. The way he arched upward into her mouth sent a rush of pleasure through her. Heat and a light taste of salt caressed her tongue as she swirled it around his hard length. Another groan rumbled out of him as his hands slid through her hair, and he murmured something incoherent. Releasing him, she lifted her head and smiled at the expression on his face.

"Are you all right, Eminence?" She used the title in a playful manner, and he groaned as she cupped him and rolled his sacs around in her hand.

"*Christus*, woman, are you going to make me beg for it?"

"Actually, I like the thought of that very much," she whispered.

"It's not in my nature."

His dark growl made her laugh, but a moment later she gasped with surprised pleasure as a powerful, invisible force lifted her up and he thrust upward into her. Desire coursed its way through her veins as her body welcomed his. A shiver of delight raced across her skin as she saw the triumphant smile on his face. He knew exactly how much she'd enjoyed his masterful behavior. Hunger glittered in his eyes as he reached out and rubbed his thumb against the sensitive flesh of her sex. The touch made her jump, and a wicked smile curved his mouth.

"Now who's on the edge of begging, Madame Consul?"

"You're not playing fair," she gasped as he increased the pressure of the touch while slowly pressing deeper into her.

"Shall I stop?"

"No," she whispered, rocking her hips against his.

He matched her slow rhythm, one hand pressed into her breast-bone as he gently forced her backward to enhance her pleasure. A relentless pressure began to build in the spot where they were joined at the hip. With each stroke of her body against his, she slowly increased the pace until she rode him with a wild abandon that answered the fevered pitch of the passion burning between them.

The first ripple of her orgasm caught her by surprise, and she cried out his name. His fingers biting in her hips, he forced her to ride him at a blistering speed as one violent tremor after another crashed through her. The explosion of ecstasy spiraling its way through her body left her trembling as he shouted with pleasure and came inside her. For a long moment they shuddered against each other while the aftermath of their combined pleasure ebbed away.

Atia sighed with contentment as she unseated herself from Marcus and shifted her body off his to lie beside him. His arm curled around her shoulders to pull her into his side as his mouth brushed against her forehead. Eyes closed, she murmured a soft sigh.

"Is that a sigh of happiness or satisfaction?" he asked with a chuckle.

"Both." She kissed the edge of his chin then came up on one elbow to stare down at him with a smile. "I don't remember you ever being quite so insatiable."

"I'm making up for lost time," he said in a dark, velvety tone that sent a lazy shiver down her back. An invisible warmth stroked the side of her breast before it moved to brush across her stiffening nipple.

"Stop teasing," she admonished him with a mock glare that made him chuckle.

"That's rather difficult when I'm presented with two such delightful opportunities."

This time he stretched out his hand to lightly circle the tips of each breast. She laughed and playfully smacked his hand away. A quick glance at the clock said it was past one, which meant they'd spent half the day rediscovering each other. She scooted off the bed and moved toward her closet.

"Where do you think you're going?" he growled.

Powerful, invisible hands gently dragged her back to the bed, where she tumbled on top of him. Hands braced against his solid shoulders, she strained away from him and shook her head.

"In case you've forgotten, we still have a puzzle to solve, and I wanted to get Lysander to come look at the document right away."

"A puzzle that's gone unsolved for almost two thousand years can wait another day," he growled.

"It's not just the document. There are other business matters to attend to."

She brushed her mouth over his before she escaped his grasp and went to her closet. Her fingers stroked soft silk as she hesitated to voice what the other matters were. Breathing out a quiet, resigned sigh, she pulled her robe off a hanger.

"I need to talk to Ignacio and ask him to reconsider his resignation." She bit down on her lip when Marcus didn't reply, and she slowly slipped into her robe, afraid to turn around.

"Do you think it wise to ask him to come back as your advisor?" he asked with a hint of jealousy in his voice.

Atia immediately whirled around to reassure him. At the sight of him, she drew in a deep breath. He was magnificent. Stretched out across the bed, he was lean, hard muscle. Time had barely touched him. It had only made him more beautiful. She hesitated for a moment, cognizant of the sensitive aspect of their conversation.

"Ignacio has been my eyes and ears in the Order since Cleo was little. He always knows everything before it happens, and that kind of help is irreplaceable." She kept her tone gentle and matter-of-fact as she tied the belt around her waist. "Without him, my leadership of the Order will be much more difficult."

"And do you really think he'll even consider your request?" He asked harshly. Following her lead, he got out of bed and tugged on his pants with a sharp gesture. "The man's in love with you. If I were him, I'd tell you to go to hell."

"Then what do you suggest I do?" She met his gaze steadily.

"Ask Lysander or Ares to take his place." His response wasn't what she expected. She tipped her head to one side to study his hardened profile. Was he angry she'd not asked him to take over Ignacio's responsibilities?

"What if I asked you?"

"I'm not a good candidate," he bit out. Frowning, she glared at him.

"Is that because you'd have trouble reporting to your wife?"

"*No.*" He scowled at her as he zipped his slacks. "I can't take the job because I'd kill you in a matter of weeks. A *Celeris* isn't just the eyes and ears of the *Prima Consul*. The *Celeris* protects. And we'd butt heads every time I'd try to do my job and keep you safe."

"We would not," she snapped.

"No?" Marcus snorted with skepticism. "Firmani didn't do a very good job keeping you safe."

"That's not true. Ignacio has always protected me," she protested. A look of scorn crossed his strong Roman profile.

"Your idea of protection and mine are obviously very different. Was the man protecting you when you eluded him to meet me at the Santa Maria sopra Minerva?"

"You were the one who suggested such a dangerous place to meet." She glared at him for suggesting that she or Ignacio was at fault for doing what he'd commanded.

"It's not dangerous in the daytime if you come with an escort. Jupiter's Stone, Atia. The man should never have agreed to let you go to Rome in the first place. Of all the cities in the world, Rome is where the *Prima Consul* should be well guarded at *all* times, and yet you were alone at La Terrazza del Ninfeo."

"I was not," she denied fiercely. "Ignacio was standing guard at the foot of the hill."

"The man should have been *no more* than twenty feet away from you. If I'd been a Praetorian that morning, you would have been dead or worse."

She shook her head at his rebuke and murmured a wordless protest. Satisfaction swept across his features as he jabbed his finger in her direction. "Ah ha. See. You can't even deny the fact that Firmani never had a chance in hell of stopping you from going to Rome. If it had been me, I would have tied you down to keep you here."

"You'd have liked that, wouldn't you?" she snapped.

"Actually, come to think of it, it might have been quite pleasurable for both of us." He growled in exasperation, but there was a dark, sensual edge to his voice that sent a warm frisson across her skin.

She swallowed hard, unable to think of a retort. They stared at

each other for a moment before Marcus made a gesture of disgust
and turned away to finish dressing. The silence in the room was
thin and brittle, leaving Atia feeling as though the floor beneath her
would give way at any moment. They'd only just reconciled. Did she
want to let anything come between them?

He would never admit it, but she was certain Marcus was feeling threatened by Ignacio when it came to her feelings. The thought
of him being unsure of her made her heart ache. For the first time
in years she was doing what was right—what made her happy. She
took a step forward. The moment her hand touched his arm, his
body went hard and rigid.

"I don't want to argue with you," she said quietly. He turned his
head to look at her for a brief moment before he pulled her into his
arms with a combined move of mental and physical motion.

"I love you, Atia." His voice was soft velvet in her ear as his
mouth grazed her earlobe. "But you said it yourself. Firmani helped
you keep your finger on the pulse of the Order. I can't do that when
I already have a full-time job keeping you safe. All I ask is that you
find someone else other than Firmani to help me protect you."

Atia tipped her head back to study his resolute expression, not-
ing the fierce, adamant glint in his eyes. She reached out with her
thoughts to lightly stroke the frown on his brow.

"All right," she said with a nod. "Then I'll ask Lysander to be
my *Celeris*. Ares would do it if I asked, but he'd hate the politics.
And frankly, the thought of refereeing arguments between you and
Ignacio holds little appeal."

Marcus released a soft laugh at her wry tone, and the furrow
on his forehead slowly disappeared. The moment his tension ebbed
away she breathed a sigh of relief. Gently freeing herself from his
embrace, she headed toward the bedroom door.

"I'm hungry. Do you want something to eat before we call
Lysander to the research lab?"

"Just you." The sinful note in his voice made her blush as she met
his gaze over her shoulder.

"Be serious," she said with an unsteady laugh.

"I am serious. Just as serious as I was a moment ago when I said
tying you down would be pleasurable." A playful smile curved his

lips as his gaze swept over her from head to toe. A blistering heat rushed into her cheeks, and she sent him an exasperated look. His wicked smile simply widened.

"I'm going to get some lunch," she choked out, flustered by his teasing. "Do you want me to fix you something or not?"

"A sandwich, if you please, Madame Consul." He reached for his shirt and shrugged his way into it.

"Turkey on rye?" She smiled at the surprise that swept across his face before he grinned like a schoolboy. Clearly he was pleased that she'd remembered his favorite kind of sandwich.

"That sounds good," he said with a nod. "While you're fixing us lunch, I'll call Lysander and ask him to be here in a half hour."

She nodded and turned away as he started to fasten the buttons on his shirt. She'd barely gotten out of the bedroom before she heard him humming "Volare" under his breath. Atia suppressed a laugh and walked out of the bedroom in the direction of the kitchen. Behind her, Marcus broke out into song, and this time she laughed softly. Life was good. The only thing missing was Cleo. Perhaps Marcus was right. Maybe all Cleo needed was time. Atia simply wished her daughter would come home soon so she could make amends.

LYSANDER smiled at Atia as she opened the door to her suite. He gave her a hug and as she pulled back she stared up at him with a look of assessment on her face.

"You look happy," she said, her mouth curving into a pleased smile.

"I am." He looked over her shoulder and saw Marcus waiting to greet him. As Atia stepped aside, Lysander strode forward to grasp the Sicari Lord's forearm in the traditional greeting of Sicari warriors. "Marcus, it's good to see you again."

"And you, old friend." The Sicari Lord gestured toward the couch. "Have a seat. There's something Atia and I want to discuss with you."

"That sounds ominous," he said with a chuckle. Seating himself on the edge of the sofa cushion, Lysander rested his forearms on his thighs to clasp his hands in front of him. "What is it you want to talk about?"

The couple looked at each other for a moment before Atia shook her head and stepped forward.

"Ignacio has resigned as my *Celeris*, and I want you to replace him."

"Resigned?"

He stared at the *Prima Consul* in amazement before narrowing his only eye at the woman then turning to study Marcus's face. The impassive look on the Sicari Lord's face didn't fool Lysander for one minute. Ignacio had quit because of Marcus. He couldn't blame the man. He'd known for some time that the *Celeris* was in love with Atia. It would have been hard for Ignacio to continue as her bodyguard with Marcus back in the picture. Lysander turned his head back to Atia.

"So why me?" At his question, Atia assumed her politician face as she matter-of-factly proceeded with her explanation.

"I want someone I can trust, and I can't think of anyone better suited for the task."

"I'm not sure I want the responsibility," he growled as he considered just how difficult a job being Atia's *Celeris* would be. He'd seen Ignacio's frustration in the past. "You don't listen, which means protecting you is going to be harder than fighting off a dozen Praetorians."

Marcus snorted loudly with what Lysander knew had to be suppressed laughter. Her expression dark with annoyance, the *Prima Consul* shot the Sicari Lord a withering look before she turned back to Lysander.

"I've already been informed that I take too many risks, thank you," she snapped. "Marcus has seen fit to assign himself as my full-time bodyguard. So you won't be alone in your efforts to protect me."

"I'm still not sure I want the job. I'm not a politician."

"You don't have to be." Her irritation receding, she offered him a small smile. "That's my job. All I ask of you is that you help me keep my finger on the pulse of the Order."

Lysander stared up at the woman he'd known since he was a boy.

She'd always been there for him. Like Ares and Phaedra, the *Prima Consul* had taken him into her home when he was all alone. Could he really refuse her request? He nodded slowly.

"I'll accept on the condition that you at least listen to me and consider any recommendations I make when it comes to your safety." His tone was stern, and he saw a hint of rebellion cross her face before she scowled in Marcus's direction. The Sicari Lord had apparently used his telepathic ability to encourage Atia to agree to his condition. Although he wasn't sure *encouraged* was an accurate term based on the *Prima Consul's* scowl.

"Agreed." She jerked her head at him in a sharp nod. At her reluctant acquiescence, Lysander stood up and bowed slightly.

"Then I accept the *challenge* of being your *Celeris*," he said, biting back a smile as she scowled at his dry response. "So how do we proceed?"

"I'll need to inform the Council," Atia said with a wave of her hand. "It's just a formality, since my choice of *Celeris* needs no confirmation. In the meantime, there's another matter we need to discuss."

The Prima Consul bit down on her lip and studied him for a long moment with an uneasy expression on her face. Normally, Atia presented a confident face to the world, and seeing her hesitate struck him as completely out of character. Frowning, he arched his eyebrow at her with a fair amount of suspicion. What was the woman up to now? She glanced at Marcus before looking back at Lysander, her discomfort obvious.

"I'm afraid I have some news that will come as a shock . . ." The *Prima Consul* hesitated again, and Lysander stiffened. Something had happened. It couldn't be Phaedra, he'd just left her in their apartment.

"Who is it?" he rasped. "Who's dead?"

"It's nothing like that," Atia said with a shake of her head. "In fact, it's the exact opposite."

"What in Juno's name is that supposed to mean?"

Puzzled, he watched the woman he'd known since childhood struggle with something she wanted to say. Atia never had trouble speaking her mind. The *Prima Consul* was as tough as steel. With a heavy sigh, she paced the floor slowly.

"I've wanted to tell you this for a long time, but I'd . . . we'd promised your mother that we wouldn't tell you." Again she hesitated. Lysander narrowed his eyes at her.

"It would be a hell of a lot easier on me if you just spit it out," he snapped. "What are you trying to say?"

"You have a half brother."

Atia's quiet words were a bombshell going off in the room, and he stared at her in disbelief. The whole time they were in Rome hunting for the *Tyet of Isis* he'd been wondering if the *Prima Consul* was losing her grip on reality. He was now convinced she'd snapped, and proven him right. Where the fuck would she get the idea he had a brother? He shook his head in denial.

"I don't have a brother." The emphatic harshness of his statement made Atia wince.

"He was four when you were born, and he didn't even know about you." Atia rushed on with her explanation when he opened his mouth to reject her statement. "After Nicostratus . . . after your mother became pregnant with you, she took your brother to Rome to be trained by Marcus."

"In the *Absconditus*?" Lysander snorted and arched his only eyebrow in disbelief. The woman was deranged. Atia moved quickly to sit down on the sofa next to him, and she lightly touched the back of his hand.

"It had already been decided that your brother would be sent to the *Absconditus* for training. Then Nicostratus killed Dante's father and raped your mother. Aurelia had planned to go with Dante to Rome, but when she learned she was pregnant with you, she chose to raise you alone, and left Dante in Marcus's care."

"Okay, this has gone far enough," he snarled as he sprang to his feet. "I don't know what the fuck you're playing at, but I don't have a brother."

A firm, unseen pressure on his shoulder made him jerk his head toward Marcus. The moment he met the older man's sympathetic gaze he knew Atia was telling him the truth. Even though it had been centuries since he and Marcus had served together in the Roman army, he recognized the candor in the Sicari Lord's eyes.

"Your mother knew Nicostratus would try to take you away if

he realized you were his son. That put Dante at risk too," Marcus said quietly. "Dante is as powerful as Gabriel was. If Nicostratus had taken you *and* Dante as he did Gabriel, the threat to the Order would be beyond measure. Aurelia knew that. It's why she made the decision she did."

"That doesn't explain why she never told me I had a brother or why you've chosen to tell me all this now," he rasped. *Christus*, all this time he'd had a brother. A brother in the *Absconditus*.

"You were just a boy when your mother was killed. And I think in time she would have told you about Dante. But she made Marcus and me promise not to tell you." Atia was on his blind side, and Lysander turned his head toward her. Regret darkened her gray eyes. "A promise we've broken."

"Why? Why break your word now? What do you stand to gain, Atia?"

He didn't care that she flinched as he glared at her. She'd taken him in after his mother died. He'd grown up in her house, and yet he was beginning to realize he didn't know this woman at all. His face ached from the way the thin layer of skin on his cheek was taut with tension. He turned his head back to Marcus as Atia shifted her gaze to the Sicari Lord.

"Because it's the right thing to do," Marcus said quietly. "Dante is in line to become the next Sicari Lord, and as *Celeris* to the *Prima Consul* it's more than likely the two of you will meet at some point in time. Would you have preferred that we let the two of you figure it out on your own?"

The question made Lysander frown. He could see the logic in everything they were telling him, but he didn't like it that they were only just now presenting him with the truth. Although he'd not talked to Cleo since that night in the Pantheon, he could understand how his friend must have felt when Atia had told her about Marcus.

"I'm sorry, Lysander," Atia said quietly as she met his gaze with obvious regret. "It was done to protect both of you. I wanted to tell you numerous times, but I'd promised your mother we'd keep you safe. Things are different now. The last thing I wanted to happen was for you to meet Dante unprepared."

"Does he know? Know about me?"

"Not yet," Marcus said quietly. "I intend to tell him at the earliest possible moment."

"I need time to think about all this," he growled. "Excuse me."

Lysander didn't wait for either of them to give their permission for him to leave. He simply turned and stalked out of the apartment. He had a brother named Dante. Unbelievable. Until Phaedra, he'd thought himself alone in the world.

He understood why Atia and Marcus had kept him in the dark about his brother, but it didn't change the emotions that were slamming through him at the moment. Phaedra. He needed to be with his wife. She'd help him make sense of this unsettling news. In her, he'd found a safe harbor. The woman had saved his soul, and right now he just wanted to hold her and have her help him heal one more open wound.

Chapter 18

THE tunnel ended abruptly just below the stone balcony that was part of the Convent of the Sacred Mother. A part of the rock face, the balcony was in the dark. The last time she'd been here was in the daylight, but she knew from the photos she'd taken from her boat that there was a door leading into the convent itself. The only thing she didn't know was whether the portal was locked.

No one spoke a word, but Dante's arm suddenly pressed against her chest and forced her back against the wall. She released a soft sound of annoyance and earned herself a stern look from Dante as Tony and another fighter moved forward. Dante looked at his two fighters, and as she watched their expressions, she realized they were communicating telepathically. She grimaced at her inability to hear the conversation.

With a nod, Tony turned slightly and gestured at a younger member of the team. Without hesitation, the woman passed forward two coils of rope with a metal anchor on each one. Tony took one, while the fighter next to him accepted the other.

Dante gently forced Cleo away from the entrance as the rest of the team retreated deeper into the tunnel as well. From where she stood with her back pressed into the roughly carved wall, she watched Tony swing his anchor-weighted rope back and forth then toss it upward. The soft sound of the three-pronged grappling hook against stone made her tense as she waited for a Praetorian to suddenly charge out onto the balcony.

When nothing happened, Tony nodded at Dante then swung across the fifteen-foot divide and quickly scaled the solid stone railing of the balcony until he disappeared over the top. Seconds later the other fighter tossed his grappling hook over the stone railing and repeated Tony's movements.

Nothing happened for a long moment until she saw Tony straighten upright. An unseen hand swung the rope back toward the tunnel entrance, and Cleo tried to step forward, but Dante's arm pressed her back into the wall for a second time.

"You and I go last." His abrupt thought filled her head, and she frowned. The man was going to be difficult tonight. He returned the look, his expression harsh with determination.

"I'm not being difficult. I told you from the start that if you wanted to be a part of this team you had to obey my every command."

"Well, I don't need a babysitter. Just let me do my job," she whispered tersely as one fighter after another swung over to the balcony. When they were the only ones remaining, Dante passed her a rope.

"You're to wait for me once you're on the balcony."

"Fine," she muttered.

A moment later she landed in a crouched position over the rail of the balcony. She glanced around, expecting to see every fighter still on the balcony, but to her surprise the door of the convent was open. Several of the team members had already entered the facility, and she chafed at not being able to move forward.

"You're about to get your wish, but stay behind me. And stay close to the edges out here. Tony says the center of the balcony is unstable."

She nodded at his mental instructions as she followed him to the partially opened door and slipped through into a darkened corridor. The shadowy figures of the rest of the team lay ahead of her. A thin stream of light appeared in front of her, and she realized someone had opened another door, this time into an occupied part of the convent. With bated breath she waited for the sound of fighting to begin, but nothing happened.

"This is too easy," Dante's thoughts whispered through hers. *"How many men did you say Angotti told you were in the convent at any given time?"*

"Twenty to twenty-five on the inside," she responded silently. He didn't comment as he jerked his head in the direction of the door in an obvious command for her to follow him.

As they stepped out into the dimly lit hall, she saw Tony disappear around the corner of the short hallway. A sharp clang echoed in the air followed by a soft scraping sound as the fighter reappeared dragging a limp body after him. Unceremoniously dumping the body, he gave a thumbs-up and with a grin darted back the way he'd come.

"Right. Let's move," Dante commanded in her head, and as the entire team immediately moved forward, she realized he issued the order to everyone.

Without thinking, she pulled the sword from the scabbard on her back and retrieved the stiletto she'd placed inside its protective sheath in her boot. As she moved forward, the only thing she could hear was Dante's cloak whispering against the stone floor. He was the only member of the team who wore one, and she found it a comforting sound for some reason.

Once more Tony disappeared around another corridor, and again there was a soft scuffling noise before he pulled another Praetorian out of sight. Dante was right. This *was* too easy. But then maybe they really did have the element of surprise.

"I'm not betting on it."

His words intertwined with her thoughts, and for once in her life it didn't bother her that someone had read her mind without permission. If anything, it felt natural when he did it. The moment that thought filtered its way through her head, she felt him withdraw from her mind.

Instantly, she felt as if a piece of her had gone missing. It was an acute sensation that made her heart skip a beat. She glanced in his direction, and his face looked as if it were chiseled out of the stone that lined the hallway. Was he feeling the same sense of loss? It might explain his stony expression. She was being ridiculous. As planned, the team explored first one corridor and then another as they moved in the direction of the control room.

The sudden sound of raucous laughter and a woman's screams made Cleo's stomach churn. She automatically turned toward the sounds, and Dante's physical touch startled her as he gripped her arm tightly.

"Not yet. We secure the perimeter first, Cleopatra. Then we rescue. If they get word out of an attack, Nicostratus will send every available fighter he has." The quiet words in her ear made her jump. She glanced up at him and nodded.

Together they moved forward with fighters in front of and behind them. Somehow she was certain it wasn't the usual order of things. She didn't know whether to feel cherished or irritated by Dante's protective manner. They were within a hundred feet of the control room door when a screeching alarm went off in the building. In seconds, three Praetorians appeared at one end of the corridor while five more launched themselves into the hallway behind them. Dante looked first one way then the next.

"*Fotte.* There's not much room for swords, people. Tony, you deal with those *bastardi*." Dante nodded toward the Praetorians at one end of the corridor. "Cornelia, take up the rear."

With Dante's attention occupied, Cleo bolted toward the control room. Her hand gripped the slender door handle and she pushed down. Locked. One look at the deadbolt told her there was only one way to open the door. She sensed Dante behind her, and she stepped aside as with a wave of his hand he unlocked the door. The moment Dante threw the door open, a sword split the air inside the doorframe.

Fingers splayed, Dante threw his hand out, and there was the sound of a body crashing into a piece of equipment. As he lunged into the room, a Praetorian charged at him from behind the door. While the two of them struggled, Cleo darted forward to finish off the Praetorian that Dante had sent flying into the console. She shoved the dead man to the floor in order to study the monitors above the equipment console.

The camera focused on the front gate showed the second Sicari team meeting little resistance from the five Praetorians guarding the entrance. Quickly scanning the console, which some anal-retentive Praetorian security officer had clearly labeled, she pressed the button that sent the gate sliding open. Her senses on full alert, she felt rather than saw the Praetorian she thought dead pull himself up off the floor. Her movements swift, she drove her stiletto deep into the man's chest straight into his heart. As she watched, the light went out in the man's eyes, and he sank to the floor without another sound.

"Damnit, Cleopatra, watch out." Dante's words were followed by a loud grunt, and she whirled around to see the Praetorian's sword slice into his shoulder.

"*Fuck*, will you stop worrying about me and start paying attention to what you're doing?" She shouted over the siren still wailing in the hallway as she realized he'd been concentrating on her and the Praetorian at the same time. "Finish that *bastardo* off."

Turning back to the console, she quickly silenced the alarm. As the shrieking siren went dead, the sound of the battle in the corridor was easier to hear. She looked up at the front gate monitor and saw that the second Sicari team was already driving the van into the front courtyard. Her gaze shifted to the other monitors where she saw Cornelia and the Sicari with her fighting their way out of the hall into other corridors.

The monitor flickered as it changed views, and she froze at the sight of two Praetorians entering a room of cribs. The nursery. A sharp, stabbing pain sliced through her belly, and she looked downward expecting to see blood. When she didn't, ice slugged its way through her veins. Whirling around, she charged out of the control room and turned left.

A map of the complex filled her head, and she leaped over fallen Praetorians as she raced toward the nursery. In the distance, she heard screams, but her stride didn't falter. Ahead of her the sound of babies crying tore at her. A sound that grew softer with each pound-

ing step she made. Two more strides carried her into the nursery,
where she saw a Praetorian send his sword downward into a crib.

The cry of fury she released was like that of a wild animal. The
Praetorian jerked his head up, the surprise never leaving his face
as Cleo used her momentum to leap into the air and plant her feet
in the man's chest. As he hit the floor, she buried her sword in the
man's throat.

Her breathing ragged, she stood up and stumbled from one crib
to another. With each step she took, the horror of it numbed her
until she couldn't feel anything. Even worse was the silence. After
passing the sixth crib, she turned and stumbled out of the nursery
unable to bear any more. In the hallway, she leaned against the wall
and closed her eyes. Her hand clutched at her churning stomach as
she heard the sound of her heart bleeding in her ears.

Suddenly, a woman's scream and a baby wailing made her go
rigid. Her nausea subsided almost instantly as she pushed herself
away from the wall and ran toward the sound. At the end of the corridor, she heard another scream and followed it into a room where
a young woman lay in a hospital bed sobbing wildly as a Praetorian
tried to pull a crying baby from her arms.

"Why don't you try me on for size, Praetorian?" Cleo said quietly. "Or are you a coward who only kills those who can't fight
back?"

The Praetorian jerked his head up, and her body tensed as she
remembered him from the monitor as the second man who'd entered
the nursery. He released his grip on the baby then lunged in her
direction with his sword. Cleo darted to the left, her blade lightly
grazing the man's arm. She shook her head.

"You'll need to move a little faster than that."

The quiet, emotionless sound of her voice surprised her. Inside
she was screaming, but on the outside it was business as usual. No.
Not quite. The wails reverberating in her head created a chaos she
knew would hide her thoughts from her opponent. Her eyes met the
Praetorian's, and she could see the frustration in his gaze. The man
couldn't probe past the screams of chaos in her head. He grunted
with anger and thrust his sword at her again. She leaped back as the
tip of his weapon sliced a hole in her black knit shirt.

"I can tell right now you're going to be a good fuck, bitch." The man's smile was cruel as he chuckled.

Any other time she would have found his confidence irritating. Now she felt nothing. Deep inside, the newborn wailing in her head was a finely honed blade cutting away at her heart. She ignored the Praetorian's glee and lunged forward to send the sharp edge of her blade across the man's side. It wasn't a deep cut, but she knew it had to sting.

A cold rush of emotion streamed through her body as a grimace of pain replaced the Praetorian's smile. He uttered an oath and swung his sword in a vicious arc toward her head. In a flash of movement, she did a quick somersault past him then sprang to her feet in one smooth move. As she whirled around, she dragged the tip of her sword across his back.

She knew she'd barely grazed him with her blade when she could have easily finished the man off with one stroke. But she didn't want to finish him that quickly. The cries in her head urged her on. She took a step backward as the Praetorian whirled to face her.

The fury on his face didn't faze her, and she crooked her finger at him in a gesture for him to attack. Rage darkened the Praetorian's expression as he threw himself forward to wield several fierce swings of his weapon at her. Cleo easily blocked his blows then countered with a flurry of strikes that drove the Praetorian several feet backward. He recovered swiftly to slam his weapon into hers.

Sparks flew off their weapons as the blades skated downward against each other until the hilts of their swords were locked. Triumph lit the man's features at the same time a cold malice swept through Cleo's limbs, and she viciously drove her knee up into the man's groin. The Praetorian released a shout of anger and pain as he struggled to remain standing.

For a long time there had been a thin veil between her and the darkness buried deep inside her. Over the last three years she'd fought the enjoyment of killing when she assassinated her targets. This time there was nothing keeping her dark pleasure at bay. It was a seduction she welcomed as she sent her fist slamming into the man's face.

Blood gushed from the Praetorian's nose, and with a deft twist of her hand, Cleo unlocked her sword from his. She saw him tighten his grip on his sword, but he never got a chance to do anything, as she brought her sword up and sliced through the man's wrist.

Another roar of pain flew out of the Praetorian as Cleo tugged the weapon from his useless fingers and flipped it so as to catch the sword in her free hand. One more time, Cleo kneed the man in the groin, and with a guttural sound her opponent fell, his hand clutching at his crotch. She bent over to grab his chin, forcing him to look at her.

Silently, she showed the Praetorian his sword then lightly dragged its blade across the side of his neck. The wailing in her head continued as a thin but steady stream of blood rolled downward and spread across the Praetorian's skin. She saw fear flicker in his eyes, and for the first time, she smiled. Cleo straightened upright then kicked the man in the jaw. His head snapped back, and he crashed backward to the floor with a moan.

"How many babies have you killed in your lifetime, Praetorian?" she asked softly as she threw the man's sword off into the corner of the room and stared down at him. "How many Sicari women have you raped?"

When he didn't answer her, she jammed her sword into his shoulder. The shout of pain he released made her smile grimly, but the Praetorian's agony didn't help silence the cries echoing in her head. She withdrew her blade from her opponent's shoulder and took a step back. For the first time she remembered the young woman and her baby. Cleo glanced in the direction of the woman, who was staring at her with a stunned look on her face.

"Is the baby okay?" Cleo asked in a mechanical voice.

"Yes," the woman whispered.

The Praetorian shifted on the floor, and Cleo drove her sword down into his leg just below the kneecap. He writhed on the floor and screamed with agony. She took a step back from the Praetorian and looked at the woman again.

"Do you recognize this *bastardo*?" She waited as the woman nodded. "Did he ever touch you?"

"Yes, he was . . . he . . ." The woman's voice trailed off as a blank look swept across her face. Cleo's gaze scanned the room, and she pointed to the door.

"Wait for me in the hallway."

"I will serve as a witness," the woman said.

"No. Outside. Now," Cleo said emphatically. The younger woman blanched as she met Cleo's eyes, then, clutching the baby to her chest, she turned and left the room. Now alone with the Praetorian, Cleo returned to his side and dragged her blade up along his leg to his thigh. Gently, she used her sword to nudge at the apex of his legs. A moan rumbled out of him.

"Shall I castrate you, Praetorian?"

"Do what you want," he spat at her with renewed strength.

The son of a bitch had told her to do what she wanted. She wanted to make him and every Praetorian die a long, slow death. She stared down at him as she remembered the nursery. The blood. Precious lives extinguished because of this monster and the one she'd killed before him."You sound like you might recover," she murmured. "We can't have that now, can we?"

Again her sword made contact with his balls, and in a split second, she sent the sword barreling downward. The man's agonized scream didn't give her the satisfaction she was looking for. She drove her sword into his other testicle, or perhaps it was his cock. She didn't care. It still didn't ease the torment consuming her. He gurgled something, and she arched an eyebrow at him.

"What? Do you object to my method of execution?"

"Sicari . . . Code . . . wrong . . ." His voice trailed off as he stared up at her with a pleading look on his face.

"Ah . . . but there you're wrong," she said with a bitter laugh. "I'm not Sicari at all."

"But—"

"No buts," she snarled. She had no intention of showing this monster any mercy.

She drove her sword through his arm until the blade hit the stone floor. The man's cry of pain still wasn't as loud as the screams echoing in her head. Cries of horror that had started the minute she'd entered that nursery.

Her sword sliced through the man's side, and he started to sob. The sound simply hardened her heart. The Praetorian's cries were a vivid reminder of the night she'd woken up in a hospital bed knowing her baby was gone. She pulled her sword out and plunged it into his other arm.

"Cleopatra." The quiet sound of Dante's voice made her freeze, and she jerked her head toward the door. She didn't want him here. Didn't want him to see her like this. Trembling, she stared at Dante's outstretched hand.

"He killed them," she said. Somewhere beneath the wails inside her mind, she heard how cold and mechanical her voice was. Heartless.

"I know, *carissima*." Dante's expression was tender and compassionate as he gestured for her to come to him. "But this isn't you. Don't let them eat your soul, *bella*. Show him the mercy he didn't show the little ones. Let Tony put this sorry *bastardo* out of his misery."

She stared at Dante for a moment then looked back down at the Praetorian. Mercy? The son of a bitch had shown no mercy, so he deserved no mercy. The Praetorian began sobbing with pain as she jammed her sword into untouched parts of his body.

"Burn in hell, you sorry fuck," she said as she bent over and spat in the man's face.

With swings sharp and vicious, her sword sliced its way through first one side of the man's cheek then the other. His screams echoed in the room, and her own cry of fury merged with the Praetorian's as she drove her sword down into the man's chest and he went limp.

Straightening upright, she pulled her sword out of the Praetorian and meticulously cleaned the blade on the sheet of the hospital bed. Inside her head the wailing ebbed to a dull roar, allowing her to feel the familiar frisson of Dante's body close to her. The weight of his hand fell on her shoulder, and she shrugged him off.

"Have they found Marta?" She turned to face him, expecting him to tell her the worst.

"Yes, she's alive and already in the van with the others."

"Beatrice?"

"Cornelia's with her in the hallway. You saved her."

His words made her look down at the dead Praetorian. She should feel remorse, but she didn't. The pain inside her was too raw for her to be sorry for what she'd done. The Sicari Code didn't apply to Praetorians. She was free to kill them without asking the *Rogare Donavi*, but she knew what she'd done had crossed an unspoken line. She didn't care. She wasn't really Sicari. She was just a woman pretending to be.

Chapter 19

DANTE paced the floor of the *Absconditus*'s main salon. Sunshine illuminated the room, but it did nothing to improve his grim mood. It had been three days since the rescue operation. Three days since he'd watched Cleopatra coldly and methodically torture a Praetorian.

The connection between him and Cleopatra had continued to strengthen with her reaction to the massacre heightening his own feelings about the bloodbath. His stomach knotted at the memory of the quiet nursery filled with murdered infants. It was the worst slaughter of innocence he'd ever seen, but he was certain it was Cleopatra's first.

The way she'd been torturing that Praetorian had revealed more about her than any words might have. Without their telepathic connection, he would have simply assumed her torture of the Praetorian was rooted in the trauma of the moment. But knowing about the loss of her baby, and how a Praetorian sword had rendered her barren, helped him understand some of what had driven her brutal response to the massacre. She had to be enduring the fires of Tartarus at the moment.

The moment they'd arrived home, Cleopatra had gone into seclusion. Not once since then had she emerged from her rooms. Not even to check on her friend. That alone was enough to worry him deeply. She'd been so determined to rescue her friend that her present lack of concern for Marta's well-being alarmed him.

It didn't help matters that Marcus was becoming increasingly concerned about his daughter's withdrawal. Cleopatra had turned off her cell phone, and when Marcus had been unable to reach her after several tries, he'd called demanding a report on his daughter. The Sicari Lord had been understanding about the situation, but if Cleopatra didn't come out of her room soon, her parents would be the ones knocking on her door, not him.

"I take it she still refuses to see you?" Placido's voice behind him made Dante turn around to face the Sicari Lord.

"She won't see anyone," Dante said with frustration as he shoved a hand through his hair.

"Cornelia has shared with me that the . . . the nursery . . . that it was the worst massacre she's ever seen."

It was the first time Placido had broached the subject with him. The old Sicari Lord had instinctively understood Dante's need for time before he was ready to talk about the horror he'd seen. Now, Placido's somber words vividly brought back the terrible sight he'd witnessed in the nursery.

In the past, there had been only two or three infants murdered by the Praetorians, which was always a punch to the gut. But at the Convent of the Sacred Mother, with the exception of two infants, more than twenty Sicari male babies had been slaughtered in their cribs. It was terrible enough that the *bastardi* murdered the female children shortly after birth, but to slaughter the males simply to keep them out of Sicari hands was incomprehensible. He nodded. "There aren't any words for what I saw," Dante rasped as he swallowed the knot lodged in his throat.

Placido heaved a deep sigh of sorrow as he studied the marble beneath his feet. The fragility Dante had witnessed in the old man almost a month ago seemed even more pronounced, as Placido was clearly mourning the loss of innocent lives. The Sicari Lord lifted his head and met Dante's gaze wearily.

"At least Theodorus and Dorothea were spared."

He simply nodded at Placido's observation. Theodorus and Dorothea were the only two bright lights to emerge from the darkness he'd witnessed at the convent. Cleopatra had slain the Praetorian in the nursery before Theodorus had met the same fate as the others, while Dorothea had been in her mother's arms when Cleopatra had saved them.

Cornelia had found her daughter and a new grandchild as well. With his *Praefect*'s help, the odds of Beatrice overcoming the trauma of her time in the convent were strong. The fact that she wanted to keep Dorothea said a great deal about Beatrice's strength to overcome the horrors she'd endured. Placido interrupted his thoughts.

"They are aptly named," Placido said as he referenced the fact that the rescued infants' names meant "gift of the gods."

"I don't know how Theodorus escaped that nursery without a scratch. Cornelia named him well. He's a lucky baby. As for Dorothea and Beatrice, they're alive only because of Cleopatra."

"I think Cleopatra's been in isolation long enough." Placido's quiet statement sounded more like an explosion in the room.

"And how do you propose to coax her back into the world of the living?"

The old man didn't answer him. Instead, the ancient Sicari Lord's eagle-eyed look pinned itself on Dante. It was clear what his friend wanted. He shook his head in silent objection, and Placido frowned.

"You're the only one who can reach her." The man's words made Dante flinch.

"I don't know how to do that." This time he shook his head more sharply. "She's not responded to me any more than she has to you or Cornelia."

"You're the only one she's actually spoken to, which means you can convince her to come out of her seclusion," Placido said in an unrelenting tone.

"What the hell makes you think that?" he snarled. "Another one of your prophecies?"

"No. Simple observation. You're in love with her."

Speechless, Dante stared at his friend. What the hell was the old man thinking? He wasn't in love with Cleopatra. *Christus*, he barely knew the woman. Somewhere in the back of his mind Dante heard a chorus of protests. He shut the door on the cries. How in the name of Juno could he possibly be in love with her? He glared at the Sicari Lord.

"You're mistaking my concern for her as something it isn't," he said in a stilted voice. "She's Marcus's daughter. That alone warrants concern on my part. My desire to ensure her safety is no different than that of any Sicari under my care in the *Absconditus*."

"So you say. But I'm not convinced. You're in love with the woman," Placido said emphatically.

"You're wrong," he growled, ignoring the laughter crashing its way through his head like a loud church bell. "Even if you were right, *which you're not*, I know where my duty lies. I can have only one mistress. I swore to serve the guild and the Order."

"The *Absconditus* and the Order have survived almost two thousand years without the reigning Sicari Lord blindly throwing himself on the altar of celibacy," Placido said with disgust.

"I don't see myself as a sacrifice, but I do find this conversation as wearisome as the last one we had on the subject." Dante's comment made the Sicari Lord snort harshly.

"*Va bene*, but you're to go to her. Convince her to come out of her rooms before Marcus tells you to do so." The old man turned and walked away, leaving Dante to glare at his elderly friend's retreating back.

Cleopatra had refused to let him in all the other times he'd gone to her door. What made Placido think she'd see him now? He exhaled a sharp breath of fury then clenched his jaw. Fine. If the old man wanted him to drag Cleopatra back into the world of the living, he'd do it. But the Sicari Lord was wrong.

The concern he felt for Cleopatra was no different than what he felt for any other Sicari in the *Absconditus*. He wasn't in love with her. A loud voice in the back of his head argued with him, and he brutally crushed it into silence. With a muttered oath, he strode out of the salon and headed toward Cleopatra's apartment.

The main salon was some distance from her suite, and as he marched through the corridors, he tried to form a strategy for reaching out to Cleopatra. He was no closer to a plan as he turned into the hallway outside her apartment than he'd been a few moments ago in the main salon. He was only a few feet away from her door when a bleak emotion slammed into him like a nail from a high-powered nail gun.

Over the past several days, their emotional connection had grown in strength despite the door between them, but today her desolation was so stark he went rigid with shock. An instant later, the emotion vanished. She'd obviously sensed him, and whether by design or instinct, she'd shut her emotions off as easily as one might shut off a spigot. He stared at the door for a moment then drew in a deep breath and with a wave of his hand unlocked the deadbolt.

The door opened quietly, and he stepped into her apartment. The small living room resembled twilight, as the drawn curtains blocked out the sunlight. Behind him the door closed with a soft snap, and as his eyes adjusted to the low lighting, he saw her curled up in the corner of the couch with her back to him.

"Go away, Dante," she said in a voice that was devoid of all emotion.

"You know I can't do that," he replied quietly.

"Then say what you came to say and leave."

The lifeless note in her voice grabbed at him harder than if she'd been sobbing. It emphasized the wall she'd built around her feelings to keep him out. Slowly, he walked toward the sofa to squat in front of her. She averted her gaze, offering him only her profile to study. Although she'd managed to lock him out of feeling her emotional pain, the external effects were plain to see.

Her face was pale, and he could see a slight puffiness at the corner of her eye. It was a clear sign she'd been crying, but she was still beautiful. The acknowledgment tugged at his heart in a way that was strangely familiar and yet unfamiliar at the same time. It made him ache with the need to pull her into his arms.

He wanted to hold her close until her pain eased out of her body into his. He swallowed hard. The thought of her bearing her burden alone struck a nerve deep inside him that he'd never thought anyone could reach. It scared the hell out of him, and he didn't frighten easily. His muscles tightened and braced themselves against the need to gather her up into his arms. Instead, he rested his forearms on his thighs and clasped his hands in front of him.

"You can't stay locked up in here forever, *carissima*," he said softly. "It will only make it worse."

"I doubt that." She turned toward him, her face cold and stony. "It doesn't get any worse than this. Now that you've said your piece, please leave."

"I'm not going anywhere until you understand that I *know* what you're feeling." His admission made her eyes narrow as she directed a cold look at him.

"*No*," she bit out. "You *don't*. No one knows what this feels like."

"*I* do." He didn't move. Instead, he reached out with his thoughts to touch the back of her hand in a light caress. "The rage, the sorrow, the pain, the helplessness. I felt everything before you closed yourself off to me."

"Even if you did feel some of those things, you're not me. You can't possibly know what *I'm* feeling. No one can." This time the contempt in her voice was raw and brutal despite her stoic expression. Gently, he reached out and caught her hands in his. He half expected her to jerk away from him, but she just stared at him as if he wasn't even there. It made his heart ache that much more.

"I know exactly what you're feeling, because ever since that day outside of the training room, we've been connected. It's how I knew where to find you in the convent the other night."

His throat tightened as he remembered the violence of her emotions when he'd raced toward the nursery then to the room where he'd found her torturing the Praetorian. Despite the distance between them, her horror, torment, and raw fury had pulsed through him as if he'd been at her side deliberately reading her thoughts.

"We don't have a connection," she said with the icy reserve of an automaton. "You're imagining things."

"Then why did you shut down your emotions the minute you sensed my presence outside your door?" he asked with an edge to his voice.

He hadn't meant to speak so roughly to her, but her emotionless manner was slowly eating away at his restraint. This was a stranger staring back at him, her violet eyes dark and unreadable. He wanted the feisty, confident Cleopatra back. The fearless woman who saw what she wanted and reached out for it. A flicker of emotion brightened her eyes before she turned her head away from him.

"Go away, Dante," she said in that dispassionate voice. "Just go away and don't come back."

"I'm not going anywhere, Cleopatra," he growled as he instinctively reached for her and dragged her out of the corner of the couch to the edge of the cushion. The stoic expression on her face vanished as his movement startled her.

"Let. Me. Go." She enunciated the words fiercely and shoved hard against his chest in an attempt to break free of his grasp.

Her struggle knocked him off balance, and he tumbled back onto the floor, dragging her with him. As she fell on top of him, her angry gaze met his, and relief streaked through him. The fury in her eyes was the first real emotion he'd seen her exhibit since he'd entered the room. It meant he'd reached her. The realization strengthened as her violent emotions reverberated against him with the same sledgehammer force he'd experienced outside her apartment a short time ago.

"I'm not letting go of you until you agree to stop hiding from what happened the other night." He kept his voice soft yet inflexible.

"Hiding? You think you have me all figured out, don't you?" she snarled with a ferocity that gave him an even greater sense of the rage boiling inside her.

"Figured you out?" *Deus*, if the woman only knew how clueless he was. He released a harsh snort of laughter. "Half the time I don't know whether I'm coming or going where you're concerned. The only thing I know is that you're hurting, and I can't stand the thought of you in pain."

The confession pounded its way through him as if a car had struck him from behind. Her beautiful violet eyes widened with surprise, and his mind reeled at the significance of his admission. It wasn't possible. Placido couldn't be right.

His throat began to swell closed, and his chest felt like someone was standing on it. He saw her gaze narrow at him, and in a swift move she was free of his arms. With a lithe movement, she rolled away to come up in a low crouch before springing into an upright position. Arms folded, she watched him as he got to his feet.

"Thanks for the sympathy, but I don't need it," she said quietly, her stoic expression in place once more. "What I *do* need is for you to get the hell out of here and leave me alone."

"Why? So you can crawl back into your hole and feel sorry for yourself?" He blew out a harsh breath at the way his sharp words made her head jerk back as if he'd struck her.

"Who the fuck do you think you are?" Her voice was little more than a whisper, but her eyes were blazing with the same anger he'd seen just moments ago.

"Someone who's not going to let you keep running away from the fact that you can't control everything that happens to you," he rasped.

Was he pushing her too hard? He sensed the rising anger that covered the pain she fought to keep locked away from him. From herself. The bleak despair he'd sensed in her earlier had only emphasized to him how much she was struggling with.

The discovery that Marcus was her father had simply strengthened the irrational notion that because she lacked special abilities she wasn't Sicari. Then the slaughter she'd witnessed in the nursery had only magnified the pain and anger she'd been feeling about the loss of her own child as well as the consequences of her injury.

Again, the overwhelming need to draw the pain out of her and into his own body flooded his senses. He closed the distance between them, his eyes locked with hers. She flinched but didn't back away from him. Gently, he cupped the side of her face with his hand.

"I told you the truth when I said I could feel everything you were feeling," he said softly. A pulse of electric current zipped through his fingers to spread through his entire body as he grasped her by the arms and pulled her toward him. "I don't understand how that's possible. But what I do know is that I can't stand by watching you deal with all the pain alone."

"Don't," she murmured as her eyes closed. "Please don't ask me to bare my soul to you."

"You already have, *carissima*," he rasped.

He didn't tell her how hard he'd fought not to come to her in the dark of night when her emotions had been so strong they'd woken him out of a sound sleep. Not that he'd had a good night's sleep since the first night they'd met. A shudder rippled through her as she sagged against him. The sharp bitterness of her pain was a tidal wave engulfing him. His senses reeled, but he simply tightened his embrace and held her close.

Deep, agonizing sobs echoed out of her as she trembled violently in his arms. With each tear she shed, she opened herself up to him freely, and the trust she placed in him was humbling. Her darkest emotions became his as he experienced the horror she felt the moment she entered the nursery. The sensation was so acute it was as if he were standing in that silent room seeing the bloodbath all over again. But this time he saw it through her eyes and felt the agony that had assaulted her from the innocence lost. Just as knife-like was her rage and vicious satisfaction as she'd tortured the Praetorian before taking his life.

Dante wasn't sure how long she sobbed in his arms, but the depth of emotion she released drained him. If he'd battled more than a dozen Praetorians he couldn't have been any more exhausted. Even his reserves were depleted.

Ever so slowly, she grew quiet and still in his embrace, and relief spread through him as her savage emotions ebbed away from them both. As her crying abated, she didn't stir. If anything, she clung to him as if afraid to let go. Her vulnerability made him tighten his hold on her. It was a silent signal that he wouldn't let go of her until she was ready.

Time stood still, and with his senses completely open to her, he could feel her turmoil give way to a serenity he knew she'd not experienced for a long time. He offered up thanks to the gods that her pain had subsided to a dull ache as he pressed his face into the soft silk of her hair. The scent of exotic fruit filled his nostrils, and the smell quickly banished all thoughts of the gods.

Desire and something else he didn't want to confess to surged its way through him. The sensation was already a well-defined one where she was concerned. No matter how hard he fought the emotions stirring deep inside him, they'd become impossible to ignore. If it weren't for his oath—a shock wave of emotion slammed its way through him as he crushed his thoughts.

He froze as Cleopatra lifted her head off his shoulder to stare up at him with a hint of surprise before her eyes softened to a deep purple. The emotion he saw shimmering in her gaze made his gut clench with something that bordered on the edge of fear and excitement.

Christus, she knew. Almost as if she didn't trust her senses, she hesitantly reached up to trace his mouth with her fingertip. Somewhere in the back of his mind, he knew he was about to cross the dangerous line between sanity and madness.

With a low groan, he bent his head and caught her lips in a hard kiss. She tasted as sweet as she smelled. How in the hell had he managed to resist her this long? Pleasure swept through him as her teeth gently tugged at his lip so he would grant her access to his mouth. In an instant, her tongue danced with his. Tentatively, he responded to the intimate caress.

Hot and sultry, the kiss made him tremble with a need that left him helpless to fight her or himself, even if he'd wanted to. Instinct and a primal craving were the only things guiding him as his hands slid beneath her blouse to explore the softness of her skin. A small mewl escaped her when his mouth brushed across her cheek and lightly nipped at the side of her neck. Pomegranates. That's what she tasted like. Tart, sweet, and exotic. The frantic movements of her hands against his shirt made him quickly shrug it off and toss it aside.

The cool air breezed across his skin, but it didn't curb the heat in his body as he watched her jerk her shirt up and over her head. An instant later, the air left his lungs as she slid her jeans off the sensual curve of her hips. Black lace. It barely covered her breasts, and the small triangle of silk at the apex of her thighs—a G-string. He gulped. There was just enough lace to let his imagination run wild. Immediately, his cock swelled and stiffened at the sight of her.

Her violet gaze never left his as she reached for the belt at the waist of his trousers. The touch sent a jolt of electricity through him. Somewhere in the depths of his mind a voice commanded him to remember his oath. A primal need silenced the voice without mercy as his senses went into overdrive once more. But this time the sensations were much more powerful. They were fiery, urgent, and demanding.

As she undressed him, his desire grew stronger, more savage.

With a rough gesture, he pushed her hands away and finished removing his clothes with sharp, choppy movements. Need pummeled him from every direction as he tossed his clothes aside and tugged her into his arms. The mental connection between them merged with the physical as he kissed her hard. Erotic images flooded his head, and it no longer mattered whether they were his thoughts or hers. The only thing he understood was the way his body clamored for satisfaction.

The demand blinded him to everything but the sweet scent and taste of her. The softness of the room's carpet scratched lightly against his skin as they sank to the floor together. He leaned over her and stared down at her with a sense of possession he'd never felt for anyone or anything in his life. His hand curled around her gently rounded hip, and with a firm squeeze, he mentally marked her as his.

A soft gasp escaped her, and as their gazes locked, he knew she understood the significance of his caress. He wasn't sure whether she'd read his mind or simply sensed the touch's primal meaning. Her eyes darkened with passion, and she tugged his head down to kiss him with an intensity that heightened his desire even more.

Her mouth was hot against his as she discarded her bra in a frantic movement, and a moment later, the sight of her beautiful breasts made it almost impossible to breathe. Like an explorer marveling at a new discovery, he cupped her and studied the full curve of her breast. From there his gaze traveled down along her side, hip, and finally her beautiful legs.

He memorized every inch of her that his gaze caressed. She was exquisite. He jumped as her hand slid over his hip to lightly touch the small of his back. A small laugh escaped her, and the moment he stiffened, she kissed him softly, a silent reassurance that she'd found pleasure in his reaction, not amusement. Slowly, she began to trace gentle circles across his back and down over his buttocks.

The erotically languid caresses made his breathing grow ragged as he responded to her touch. *Deus*, the woman was Venus incarnate. Rock hard, he groaned at the way her body made his respond so easily. Eager to explore her in a similar fashion, his hand slid from her breast down to the gentle curve of her waist where his overzealous fingers fumbled and broke the elastic band of her G-string. As the fragile strip gave way, he froze. He'd been too rough.

A brief second later, his heart restarted as she guided his hand to the incredibly creamy spot between her legs. His mouth went dry at the way her liquid heat coated his fingers as he pressed into her warmth. A soft whisper of sound passed her lips, and he froze again, realizing how clumsy his attempt to please her must be. Her eyes met his, and he trembled at what he saw in her gaze.

Excitement and desire glowed in her violet eyes as her hand trailed its way lazily down to where he was awkwardly stroking her. Her eyelids fluttered downward as she guided his fingers to a small piece of flesh within her sleek folds and encouraged him to apply a slight amount of pressure to the spot.

The silent request made him gently rub the swollen nub with his thumb. She jerked against his hand, and he repeated the caress. Another hard tremor wracked her lovely body, and the low moan that echoed out of her throat vibrated over his skin. He didn't have to be experienced to understand that sound. His touch pleased her, excited her. It was a sound of delight that ignited a blaze inside him and obliterated everything but the craving to know every inch of her.

Suddenly, she rolled her body into his and forced him onto his back to hover over him. Black, silky hair fell forward until it formed a curtain around his face, and the only thing he could see was her beautiful features. Desire blazed hot in her violet eyes, and in the next heated instant she sank her creamy center down over his cock.

A sharp hiss of air passed its way through his clenched teeth as tension locked his body rigid. He was uncertain whether it was from surprise or pleasure. Possibly both. Eyes closed, he shuddered at the intense sensations clutching at him. Desire. Pleasure. Exhilaration.

Christus. Was this what being in the Elysian Fields was like? A second later, she slowly rocked her body over his, and he knew the answer was no. *This* was a heaven not even the Elysian Fields could bring. The friction of her body against his defied description. It stirred something dark and primal inside until it consumed his body.

Fingers clutching at her hips, he groaned and urged her to move faster. A moment later his mind reeled at the pleasure flooding his brain as she arched backward until he was penetrating her even deeper. She uttered a soft cry and moved faster, riding him at a frenetic pace that pushed him to a place he'd never been before.

A familiar pull tugged at his cock, making his fingers dig deeper into the soft flesh of her hips. *No. Not yet. It was too soon.* But he had no control. For a fraction of a second he stood poised on the edge of a high cliff before he exploded inside her and tumbled down into a blinding light that pulled a shout of intense pleasure from his lungs.

Seconds later, she shuddered and her body clenched tightly against him. It pulled another cry from him as her orgasm sent shock waves racing along every nerve ending in his body. Wave after wave of unbelievable pleasure rolled over him, and he lay spent on the carpet as she came forward to rest her forehead against his. Her rapid breathing matched his own, and he wrapped his arms around her to hold her tight.

They remained like that for some time before she slid off him to curl her body into his. Without thinking twice, he kept his arms around her. Deep inside he knew this was the only place he wanted to be. She made him feel as if he'd been in a deep sleep, and he was only just now beginning to realize what it was like to be alive.

In the simple span of just a few short minutes, his entire life had changed. It wasn't simply the fact that he'd broken his vow. It was the fact that Placido had been right. He was in love with Cleopatra. It didn't seem possible, but he couldn't deny what his heart was telling him.

Now he had to come to grips with the consequences. The knowledge made him close his eyes. Her hand brushed across his brow, and he turned his head to meet her troubled gaze.

"Are you all right?" Her soft question made him nod abruptly before he looked up at the ceiling.

"Yes," he rasped. He wanted to share everything he was thinking and feeling but couldn't find the words. A fragile silence stretched between them for a long moment.

"You're regretting what happened." The flat vulnerability in her voice made him jerk his head back in her direction. He quickly shifted his body to hover over her and shook his head as he stroked her cheek.

"No, *carissima*. How could I ever regret the most incredible experience of my life?" He swallowed hard. It was the truth.

"But you still feel guilty."

Her voice was soft as she turned her head away from him. The remorse on her face said she believed she was partly responsible for his decision. His fingers caught her chin in a firm grip as he forced her to look at him.

"It was my choice, Cleopatra," he said firmly. "I made the decision to break my oath. You're not to blame."

He pulled away from her to sit up and wrap his arms around his knees. A jolt of pain surged through him, making him close his eyes as he struggled to accept that he'd broken faith with those he'd pledged to serve. He didn't regret for one minute making love to Cleopatra, but his guilt at not absolving himself of his oath beforehand made the experience bittersweet. She moved behind him to press her cheek against his shoulder and wrapped her arms around him.

"*Whose* trust did you break?" she asked quietly. "The *Absconditus*'s? Placido's? My father's? Or yours?"

"Mine?" He opened his eyes in surprise as she quickly moved to kneel in front of him.

"Yes, yours. What makes a fifteen-year-old boy take that kind of an oath? I think you did it because you were afraid." There was a gentle understanding in her expression that he didn't feel worthy of, and he shook his head.

"Of what?" he said tightly as he realized her observation had struck a little too close to home.

"Of being abandoned again like your mother abandoned you." He flinched as she reached out to stroke his cheek with her fingers. "Taking that oath meant you wouldn't have to risk caring about anyone who might stop loving you, or worse, leave you."

"You're wrong." Rigid with tension, he shook his head as she ignored his sharp denial.

"It's why you always want to please my father and Placido," she said gently. "I think deep down you've always been afraid they might send you away if you didn't do everything they asked."

"They wouldn't have done that." His voice was harsh with emotion as he struggled with the truth of what she was saying.

"You're right. They wouldn't have." She cupped his face in her hands, her violet gaze never wavering from his. "But that fifteen-year-old boy didn't know that. All he knew was that his mother had left him alone when he was four years old, and she never came back. That boy believed the only way he could avoid losing everyone he loved was by devoting his life to them. To the *Absconditus*."

He didn't move as Cleopatra's voice died away and she leaned forward to kiss him softly. The touch of her mouth on his didn't alleviate the guilt holding him hostage, but it softened the shackles. Deep inside, he knew she was right. He'd been a boy when he'd made his decision, and he'd been lying to himself about his motivations for taking his oath ever since. The question was, could he forgive himself for his lie?

Wrapping his arms around Cleopatra, he buried his face in her neck, breathing in her sweet fragrance. He didn't have to hear her voice to know she was still worried she was to blame for his decision to cast aside his vow. Their mental connection seemed to be growing stronger by the hour, which made it so easy to sense her concern.

"I don't regret making love to you, *dolce cuore*," he murmured in her ear.

It was the truth. He could never regret the choice he'd made. How could he regret being with her when he loved her so much? The only real regret he had was the fact that he'd been living a lie all these years. He'd deceived not only himself, but his family as well. He pushed the guilt into a dark place to hide it from her. Skepticism darkened her face as she raised her head to look at him. He brushed his fingers across her cheek.

"It's one of the few things I've done right in my life," he said with a small smile. She studied his face for a moment before he sensed the relief in her.

"I'm glad," she said in a husky tone. "Because I thought it was pretty amazing—*you* were amazing."

The compliment made his cheeks burn. *Christus*, he was blushing like a teenager. He grimaced as she laughed and touched his cheeks.

"There's no need to be embarrassed. When I say it was amazing, believe it."

Cleopatra reached out and slowly explored the curve of his lips with her fingers in a sweet caress that carried with it a heat that penetrated his skin. He gently nipped at her fingertips with his teeth. The warmth of her touch spread slowly through his veins until need consumed his body and had him hard in seconds. He lowered his head to kiss the side of her neck.

"Perhaps we should repeat it just to be sure."

"Hmm . . . are you up for it?" Despite her teasing, he could still sense her uncertainty.

"I think so," he growled as he caught her hand and made her stroke his swollen cock.

"*Yes*, I think you are." Her breathless tone said she liked touching him, and a rush of triumph surged through him as he saw the anticipation in her eyes. Somewhere in the back of his head, guilt tried to steal the pleasure her touch gave him. Without a second thought, he closed his mind off to everything except the delicious taste and scent of her as he captured her mouth in a hard kiss. Later he would find a way to come to grips with the choice he'd made. For the moment, all he wanted to do was love her.

Chapter 20

ALIVE. It was the only word Cleo could think of for the way Dante made her feel. It was something she'd never experienced before. This emotional and physical sensation of being a part of someone else. The connection between them was one she didn't understand, but it was there just the same. It had been since that day in the hallway when their thoughts had merged and he'd seen her painful past. With each passing day it had grown stronger, despite her best efforts to ignore it.

Intense delight banished every thought from her mind as his fingers brushed across her breast. It was a caress of exploration, slightly tentative and unbelievably sensual. That she was his first was a heady thought. It meant she was special. She flinched inwardly and quickly shoved the thought aside. Instead she focused her attention on Dante's face as he gently, almost reverently, cupped her breast. The fascination on his features sent a small shiver down her back, which became a shiver of pleasure the moment he circled her nipple with his thumb. The light touch pulled a sharp breath from her, and their gazes locked for a brief moment before he slowly lowered his head to take her into his mouth.

Her back arched toward him as a sensuous delight spun its way through her limbs. The lazy heat of the sensation wrapped itself around her, sending her heartbeat skidding out of control. The man was definitely intent on making up for lost time when it came to his lack of experience. She wasn't about to protest. Another harsh breath filled her lungs the instant his tongue swirled around the tip of her. She couldn't remember ever enjoying a man's touch as much as his. The thought had barely registered when his fingers gently probed for the nub of flesh between her legs. The touch tugged a low cry of excitement from her.

She bucked her hips upward as his thumb rubbed firmly against the sensitive flesh. Sweet Vesta. For an innocent, he learned quickly. She'd never wanted a man more. Sex had always been pleasurable, but not even Michael had created this constant craving inside her. A need to possess and be possessed. It stirred a white-hot heat deep inside of her that she knew would never go away. Her next breath was ragged as he slid a finger into her.

"*Deus*," she cried out sharply. The moment his mouth left her breast, her eyes fluttered open to look at him. Desire glittered in his gaze.

"I take it you like that?" His voice was a husky caress.

"Yes, very—" she gasped as he slipped another finger inside her and increased the pressure of his stroke between her legs. "*Sweet mother of Juno*."

He lowered his head to nip at the side of her neck. Other men had administered similar caresses, but they'd never stirred her body into such a frenzied state. What the hell was happening to her? Desire coiled deep in her belly until she ached with the need to have him throbbing inside her.

She pressed her hands against his shoulders in an effort to shift the balance of power between them, but he resisted. An instant later he was on top of her and settled between her legs. It was a startling display of confidence from him. Arms braced on either side of her, he stared down at her with an expression that thrilled and terrified her at the same time.

In a leisurely fashion, he bent his head to kiss her lightly. She wanted it to last longer, but his mouth moved on to explore the side of her neck and then her shoulder. His cock jumped against her thigh, and she whimpered.

"Please . . . I need you inside me now," she choked out harshly. His response was to press the tip of his erection lightly against her. *Christus*, hadn't the man heard her? "Please . . ."

"I like the way you say please." His whisper was a warm, teasing breath across the top of her breasts. The tip of his tongue dampened the skin there. "And I like the way you taste."

His mouth was like a hot summer breeze against her skin, drawing her into a whirlwind of fiery sensations. She moaned as his cock pressed harder against the very edge of her. The anticipation tightened every muscle in her body as she pressed her hips forward in silent demand. He lifted his head to look down at her.

Hunger darkened his eyes before he suddenly thrust hard into her. Sharp and exquisite, the feel of him buried inside her made her cry out with intense pleasure. He remained still for the longest moment then with slow strokes moved his body against hers. She arched her hips up into him with each thrust. Desire coiled tight and hard inside her.

Deus, she'd never felt like this before. Every part of her craved him to the point where she was certain she'd stop breathing if he pulled away from her. Need burned its way into every inch of her, blinding her to everything but the hard heat of him inside her. His hips continued to move against her as he lowered his head to suckle one stiff nipple.

Pleasure thundered its way through her as his tongue abraded the rigid peak. The desire pulsing its way through her made her clutch at his hips in a frantic demand for him to increase the pace of his strokes. Each breath she took was more ragged than the last as her body cried out for a release from the exquisite torment spiraling through her veins.

With a loud cry, she thrust her hips upward as her body clenched around his cock. Like a wild storm, her orgasm took her to a high peak of intense delight. One tremor after another crashed through her as she fell off the summit. Seconds later, the pleasure tugged her upward again as his body began to rock against hers in hard, fast strokes.

Each thrust of his body sent delight curling its way into every inch of her body, but it was the flash of hot emotion caressing her senses that made her gasp. The intimacy of the mental touch increased her pleasure as his thoughts melded with hers. Not only was she experiencing her own pleasure, but his as well.

It was as intense as it was sensual. She could feel everything he felt. The friction. The heat.

The need.

Another emotion fluttered on the edge of his need, but it was impossible to fully define, as pleasure carried her to a place she'd never been before. The moment her body clenched tight around him, he jerked against her hips and throbbed inside her.

Brilliantly colored lights flashed inside her head as her eyes fluttered closed. Their connection made her uncertain whether the vivid colors were her own reaction to the acute waves of pleasure engulfing her or his. As the intensity of her climax ebbed away, a warm lethargy filled her limbs. She couldn't remember ever feeling so satiated.

As his harsh, ragged breathing slowed, he rolled to the side, taking her with him to cradle her in his arms. The silence between them was warm and comfortable, as if they'd been lovers a very long time. Eyes closed, she snuggled into his chest. His spicy aroma and the soft, warm scent of their lovemaking filled her nostrils. She felt complete and whole. Something she'd never felt before. The thought frightened her.

In the short time she'd known Dante, she'd developed feelings for him. Feelings that ran deeper than she'd realized until now. And that complicated things. It took her relationship with him to a whole different level. Something she hadn't been prepared for. Worse, the man had broken his vow because of her.

Logically she knew he'd made the choice of his own free will. It had all happened so fast, but somehow she still felt like Lilith seducing Adam in the Garden of Eden. Not a pleasant feeling. It cheapened what they'd just shared. And *that* she didn't like at all, because it had been the most wonderful experience she'd ever had with a man.

A quiet thought caressed hers, and she stiffened in his arms. It was the same feeling she'd sensed before, just as that final moment of intense pleasure had blotted out every other thought in her head. She drew in a sharp breath. *Deus*, he couldn't possibly . . . was that why he'd broken his oath? Quickly shoving herself out of his arms, she scrambled to her feet. Her gaze fell on their tangled clothing, and she sorted through the items in a frantic effort to find her things.

"What in Jupiter's name is wrong?" Dante said in a gruff voice. She snatched up several articles of his clothing with shaking hands and threw them at him.

"You need to get dressed."

She jerked her jeans on and found it almost impossible to zip them because her fingers were trembling so badly. Strong hands spun her around to face him. He towered over her with a grim expression on his face.

"I'm not doing anything until you tell me what's wrong."

"You're in *love* with me," she exclaimed. His brow wrinkled with a frown of puzzlement.

"Is that a bad thing?"

"Yes . . . no . . . *yes*." She tried to break free of his grip.

"Which is it? Yes or no?" he asked with exasperation.

"You can't love me."

"Why not?" His mouth thinning with irritation, he shook her gently.

"There are lots of reasons why not."

"Such as?"

"Such as . . . I can't have children." The words were like a blade cutting through her heart. It wasn't just that she couldn't have children. She couldn't have *his* children. It made her want to cry. And she'd already cried enough.

"I know that, *carissima*. It doesn't matter." The gentleness in his voice only made things worse. Fuck, why did he have to be so goddamn understanding and . . . wonderful. She tugged one arm free.

"Don't be ridiculous," she snapped. "Of course it matters. Not only that but I'm not Sicari."

"Now who's being ridiculous?" The sharp note in his voice indicated his frustration was growing.

"You know what I mean."

"No, I don't," he bit out. "You have the blood of a Sicari Lord flowing through your veins. I don't know how much more Sicari you can get. But even if you weren't Sicari I'd still love you."

"*Goddamnit*. Don't say that." This time she jerked completely free of his grasp.

Pain and humiliation hardened his face, making her eyes water. *Deus*, if she cried now . . . She wouldn't. She swallowed the knot of bile rising in her throat. Maybe she was being ridiculous, but she was the worst thing that could ever happen to him. He'd already broken his oath for her. She wouldn't let him give up anything else. The next thing she knew he'd be talking about a blood bond.

"Of course I want to blood bond with you. It's the natural order of things."

"*No*. It's not." She glared at him, angry that he'd read her thoughts.

Their connection was only going to make things all the more difficult if she didn't find a way to keep him out of her head. The sound of a cell phone going off pierced the air, and she breathed a sigh of relief. With a muttered curse, he picked up his pants and dug into the pocket for the small handheld device.

"What is it?" he growled.

It was impossible to hear the other side of the conversation, but the minute his face grew ashen, her heart leaped into her mouth. Something was terribly wrong. Fear gnawed at her as she felt him reeling with grief. She stepped forward and grabbed his arm.

"My parents?" she hissed softly. As she asked the question, she realized she'd included Marcus in her concern. He shook his head at her.

"Inform Marcus. Put the compound on full alert, and I want two teams ready to go in fifteen minutes. I'll meet you at the garage." Even before he ended the call, Dante was already getting dressed.

"What's happened?"

"Nicostratus attacked the city's main installation. There are only a few survivors, most of them *Vigilavi*."

"*Sweet Vesta*," she breathed in horror. She remembered the friends she'd made more than a year ago while staying at the facility. Salvatore, Stefano, Maria . . . were any of them still alive?

"*Fuck*." Dante's harsh oath was a mixture of rage and grief all rolled into one. "That facility has some of the strongest security measures in the Order."

"How could they have possibly broken through their defenses unless . . ." Her voice trailed off at the terrible thought.

"Unless the *bastardi* had help from the inside."

He finished her thought, and she met his gaze with a sinking heart. Had a *Vigilavi* betrayed the Order, or even worse, a Sicari? Dante turned away from her and resumed dressing. The connection between them had never been stronger, and his cold rage assaulted her senses.

Cleo understood his fury far too well. It had consumed her the other night at the convent. A shiver ran down her back. Was that why Nicostratus had attacked the Rome facility? Whatever the reason, she wasn't about to stay behind. She was a skilled fighter, and if the Praetorians returned, Dante would need her.

"I'm coming with you."

"No." The single word was an angry thunderclap in the room. She stared at him in shock. Dante shot a quick glance in her direction as he tugged his trousers on. "You're staying here."

Cleo narrowed her eyes as she watched him tug his shirt over his head. His tension was a harsh, invisible vibration against her skin. The man wasn't just being unreasonable. He was doing exactly what she feared he would do. He was trying to protect her. It was an impossible task.

"*This* is why I won't blood bond with you," she said quietly.

"I don't have time for this, Cleopatra. We'll discuss this later." The vicious snarl told her exactly how much he wanted to protect her.

"No. We won't. Because there's nothing to discuss. You can't favor me over others when it comes to situations like this. You know that. It comes with the territory."

"I'm not about to take you into a situation like this where your lack of abilities could get you killed."

If he'd slapped her face she couldn't have been more stunned. Dazed, she immediately recoiled from him as he took a step toward her. The instant she retreated, anguish flashed across his face.

"*Christus*, I didn't mean it like that, Cleopatra."

His torment rolled over her before she cut their connection by closing herself off to him. It was difficult to do, but she'd had plenty of practice learning how to hide her thoughts from Praetorians. He might regret his words, but they illustrated precisely why she could never bond with him. The fact that she was Sicari simply by blood and nothing more would always stand between them.

"I know exactly what you meant," she said in a voice devoid of emotion. She turned away and quickly gathered up her clothes. "I'll meet you in the garage."

The silence in the room was thick with tension as she turned and walked toward her bedroom to dress for the mission. Ruthlessly, she shut out every emotion she possessed except for a steely resolve to do what she was trained to do. The Praetorians had declared war by launching an assault on the Rome installation, and she needed to prove once again that she was worthy.

In her bedroom, she moved with a speed that years of discipline had taught her. As she tugged on a black knit shirt, she heard the door to the suite slam shut. Turbulent emotions threatened to break through, but she crushed them before they had a chance to surface and threaten her composure. She had a job to do, and Sicari abilities or not, she intended to do it to the best of her ability.

Cleo finished dressing in record time, and in less than ten minutes she was following other members of the *Absconditus* into the garage. There was no talking, just a grim silence that reflected the seriousness of the situation. Without any instruction, the teams launched themselves into four vehicles. Cleo made specific note of where Dante was and deliberately avoided his SUV. Her gaze met his across the distance between them, and he jerked his head in the direction of his car. She ignored the silent command and climbed into the nearest vehicle. Moments later the two teams roared out of the compound.

AS Atia walked down the corridor toward the research lab, she playfully nudged Marcus with her elbow.

"You're doing it again."

"I always hum when I'm in a good mood or feeling *satisfied*," Marcus said and flashed a wicked grin at her. "I've enjoyed not having to think about work for a change."

"Something I should have been thinking about, rather than giving into your every whim for the past three days." She shot him a quick glance of exasperation then softened her voice. "But I don't regret it."

"As long as you never do," he murmured as they stopped in front of the lab door.

"Never." Her fingertips brushed across his mouth before she punched her private code into the security panel on the wall. When she heard the soft click of the lock releasing, she pushed the heavy steel door open and entered the dark room. She immediately froze. Something was wrong. She could feel it.

Mentally she envisioned the light switch and flipped it upward without touching it. The fluorescent bulbs overhead flickered briefly before they steadied and illuminated the lab.

"Something's not right," Marcus growled as he entered the room.

Her husband's words simply confirmed what her senses were telling her. Fear streaked through Atia as she didn't reply but hurried toward the secured storage box that held the *Tyet of Isis*. The moment she touched the electronic security panel, she knew the document was gone. It didn't stop her from frantically opening the lockbox, hoping she was wrong. She wasn't.

"*Fuck*." Marcus's anger was a palpable sensation on her skin. She whirled around to see him standing at the computer as he slammed his fist against the steel countertop. He looked at her, his face grim. "The hard drive's been wiped clean."

"Sweet Vesta."

He jerked upright in fury. "The document is gone?"

When she nodded, Marcus uttered another oath. He immediately pulled his cell phone from his pants pocket. Fingertips pressed against her lips, Atia paced the floor in front of the empty lockbox. Whoever had killed Sandro had to be the same person who'd stolen the *Tyet of Isis* document.

"Lysander, find Firmani. The document is gone," Marcus snapped. A second later his brusque voice became a vicious snarl. "*When?*"

Another long pause occurred in the conversation, and Marcus met her gaze with an expression she remembered from the day Gabriel was taken. He was ready to kill someone.

"Have the car brought around and call the airport. I'm going after him." Marcus tapped the screen of his phone to end the conversation, his features dark with fury. "That Councilman who's a thorn in your side, Cato, is missing. He disappeared three days ago. Apparently Firmani tracked him down to a commercial flight to Rome out of O'Hare. He took one of the Order's planes yesterday to follow him."

"*Cato?*" Atia frowned. "The man is a despicable, overbearing ass, but a traitor? No. And he's too much of a coward to kill anyone. Whoever killed Sandro was highly skilled. Cato hasn't used a sword in years."

"Then who else could it be?" There was a darker note underlining Marcus's voice that made her flinch as she felt the blood drain from her face, leaving her skin cold.

"*No. Not Ignacio.*" She shook her head sharply. "It has to be someone else. I can't believe he'd betray the Order like this."

Or me. Although she didn't say the words, they hung in the air like bells ringing loudly in a church. Marcus's features hardened as though they were set in stone. It was evident to her that he believed her defense of her onetime *Celeris* was rooted in emotions she didn't really feel for Ignacio. Was he still so uncertain of her? She quickly stepped forward and grabbed his hand. He didn't reject her, but the rigid tension in his body didn't ease.

"Marcus, please. He's been my friend for more than twenty-five years. Would you have thought the worst of Placido after all this time? Of Maximus when you lived in ancient Rome?"

He uttered a soft oath and pulled her into his arms. "No. I would find it impossible to believe either of them capable of any traitorous act. But I don't like Firmani. I should have been the one you relied on all these years. Not him."

"Wasn't it you who said we can't erase the past?" she said quietly. "You're here now, and that's all that matters. My heart has *never* belonged to anyone except you."

"*I love you, Atia.*" His thoughts stroked hers as he crushed her against him. "*I can't lose you again.*"

"*You won't.*"

Marcus held her for a long moment then bent his head to kiss her tenderly. "I need to go. The car will be ready by now."

"I'm going with you."

"No. You're not," he said in a tight voice. "It's too dangerous."

"I know it's dangerous, but you need me. I know Ignacio well. I know how he thinks." Atia met his harsh look steadily. "And he's *my* responsibility. If he's betrayed the Order, I want to hear it for myself."

The forbidding look on his face said how much he wanted to refuse her. With a vicious shake of his head, he released a soft growl of frustration.

"*Christus*, if I refuse you, you'll just follow me, won't you?"

"Yes."

"Very well, but it's against my better judgment," he bit out. "Go pack an overnight bag. I'll notify Lysander that his duties as the new *Celeris* just started."

"If Ignacio really is working for the Praetorians . . ." Her voice trailed off.

"If he is, we'll find him." Marcus touched her cheek before jerking his head toward the door. "Now go. We need to move quickly."

With a nod, she hurried out of the lab and headed toward her room to gather some fresh clothes. It couldn't be Ignacio. It couldn't. There had to be some explanation. Perhaps Cato was capable of more than she realized. But what if she was wrong? She flinched. Ignacio knew practically everything about the Order. Defenses, security codes, all of it. He could destroy them all. And if that happened, it would be her fault for trusting him.

Chapter 21

CLEO stepped through the door of the Rome installation and drew in a sharp breath. The slaughter was horrifying. The Praetorians were easily identifiable by the insignia on their shirtsleeves, but they were few and far between. The majority of the dead were Sicari and *Vigilavi*. It was obvious no one had been spared.

Dante and several other members of the *Absconditus* had moved deeper into the facility to secure the installation. Just before he'd disappeared through one of the doorways, he'd looked at first her and then Cornelia. It was obvious that he'd used telepathy to instruct his *Praefect* that she was to watch over Cleo, because she saw Cornelia dart a quick look in her direction as she nodded her head. Dante's eyes met hers briefly, but she turned away. The sting of his words still cut deep.

Gingerly, Cornelia knelt beside a fallen Sicari to check the man's pulse. Cleo followed her lead and moved to check on a warrior close to her. The man was dead, so Cleo gently closed his eyes and crossed his arms across his chest in the traditional ceremonial position. When she'd finished, she moved to the next body, hoping and praying she would find someone with a faint heartbeat whom they could still save.

With each dead warrior or *Vigilavi*, her heart grew heavier. Then she heard it. A faint rasp. Her gaze darted toward the sound, and she saw a face she recognized covered in blood. At his side in less than a second, she gently touched Salvatore's forehead.

"Cornelia, I need a healer. *Now*," Cleo said as she glanced over her shoulder at the *Praefect*. The other woman nodded and hurried off. Cleo turned her attention back to her friend.

"Sal, it's Cleo. You're going to be fine." She could only hope it wasn't a lie.

She winced as his hand caught her arm in a vicious grip, but she didn't try to pry his fingers away. Instead, she quickly assessed his injuries. His wounds were deep, and he'd lost a great deal of blood, but there was still a chance he might make it if the healer arrived soon. Salvatore's mouth moved, and Cleo leaned forward.

"Shh . . . It's going to be all right. A healer will be here any moment."

She offered up a quick prayer that she was right then drew in a sharp breath as his grip on her arm tightened further. His eyes opened wide with a stare that frightened her. His look said he knew it was too late for him. *Deus*, where was that healer?

"Hang on, Sal, *please*. Just a moment longer," she pleaded. His lips moved again. It was less than a whisper, and she had to put her ear close to his mouth in order to hear him.

"Don't . . . trust . . ."

An instant later, air rattled in his lungs before he sighed his last breath. The pressure on her arm eased as Sal's grip grew limp in death. Head bowed, she squeezed her eyes shut against the sorrow washing over her. Sal had been a gentle giant. Always looking out for everyone like a big brother might.

Drawing in a deep breath, she fought to regain control of her emotions. Sal had always been fatalistic about death. He wouldn't want her to spend more than a minute grieving for him, because he'd always been of the opinion that the fallen meet again in the Elysium Fields. Gently removing his hand from her arm, she laid it across his chest before crossing his other arm over it.

As she lifted his arm, his fingers uncurled and something gold slipped from his hand to hit the marble floor with a soft sound of metal against stone. She finished tending to her friend then reached for the piece of jewelry lying next to him. The ring looked familiar, and she stared at it for a few seconds before her heart became a roaring thunder in her ears.

Ignacio. It was his ring.

She snatched the ring up in her hand then sprang to her feet to search through the carnage to find the man who'd been her surrogate father since childhood. Frantic, she moved from one still figure to another, hoping against hope that Ignacio wasn't among the bodies on the installation's main entryway floor. When she didn't find him, she stood in the middle of the room with panic rising inside her. Where was he? A scraping sound behind her made her draw her sword from the sheath on her back as she whirled around to face the unknown. The sight of Ignacio leaning against the installation's front interior doorway covered in blood made her gasp with a mixture of fear and relief. She leaped forward to assist him, but he waved off her assistance.

"*What the fuck are you doing here?*" he asked fiercely, an odd look on his face.

"I've been staying at the *Absconditus.*" She bit down on her lip with worry as she saw the blood seeping through his fingers where his hand pressed into his side. She pulled him deeper into the house and secured the door behind him.

"I'll be fine, just a few cuts," he growled with a shake of his head. "I arrived too late. I . . . . chased two of the *bastardi* as they came out of the house. I left one of them dead in an alley a couple of blocks away."

"When I found your ring, I feared the worst," she exclaimed as she ignored his protest and bent over to examine his injury. Her touch gentle, she pulled his hand away from the wound. It was deep, but in a spot where none of the major organs might be damaged.

"You found *my ring*?" There was a strangled note in his voice that barely registered with her as she quickly examined the remainder of his wounds.

"Yes." She straightened upright and opened her hand to stare at the ring in her palm. "I thought for certain you were dead."

The gold jewelry was covered with blood, and for the first time it struck her as odd that Sal would have been holding it in his hand. The moment she'd seen it, she'd been so afraid for Ignacio's safety that the question as to why her friend had the ring hadn't even occurred to her. Cleo's gaze slowly shifted from the ring to Ignacio's face. Something in his expression struck a chord of horror deep inside her.

Tension sped through her body with the speed of a poisonous snake preparing to strike. The idea slithering into her consciousness was too unbelievable, and she immediately rejected the thought. It was ludicrous. Ignacio could never betray the Order. He stretched out his hand to her, and instinct made her take a quick step backward.

"I can explain, *carissima*." The pleading note in his voice made Cleo flinch.

"I'm listening," she said quietly, praying he had a solid explanation for why his ring had been in Sal's hand.

"Salvatore has been working for the Praetorians."

The bald-faced lie made Cleo's stomach churn as though she were physically ill. Sal would never have worked for the Praetorians. He hated the Praetorians more than any Sicari she'd ever met. The *bastardi* had left him an orphan when he was thirteen, forcing him to watch as they'd raped and murdered his mother and sister before they'd left him for dead.

He'd only mentioned it to her one time, but the manner in which he told his story would be forever seared in her memory. Even Ares didn't hate the Praetorians as deeply as Sal did. Now Ignacio was trying to convince her that Sal was the one who'd betrayed the Order? She knew better, and it left only one alternative.

Denial scraped at every one of her senses as the word *traitor* whirled its way through her head. It wasn't possible. She would have known. *Fuck*, her mother would have known. The man had been a part of their family since she was old enough to walk. It just wasn't possible. But everything pointed to it. The ring, his injuries that were superficial at best, his appearance here in Rome without her mother. None of it made sense.

As she stared at Ignacio in horrified silence, her chest hurt as if someone had ripped her heart out. In the back of her mind, Dante's thoughts brushed against hers. It was clear he sensed something was terribly wrong, but she pushed him out of her thoughts and blocked him from probing deeper. If what she feared was true, *she* would be the one to take Ignacio's life. No one else.

"Didn't you hear what I said?" Ignacio's voice was harsh as he took a step toward her. Cleo recoiled from him, and Ignacio's eyes narrowed.

"You're a liar," she rasped. "A liar and a traitor."

Unfazed by her words, he studied her in silence with a cold, stony expression on his face. "A traitor is someone who betrays his own people. I've not done that."

"What the *fuck* do you call this?" She spat out the words as she gestured angrily at the carnage surrounding them.

"Necessary."

"Necessary?" she whispered as bile rose in her throat.

The denial she'd been struggling with evaporated as she absorbed his brutal, matter-of-fact response. How could he admit his guilt so calmly and without any evidence of remorse? He'd betrayed the Order. Her mother. *Her.* A knot developed in Cleo's throat, making it difficult to breathe as she struggled with the scope and depth of Ignacio's treachery.

"Yes. Necessary," he snarled. "The *Tyet of Isis* document was a threat to the Collegium. I couldn't let it remain in Sicari hands. I never condoned this slaughter. This was Nicostratus's doing." The last part of his statement barely registered with her.

"The *Collegium*? You stole the document just so you could give it to those fucking Praetorians? Why?" Her throat scratchy from unshed tears, she stared at him in horror. He'd betrayed them. Betrayed *her.*

"Because I'm not Sicari." The grimly spoken words only served to add to the turbulent emotions stampeding their way through her. "For more than thirty years I've pretended to be one."

"How in the hell can you pretend to be a Sicari?"

"It was quite easy." His words pierced her thoughts easily.

"But your telekinetic abil—" A light pressure encircled her throat to choke off her words, and for the first time fear spiraled through her.

"I'm not anywhere near as strong as Vorenus or others of my kind, but it was enough to deceive members of the Order."

She clawed at the invisible grip around her throat as Ignacio's cold words filled her head. Her fear made her vulnerable and allowed Dante to break through her mental block, his thoughts a reassuring caress.

"It will be all right, carissima. *I'm coming."*

Dante's promise drifted into the background as Cleo struggled with a new torment. The man she'd revered as a father wasn't even a Sicari. The realization reemphasized her sense of being an outsider. Everything Ignacio had said and done from the time she was a child had been built on a lie. It was all lies. It was as if someone had come along and ripped her entire childhood away from her. For the first time, regret crossed his face as he shook his head.

"That is the one thing that wasn't a lie," he said quietly. "You are the daughter I never had, and if your mother had loved me, I would have willingly betrayed my vow to the Collegium for her. For both of you."

"You sorry son of a bitch."

She leaped forward and delivered a hard blow to his solar plexus. He grunted before his fist connected with her jaw. Stunned, she stumbled backward, the salty taste of blood filling her mouth.

"Don't make me hurt you, Cleopatra." He drew his sword as regret darkened his face once more.

"Why did you come back?" She spat blood from her mouth as she glared at him, her hate smothering the pain of his betrayal.

"For my ring. You might not believe me, but it means something to me."

"You're right. I don't believe you," she said in an icy voice.

The words were barely out of her mouth when she sensed Dante. A calculating look crossed Ignacio's face before an unseen hand grabbed her braided hair and yanked her toward him. Pain ripped at her scalp as she instinctively fought to twist free of Ignacio's invisible grasp, but her futile attempts only made her head hurt worse.

A strong hand combined with the unseen force twisted her around until her back pressed into Ignacio's chest. With his arm locked around her, he pressed the sharp edge of his sword into her throat. The moment Dante charged into the room, Cleo's senses reeled with the strength of his emotions. His anger, fear for her safety, and a helpless indecision she knew was unfamiliar to him crested over her. The moment her gaze locked with his, her heart ached, because she realized she'd caused this to happen. She'd taken away the one thing he'd fought to preserve. His ability to distance himself from his emotions in a crisis situation was in jeopardy because of her.

Chapter 22

DANTE straightened from checking yet another lifeless body on the floor, this time a young *Vigilavi*. The girl couldn't have been much more than sixteen, her life ended by a slit throat. He was beyond fury. Every part of him longed to find the nearest Praetorian and slowly carve the *bastardo* up for the atrocity he'd found here in the Order's Rome facility.

Although the installation was only a quarter of the size of the *Absconditus*, the silence was a tangible sensation on the skin. It cried out murder in a way that was only surpassed by the deaths of the innocents at the convent. But this time there were no miracles to be had. A sudden sharpening of his senses made him grow still as Cleopatra's fear swept through his head. He immediately strode out of the room and down one of the facility's many hallways. A couple of quick turns later, he saw Cornelia hurrying toward him.

"Where's Cleopatra?" He didn't even try to hide his concern. His *Praefect*'s eyes were reassuring and sympathetic as she raised her hand in a placating gesture.

"She's fine. I wouldn't have left her if the main entrance wasn't secure. She found a warrior who's still alive, and I'm looking for Noemi. You know my telepathy skills aren't the strongest."

Dante nodded and concentrated his thoughts on reaching the healer in the building. He had barely brushed Noemi's mind to summon her when he sensed a change in Cleopatra's emotions. Fury, disappointment, pain, and other feelings clamored like a warning bell inside his head. He tried to enter her thoughts, but she pushed back, shutting him out. He jerked his head toward Cornelia.

"Something's wrong," he snarled. "Are you certain the front door was secured?"

"Yes, Mario was the last one through the door, and I made sure the alarm was set." Cornelia's expression was one of confusion as she met his gaze. "The only person who can get in here is either a member of the installation or one of the *Prima Consul*'s senior officers."

For a moment, Dante considered that possibility. Again Cleopatra's emotions crashed through his head. This time her fear was so strong that he was able to see what she saw. Although he didn't recognize the man she was confronting, he could tell the man was someone she knew and trusted. No. She no longer trusted him. *Christus*, the son of a bitch had her in a telekinetic choke hold.

"Bring Noemi to the front hall. *Now*."

Dante didn't bother to explain his command as he darted past Cornelia and raced toward the main entrance. His heart pounding with fear, he reached out with his thoughts to touch Cleopatra's mind.

"It will be all right, carissima. *I'm coming."*

Her thoughts were chaotic and incoherent, and it was impossible to tell if she'd heard him. It was even more difficult to understand what he was seeing in his head. The fact made him run even faster. In the back of his mind, he remembered his responsibility to protect his people equally and without favoritism. But his fear shoved the thought aside. All he knew was that the woman he loved was in trouble, and he wasn't about to let anything happen to her.

As he pounded his way down the hall that led to the entryway, Cleopatra's fear became an anguish that terrified him. *Deus*, if someone were hurting her . . . He flew through the open doorway of the entryway, his boots slipping on the blood-soaked marble floor. Effortlessly, he regained his balance and came to a halt just inside the room to see Cleopatra held hostage with a sword at her neck.

His initial reaction was to reach out with his thoughts and yank the blade away from her throat. Nothing happened. Stunned, he stretched out his hand and gestured at the deadly weapon to fly out of the man's hand. Again, nothing happened, and unfamiliar threads of panic twisted their way through his body. The stranger smiled pleasantly at him.

"No need to worry. You've not lost your powers. I happen to possess some abilities such as yours as well."

Dante steeled himself not to react to the man's congenial tone, but his insides were coiled as tight as a spring ready to be released. Jupiter's Stone. The man was a Praetorian Dominus. How in the name of Juno had he gotten into the installation? He stood silent as he assessed the situation, the indecision sweeping its way through him a foreign emotion.

He'd been in plenty of situations such as this, and not once had he ever hesitated to take action. That was until now. His instincts made him want to charge forward and kill the *bastardo* threatening Cleopatra, but he didn't. He couldn't risk her safety. Cleopatra's gaze met his, and the moment her eyes darkened, Dante knew she understood his indecision. A soft fluttering against his thoughts made him realize she was trying to reach out to him with her thoughts, and he opened himself up to her.

"Don't let him use me against you. The preservation of the Order and the Absconditus must come first."

"I'm not going to lose you." He met her gaze with determination as he saw a stubborn expression sweep across her face.

"Dante Condellaire, meet Ignacio Firmani, *Celeris* to the *Prima Consul*, but most important of all, traitor to the Sicari Order." Cleopatra's words sounded like icicles snapping off an icy roof before they crashed to the ground. Her expression was cool and composed despite the frenzied emotions he sensed flowing inside her. Then the full impact of her statement slammed into him. *Celeris* to the *Prima Consul*.

"Sweet mother of the gods," he breathed.

As *Celeris* to the *Prima Consul*, the man was privy to almost as many secrets as the Sicari Lord himself. He had clearance to access any Sicari installation in the world, except for one—the *Absconditus*. Dante struggled with the knowledge that the Collegium had a mole so high up in the hierarchy of the Order. How much damage had been done and for how long?

To be chosen *Celeris* was a sign of trust, and it was a job rarely given to someone who wasn't well known to the *Prima Consul*. Sorrow making her face pale, Cleopatra looked like she was fighting back tears. Clearly, Firmani's betrayal was a crushing blow to her. If the man had served as her father figure, his treachery would be all the more heartbreaking. And what of the *Prima Consul*? Was it possible she was a part of something Marcus wasn't even aware of?

"No. Atia didn't know any more than Cleo did." Firmani snarled, and Dante couldn't be sure whether the man had read his mind or if his expression had given away his speculation. "Neither one of them are responsible for anything I've done."

"At least you have the balls to admit that." Cleopatra's vicious disgust was evident in her response, and Dante reached out to her with his thoughts.

"Jupiter's Stone, Cleopatra, will you shut the fuck up? The man has a sword to your throat. Don't give him a reason to use it." His harsh mental command made her narrow her gaze at him, and despite the glare she sent his way, he knew she would do as she'd been told.

"Condellaire?" The *Celeris* said his surname with a note of curiosity as he eyed Dante carefully for a moment. "I didn't realize Lysander had a brother. You look like him. Or at least the way he used to look until Nicostratus got ahold of him."

"I don't have a brother," he said harshly. His gaze flickered toward Cleopatra as her amazement flooded his senses. Did she actually believe Firmani? Impossible.

"Think what you like, but I know Lysander too well not to recognize a sibling of his. The resemblance is striking." Something about Firmani's pragmatic tone sent a chill streaming through him, but he ignored the sensation as he stared at the man.

"Let Cleopatra go, and I give you my word that I won't stop

you from leaving." Dante deliberately closed his thoughts off to prevent the traitor from realizing that Cornelia and Mario were racing toward the front hall.

"We both know I can't do that." The *Celeris* shook his head. "At least not until I'm safely out the door."

"Do you really think you're ever going to be safe?" Cleopatra asked in a flat voice. There was a haunted look in her eyes that made Dante's body go hard with tension. She was clearly on the edge, and the thought of her doing something reckless scared the hell out of him.

"A comment worthy of the woman I raised as my own," Firmani said with pride, but his grasp on her didn't ease.

If anything, he seemed to tighten his grip, and as Cleopatra shifted slightly, a speck of blood appeared on her throat. She didn't even flinch at the scratch, which only intensified the fear twisting Dante's gut into knots. *Christus*, if he lost her—no, he wasn't going to let that happen.

"You say that like a proud father, and yet you're holding a blade to her neck," Dante said quietly.

"It's necessary." Firmani shrugged his shoulders.

"Like stealing the *Tyet of Isis* document and ensuring the Order's annihilation is necessary?" Cleopatra snapped. At her accusation, Dante's throat closed. If Firmani had the document, they had to get it back.

"The document will ensure the survival of the Collegium. It's already being reviewed as we speak."

Firmani's matter-of-fact statement made Dante clench his fists and bite down on the inside of his cheek in an effort to remain still. If the man hadn't been holding Cleopatra's life in his hands, Dante would have torn him to bits by now. Behind him he heard the sound of running feet, and the traitor arched his eyebrows.

"So you've summoned help."

"Release Cleopatra and I'll see to it that you're allowed to leave unharmed."

"We both know you won't do that." Firmani shook his head, and Dante sent the man an icy glare.

"I'm a man of my word," he said coldly. "If I say you'll go free, then you will."

"*No!* You can't do this," Cleopatra cried out sharply as she tried to twist free of Firmani's grasp.

Her action only caused the sword at her throat to bite into her skin deeper, and Dante's heart slammed to a halt inside his chest. As a thin stream of blood trickled down her neck, Dante reached out with his thoughts to grip her shoulders and hold her still. Across the short space between them, her gaze locked with his, and a wisp of a thought drifted its way through his head, making him latch on to it like a ship seeking an anchor.

"*Don't do this, Dante. You'll never forgive yourself . . . or me.*" There was a bleakness to her thought that made Dante shake his head slightly as he met her anguished gaze.

"*I'm doing this because I love you.*"

"*Then if you love me, let me go.*"

He ignored her unspoken plea and turned his attention back to Firmani. The *Celeris* eyed him carefully for a long moment before he nodded his head.

"Very well. Once I'm through the door, I'll let her go."

"*No.*" Cornelia's voice was cold with bitterness as she entered the entryway from a door on the left. Her appearance startled both Dante and Firmani. "He cannot go free. The dead deserve justice."

"I gave my word," Dante growled.

"But I didn't," his *Praefect* replied.

Without any other warning, Cornelia hurled herself toward Firmani, her sword swinging horizontally toward his head. His sole thought being for Cleopatra's safety, Dante mentally yanked Cornelia to a halt less than a foot away from Firmani. About to order his *Praefect* to stand down, the *Celeris*'s sword fell away from Cleopatra's neck in a blinding flash of speed and plunged into Cornelia's chest.

Stunned, Dante watched Cornelia sag against the blade before Firmani withdrew his sword from the *Praefect*'s body. The next few seconds took place in slow motion. Dante lunged forward to catch his friend as she crumpled to the floor. Blood spurted between his fingers as he pressed his hand over her wound and called out for Noemi. His eyes met Cornelia's as she moved her lips and tried to speak.

"Don't talk. Noemi is here." He looked up at the healer who'd reached Cornelia's side. The look on her face was grim, and he rejected the idea that nothing could be done.

"*It's too late*." The *Praefect*'s words whispered faintly through his head.

"*No. Noemi's here*." Dante refused to accept that she was dying. Dying because of him. In his attempt to save Cleopatra, he'd made Cornelia vulnerable by preventing her from protecting herself.

"*Don't let him leave*." Cornelia's thoughts made him jerk his head toward Firmani and Cleopatra.

The *Celeris* was already more than halfway through the door, dragging Cleopatra with him. A raw, primitive fury blasted through Dante, and he was on his feet in an instant. He charged toward the door, only to slam into an unseen wall. He stumbled backward then leaped forward again, applying his own abilities as an opposing force against the invisible barrier.

The resistance he met was minor, but the effort to break through cost him precious seconds as Firmani pulled Cleopatra out of the house. When Dante charged out of the Sicari installation, he saw Cleopatra being dragged into the backseat of a black SUV.

Before he could reach the vehicle, the door slammed shut and the car squealed loudly as it roared away from the curb, barely missing an oncoming vehicle. Desperately, he stretched out his thoughts before the distance between them made it impossible to reach her.

"*I'll find you, carissima. I promise*." In the back of his head he heard the faintest whisper of her saying his name, and then she was gone.

Chapter 23

THE late-afternoon sun warmed one of the main rooms in the *Absconditus* complex as Atia passed through the door. Seated in a chair across the room, Placido rose slowly to greet her. Gnarled hands clasping hers as she halted in front of him, she kissed him on both cheeks. Although his features were roughly hewn with age, his smile was as mischievous as it had always been.

"You're glowing just like you did the first time Marcus introduced me to you."

"Always the flatterer," she said with a smile.

Placido held a special place in her heart because he'd tried desperately to reunite her and Marcus after Gabriel had been taken. He'd aged drastically since the last time she'd seen him, but his eyes were still as bright and sharp as an eagle's. Behind her, the muffled sounds of Marcus's angry voice startled her, and she turned toward the door. Even from here, his anger made the hair on the back of her neck stand on end. The last time he'd been this angry was the day Gabriel was taken. Her heart slammed to a halt in her chest as Marcus strode into the sitting room followed closely by Lysander.

"Why in Jupiter's name wasn't I told about the attack the minute

I got off the plane?" His words were a low, rumbling thunder of anger, but Placido seemed unconcerned.

"Was there anything you could have done between the airport and here?"

"Don't play games with me, old man," Marcus snarled. "I should have been told."

It was the first time Atia had ever heard him lose his temper with the ancient Sicari Lord, and it frightened her. Beneath his anger, Atia sensed something darker stirring inside her husband. Something terrible had happened, and he was deeply worried.

"What's happened?" she asked quietly. He kept his eyes pinned on Placido as he released a low growl of anger.

"Nicostratus has declared war on the *Absconditus* and the Order. The Praetorians gained access to the city's main installation and slaughtered everyone inside this morning."

"Everyone?" she gasped in disbelief.

"No one was spared," Marcus's words cracked sharply like ice giving way on a frozen lake. "Not even the *Vigilavi*. And the only possible way the *bastardo* could have done what he did was if he had help on the inside."

He shifted his gaze to her, and she knew exactly what he was thinking. Ignacio. Her heart sank as she struggled to accept the ever-increasing likelihood that her old friend was responsible for stealing the *Tyet of Isis* document and for the barbaric atrocity in the Rome installation. She could only hope that Cleo hadn't—her lungs tightened until it was impossible to breathe. Suddenly feeling light-headed, Atia swayed on her feet as fear made her skin grow cold.

"*Cleo*. Where is she?"

"She and Dante went to the installation after we received word of the massacre." Placido, despite his age, moved quickly to take her arm and guide her to a nearby chair.

"I want to see her."

At her demand, a grim look settled over Placido's worn features. The old Sicari Lord looked at Marcus, and a brief second later, Marcus went white. Certain Placido had communicated something to Marcus with his telepathic abilities, she started to stand up, but a powerful force held her in place.

The minute Marcus stepped toward her, she shook her head. It wasn't possible. Their daughter couldn't be dead. She'd gone to the facility *after* the massacre. Marcus squatted in front of her and grabbed her hands in a tight hold.

"Firmani has her," Marcus said in a grim voice.

A rush of relief eased the tightness in Atia's muscles. Cleo was alive. Ignacio had taken care of her just as he had when she was a child. Her relief evaporated as she saw a familiar torment in Marcus's eyes.

"*Mea amor*, he took her to Nicostratus."

The words didn't register for a moment as Atia stared at her husband's harsh, anguished features. No. Marcus was wrong. It wasn't possible. Ignacio would never do something that cruel. He knew how devastating Gabriel's kidnapping had been for her. Family didn't do things like that, and he was family, not by blood, but family nonetheless. She'd relied on him. Cherished their friendship. And Cleo adored him.

"You're wrong. He wouldn't hurt Cleo." She barely recognized her own voice from the way it vibrated with fear and denial.

Marcus tried to speak but clearly couldn't. Instead, he pulled her forward into his arms and held her tight. She trembled violently in his embrace but didn't cry. A numbness crawled through her limbs until she couldn't feel anything. It was Gabriel's kidnapping all over again. Their child was in the hands of Praetorians, and the odds of rescuing her were slim.

"I'm afraid there's more bad news, my friend." Placido's quiet words made Marcus pull away from her and look up at the old Sicari Lord. "Cornelia is dead."

Marcus slowly stood up, a stunned expression on his face. Although Atia had only met the woman once, she knew how well liked she'd been in the *Absconditus*.

"*Dead?* How?"

"I'm responsible for her death." Dante's voice was quiet and devoid of emotion as he entered the room and strode forward.

Still struggling with her fear for Cleo, Atia stared blankly at the man who'd just arrived. It took her a moment to realize who he was. The last time she'd seen Dante, he'd been much younger. What struck her was his strong resemblance to his brother. It wasn't so much their physical features that were so remarkably similar as the way they carried themselves. Their stoic manner. Her gaze flitted to Lysander, who was standing rigid just inside the doorway. His expression revealed nothing, but a slight tic in his scarred cheek indicated he was finally convinced he had a brother.

"Explain," Marcus commanded harshly.

"I gave Firmani my word he could go free. Cornelia disagreed with me. When she tried to kill Firmani, I stopped her, and he killed her."

"You told that *bastardo* he could go *free*?" Marcus took a step toward Dante as if he were going to strike his apprentice, but Placido's gnarled hand held him back.

"The prick had a sword at Cleopatra's throat. Dante was trying to save your daughter's life," the old man snapped. "She'd discovered Firmani was a traitor, and the *bastardo* was using her to escape."

Stunned, Atia stared at Placido as her mind struggled to cope with the reality of the ancient warrior's words. Slowly her numbness gave way to a fierce anger as she accepted the truth about Ignacio. He'd betrayed not only the Order, but her as well. How could she have been so blind?

Marcus stiffened at Placido's chastising tone, and his gaze jerked from his old mentor back to Dante. The conflicting emotions at war inside Marcus stretched across the distance between them like an electric shock. His emotions dueled with her feelings of anger, pain, and fear. No Sicari was so important as to be saved if doing so threatened the existence of the entire Order. Dante had ignored that fact by agreeing to let Ignacio go free in order to save Cleo's life.

She had never been so grateful to anyone in her entire life. Her daughter was still alive thanks to Dante. A tendril of relief slipped its way into her head as Marcus's thoughts mixed with hers. Intertwined with his relief was the same fear that they would never see their daughter again.

"I don't know whether to thank you or have you run the gauntlet," Marcus snapped as he glared at Dante. The stoic expression didn't leave Dante's face as he bowed slightly.

"Whatever punishment you choose, Eminence, will not be as

harsh as the burden I carry for Cornelia's death and my failure to save your daughter."

There was something in Dante's voice that made Atia take a closer look at him. His mouth was a thin line of tension that reflected he was hiding something from them. Whatever it was, his ability to conceal his emotions made it impossible to determine what he might be thinking. Marcus frowned before his expression softened slightly.

"You've never given me or Placido any reason to doubt your decision making before, and I'm sure you did what you thought was the right thing to do. I know how close you were to Cornelia. Her death is a blow to all of us."

Dante flinched at Marcus's words, and Atia noted how rigid his stance was. He had the look of a man weighed down with guilt. Dante didn't answer but simply jerked his head in acknowledgment. Marcus studied the younger man for a moment longer before he drew in a deep breath and exhaled it.

"I want the complex on full alert, and double the security teams. If Nicostratus was bold enough to attack the Rome installation, it's possible he might consider launching an assault on us here. Dante, I want you to—"

Marcus abruptly stopped issuing orders and frowned as he shot a look in Lysander's direction. Dante followed the Sicari Lord's gaze then stepped forward and extended his arm to Lysander.

"I think it's time we introduced ourselves. I'm Dante. Your brother." It was a sharply worded greeting, and Dante grimaced in apparent regret for his abrupt manner.

Startled, Atia looked at Marcus, who shook his head in bewilderment. When it was evident Marcus hadn't said anything, she turned toward Placido. From his slack jaw, it was clear he was equally stunned by Dante's revelation.

"I didn't realize you knew," Lysander murmured as he grasped Dante's arm in the ancient Sicari greeting.

"Firmani told me I had a brother." His jaw locked with tension, Dante sent Placido and Marcus a hard look. "I didn't believe him until a few minutes ago. I simply wish someone had told me sooner."

Both of the Sicari Lords looked decidedly uncomfortable, and Atia stood up and crossed the floor to stand at Dante's side.

"You might not believe me, but we didn't tell either of you the truth because we were trying to protect you," she said gently. "Your mother wanted to keep both of you safe."

"Forgive me, Madame Consul, but I find it hard to believe my mother spared one thought for my safety considering she left me here in the care of others and never came back." Dante's steely words left Atia speechless, and when she didn't respond, he offered her a nod. "If you'll excuse me, I have work to do."

As Dante strode from the room, Atia looked helplessly over her shoulder at Marcus. He immediately moved forward to lightly touch her shoulder in silent reassurance then turned to Placido.

"He'll listen to you better than he will me," Marcus said quietly. "See if you can mend some broken fences."

"I'll go with him," Lysander said. "Maybe it'll help if he has someone who can empathize with him about not being told the truth."

Atia winced at Lysander's none-too-subtle reference to his own recent discovery that he had a sibling. She took a step toward him, but Marcus's invisible touch prevented her from going after her new *Celeris*. As she watched Lysander and Placido leave the room, the full impact of everything that had just happened rolled over her. It was like reliving those first few hours after Gabriel was taken. The numbness, the anger, and the fear. The fear was the worst part. Perhaps even more so now because she knew her son had never come home, and the thought that Cleo was lost to her as well was like a knife slicing into her heart. She drew in a sharp breath at the tangible pain in her chest.

"Talk to me, *mea amor*." Marcus's voice was a soft stroke on her senses as he closed the distance between them. When he wrapped his arms around her, Atia leaned into him and pressed her cheek to his chest.

"She's not coming back, is she?" she whispered. Marcus didn't answer her for a long moment.

"I won't lie to you, Atia." His voice cracked with emotion. "I don't know. But I'll do everything in my power to bring her back safe and sound."

"We both will." She lifted her head and stared up into his blue eyes dark with pain. "I love you, Marcus."

"And I you, *carissima*. With all my heart and soul." He kissed her gently then pulled her close again, and Atia leaned into him, taking solace in the comfort of his arms.

Chapter 24

MOONLIGHT filled the inner courtyard of the *Absconditus* compound as Atia sat on a bench staring up at the sky. Unable to sleep, she'd left Marcus in their bed to come out into the garden to think. She stretched her hand out toward the moon.

It was so close she was certain she could almost touch it. Just like Cleo was so close and yet unreachable. Atia closed her eyes against the fear of what might be happening to her daughter. Would Ignacio allow Nicostratus to hurt her?

He couldn't have been pretending all this time that he cared for Cleo as if she were his own child. He'd always doted on her. His affection for Cleo had to have been real, hadn't it? She blinked back tears as she realized her own blindness had put her daughter's life in jeopardy.

This time, though, she wasn't going to let Nicostratus win. The Praetorian son of a bitch had taken her son from her. She wouldn't let him have her daughter, too. She glanced down at the cell phone on the stone bench beside her then picked it up, pressed one of the speed-dial keys, and put the phone to her ear.

The first ring made her mouth go dry as she realized what she was planning. If Marcus knew, he'd lock her up to keep her from following through with her plan. She pushed the thought of him out of her head. She loved him, but this was something she had to do to make amends for her failure to protect Gabriel. She couldn't change the past, but Cleo was the future, and saving her daughter was all that mattered.

"Hello, Atia." Ignacio's voice was quiet with resignation and guilt. She hadn't thought about what she would say when he answered, but the sound of his voice sent a rush of anger through her.

"I want my daughter back."

"It's out of my hands."

"Is it?" she said in an icy voice. "Tell Nicostratus that I'm willing to trade my life for Cleopatra's."

"Are you mad?" Ignacio rasped. His voice was dark with an emotion that gave her hope he cared enough about her and Cleo to save them both.

"Perhaps. But I love my daughter. Can you blame me for wanting to save her?" She kept her voice cold, and a long pause followed her question before she heard him utter a soft oath.

"No. Let me see what I can do."

"How soon?"

"*Christus*, Atia. It's two o'clock in the morning."

"You're awake. Guilty conscience, perhaps?" This time she didn't hide her rage. "Wake the *bastardo* and let me know where we can do the exchange. I want my daughter free before dawn, or I swear to Juno, I will destroy the Collegium in a matter of months."

"We both know that's impossible," Ignacio replied with a snort of disbelief.

"I have the formula," she said in a quiet voice.

"You forget how well I know you, Atia. You always were good at bluffing."

"Am I?" she responded coolly. "We e-mailed Lysander images of the standards the morning after we digitized the document. As the first Sicari Lord reincarnated, he remembered even more than we'd hoped. Tell Nicostratus that if anything happens to my daughter, I'll make his death a prolonged experiment in agony."

Her voice hardened with each word until she was finished. From the silence on the other end of the phone, she was certain Ignacio was trying to determine whether she was telling him the truth or lying.

"I expect an answer in the next half hour," she said coldly then ended the call.

Sagging downward, she rested her elbow on her knee, her head cradled in her hand as she prayed Ignacio had believed her and that he could persuade Nicostratus to accept her lies as the truth. Behind her she heard a soft sound, and she was on her feet in a split second whirling to face the potential threat. The sight of Lysander made her pounding heart slow to a more normal rhythm.

"Sweet Vesta, you scared me half to death. What are you doing here?"

"I just got off the phone with Phaedra, and I needed a place to think about everything that's happened. This seemed like a good spot." The scarred side of his face hidden from her, he stared up at the moon with an odd expression. "Cleo found Marta and rescued her."

"Marta's *alive*?" Flabbergasted, her mouth fell open in surprise as Lysander looked at her with a bemused expression and nodded.

"She's here in the compound. I saw her earlier this evening. She and Dante told me how Cleo found out where Marta was being held and planned the whole rescue operation." He released a soft sound of amazement. "From what I can tell, Marta's going to be okay. She told me about this Praetorian who protected her while she was held prisoner."

"Since when do Praetorians protect Sicari, particularly Sicari women?" she bit out fiercely in disbelief.

"Apparently the Praetorian told Marta that there's a growing faction inside the Collegium that wants an end to the fighting between the Praetorians and the Sicari."

"I don't believe it." Atia dismissed the idea with a sneer.

"Marta's convinced this Praetorian, Draco I think was his name, is telling the truth."

Lysander wore an expression of someone not sure what to believe, but Atia didn't trust the word of any Praetorian. Ignacio's actions had simply cemented her belief that the only good Praetorian was a dead one.

"How in Juno's name did Cleo get Dante to go along with her plans? I'm certain he didn't clear it with Marcus. If he had, Marcus would have told me." Lysander cocked his eyebrow at her, and she exhaled a sharp breath that demonstrated her irritation. "Fine. He would have told me *after* the fact."

"Cleo discovered Marta was being held in the Convent of the Sacred Mother down off the coast of the Tyrrhenian Sea. She convinced Dante to take a team in and rescue Marta and others." Lysander shook his head as if he still had trouble believing what had happened. "Dante had been working on a similar plan because the daughter of the woman Ignacio killed today was a prisoner in the convent as well. They pretty much laid waste to the place. They only lost one team member in the raid."

"*Jupiter's Stone*. Nicostratus had to have been furious and eager for revenge. With Ignacio's delivery of the *Tyet of Isis* document, the *bastardo* must have struck the Rome installation because he believes he's invincible." Atia bit down on her lip for a brief moment as she tried to figure out how she could use this information to her advantage.

"You know I'm not letting you go alone, don't you?"

"What are you talking about?" she asked with a shake of her head, trying to hide how he'd caught her by surprise.

"I heard you talking with Ignacio, and if you think I'm letting you do this without an escort, you're mistaken." The black patch on Lysander's face only intensified the hard, unflinching look of his one eye. Resigned to the fact that he'd heard her conversation, she shook her head.

"There's no point in you risking your life," she said.

"I disagree. It's my job to protect you, and I owe Cleo big-time for saving Marta," he said quietly. "And if he has the *Tyet of Isis* document like you think, then I'd say he *is* in a very powerful position."

"But he doesn't have *you*, which is why you can't go with me," she said in an emphatic voice as she gestured toward him. "I truly believe you'll recognize one or more of the standard positions in the document's message. We can't risk it."

"You know me well enough that I'll tell that son of a bitch nothing." His green eye was a hard emerald in the moonlight. The taut line of his mouth stretched his scarred features into a vicious mask. "This is one argument you're not going to win, Atia. If you refuse to listen, then I'll wake up Marcus, and we'll see exactly how far you get with this scheme of yours."

"Don't you dare threaten me, Lysander Condellaire," she snapped.

"It's not a threat," he said in a quiet, unrelenting voice. "I'm not coming just because I'm your *Celeris*. I've got a personal stake in this, too. Cleo is the closest thing to a sister I have, and I also have a score to settle with Nicostratus."

"And what if that *bastardo* settles the score first? What about Phaedra? You're willing to leave her alone after everything the two of you have been through?"

Lysander didn't say anything for a moment before he rejected her question with a firm shake of his head. "Phadera's known since that night in the Pantheon that I would eventually have to settle the score with Nicostratus. She'll understand."

"You're a stubborn fool," Atia said with a harsh sound of disgust.

"So Phaedra keeps telling me," he said ironically, his mouth curled in a slight smile.

Atia uttered a soft oath of frustration and angrily turned away from him. How in Juno's name did Phaedra put up with the man's stubborn streak? A soft chirp sounded in her pants pocket, and she froze. Ignacio.

The only reason he could be calling back so quickly was that Nicostratus had said no. Her heart contracted with fear before it started to race at a frightening speed. Slowly, her hand slid into her pocket and pulled out her cell phone. It continued to ring as she stared at it in silence. After the fourth chirp, she lightly tapped the screen to answer the call.

"Yes."

"The Patriarch has agreed to your request." Ignacio's formal tone was an excellent indicator that Nicostratus was standing close by. The concern she'd heard earlier in Ignacio's voice had been replaced by a flat tone that revealed no emotion at all. "You're to come alone."

"Am I?" She couldn't help the small laugh of sarcasm. "Tell Nicostratus he's a fool if he thinks I'm coming alone. My new *Celeris*, Lysander, will be there just to ensure your Patriarch sticks to his side of the bargain."

"Very well." Ignacio's stilted response made it obvious he wasn't about to relay her every word to Nicostratus. "Meet us at the top of the Tarpeian Rock in an hour."

"*What?* He's not going to torture me to learn all the Order's secrets? No, he has you for that, doesn't he?" She paused to let her sarcastic accusation sink in. "The Tarpeian Rock? At least the *bastardo* hasn't lost his twisted sense of humor. I'll be there."

Atia grimaced as she tapped the phone to end the call. The Tarpeian Rock was where criminals of ancient Rome had been thrown to their deaths as a punishment for their crimes. At least she knew how Nicostratus intended to execute her. And she had no doubt that she would be dead by sunrise, despite Lysander's determination not to let anything happen to her. Her mouth dry with fear, she met the gaze of her *Celeris* serenely, although she was far from calm inside.

"We're to meet them at the top of the Tarpeian Rock in an hour," she said quietly.

"Why in Juno's name would he pick that place?"

"You said you heard my conversation with Ignacio."

"Obviously not the whole thing," he growled. "What the fuck did you promise him?"

"My life for Cleo's."

Lysander stared at her, speechless. She turned away from him, afraid she wouldn't be able to keep her composure in the face of his horrified expression. And she was definitely having trouble maintaining her usual unflappable manner. She wasn't afraid to die, as long as she knew Cleo was safe and out of Praetorian hands. Nothing else was important. Saving Cleo was all that mattered now.

Chapter 25

ATIA'S cold words were still ringing in Ignacio's ear almost an hour later as he sat beside Cleo on the way to the Tarpeian Rock. Although he had no one to blame but himself, the loathing in Atia's voice had cut him to the core. What did he expect? The man she'd known for almost thirty years had betrayed her. His gaze shifted toward Cleo, sitting scrunched up in the far corner of the backseat. Her body language said she wanted to put as much distance between them as possible.

Ignacio turned his head to look out the car window. How was he supposed to explain that he hadn't meant for any of this to happen? A part of him had always hoped he wouldn't ever have to betray their trust. He'd thought being Nicostratus's spy would be easy. He hadn't counted on loving the enemy.

He'd built a life for himself with Atia and Cleo. He loved them both, and the fact that he'd used Cleo as a shield in his efforts to escape Condellaire was something Ignacio would never forgive himself for. He'd panicked. The moment Cleo had realized he'd betrayed them, her expression of horror and disgust had nearly ripped his heart out. His gaze flickered back in her direction.

"I'm sorry." He wasn't sure she'd heard his apology until she slowly turned her head toward him.

"Go fuck yourself, Praetorian." Her response made him grow cold.

"I don't expect you to understand. I didn't mean for any of this to happen."

"You're a spy and a traitor," she bit out in a detached voice. "Now do me a favor and shut the fuck up. I don't care that you might be feeling a bit guilty. Although it would surprise me if you were even capable of remorse."

"You're like a daughter—"

"Don't you *even* go there, you *bastardo*." Cleo almost shouted the command, and the Praetorian in the front passenger seat turned around. Ignacio gestured for him to ignore what was happening in the backseat. Leaning forward, he closed the glass window separating the front and rear seats.

"I panicked, Cleo. I wouldn't have taken you hostage if I'd been thinking right. I should have just forgotten about the ring, but I couldn't."

"Ask me if I care."

"I know you do," he said with a crack in his voice. He knew exactly what she was thinking at the moment. She was hurting, and he was responsible. "If you didn't care, you wouldn't be so angry with me right now."

"Don't flatter yourself. And you can't care too much, since you turned me over to Nicostratus."

"It's not like that."

"Truthfully, I don't give a fuck. So why don't you just shut up and leave me be."

Ignacio turned away from her, and closed his eyes. There had to be a way out of this. Somehow he would find a way. . . he immediately closed off his thoughts. He was so used to being in Sicari company, he'd forgotten that he needed to shield his mind from other Praetorians. Nicostratus had spies everywhere. He needed to remember that.

The car came to a sharp halt, throwing him and Cleopatra forward. His gut knotted up with a tension that hurt. They'd reached the Tarpeian Rock a lot faster than he'd expected. He looked over at Cleo, and as if aware of his gaze, she turned her head. The hate in her eyes sickened him. Without a word, he got out of the car, and walked around to open the door for her. As Cleo stepped out of the vehicle, she jerked away from his touch.

"Don't touch me, you sorry fuck."

Nicostratus had just gotten out of the other car, and heard Cleo's harsh comment. The Patriarch joined them with a smirk on his face.

"Is the bitch giving you trouble, Firmani?"

"No, Excellency." Ignacio shook his head.

"How unfortunate. It might be quite pleasant disciplining her."

"Who knew the Collegium's Patriarch is into kink," Cleo sneered. "The next thing you know someone is going to tell me how much he loves sucking cock."

The minute Cleo's crude comment rent the air, Nicostratus went white with fury. In a flash of movement, the Patriarch closed the distance between him and Cleo and slapped her hard. The blow wasn't so much a surprise as the strength of it.

Cleo could have sworn a fucking hammer had slammed into her jaw as her head jerked to the side from the blow Nicostratus delivered to her face. Who knew the Patriarch didn't have a sense of humor? If her hands hadn't been bound at her wrists, she would have slugged the *bastardo*. Instead, she had to settle for glaring at his back as he walked away from the vehicle she was standing next to.

The soft thud of a car door made her jump. It was a vivid reminder of how she'd been hustled in and out of a Praetorian vehicle twice now in less than twenty-four hours. The first time had been at the Sicari installation when Ignacio had used her as a human shield. After throwing her into a car, he'd remained silent the entire time she'd blasted him with her angry words.

When they'd arrived at the Collegium's complex, he'd given an order she couldn't make out then walked away without looking back. For some reason, that action hurt even more than finding out he was a traitor. Furious, she'd decked both of her guards before three more showed up to knock her senseless.

She'd woken up in a windowless room that she'd assumed was a novitiate's cell. She'd paced the floor for several hours before logic reminded her she needed sleep if she wanted to capitalize on any escape opportunity. Although it had been difficult, she'd napped on and off for several hours. It wasn't much rest, but it was better than nothing.

At least she'd been able to remain standing as Ignacio had just stood by and allowed the Patriarch to slug her. Obviously, Nicostratus hadn't appreciated the reminder that he'd gotten his ass kicked at the Pantheon a few weeks ago. The coppery taste of blood ran over her tongue, and she spit it out on the ground.

"Praetorian asshole," she muttered. Nicostratus whirled around and started to close the distance between them, his fury twisting his features into a hideous mask. To her surprise, Ignacio immediately stepped in front of her.

"Excellency, she's no good to us if she's dead."

Looking over Ignacio's shoulder, Cleo saw Nicostratus study her with a malevolent expression before he smiled. The feral look on his face sent an icy chill down her spine in spite of the hate boiling inside of her. The *bastardo* was plotting something, and she knew she wasn't going to like it. After a moment, Nicostratus nodded and turned away again to head up the steep path in front of them. Wheeling about on his heel, Ignacio glared at her.

"Goddamnit, Cleo. Keep your mouth shut. I'm trying to keep you alive," he whispered.

"Don't do me any favors, you fucking traitor," she mumbled.

"*Christus*, you're as stubborn as your mother." Ignacio grabbed her arm and forced her to walk beside him as they followed Nicostratus.

"Don't you *dare* mention my mother. If anyone trusted you more than me, it was her." She spat more blood out of her mouth. Sweet Vesta, for an old man, the Patriarch had one hell of a punch. "Where are we going?"

Ignacio grunted something she didn't hear, and she stumbled on the rocky path.

Behind them six Praetorians followed. She overheard one of the men say the name Alessandro, and ice immediately coated her skin. Whatever Nicostratus had planned, if he was bringing a Praetorian Dominus along, it wasn't going to be pleasant. She glanced around her trying to figure out exactly where they were. Despite the brightness of the moon, it was still dark with all the trees shrouding the path. As they trudged upward, she recognized something familiar about the place, but she couldn't pin down what it was.

Cleo stumbled again, and Ignacio caught her and set her upright. She jerked away from him with a vicious tug, her eyes meeting his. There was a sorrow there that tried to chip away at the layer of granite she'd encased her heart in. Not a chance in hell she was going to let him fool her again. She'd had a lot to think about in that tiny room at the Collegium. Ignacio's betrayal made her mother's lie about Marcus pale in comparison.

Her mother had been trying to protect her. Ignacio had simply been using them. Worse, the fucking *bastardo* had killed a good woman. When Cornelia had sagged against Ignacio's sword, Cleo had known she was beyond a healer's touch. She'd seen the life flicker out of Cornelia's eyes just before she'd looked in Dante's direction. The anguish on his face made it clear that he'd done the one thing Cleo was afraid he would do. He'd chosen to protect her rather than think of the safety of others on his team. It had been a terrible moment for her.

An image of Dante filled her head. *Deus*, how had she fallen in love with a Sicari Lord? She didn't know whether to laugh or cry at the thought. The chill layering her skin eased when she remembered his thoughts entwined with hers as Ignacio and his henchmen had taken her away. Cleo knew he'd come looking for her, but she was certain he was going to be too late. It would be better that way. She didn't want to see anyone else die because of her.

The path they were on gave way to a plateau sparsely littered with trees and bushes. The moment she entered the area, she knew exactly where they were. The *bastardo* was going to throw her off the Tarpeian Rock like an ancient Roman criminal. Her gaze flitted around her as she tried to find some method of escape.

There wasn't one. What was it Ignacio said? He was trying to save her life? If this was what he had in mind, it wasn't much of a plan as far as she was concerned. The only way out was the path behind her. With her bound wrists, she'd find it damned difficult to get past five Praetorians and one Praetorian Dominus.

Then there was the Praetorian next to Nicostratus. The Patriarch turned his head and addressed the man as Draco. For some reason, she found it amusing that a dragon was guarding the Patriarch. A sound from the far left made her turn her head, and despite her attempt not to react, she gasped. Across the small distance between them, she met her mother's gaze.

The relief on Atia's face was plainly evident, and when Cleo saw Lysander emerge from the darkness, her heart skipped a beat as she looked for Dante to follow him. Several seconds passed, and her heart sank as she realized he wasn't with them, but then neither was Marcus. It didn't make any sense. The tension in the air was heavy, and Cleo jerked her gaze toward Nicostratus. The *bastardo* looked like he'd just won the lottery.

"What are you doing here, Mother?" Cleo called out as she continued to study Nicostratus. The Patriarch sensed her gaze and turned his head toward her.

"It's quite heroic, really," he said with a beguiling smile. "Atia has agreed to be traded for you."

"*What?*" She snapped her head back toward her mother to stare at Atia in horror. "Are you insane?"

"You might be an adult, Cleopatra, but I'm still your mother *and* the *Prima Consul*. Show me the respect I've earned." The sharp words made Cleo wince as she stared helplessly at her mother. The harsh look on Atia's face eased, and Cleo felt a soft, invisible stroke on her cheek. For the first time, Cleo realized where her mother's rare telekinetic ability had come from. Bonding with Marcus had given Atia an ability that few Sicari women possessed. The touch immediately made tears well in her eyes, and Cleo blinked hard to prevent them from falling.

"I'm delighted to see you, Lysander." The Patriarch smiled at the scarred Sicari fighter, and Cleo could have sworn there was a look of real pleasure on the Praetorian's face.

"I can't say the same," Lysander replied in an icy voice.

"Why don't we stop playing games, Nicostratus," Atia said with a steely calm that seemed to impress even the Patriarch. "I came as agreed. Let my daughter leave with Lysander and I'll remain."

"No. I won't let you do this, Mother." Cleo shook her head as panic swept through her.

"It's all right, *carissima*. I know what I'm doing."

"No. You don't. This fucking *bastardo* is going to kill you."

Cleo took a step toward her mother only to have Ignacio hold her back. She sent him a blistering look of hate over her shoulder, and he immediately released her. Stumbling forward, she reached her mother in just a few steps as Atia met her halfway. Enveloped in her mother's warm hug, Cleo buried her face in Atia's shoulder and fought back tears.

"It's all right, *bambina*. I'm here now. Everything is going to be all right." Her mother's voice was soft and loving in Cleo's ear as Atia held her tight.

When Cleo lifted her head, a dark rage swept across her mother's face as she gently touched Cleo's bruises.

"Who hit her?" Atia directed a harsh look at Nicostratus.

"She had trouble getting out of the car." The Patriarch's answer made Cleo shoot him an angry look over her shoulder before she returned her attention to Atia.

"Please don't do this, Mother," Cleo pleaded. "You're more valuable to the Order than I am. I'm not even Sicari."

"Not Sicari?" Atia's appalled expression made Cleo wince. "Don't be ridiculous. You were always too sensitive about your abilities. Your heart is more Sicari than you realize. Only a Sicari would have risked so much to save Marta or relieve Lysander of the guilt he's carried ever since Marta was taken on his watch. I have never been so proud of you as I am now."

At her mother's words, Cleo's fight to hold back her tears weakened considerably, and a tear slid down her cheek. She gulped back more tears as her mother gently brushed the teardrop from her face. Love glistened in Atia's eyes as she steadily met Cleo's gaze.

"I couldn't save your brother, *carissima*, but I can save you."

"I don't want to be saved," Cleo snapped as fear clawed its way through her. "I want you to get out of here. Now."

"My mind is made up, Cleopatra."

She sucked in a sharp breath. Her mother never used her whole name unless she was determined to have her way. Cleo met Lysander's gaze over the top of her mother's head. Her friend's expression was grim as he shook his head slowly. Obviously, Lysander had fought this same battle and lost just like her.

"I grow weary of this emotional display. Either your daughter leaves or I'll execute you both," Nicostratus said in an impatient voice.

Atia pinned him with an icy look before returning her gaze to Cleo's. The warmth in her mother's eyes made Cleo's heart twist with a grief that had already spread through her body until she ached. The pain in her jaw was nothing compared to the pain of saying good-bye to her mother.

"I love you, Mother." She whispered the words, and Atia kissed Cleo on both cheeks.

"Not half as much as I love you, *bambina*," Atia whispered as she stepped to one side and gently pushed Cleo toward Lysander. "Go on now. Lysander will take you home."

Her gaze fixed on her mother, Cleo moved toward her friend, her heart breaking with each step she took. When she reached Lysander, he enveloped her in a bear hug that hardly eased the sorrow numbing her body.

"Don't give up hope just yet, Cleo," her friend murmured in her ear. "Have a little faith."

Cleo raised her head to see Lysander's look of determination. His black eye patch emphasized the white scars covering half of his face, his skin pulled tight with tension. There was a reflection of something else in his green eye that made her take heart. Had he planned something, or was he simply trying to ease her pain? She shook her head as he pulled a knife from his boot and cut the rope binding her hands together.

"I confess I never thought I'd have the pleasure of seeing the Order's most prestigious member come before me without so much as a sigh of resistance."

As Nicostratus's gloating words drifted through the air, Cleo jerked away from Lysander and turned to see her mother standing in front of the Patriarch. There was a fierce, proud look about Atia that filled Cleo's heart with admiration at the courage her mother was showing in the face of Nicostratus's gleeful triumph.

"Shall we get this over with?" Atia said coolly. "I grow weary of your games."

"As you wish." Nicostratus turned his head toward Ignacio. "You shall do the honors, Firmani, since you arranged this little gathering."

Cleo saw a haunted look flit across Ignacio's face at the order, and he didn't move. The Patriarch frowned as he nodded his head in the direction of Atia. For a moment, Cleo thought Ignacio would refuse the order, but he didn't. His expression devoid of emotion, he walked toward Atia, and the moment her mother instinctively cringed backward, Cleo started forward. She didn't get far, as Lysander's fingers dug into her shoulder.

"Patience," he whispered.

She glanced up at him and froze at the hint of satisfaction on his face. A second later, a familiar tendril of emotion wound its way through her thoughts, caressing her with a tenderness that made her heart swell with what she knew was a dangerous emotion.

"*I told you I'd find you, dolce cuore.*"

"*So what took you so long?*" She buried her vulnerability deep, unwilling to accept what her heart was telling her. When Dante didn't respond to her sarcasm, fear suddenly gripped her that she'd dreamed his voice in her head.

Behind her there was the soft sound of rock crumbling as someone approached the clearing. She turned her head toward the noise to see Marcus and Dante emerge from the trees. In a split second the area exploded with oaths and the loud whisper of swords drawn from leather sheaths.

"You deceitful Sicari bitch," Nicostratus roared with fury as he pulled his sword and swung it at Atia. With a cry of horror, Cleo leaped forward. Before she even reached her mother, Ignacio's sword stopped Nicostratus's blade from touching Atia.

The surprise on the Patriarch's face instantly twisted into one of murderous rage, and with a quick feint, Nicostratus tricked Ignacio into leaving his chest vulnerable to the other man's blade. In a single thrust, the Patriarch drove his sword home. As Cleo reached Atia, Lysander passed them in a blinding flash of speed to confront Nicostratus.

The sudden clash of swords exploded in the clearing as she tried to pull her mother clear of the combat. Atia viciously jerked free of Cleo's grasp and scrambled forward to pull Ignacio away from the fighting.

"Jupiter's Stone, Mother. I need to get you out of here."

"Not yet," Atia snapped as she bent over her old friend.

Conflicting emotions lashed through her as she watched her mother kneel beside Ignacio and take his hand. A part of her wanted to kill the man where he lay, but another part of her wanted to cry because he was dying. She quickly picked up Ignacio's sword then circled her mother to kneel at her mentor's side, making sure she had a clear view of the fighting. Ignacio grabbed her arm with his hand, and she looked down at him.

"Forgive me," he rasped. The plea tore at her heart, but she shook her head.

"No. What you did was unforgiveable," she whispered. "You made me think you loved us. I can't forgive that."

"I do . . . love you." Ignacio coughed hard for a moment, and a trickle of blood flowed from his mouth as his breathing grew labored. "I love both of you. But he . . . took you away from me. There was . . . nothing left for me."

His gaze shifted to Atia's, and he lifted his hand to touch her face. With a sorrowful expression, Atia took his hand in hers and gently stroked his sweating forehead.

"You saved my life, old friend. Thank you for that."

"Would do it . . . again," he murmured. "Would do it . . ."

Ignacio's voice died away as his head lolled to the side, and Atia released a small cry of grief. Dante's familiar thoughts mingled with Cleo's in a frantic warning. She immediately jerked her gaze up and saw one of the Praetorians charging toward her and her mother. Cleo was on her feet in one fluid movement, the sword she held scraping against the Praetorian's blade as she stopped his weapon from cutting Atia in two.

The awkwardness of her position prevented her from pushing the other fighter back, and his gloating smile irritated the hell out of her as she fought to keep her balance. The Praetorian's smile vanished as Atia's foot plowed into the middle of his crotch. With a grunt of pain, the fighter clutched at his groin, and Cleo twisted her sword against his. Her weapon circled the Praetorian's in a swift move that disarmed the fighter. Not waiting for him to recover, Cleo was behind him with the tip of her sword pressing into the back of his neck.

"You are beaten, Praetorian, and I must ask your forgiveness. Do you give it?" Cleo bit out then waited for the man's reply.

When he muttered a harsh no, she bit down on the inside of her cheek and drove the sword straight down, killing the Praetorian instantly. As the man crumpled to the ground, Atia called out a warning, and Cleo whirled around prepared to fight off another Praetorian.

"Fuck," she snapped as she saw two Praetorians charging toward her.

The first one to reach her nearly took her head off, but she dropped and rolled past the fighter. As she came up in a swift spring-board movement, her mouth gaped open as the second Praetorian ran his sword through the other fighter. As the Praetorian turned toward her, she recognized him as the man called Draco. Her savior didn't speak. He simply bowed slightly and offered her a small smile before he ran off to help Marcus and Dante, who were fighting the remaining three Praetorians and the Dominus.

Cleo whirled around as Atia called her name and saw her mother pointing to where Lysander was battling Nicostratus. She took a quick step forward only to halt as she saw the Patriarch leave his guard open and Lysander strike the man a blow that left Nicostratus with a useless arm.

Not about to interfere with Lysander's personal demons, she turned toward the other battle raging a short distance away. The sight of Draco deflecting a Praetorian sword aimed for her father's back made her want to hug the man before she questioned her sanity for wanting to hug a Praetorian. When she saw Marcus falter slightly, she knew it was from surprise. The Sicari Lord barely gave Draco a nod of thanks before he launched a new attack on his Praetorian opponent.

As the Praetorian crossed swords with Marcus, the man thrust out his free hand and sent Draco flying backward. She grimaced.

The Praetorian Dominus. Her gaze flitted toward Dante, who was battling the remaining three fighters by himself. He fended off one vicious attack while leaping up into the air and landing a powerful kick to the side of another fighter's head. In the process, the third Praetorian sliced into Dante's back. She heard him grunt with pain before he whirled about to strike out at his attacker.

Fear snaked through Cleo, and she raced forward to throw herself into the fray. Her sword clanged loudly against a Praetorian blade meant for Dante's neck as she prevented the weapon from doing any damage. Clearly surprised by her attack, the fighter turned his head toward her.

"Time to die, bitch," he growled fiercely.

"Not today, asshole." Her sword raised to shoulder level, Cleo smiled and gestured at the Praetorian to attack. Inside her head, she felt the touch of Dante's thoughts mix with hers.

"*Christus, Cleopatra, will you get the fuck out of here? I can handle these* bastardi." His mental order was a vivid reminder of the argument they'd had about her going to the Sicari installation.

"*Sure you can, and if I hadn't stepped in to help, you'd be headless right now.*" She didn't bother to hide her contempt for his command as she countered the Praetorian's oncoming blade then slammed her free hand into the man's throat.

"*Goddamnit, Cleopatra. Get out of here now. That's an order.*"

His thoughts were easy to ignore, as she was caught by surprise when the Praetorian she was fighting recovered from her blow faster than she expected. Gritting her teeth, she jammed the bottom of her foot into the Praetorian's knee and heard a loud crack.

"*Just because we slept together, Dante Condellaire, doesn't give you the right to tell me what to do.*" Her sword crashed against the Praetorian's who was struggling to stand. "*Now get the fuck out of my head and let me do my job.*"

Closing her thoughts off to everything but the task at hand, Cleo danced to the right to avoid the Praetorian sword heading directly for her chest. Spinning about on her heel, she ended up behind the Praetorian and dragged her sword across the back of his leg. Her blade left a deep cut that severed the fighter's leg muscles, and he crumpled to the ground. With the tip of her sword against his throat, she saw the look of resignation on his face. This time when she asked forgiveness, her opponent granted it to her.

A quick glance in her father's direction showed that Draco was hurt but standing, while Marcus had the Dominus on the defensive. To her far right, she saw Lysander locked in close combat with Nicostratus. As she watched, she saw Nicostratus sink to his knees, and a moment later Lysander executed the Patriarch. The loud grunt of pain behind her made her whirl back around to Dante.

Of the three Praetorians Dante had been fighting, only one was still standing. Her relief was short-lived as she saw Dante fly backward several feet without the Praetorian touching him. *Deus*, another Dominus. She'd thought there was only one.

Her heart sank to the pit of her stomach as she watched Dante regain his balance then circle the Praetorian with a wary expression on his face. She could tell they were equally matched, but the idea of something happening to Dante scared the hell out of her.

"*Goddamnit, Cleopatra, I'm not going to tell you again. Get back.*"

She didn't answer his mental command. Instead, she remained rooted to the spot she was in, feeling more helpless than she'd ever felt in her life. A moment later, Cleo's mouth went dry as the Dominus sent Dante flying backward and into the trunk of a nearby tree. Before Dante could recover, the Dominus leaped forward to send his sword biting into Dante's arm. Grunting with pain, Dante countered with a strike of his own, but his sword missed the other man's chest by a mere inch. As the Dominus jumped out of range of Dante's weapon, he jerked his head in Cleopatra's direction.

"Cleopatra, is it?" The Dominus eyed her with cold amusement. A cruel smile slowly curled the man's lips as he looked back at Dante. "It appears you have a weakness, Sicari."

Dante didn't answer the man. He simply threw his sword up into the air, and it whistled toward the Dominus. The Praetorian easily countered the weapon's hard blows as Dante controlled the sword with his telekinetic ability. The Dominus snarled with anger as he battled Dante's weapon, giving Dante enough time to throw himself forward in a tight somersault to slam his body into the other fighter's legs.

Caught by surprise, the Dominus stumbled and fell onto his back. As he hit the ground, the Praetorian's sword clashed with Dante's. The force of the Dominus's blade sent Dante's sword spinning away until it slammed into the ground, the weapon quivering wildly. Dante was on his feet in a split second, but in a blurring flash of movement, the Dominus arched his back and flipped himself backward and onto his feet.

Cleo swallowed hard as she saw Dante extend his hand for his sword. The weapon barely moved, and panic coiled in her stomach. *Christus*, he'd expended most of his telekinetic energy. Without a second thought, she raced toward the weapon, ignoring Dante's command to stay back. Her senses heightened, she knew the Dominus was close on her heels.

The moment her hand wrapped around the warm grip of Dante's sword, she tugged it from the ground. All too aware of the Praetorian heading straight toward her, she threw her body into the air in a horizontal roll that landed her on her feet and facing both men.

Effortlessly, she threw Dante's sword to him while preparing to fight the Praetorian. The Dominus stopped the minute she lifted her sword. A malicious sneer on his face, he snorted with dark laughter then extended his hand in a sharp gesture. The air whooshed out of Cleo's lungs as an invisible force crashed into her chest. She was certain an elephant sitting on top of her couldn't have been any more painful as she hit the ground hard.

A loud oath from Dante pulled her out of the pain, and she jerked her gaze to see him attacking the Dominus with one vicious blow after another. Surprised by the strength of Dante's attack, the Praetorian retreated several steps. As Cleo staggered to her feet and stumbled forward, she saw the Dominus find an opening in Dante's defensive stance.

His smile vicious, the Dominus drove his sword into Dante's thigh. As Dante released a growl of pain, the Dominus twisted his blade in the wound, forcing Dante to his knees. With his free hand, the Praetorian landed a hard punch to Dante's jaw, and Cleo watched in horror as Dante hit the ground. Adrenaline pumped through her body as she blocked out her pain and ran forward.

The Dominus jerked his sword out of Dante's leg, and just as he thrust downward, Cleo threw herself in front of Dante. Both men were surprised by her action, and as her back pressed Dante into the ground, she glared up at the Praetorian as his sword pierced her shoulder.

"Fuck," she cried out in renewed pain before anger ripped through her. "You are *really* beginning to piss me off, asshole."

Her fury added force to the kick she landed in the Dominus's crotch. The minute he bent forward in pain, Cleo rammed her sword up into the man's chest, straight through his heart. Astonishment forced the Praetorian's mouth open in surprise before the light in his eyes flickered out. As he fell forward, Cleo used both feet to push him away from her and withdraw her sword at the same time.

The daggerlike pain in her chest renewed with each breath she tried to take. *Christus*, the *bastardo* must have driven one of her ribs into a lung. She rolled off Dante to curl up on the ground and tried to control the pain battering her body. Her shoulder was on fire, while a tight band had wrapped itself around her chest, making it difficult to breathe.

A strong hand gently rolled her onto her back, and she moaned as pain spread its way into every inch of her body. Anguish, and a small bit of anger, darkened Dante's features as he bent over her.

Was the anger in his gaze for the Praetorian or her?

Cleo wasn't sure she wanted to know, because if he was angry at her, the last thing she could handle at the moment was an argument. Besides, she'd done what any Sicari would do. She'd protected the heir to the Sicari Lord title. It wasn't just that. She'd been willing to give her life for him because she loved him. With a sigh, she closed her eyes. *Deus*, she was a fool.

Chapter 26

AS Cleopatra's eyes fluttered shut, panic became a red-hot iron burning its way into Dante's chest. A quick examination of her shoulder wound showed she was in no danger from the injury, but he couldn't find any other open wounds on her. That worried the hell out of him as he recalled how the Praetorian Dominus had sent her flying through the air like a sack of flour. The sound of her harsh wheezing made his gut knot up with fear. She probably had several broken ribs, and if one had punctured a lung, it would account for her difficulty breathing. Even worse, she could have a lacerated liver.

"Goddamnit, Cleopatra, why didn't you listen to me?"

"Instead of yelling at me, do you think maybe you could say thank you?" she rasped. Her eyes were still closed, but relief swept through him at the obvious irritation in her voice. He gently probed her side, and pain slashed across her beautiful face. "Fuck a Praetorian. Are you trying to break another one of my ribs?"

"Stop complaining," he bit out. "I told you to stay out of it, but you didn't listen, did you?"

"You're welcome," she said with a cough, and the sarcasm in

her voice made it clear she wasn't happy he'd not acknowledged her sacrifice.

"Thank you," he growled.

Dante didn't need a reminder that she'd saved his life. She'd almost gotten herself killed doing it. And if he didn't get her to a healer, she still might. From the way she'd just responded to his touch, there was a strong possibility she had some internal bleeding. A shadow blocked out the moonlight shining on Cleopatra's face as Atia reached them and knelt at her daughter's side. The *Prima Consul* carried Cleopatra's hand to her cheek.

"*Carissima*, what were you thinking?" she breathed as she stared down at her daughter. With her free hand, she brushed her fingertips across Cleopatra's pale cheek and met Dante's gaze. "I saw what the Dominus did to her."

"I'll be . . . all right." Cleopatra coughed hard as she squeezed her mother's hand. "I'm . . . sorry, Mother."

"Hush, *bambina*. I'm the one who's sorry." Atia pressed her mouth to the back of her daughter's hand. "I should have told you about your father a long time ago."

Another cough wracked Cleopatra's frame, and a look of fear flashed in Atia's gray eyes as she met Dante's gaze. He shook his head.

"She's going to be fine. I just need to get her to Noemi. I'm pretty sure she has some broken ribs and possibly a punctured lung," Dante rasped. He glanced down at Cleopatra, who opened her eyes to look up at him. He grimaced.

"I'm not dying," she wheezed. "Now help me get up so I can walk to the car."

"You're not walking."

"And I suppose you're going to carry me on that sliced-up leg of yours?" Another coughing spasm made her face twist in pain. Dante swallowed the knot of fear lodged in his throat.

"*Just shut the fuck up*, and let *me* worry about my leg," he snapped viciously.

He ignored Atia's expression of astonishment as he got to his feet. The pain in his thigh was excruciating, but he knew he could get down the hill with her in his arms. Another shadow appeared over his shoulder, and he glanced up to see Marcus as well as the Praetorian called Draco join the circle around Cleopatra. Both men were bleeding, but they were still standing. Behind them was the body of the Dominus, Alessandro. He barely acknowledged either man as he bent over to lift Cleopatra up. Lysander suddenly appeared next to Atia and gently pushed the *Prima Consul* aside.

"Here, let me carry her." A single green eye met his gaze, and Dante glared at him.

"*I'll* do it," Dante rasped. His half brother arched his eyebrow slightly as he stared at him for a long, drawn-out second then nodded.

"Okay, but at least let me help you get her up off the ground," Lysander said quietly.

It was an offer Dante was more than willing to accept, as he'd known picking Cleopatra up would have put even more stress on his leg. With an abrupt nod, he straightened and watched as his brother carefully lifted Cleopatra up off the ground.

She cried out in pain, and Dante quickly stepped forward to gently take her from Lysander. As he turned to carry Cleopatra to the car, Dante met Marcus's astute gaze. It was easy to read the curiosity in his mentor's eyes, and he didn't miss the Sicari Lord's quick look at his wife. Dante released a small oath beneath his breath and started down the hill, keeping his tread as steady as possible. Cleopatra moaned softly, and when he glanced down at her, she was staring up at him. The connection between them was as strong as ever, and he entwined his thoughts with hers.

"*Am I hurting you?*"

"*Not any more than someone else would. I could have walked, and I don't understand why you wouldn't let me.*"

"*Christus, you are one hardheaded woman.*"

"*And you'd be dead if I wasn't.*" The intensity of her annoyance swept through him like a wildfire as she closed her eyes again.

"*You're right. Thank you.*"

He kept his mental response gentle as he looked down at her. Cleopatra's expression softened with satisfaction. He had no doubt that if she'd not thrown herself between him and the Dominus, the Praetorian's sword would have sliced him open.

"*And you didn't think I was up to the task.*" Bitterness lightly tinged the thought, and he glanced down at her pale face.

"I didn't mean it like that."

"Shall I quote you?"

She coughed and her wheezing increased, but her emotional pain lashed at him like a whip. He clenched his jaw, knowing he was responsible for her mental anguish. A small dip in the ground made his stride jerky, and Cleopatra uttered a sharp cry. Remorse rolled through him, and he stopped for a moment.

"All I wanted was to keep you safe, dolce cuore. I love you."

The instant he shared his feelings, she shut herself off to him. Frustrated, he released a harsh sound of anger, and a tense silence settled between them as he carried her toward the car. It didn't take long for Lysander to catch up with him, and he helped get Cleopatra settled in the back of the SUV. When his brother offered to drive, Dante nodded and slid into the vehicle beside Cleopatra. As Lysander carefully shifted into gear, Dante saw Marcus and Atia hurrying to the other vehicle.

"Someone needs to call for some sweepers to clean up that mess," Dante said quietly.

"Marcus already took care of it."

"Good." His gaze fell to Cleopatra's lovely face, and he brushed a stray hair off her cheek.

"Cleo's like a sister to me."

Lysander's quiet statement made Dante look up into the rearview mirror. He stared into his brother's steely green gaze. It was clear Lysander was putting him on notice not to hurt Cleopatra. The sudden snort of laughter from Cleopatra followed by a spate of coughing and wheezing startled him.

"Tell the dumb bacciagalupe *that I don't need him protecting me."*

"She said she doesn't need you *or* me to protect her." He met Lysander's gaze in the mirror again, and his brother glared at him.

"I didn't hear her say anything."

There was an unspoken question in Lysander's observation that Dante didn't want to answer. Instead, he just shrugged and returned his gaze to Cleopatra. Her eyes were open, and she was staring up at him with an emotion that took his breath away before it vanished. Dante reached out to touch her cheek, but with a grimace of pain, she turned her head away from him. For the briefest of moments, he thought he heard her whispering something in his head, but it was too faint a thought for him to know what she'd said.

IT had been more than forty-eight hours since the battle at the Tarpeian Rock, and Dante was determined to settle things with Cleopatra. He was going to make the woman admit they belonged together. Dante quietly entered Cleopatra's apartment without knocking. She already knew he was here.

The closer he'd gotten to her suite, the stronger his senses had reacted to her close proximity. Her response had been equally strong, but by the time he reached her door she'd erected a mental shield between them.

He waited for her in silence. Seconds later, Cleopatra emerged from the bedroom. As always, she took his breath away. Her dark hair was a black cloud of silk that tumbled down over her shoulders. She was the most beautiful woman he'd ever seen.

Today she was dressed in blue jeans and a plain long-sleeved shirt. She'd rolled up the cuffs to expose her forearms, and although she looked completely relaxed, he knew she was anything but. A bird fluttering in its cage at the sight of a cat wasn't half as frantic as Cleopatra was at the moment. It was the only thing he could sense with the mental barrier she'd erected between them.

"How are you feeling?"

"I'm fine," she said in a cautious tone. "A little sore around the ribs. Noemi was weak, and I made her stop the *Curavi* when I knew I was able to finish healing on my own."

"Good," he said then immediately shook his head. "I mean I'm glad you're better. You took some hard knocks the other morning."

"I've had worse." She shrugged.

If he hadn't known her well enough, he would have missed the haunted look that flitted across her face. Just as quickly as it appeared, it was gone. In its place was a deep regret.

"I'm sorry about Cornelia."

The unexpected reference to his *Praefect* made him start, and he jerked his head to acknowledge her sympathy. "Thank you."

Cornelia's death was something he'd kept buried in the back of his mind for days now. His friend's *Rogalis* had been carried out the night after he'd brought Cleopatra home. As Tribune and her friend, he'd performed the duties of Orator, but his guilt had made the task almost unbearable.

"It wasn't your fault." Cleopatra's statement made him stiffen.

"You're wrong."

It was definitely his fault. In his efforts to keep Cleopatra safe, he'd interfered with Cornelia's attack. The death of his friend illustrated why he never should have taken Cleopatra with him that day. He'd lost a friend, and he'd almost lost the woman he loved.

"I'm not wrong," she replied sharply. "Cornelia made her own choice. She didn't obey your orders, and it got her killed."

"It's not that simple."

"Yes. It is." She narrowed her gaze at him. "You gave a command, and Cornelia chose to ignore it. You could just as easily blame me for her death."

Shocked by her declaration, he shook his head. "How in Jupiter's name could I blame you for Cornelia's death?"

"You said my lack of skills could get me killed. They didn't, but Cornelia's dead because I didn't have the ability to keep Ignacio from taking me hostage. Doesn't that make me responsible?"

"Sweet mother of Juno," he rasped. "I said that because an entire Sicari installation had just been wiped out. Fighters *with* skills were all dead. You could have had the skills of a goddamn Sicari Lord, and I still would have ordered you to stay behind. Taking you into a situation like that scared the hell out of me. The thought of losing you scared me even more."

Cleopatra didn't say anything, but her shield slipped slightly at his words. For a fleeting instant he caught a glimpse of her conflicted feelings. She quickly recovered to study him with an inscrutable gaze. He took a step toward her, and she immediately retreated. Fear gutted him. The gulf between them seemed to widen by the second, and he didn't know how to reach her.

"Damnit, say something," he demanded.

"Cornelia's death isn't any more your fault than it is mine. It wasn't my lack of abilities that made Ignacio betray the Order or kill Cornelia. Both of them chose their paths." She spiked one hand through her hair to sweep the black tresses off her face. "It was her time, and there wasn't anything you or I could have done to save her."

Dante closed his eyes for a moment as he tried to accept her rationale. Was it possible he was taking too much responsibility for what had happened? The memory of Firmani's sword against Cleopatra's neck created a knot in his throat. Up until that moment, he'd never hesitated before in battle. Not once.

But beyond that brief, indecisive instant, his response to the situation would have been the same no matter who Firmani had been holding hostage. He would never have sacrificed one of his team. That it had been Cleopatra in danger had destroyed his normal calm, but he would have made the same judgment call if it had been anyone else, and Cornelia would still be dead. The guilt he'd been carrying with him for days eased to a more bearable weight. His gaze focused on Cleopatra again, but she quickly glanced away.

"Is it true what Ignacio said?" Despite the curiosity in her voice, he recognized her question for the diversion tactic it was. "Is Lysander really your brother?"

"Half brother," he said with a nod. It was still a strange sensation to know he had family, and he could tell Lysander felt the same way. "We spent some time together yesterday talking."

"Lysander was the brother I never had growing up. He looked out for me."

"He still does." Dante's jaw tightened as he remembered Lysander grilling him about Cleopatra.

"*Christus*, he put you under the microscope, didn't he?"

"He tried." He allowed his mouth to curl in a slight smile. Lysander hadn't been happy when Dante had refused to answer any questions about Cleopatra. His half brother had finally let the matter go, but not without another warning.

"I can just imagine how *that* went," she muttered. "Lysander can be pretty intimidating when he wants."

"I managed to hold my own," he said in a wry tone. She flushed as if realizing her response had been less than complimentary.

"Sorry."

She bit down on her lip, and he knew her discomfort wasn't just because she'd inadvertently bruised his ego. Rigid with tension, she looked ready to bolt from the room the second she thought of an excuse to do so. If he didn't get to the heart of the matter soon, it would be harder than ever to find a way to settle things between them.

"We still have unfinished business between us." Dante narrowed his eyes at her then looked pointedly down at the carpet before lifting his gaze back to Cleopatra's face. She jumped slightly before she went still again.

"Do we?" she said in a careless tone that was a poor attempt to hide how nervous she was.

"Yes. We do." He cocked his head to the side to study her. Even though she'd shut herself off to him, it wasn't possible for her to keep all her emotions from seeping through the shield she'd put up. The anxiety flowing off her was almost tangible in the way it filled the space between them.

"I want to know where we go from here."

"*We* aren't going anywhere," she said in a terse manner.

"So you're willing to forget everything that happened." He noted how her violet gaze was turbulent with emotion.

"The *only* thing that happened was some great sex," she snapped, the tension in her ratcheting up another notch.

Relief and satisfaction swept through him at the words *great sex*. At least he hadn't completely embarrassed himself when it came to his initiation into the pleasures of lovemaking. More importantly, her entire demeanor convinced him that what they'd shared had shaken her deeply. For the first time since they'd met, her confidence was missing.

"Actually, I thought it was incredible, which is why we should do it again." He bit back a smile as her mouth fell open in shock. She recovered quickly with a vehement shake of her head.

"No. Not happening." Short and to the point, as always.

"So, I was nothing but a challenge to you?" His heart clenched at the sudden possibility he might be wrong about her.

"*No*," she exclaimed before bemusement clouded her face. "At first you were, but when you explained about . . . *it wasn't like that*, and you know it."

His fear subsided as he sensed the battle she waged inside her. The vulnerability she was struggling to hide made him love her even more.

"Then tell me what it *was* like." He reached out with his thoughts and traced an invisible trail along the inside of her bare arm. Cleopatra gasped, and this time he allowed himself a small smile of triumph.

"*Stop that*," she exclaimed.

"Stop what?"

He concentrated on the small indentation at the bottom of her throat, envisioning his mouth nibbling her there. The sharp breath she drew in signaled she was far from immune to him.

"Stop touching me," she snapped.

"I'm not touching you."

A small smile tipped one corner of his mouth upward. His invisible touch ran lightly across one breast straight to her nipple. Her body responded to the unseen caress despite her efforts not to show any reaction.

"I'm warning you, Dante Condellaire," she bit out as she fought the rising tide of desire surging its way through her body.

"You're fighting a losing battle, Cleopatra." Warmth enveloped her as his invisible touch skimmed across her skin and the top button of her shirt popped open. "I want you, and I know you want me, too."

The speed with which he moved startled her. One moment he was eyeing her like a tiger contemplating his next meal, and the next she was wrapped in his arms. The heat of him pressed its way through her clothes and into every pore in her body. A shudder wracked her as she saw the determination in his dark blue eyes just before he lowered his head and captured her mouth with his.

It was a hard kiss filled with passion and hunger. She recognized the same craving in herself. *Christus*, she should be trying to fight her way out of his arms. If she allowed this to continue, the situation was going to explode in her face. But her traitorous body refused to listen to what her brain was telling her, and she melted into him.

The heat inside her became a fire that streaked through her blood until it pushed its way into every fiber of her being. Reason abandoned her. Replacing it was a need so strong she was blind to anything except the hunger for his touch. Arms wrapped around his neck, she bit gently at his lower lip until he gave her access to his mouth.

Her tongue danced and swirled around his, intensifying the need that was pooling in a liquid warmth between her thighs. Strong hands gripped her hips and tugged her forward until his cock was nestled against her. A low moan rolled out of him as she shifted her body over his erection in a silent invitation.

He answered by cradling her bottom in his hands and lifting her upward. She immediately wrapped her legs around his waist as he carried her toward her bedroom. Caught up in a feverish passion, she hungrily laced the side of his neck with kisses and small nips at his skin with her teeth, while his warm, spicy scent flooded her nostrils.

She inhaled the delicious smell of him, breathing him in until he was a part of her. The mattress pressed into her thighs as he set her down on the bed then stepped back to pull his navy blue T-shirt up over his head.

Hard and muscular, he made her heart stop beating for a fraction of a second before it resumed at a faster pace. He was even more beautiful than she remembered. She reached to undo his jeans, but he caught her hands and carried them to his mouth. The touch seared her fingertips.

"Not yet, *carissima*." His unseen hands quickly undid her shirt and pushed it aside to reveal the dark red lace of her bra.

Pure lust flashed in his deep blue eyes as he stared down at her. *Deus*, if he continued to look at her like that, she was going to have an orgasm before he'd even thrust into her. Something primitive darkened his face, and she was certain he'd read her thoughts.

With an incoherent, guttural sound, he pushed her backward onto the bed to grab her jeans and pull them off her. His actions made her gasp in surprise, but it was the passionate hunger reflected on his face that caused her heart to pound wildly in her chest.

An unseen hand curled around her ankle then slowly slid upward over her leg. Tantalizing and exquisite in its unhurried pace, his invisible caress teased a soft cry from her as it glided over the silk of her panties. She'd never wanted a man's mouth on her so badly before. Hips arching upward, she pushed her panties downward until they tangled at her ankles. The image of him kissing her intimately filled her head, and a soft growl escaped him as his hands brushed across her belly.

"*Is that what you want,* dolce cuore? *My mouth on you?*" The unspoken question was a sinful pleasure that aroused her even more than if he'd uttered the words.

"*Sweet Vesta, yes.*"

"*Then show me what to do,* carissima. *Show me how to please you.*"

Her eyes closed as she visualized his mouth on her sex, his tongue stroking and swirling around the pulsating flesh between her slick folds. A mere second later, his mouth was doing exactly what she'd envisioned. Pleasure washed over her in waves as his intimate kisses made her writhe on the bed.

With each flick of his tongue he carried her to one rapturous peak after another until the intensity was so exquisite it pushed her into a place she'd never been before. The force of her orgasm was mind-numbing, and she arched upward with a sharp cry. Poised on the edge of a cloud, she tumbled downward until she lay spent on the bed, her breathing ragged.

Rough denim rubbed against her thighs, and she moaned as the heat of his mouth burned its way across her stomach and up to her breasts. His mouth suckled on a lace-covered nipple, and she whimpered with a renewed hunger. *Christus*, she couldn't get enough of him. His hair smelled of soap, and she spiked her fingers through the dark locks.

Unseen hands lifted her up slightly and undid her bra. An instant later, his teeth were lightly abrading her nipple, while he discarded the last bit of his clothing. The instant his rigid cock pressed into her stomach, a surge of desire raced through her limbs. Eager to touch him, she slipped her hand between their bodies to stroke his hard length.

He jerked at her touch, and a moment later his mouth was devouring hers with a hunger that matched her own. The muted taste of her essence was on his lips as his tongue tangled with hers, and the air instantly vanished from her lungs when he filled her completely with a hard thrust.

Her body clenched around him, rejoicing in the pleasure the joining gave her. Need spun a silky web over her body, holding her hostage as he lifted his head. Her senses reeled at the passion making his eyes dark and stormy. No man had ever looked at her like that before.

"You're in my blood, mea amor.*"* The thought brushed against her mind with the gentleness of a feather. *"You belong to me and no one else."*

She didn't have time to absorb the implication of his unspoken words as he withdrew from her slightly then thrust back into her. The action pulled a low groan from him, and she lifted her hips to welcome him again and again as he increased the speed of his strokes. The strength and power of him engulfed her as each of his thrusts pulled her toward a pinnacle she'd only visited with him.

Her body trembled against his as a wild stirring danced its way across her skin. It pulled her tight like a spring until her body clenched hard around him, and she clung to him as her orgasm made her arch toward him. Seconds later, a dark cry rolled out of his throat, and he thrust deep inside her one last time before his entire body rocked against hers as he climaxed.

He slumped forward, his face buried in her neck, and she reveled in the warmth of his strong body pressing into hers as the world slowly spun to a halt. The sultry heat settling in her limbs made her murmur a protest when he rolled away from her. A warm hand clutched hers, and she closed her eyes to savor the lingering pleasure caressing her body. *Deus,* the man was a quick learner. If possible, that had been even better than the first time.

"I have your wicked imagination for inspiration," he murmured as he read her thoughts.

"You have *no* idea," she said with a laugh as she visualized an erotic position they'd yet to try. A dark growl rumbled in his chest, and her body tingled at the possessive sound.

"We're going to have to do something about these naughty thoughts of yours." Dante rolled over on his side and grinned at her.

There was a relaxed, almost boyish look about him that made her stretch out her hand to touch the side of his face. Dante immediately turned his head to press a tender kiss in the palm of her hand.

It was a simple caress, but it frightened her. Dante didn't need her in his life. She would only complicate things for him. She'd seen what had happened when Ignacio had been holding a knife to her neck. Dante had hesitated, and it had cost him the life of his friend. She loved him too much to put him through that kind of hell again.

Quietly, his thoughts drifted across hers like a soft piece of silk. There was a deep intimacy about him reading her every thought and desire, and panic fluttered inside her as she realized how vulnerable she was. If she wasn't careful, he'd know the truth.

"Don't hide from me, Cleopatra." There was a dark intensity to his words that made her throat close up with fear. Her smile of ironic amusement was born from years of practice. She met his dark gaze.

"I'd hardly call this hiding from you." Cleo gestured at her naked body, and she saw the flash of desire in his eyes before he narrowed his gaze at her.

"You know damn well that's not what I meant."

"No, I don't," she lied.

"Then let me spell it out for you," he said fiercely. "I'm not going to let you run away from me."

"*Deus*, I am *not* running away." She scrambled off the bed to hunt for her clothes.

"You could've fooled me, because I think you're doing a damn good job of running from the truth."

"And what truth is that?" she snapped as she turned away to pull her panties on.

"That I love you. That we belong to together."

She froze. Fuck, the man just wasn't going to give up. Slowly she turned her head to glare at him over her shoulder.

"As I recall, we've already had this argument."

"No. You were trying to make a case for why I shouldn't love you."

"And I thought I did that pretty well," she said as she plunged her arms into the sleeves of her shirt.

"Did you? To my recollection your reasoning was that I couldn't love you because you can't have children and you aren't a true Sicari," he said quietly.

"Those are pretty good reasons if you ask me." Her fingers trembled as she shoved a button into the wrong buttonhole.

"No, they're not, but why bother pointing them out when all you had to do was say you didn't love me?"

Panic flashed through her, and she jerked around to stare at him. Something in his expression made her throat begin to close. She swallowed hard as a grim determination hardened his features.

"Then there's that stunt you pulled the other morning." The disapproving tone of his voice made her scowl at him.

"Stunt?" she snapped. "I was doing my job."

"Your job doesn't call for you to sacrifice yourself in order to save me." His midnight blue eyes locked with hers, and she could feel the color drain from her face as she saw the certainty in his gaze. She quickly tried to regroup.

"I saved you because you're the Sicari Lord. The *Absconditus* can't do without a leader," she lied as she turned away from him.

Before she could get too far away, he reached out and tugged her backward until he was holding her tight in his arms. Determination made his mouth a firm straight line. It said he intended to do whatever he could to make her admit the truth. One hand pressed into his muscular chest, she tried not to let her mental barrier drop as her body reacted to his.

Deus, she should have left for Chicago the morning after the battle at Tarpeian Rock. No. She should have found a different way to rescue Marta. She should have left here a long time ago. Before she fell in love with him. Before she gave him a chance to break her heart or destroy his ability to lead the *Absconditus*.

"Your reasoning doesn't hold up. I'm not the Sicari Lord. I'm the Tribune," he murmured. His penetrating gaze locked with hers, and her heart stopped at the knowledge blazing in his eyes. "You were willing to sacrifice yourself to save me. Tell me why."

Cleo turned her head away from him. If she confessed, he wouldn't let her go. But did she really want to leave? Strong fingers caught her chin and forced her to look at him again. His head descended until his mouth teasingly brushed across hers.

"I want the truth, Cleopatra." His lips trailed fire across her cheek. "Tell me why you were willing to sacrifice yourself to save me."

A tremor lashed through her at the tender way he was kissing her face. First her cheek, then her brow, then her other cheek. *Christus*, the man had no idea how defenseless his kisses made her feel. Or maybe he did. He raised his head.

"Tell me, Cleopatra." It was a quiet command, but a command nonetheless. "Tell me why you were willing to risk your life to save me."

"Because I love you," she rasped, unable to lie anymore. Beneath her palm, she could feel the tension in his body recede as he stared down at her.

"Say it again."

"I love . . . you."

"Was that so difficult?"

The warmth in his voice made her heart skip a beat, and she shook her head. Swallowing hard, she closed her eyes. After Michael, she'd made the conscious decision never to let another man into her heart again. But where Dante was concerned, she'd ignored all the warning signs. Now she was adrift in uncharted waters with only him to cling to. It terrified her. There wasn't a place for her in his life. His mind lightly touched hers before retreating.

"What are you afraid of, *dolce cuore*?" His fingers gently stroked the side of her face in a manner that made her quiver with a longing she didn't know was possible to feel.

"I'm not afr—" He frowned, and she sighed. "It's just that this isn't going to work."

"What won't?"

"Us."

"Because of some ridiculous notion that without special skills you're not Sicari? The fact that you can read my thoughts proves to me you're a Sicari."

His observation caught her by surprise. Why hadn't that occurred to her before? Because she was too busy trying not to fall in love with the guy. She dismissed it with a slight shake of her head.

"All right, we have a connection, but it doesn't mean I have any skills." It was a weak argument, and she knew it. The sardonic gleam in his dark eyes said he knew it, too.

"I love you for who you are, Cleopatra, not what you are."

"*Fine*. But I'm a liability you can't afford."

She met his gaze steadily, opening her thoughts up to the memory of Dante finding her with Ignacio holding a knife to her neck. He blanched slightly, and she knew he'd seen the images in her mind. Determination swept across his face as he shook his head.

"I'm not going to let you use that argument to keep us apart. We'll work it out."

"How? By me not taking on any more assignments?" She winced as he quickly averted his gaze. "That's what I thought."

"I can adapt," he said through clenched teeth as he met her gaze again. "Just because I don't like the thought of you taking on new assignments doesn't mean I'd ever order you not to."

"But it wouldn't stop you from trying to convince me *not* to take them on, would it?" she asked in a fierce voice.

"No more than it would stop you." His words were a dark rumble in his chest as frustration thinned his beautiful mouth. "Finish getting dressed."

His thumb brushed over her lips, and the gentleness in his touch made his command softer than it sounded. Without any other warning, he quickly got out of bed. She stared after him in amazement. That was it? He wasn't going to say anything else to convince her they belonged together? For a brief second she chided herself for being annoyed he'd stopped trying to change her mind. Still, it was impossible not to stare at him in surprise as he reached for his jeans. His gaze caught her, and he nodded at her clothes.

"I suggest you hurry up. Your parents are going to be knocking on your door any minute now."

"How the fuck do you know that?" She stared at him in horror.

"Because I can sense Marcus's presence. Your mother is arguing with him, and he's not happy about whatever she's insisting on," he said dryly as he arched an eyebrow at her. "You're a lot like your mother. The two of you like to get your own way."

Cleo glared at him as she fumbled with her jeans. She wasn't anything like her mother. Okay, maybe she was a little. She winced. Dante was right. She was a lot more like her mother than she cared to admit.

What would her mother think when she found Dante in her apartment? She'd be grilled about it the first chance Atia had. She froze. *Christus*, if her parents realized she and Dante—she refused to finish the thought. He'd broken his vow because of her, and she had no idea how it was going to affect Dante or how her father would react.

It was bad enough Dante was determined to make their relationship more permanent. What he was conveniently forgetting was how it would affect the *Absconditus* and the Order. Worrying about a family made a Sicari Lord vulnerable. And she was certain her mother and father would agree. Her mind stumbled over the fact that she was easily referring to Marcus as her father now.

Although the two of them were a long way from knowing each other well, it was a big step for her to even think of him as her father. Ignacio had always been the father figure in her life. Her throat closed up at the memory of Ignacio's betrayal and then his sacrifice at the Tarpeian Rock.

His actions showed he really had loved her and her mother. It was impossible to forgive him completely, but his willingness to give his life for her mother's made her think less harshly of him. The low chime of the apartment doorbell made her jerk upright. Dante was putting his shoes on and shot her an odd look.

"You'd better go let them in," he said with a quiet determination that put her senses on alert as he tied his shoe. He was up to something.

"But you're not even dressed yet." She eyed him with panic. The thought of him strolling out of her bedroom with her parents in the living room shot her blood pressure up. That sure as hell wouldn't be easy to explain.

"Go."

Again, that steely note of purpose in his voice. It unnerved her. The doorbell rang again, and she blew out a harsh breath then strode from the bedroom. The moment she opened the door, Atia stepped forward and enveloped Cleo in her arms. Over her mother's shoulder, she saw Marcus's stern expression and a flicker of concern in his eyes. Dante was right. The Sicari Lord wasn't all that happy about being here.

"*Carissima.*" Her mother kissed her cheek then, with her hands still grasping Cleo's shoulders, stepped back to eye her carefully. "Are you feeling better? We've been worried about you."

Cleo forced a smile at her mother then stepped aside and gestured for the couple to enter the suite. After she closed the door
behind them, she turned, expecting to see Dante greeting her parents, but he was nowhere in sight. A chill crept over her skin. Fuck,
what was the man up to?

"Cleo, did you hear me?" Atia's voice was tense with emotion,
and Cleo blinked her eyes in confusion.

"I'm sorry, Mother. What?"

"I asked you if you're going to forgive me and come home."

For a moment, Cleo stared at her mother in bewilderment. Forgive her for what? The tight expression of fear on Atia's face made
Cleo wince. After everything that had happened, her mother's revelation a few weeks ago seemed a minor transgression in the overall
scheme of things.

That her mother had lied to her still stung, but she'd offered up
her own life to Nicostratus in exchange for Cleo's. The action only
reinforced her mother's claim that everything she'd ever done was
to keep Cleo safe. Her mother might have made a bad choice by not
telling Cleo that her father was still alive, but she understood her
reasons.

Gabriel's kidnapping had shaped her mother's choices, and Cleo
couldn't fault her for that. If she'd been in her mother's shoes, she
probably would have done the same thing for her child. Her heart
clenched at the thought. As her eyes locked with Atia's, she swallowed hard then moved forward and embraced her. Atia went rigid
for an instant before she hugged Cleo close.

"Oh, *bambina*," Atia sobbed quietly. "If I'd lost you . . ."

"I'm sorry, Mother," she murmured with regret. "I was angry
and stubborn."

"I wouldn't have you any other way." Atia's cheeks were damp as
she stepped back and grasped Cleo's hands tightly. "It's all behind
us now. I'm just grateful you're safe."

"As am I," Marcus said quietly. Cleo turned her head to meet his
brilliant blue gaze. The relief she saw flashing in his eyes warmed
her heart. There was something else in his gaze that said he would
be there for her whenever she needed a friend—or a father.

"Will you come home with us to White Cloud?" Atia asked with quiet excitement. "I know your father . . . Marcus would like to get to know you better."

"I'd like that, too," she said.

A familiar tingle swept across her neck, and she jerked around to see Dante emerging from the bedroom. Painfully aware of her parents' astonishment, she glared at him. Her anger didn't seem to bother him in the least as he moved toward them.

"Eminence. Madame Consul."

Dante bowed slightly in their direction as he came to a halt at Cleo's side. The long, drawn-out silence was awkward as her parents looked at Dante and then her. Extremely uncomfortable, she shot Dante a fierce look before meeting the curiosity in her parents' eyes.

"I suppose you're wondering—"

"I'm sure they've already figured out our secret, *carissima*." Dante's arm slid around her waist and pulled her into his side.

"Secret?" Cleo looked up at him with angry confusion. He didn't look at her. Instead, he bowed his head in Marcus's direction.

"Eminence." Dante drew in a deep breath then exhaled. "I wish to ask your permission to blood bond with your daughter."

Floored, her mouth fell open as she stared up at him. His request had obviously astounded her parents as well. The older couple stood speechless as they stared at the two of them in amazement. Ignoring her parents' surprise, Cleo broke free of Dante's grasp and eyed him with outrage.

"*Christus*, but you've got a pair, don't you?" she snapped.

"I think I answered that question earlier in the bedroom."

Dante's calm reply made Cleo stare at him in wide-eyed horror. Had he really just announced to her parents that they were sleeping together? Obviously that was the conclusion her parents had drawn, considering her mother's loud gasp and the way Marcus was clearing his throat. Not about to argue in front of her parents, she reached out with her thoughts.

"*What in Juno's name do you think you're doing? You just told my parents we were making love a little while ago.*"

"*Exactly.*"

"*What?*"

"*Making love.*" His mouth tilted slightly with amusement. "*It's what people do when they love each other. When they want to share their lives together.*"

"*I've already told you I won't blood bond with you.*"

"*And I said your reasons weren't good enough.*"

"*You need an heir.*"

"*We'll adopt. There are plenty of orphans here in the* Absconditus *who need loving parents.*"

"Deus, *you're a stubborn* bastardo."

"*Not anywhere near as obstinate as you are,* mea amor."

"*You're wasting your time. You have responsibilities, and you can't afford to make me one of them, no matter how much you love me.*"

Dante stared at her in silence for a long moment, not communicating with her at all. Suddenly, his face hardened with a grim resolution that frightened her. He nodded at her then turned to her parents.

"Cleopatra thinks it's impossible for us to be together as long as I'm to be Sicari Lord." Dante's profile resembled a chiseled stone bust as he bowed toward Marcus. "Therefore, I must renounce my role as Tribune and heir to the Sicari Lord title."

Cleo didn't even have to look at her parents to know that they were just as stunned as she was. She stood frozen, unable to believe she'd heard him correctly. The man had lost his fucking mind. He'd just abdicated as the next Sicari Lord. Jupiter's Stone. Who was going to replace him? Did he expect Marcus to continue as leader of the *Absconditus*? She grabbed Dante's arm, her fingers digging into hard muscle.

"Are you insane? You can't do this."

"Yes." He nodded grimly as he peeled her hand off his arm. "I can."

"If you're trying to blackmail me, it's not going to work."

"Not blackmail, *mea amor.* I just don't know of any other way to convince you that you're more important to me than anything or anyone else in the world."

With another slight bow in Marcus's direction, Dante wheeled about on his heel, leaving Cleo and her parents staring after him in shock. The sound of the apartment door closing quietly behind him rang out with a finality that horrified her. He'd given up everything for her. His vow to the *Absconditus* and now his responsibilities as the next Sicari Lord.

It was a sacrifice she couldn't let him make. She bolted after him, the door slamming back against the wall as she ran out of her suite. Dante's long stride had already carried him to the end of the hall, and she raced after him. She caught up with him just as he turned the corner, and in three more quick steps, she planted herself in front of him.

"I won't let you do this," she said fiercely.

"It's already done, *mea amor.*" His fingers left a warm trail across her cheek as he studied her with a resigned look.

"Then undo it," she bit out. "Go back in there and tell Marcus you made a mistake."

"The only mistake I could make is letting you go, *dolce cuore.* Since the only obstacle standing in the way of you bonding with me was my title and responsibilities, I eliminated it."

"But I never said I'd blood bond with you if you weren't my father's heir."

She raked her fingers through her hair with frustration. The only other person she'd ever known who was so inflexible and determined was herself. He was going to be impossible to live with if they bonded. Trepidation flooded her veins. She was crazy to even consider the possibility. But she already was considering it.

"What are you really afraid of, Cleopatra?"

The moment he asked the question, the answer fluttered through her head with the screeching of a flock of birds. She was afraid she wasn't worthy of him. Cleo stared up at him. The love gleaming in the depths of his midnight blue eyes frightened her, too. He'd given up everything for her, simply to prove *he* believed her worthy.

Cleo had no idea whether there was anyone else capable of being the Sicari Lord, but she was certain there would be no one as good at it as Dante. He was born to lead the *Absconditus.* Tension clutched at her muscles as she prepared to speak what she hoped would be a convincing lie.

"The only thing I'm afraid of is what will happen to the *Abscon-*

ditus and the Order if I let you go through with this." The lie made her wince. His stormy blue gaze caught her grimace.

"That's not what you're really afraid of."

"*Fuck*. What more do you want from me?" she snapped. The determination in his eyes ratcheted up the tension locking her muscles into stone.

"The truth." He wasn't going to give up. Her mouth dry, Cleo drew in a deep breath then expelled it harshly as she turned her head away from him.

"I'm afraid of not being worthy of you."

In a split second, Dante crushed her against him. Cleo buried her face in his neck as he held her close. A shudder ripped through him, and she gently stroked the edges of his mind. The depth of love she sensed in him was humbling. She didn't deserve him, but she'd do everything she could to be worthy of him.

"I can't think of any woman more worthy of me."

"Oh, I'm sure there are plenty," she muttered as she pulled away from him slightly to look up at him. "But as Sicari Lord, you're just going to have to put up with me."

"In case you've forgotten, I just walked away from that title." His wry tone made her narrow her gaze at him.

"Well you're going to go right back in there and retract your resignation if you want me to blood bond with you. The Sicari need you. And I *refuse* to be the reason the *Absconditus* and the Order fall—"

She didn't get the opportunity to finish, as his mouth slanted roughly over hers. It was a kiss of possession, but it held a promise of commitment that no one had ever made to her before. The kiss deepened as her mouth parted beneath his, and his tongue mated with hers in a fiery dance that sent a white-hot heat crashing its way into every cell in her body. Desire exploded in her belly, and she moaned as an erotic image took shape in her head. An image she knew wasn't hers. It accelerated her heart to an unbelievable pace. *Deus*, she wanted him. Needed to show him with her body how much she loved him. Adored him. Bedroom. Her bedroom. The sooner the better. Dante's body suddenly shook with laughter as his mouth left hers to brush across her cheek.

"What?" she asked as she threw back her head to look up at him.

"Your parents," he groaned softly. "They're still in your suite."

"Fuck," she muttered with frustration.

"An appropriate commentary on *both* situations." His dark chuckle of amusement made her cup his face in her hands. As much as she wanted him at this very instant, she knew they had a lifetime of lovemaking ahead of them. His mind stroked hers in silent agreement. She smiled at him, her fingers rubbing against his mouth.

"I love you, Dante."

"And I you, *carissima*," he murmured as he flooded her head with more images of exactly how he intended to prove his love over and over again.

Chapter 27

"MY life for your life."

Cleo trembled slightly as the sound of her voice rang out in unison with Dante's. She'd witnessed numerous blood bonding rituals, but the words had never resonated so strongly with her as they did now. Her gaze met that of the *Absconditus*'s newest Sicari Lord as they held hands in front of the roughly hewn stone altar in the guild's ceremonial hall. Concern flickered in Dante's dark blue eyes the moment she shivered. Cleo willingly opened her mind to him.

"I'm fine. Just nerves."

"You'll fearlessly storm into a Praetorian snake pit, but you're afraid of a small cut on your palm?" Cleo rolled her eyes at his gentle teasing.

"Smart ass."

Her affectionate exasperation earned her an invisible swat on her rear. Startled, she drew in a sharp breath to keep from crying out in surprise. The wicked smile curving his lips made her heart skip a beat, but when the mischief in his eyes quickly faded to reveal his love, it left her breathless. Dante's hands tightened on hers as an overwhelming sensation of joy and happiness pulsed between them.

Turning her head back toward the altar, Cleo watched her mother reverently unwrap the Dagger of Cassiopeia from its velvet scarf. The *Prima Consul*'s careful movements emphasized the underlying solemnity of the happy occasion. Marcus stood beside her mother as an official witness to the ceremony at Dante's request. Her parents officiating at her blood bonding ceremony. It was a moment Cleo would never have dreamed possible until a matter of days ago.

Marcus met her gaze and smiled. It was easy to smile back. She'd spent time over the past two weeks getting to know her father, and she liked him. Her gaze shifted back to her mother. There was still tension between her parents, and for the first time since discovering her father was alive, Cleo found herself hoping Atia and Marcus would find the happiness denied to them for years.

With the Dagger of Cassiopeia resting on her fingers, Atia lifted the blade and held it up high. Eyes closed, Atia's lips moved in a silent prayer before she offered the blade to Cleo. Without hesitation, Cleo accepted the dagger then locked her gaze with Dante's.

"My heart for your heart," she said in a strong voice.

Withdrawing her hand from Dante's, she clenched her jaw and dragged the dagger's finely honed edge across her palm in a swift, deep stroke. Nerve endings cried out in vicious protest, but the pain faded quickly to a minor throb. His touch gentle, Dante took the blade from her.

"My blood for your blood," Dante said quietly as he cut his palm then silently added an endearment to the traditional vow. "Mea amor."

He clasped her bleeding hand in his, the blood from their lacerations mixing together in a physical manner that represented their commitment to each other. Atia beamed at them as she handed a strip of linen to Dante. His movements deft, he wrapped one end of the cloth around Cleo's wrist then over their clasped hands, binding her to him before he released the material. Using the remaining strip of cloth, Cleo repeated the movement and bound Dante to her in the same fashion. Her heart pounding, she looked up at him with a smile.

"Our blood and hearts are one."

Atia made a quiet sound, and Cleo turned her head to see her mother's eyes glistening with tears before she cleared her throat.

"Two Sicari hearts that once beat alone now beat as one." Atia smiled at them as she grasped their joined hands. "Let all who stand with you today know that Jupiter and Juno have smiled on you. May the love you share be as strong and deep as the love of Maximus and Cassiopeia."

As Atia finished speaking, applause echoed in the ceremonial hall. Cleo and Dante turned their heads at the noise, laughing at the enthusiastic reception to their bonding. With a gentle tug on their bound hands, Dante forced Cleo to look at him.

"There's never been a woman more beautiful or more *worthy* of being the Sicari Lord's wife, *carissima*," he said softly.

Cleo's throat closed up with emotion, and she wondered if it were possible to die from sheer happiness. His free arm wrapping around her, Dante pulled her tight and captured her mouth in a hard kiss. The moment he lifted his head, well-wishers surged forward. Her parents were the first to congratulate them as they circled the stone altar. Cleo smiled at her mother before Atia pulled her close in a tight hug.

"I couldn't be happier for you, *carissima*," her mother whispered in Cleo's ear. "He's a good man, and it's obvious he loves you very much."

"Thank you, Mother."

Atia stepped back and touched her cheek as Marcus stepped forward to hug Cleo and press a gentle kiss to her brow. "I expect you to keep my successor on his toes, *cara*."

"I don't think there's any question she'll do just that," Dante said with a grin as he released Atia from a warm hug. Cleo didn't respond. She simply arched her eyebrows and smiled sweetly at her new husband.

"Something tells me she's already plotting your surrender." Marcus chuckled.

"I surrendered to her a long time ago." Dante leaned into her and brushed his mouth across her cheek. The tenderness in his voice was a warm breeze on her skin.

"As I knew you would," a gravelly voice echoed over her shoulder. Cleo immediately turned her head to see Placido smiling at them with delight. With her free hand, she warmly hugged the elderly Sicari.

"If I were younger, *bella*, I would have made our newest Sicari

Lord work much harder to earn your affection." Placido playfully smacked Dante on the cheek in a gesture of fondness. A broad grin on his face, Dante squeezed the shoulder of the old warrior with his hand.

"You might have made me work harder, but I *still* would have won her heart." Dante's words made Placido wag a finger at him.

"Confidence can be a dangerous thing, my boy," Placido warned with a chuckle before he turned back to Cleopatra. "If I were—"

Angry shouts outside the ceremonial hall interrupted Placido's admonishment, followed by the harsh ring of swords crashing together. A woman screamed, and less than a second later a man stumbled into the hall. Blood darkened his fingers from where he pressed his hands against a wound in his side. His sword dragging on the ground behind him, the man staggered forward until he sank to his knees.

"*Christus*, it's the Praetorian from the Tarpeian Rock," Cleo gasped as she looked at Dante's grim features.

Another scream echoed in the hall, and Cleo jerked her gaze back toward the Praetorian to see Marta racing forward to shield the man with her body from two Sicari fighters. Dante didn't answer but strode toward the wounded Praetorian, pulling Cleo along with him. One of the fighters dragged Marta away from the man she was protecting, while the other prepared to deliver a lethal blow.

"*Stop.*"

Dante's voice wasn't loud, but it rang out clearly in the large room. The fighter appeared ready to protest, before he reluctantly lowered his sword. A frantic look on her face, Marta twisted free of her captor and rushed to the wounded Praetorian's side. She whispered something to him, but the man shook his head viciously.

"I wish to speak to the Sicari Lord," he rasped. "Where is he?"

"You're hurt." Dante turned his head toward the healer standing on the edge of the circle of people surrounding the fallen Praetorian. "Noemi. See to his wound. Angelo, you and Samuel take him—"

"*No.*" The Praetorian almost shouted the word. "I've come to speak with the Sicari Lord."

Desperation lingered in the man's voice as he rejected Dante's offer of help. Still bound to Dante by the blood bond cloth ties, Cleo quickly unwrapped the linen from her wrist. When he murmured a protest of surprise, she carried his hand to her mouth and kissed his fingertips.

"You have a job to do." Her quiet explanation made him cup her cheek.

"*I love you, Cleopatra.*"

"*I know.*"

Turning back to the Praetorian crumpled on the floor, Dante knelt down so he was eye level with the man. "Either you're a very brave man, Praetorian, or a fool. Which is it?"

"A little . . . of both, I think." The wounded man grimaced as he shifted himself up into a sitting position. "Now take me to see . . . the Sicari Lord. I have a proposition for him."

"*I* am the Sicari Lord, Praetorian."

"Vorenus?" There was a distinct note of regret in the injured man's voice, as if he expected Dante to tell him Marcus was dead and the news would sadden him.

"He has turned over his duties to me."

"Then he still lives."

"I do." Marcus stepped forward into the Praetorian's line of sight. "What is your name, Praetorian?"

"Verdi. Draco Verdi."

"Tell me, Draco Verdi," Marcus said quietly. "What is so important that you were willing to risk your life by entering the *Absconditus* to find me?"

"The *Tyet of Isis.*" The Praetorian's words made Dante inhale a quick breath, and he shot a look up at his mentor, who had gone rigid.

"What about it?" Marcus asked quietly.

"I wish to return the contents." Verdi's face contorted with pain as he shifted his body slightly.

Dante met Marcus's skeptical gaze, while a murmur of disbelief swept through the circle of warriors surrounding them. Placido emerged from the crowd like a boxer charging into the center of a boxing ring.

"Don't trust him, boy," the old Sicari Lord snapped with the vigor of a man half his age. "Praetorians can't be trusted."

"Draco Verdi is as much a man of honor as any Sicari here."

Marta stepped forward to glare at the ancient warrior. "I vouch for him."

Placido eyed her with a mix of irritation and assessment at her defiant manner. When it was clear she wasn't about to retreat beneath the old Sicari Lord's harsh stare, Placido bowed slightly in Marta's direction with a begrudging respect. A quick glance over his shoulder told Dante that his bride was as bewildered as he was by Marta's championship of the Praetorian. Beside him, Marcus bent down to whisper in Dante's ear.

"Trust isn't the issue right now. The man will die if Noemi doesn't heal him soon. Whether he's lying or telling the truth, we need him alive to find out what he really wants."

"Agreed," Dante said with a sharp nod. He turned his head back to the wounded Praetorian. "Our healer will tend to your wound, and then we'll talk."

"I don't—"

"The only reason you're still alive, Verdi, is because of your assistance to Vorenus at the Tarpeian Rock." Dante eyed the man harshly.

"My life . . . is of little consequence . . . unless I end the fighting between us." Verdi reached for the breast pocket of his leather jacket, and two swords immediately pressed against his throat. The Praetorian closed his eyes then looked at Dante. "I brought it with me."

Dante stiffened at the soft statement and stretched out his hand toward the man's pocket. Strong fingers gripped his wrist. Startled, he met Marcus's gaze.

"One can never tell where a serpent might hide. The *Absconditus* cannot afford to lose its leader."

For a moment, Dante thought of protesting. He'd sensed nothing malevolent from the Praetorian, but he also recognized the wisdom of Marcus's words. If Verdi excelled at hiding his thoughts, the man could have come here with assassination in mind. The Praetorian could have easily dusted the lining of his pocket with a poison that would penetrate the skin to reach the bloodstream.

"My word . . . I mean no harm," Verdi rasped with another contorted expression.

"We shall see, Praetorian." Slowly, Marcus reached into the man's jacket and pulled out a box.

The circle surrounding them tightened as Dante and Marcus both stood upright. Dante frowned as the two of them studied the box. His mentor looked up at him as if to ask permission, and Dante nodded sharply. His mouth taut with tension, Marcus carefully opened the case. Inside was a crumbling piece of parchment and two flash drives.

"Jupiter's Stone," Marcus breathed with amazement.

"To earn . . . your . . . trust." The Praetorian's breathing had grown increasingly labored, and in the next moment he slumped to the floor of the ceremonial hall.

"*Draco*." Although Marta's exclamation was soft, the panic in her voice made several of the fighters in the circle eye her with suspicion and disapproval.

"Samuel. Angelo. Take him to the infirmary. Noemi, do what you can." Before Dante had even finished speaking, two fighters stepped out of the crowd. As they carried the unconscious Praetorian out of the ceremonial hall, the healer and Marta followed close on their heels.

"Marta." The woman halted the moment Dante said her name, but she didn't turn to face him. "Do you know how the Praetorian gained access to the compound?"

She didn't move for a long moment. Then, as if it pained her to do so, Marta turned around to face Dante with her shoulders back and head high. "*I* let him into the complex."

Her answer didn't surprise Dante. He'd assumed as much. "And your reason for such a treasonous act?"

"Draco saved my life when I was in the . . . he protected me after . . ." The moment her voice faltered, Dante clenched his jaw with regret. He should have questioned her in private and not subjected her to an open inquisition.

"We can discuss this—"

"I have nothing to hide." Marta's chin tilted upward with defiance. "Draco Verdi protected me while I was in that Praetorian hellhole. He's a good man, and I'd trust him with my life. Draco came here to offer the Sicari a truce. He wouldn't let me be his messenger. He insisted on doing it in person."

"So you let him past our defenses." Placido's accusation was harsh as he chastised her from the edge of the circle of fighters. At Dante's hard look, the ancient warrior batted the air with his hands in a gesture of exasperation.

"Yes, and I'd do it again," Marta snapped as she sent the old Sicari Lord a rebellious look. "He knew there would be skeptics, and he believed putting his life on the line was the only way to convince Sicari such as you that he was sincere."

Placido flushed at Marta's fierce response and looked away from her defiant gaze. Satisfied that she'd silenced the old Sicari Lord, Marta turned back to Dante.

"Draco is the leader of a large contingent within the Collegium that was on the verge of overthrowing Nicostratus before he was killed. With the Patriarch gone, not even Monsignor Gregori has the power to prevent Draco from extending his hand in peace and friendship to us." She fixed her gaze on Marcus. "You above all other Sicari should believe his sincerity, *il mio signore*. He helped save your life at the Tarpeian Rock not too long ago."

Marcus met her gaze steadily as he nodded in agreement. "It's true that without Verdi's help I would have found it difficult to defeat the Praetorian Dominus."

Hands clasped behind his back, Dante's palm stung where the Dagger of Cassiopeia had sliced through his skin. It was a vivid reminder of Cleopatra and their bond. He reached out with his thoughts to brush against hers. The warmth of his wife's reflections blended with his although she offered him no advice, only her gentle support.

"Under the circumstances, I'll postpone any decision as to your punishment until *after* I've spoken with Verdi about his proposal." The flash of relief in Marta's eyes made him realize that despite her show of fearless defiance, she was more frightened than anyone suspected. "Since it's obvious you're concerned for the man's welfare, go see how he's doing."

Marta nodded her thanks before spinning around and racing out of the room. As she disappeared through the doorway, a low rumble rolled through the large hall. It was a sound of skepticism battling with hope. Beside him, Marcus cleared his throat.

"Did someone forget to order wine for the occasion, or am I mistaken?"

The retired Sicari Lord's gaze scanned the faces in the crowd that surrounded them. Almost immediately, everyone's mood lightened and the guests broke apart to head toward the buffet that had been set up at the farthest end of the great hall. Marcus turned to Dante, his expression grave.

"The document and flash drives must be destroyed."

"*You can't do that*," Atia exclaimed quietly as she moved to stand at Marcus's side. Placido, Lysander, and Cleopatra completed the circle. "As *Prima Consul*, I can't allow it."

"Would you jeopardize the possibility of peace between the Praetorians and the Sicari?" Marcus blew out a harsh breath as he met Atia's gaze.

"You can't possibly expect me to just stand by while you destroy a document the Sicari have been searching for since the time of Maximus."

"It's not your decision to make," Lysander said in a matter-of-fact tone.

"And exactly who do you think gets to make the decision?" Atia arched her eyebrow in an imperious manner and glared at her *Celeris*.

"It's the Sicari Lord's responsibility," Marcus responded in a gentle, yet firm, tone.

Snapping the box closed, Marcus handed it to Dante. His mentor's words emphasized to Dante what he already knew. The decision to destroy or preserve the document was his decision and his alone. As the reigning Sicari Lord, his word was law not only in the *Absconditus*, but within the Order itself. Even before Marcus indicated his opinion about what to do with the parchment, Dante had known what was at stake. The document and the digital files had to be destroyed if there was to be peace between the Sicari and Praetorians.

"Then Dante must choose to keep the document." Placido's voice was inflexible steel. "We can't trust a Praetorian to tell us the truth, let alone suggest there be a truce between us."

"Can we afford *not* to believe him?" Dante said as his gaze met the old warrior's.

The ancient Sicari Lord sneered with disgust but didn't reply.

Dante turned his head to meet the inscrutable gaze of his half brother. Resignation stretched the scarred tissue on Lysander's face taut, emphasizing his grotesque disfigurement. If anyone had reason to despise the Praetorians it was him.

"I don't think you really have a choice." His half brother's response made Atia and Placido both gasp with outrage, but Lysander didn't bother to acknowledge their objections. "As long as that document exists, there will always be someone trying to steal it and solve its puzzle. And that *someone* could just as easily be a Sicari as a Praetorian."

"Verdi brought us a peace offering." Marcus's forefinger tapped against the lid of the box the Praetorian had risked his life to deliver. "If the man is telling the truth about wanting an armistice between us, then we can't possibly keep the document or the digital files."

Throughout the debate, Cleopatra had remained a warm, comforting presence at Dante's side. His gaze didn't leave the box he held as he reached for his wife's hand. Their fingers laced together until the wounds on their palms connected again. A pulse of energy zipped its way up his arm, and he waited for her to say something. When she didn't speak, he gently squeezed her hand.

"*You have nothing to say, mea amor?*" He turned his head toward her. A warm, loving smile curved her mouth.

"*You've already made your decision, and that's good enough for me. It's in the best interest of all Sicari.*" There was a slight pause in her thoughts, before her eyes darkened with emotion. "*Including me.*"

Her silent response was all the more reassuring because it illustrated she'd accepted that her Sicari heritage wasn't defined by her abilities, but by her heart. Dante raised her hand to press his lips against the warm skin below her knuckles. He turned his attention back to the small group surrounding him.

"The matter can wait until tomorrow. Today is my blood bonding day, and I intend to enjoy it with my wife."

Atia and Placido sputtered with outrage, but Dante didn't give them a chance to form a protest. Instead, he slid the slim box into the breast pocket of his jacket and pulled Cleopatra away from the group. As they walked away, Marcus followed them. When they were out of earshot of the others, the Sicari Lord coughed slightly.

"Might I have a word with Cleopatra? In private?" At Marcus's request, Dante smiled and with a nod left the two of them alone. As Marcus watched his successor walk away, he clasped his hands behind his back.

"He's a good man. I'm happy for both of you."

"Thank you."

Cleopatra's voice held a note of emotion that Marcus hoped would evolve into something deeper between the two of them. The short time they'd spent together had created a tenuous bond between them, and he wanted to strengthen that connection. It was the main reason he'd asked to talk with her alone. He cleared his throat, uncertain where to begin. It was a strange sensation, but ever since renewing his relationship with Atia, he'd been feeling unsettled in so many ways.

"You want to know if I approve of you and my mother getting back together again."

Marcus found it impossible not to smile. Blunt and to the point. It was a trait of hers he'd found disconcerting at first. But he'd quickly come to appreciate it. There were so many things about his daughter that he had learned to enjoy in the short amount of time they'd spent together.

"Yes." He nodded his head.

"I heartily approve," Cleopatra said. "Mother loves you, and in spite of everything that's happened over the last several weeks, she's happier than I've ever seen her."

Marcus glanced over his shoulder at his wife, who was deep in a heated discussion with Lysander and Placido. "I'm afraid she's unhappy with me at the moment."

"She'll get over it." Cleopatra tipped her head sideways to look around his shoulder. "Although not quite yet. Here she comes."

"What in Juno's name *were* you thinking?" Atia exclaimed as she came to a halt next to the two of them and glared up at Marcus. "Dante listens to you. He's going to destroy the document based on your suggestion."

"Dante made up his mind *before* anyone told him what he should do." Cleopatra's quiet words made both Marcus and Atia look at her in surprise. Their daughter shook her head. "No, it's not transference from the blood bond. Dante and I have been linked for some time now. I don't know how or why, just that it is. But I do know he made up his mind about the document before he even sent Marta after Verdi."

"He's going to destroy it, isn't he?" Atia breathed with a sigh of grief.

"Let it go, Mother. You can't win all the time. Besides, losing can actually be fun on occasion." The devilment in Cleopatra's violet eyes made Marcus grimace slightly, while a puzzled expression darkened Atia's features. Laughing, Cleo stepped forward to kiss her mother's cheek, then did the same to Marcus. The gesture of affection made his throat close with emotion. Mischief lighting her face, she looked at her mother. "I'm going to leave the two of you alone. Father has something he wants to discuss with you, and I'm missing my own blood bonding festivities."

As his daughter grinned and sauntered off in search of her husband, Marcus and Atia were left to stare after her.

"Did she just call you *Father*?" The wonderment in Atia's voice matched his own sense of astonishment.

"Yes." Still amazed by his daughter's display of affection, he shook his head in bemusement. He entwined his fingers with Atia's and looked down into her luminous gaze. "Come, I have something for you."

"But the reception—"

"They don't need us," he said firmly and pulled her out of the ceremonial hall.

"At least tell me where we're going."

"Back in time."

A small smile tilted his mouth upward. Her hand clasped tightly in his, he forced her to follow him at a quick pace down the corridor. Atia muttered something beneath her breath as they walked toward her rooms, but he couldn't quite make out her words. Several moments later, he ushered her into the suite and closed the door behind them. Exasperation flashing in her gray eyes, Atia faced him with her hands on her hips.

"Do you want to tell me why you dragged me away from my daughter's blood bonding celebration?"

"*Our* daughter." His firm response made her wince with regret, and she nodded.

"Why did you pull me away from *our* daughter's blood bonding celebration?"

"Because we have a celebration of our own to attend."

"Celebration? You're not making any sense."

Marcus walked to the bookcase against the wall and picked up the velvet-covered blade he'd placed there earlier in the day. He turned to face Atia then slowly pulled the weapon from its soft protective sleeve. The rubies in the blade's hilt sparkled in the room's subdued lighting. The moment she saw the ceremonial dagger, she drew in a sharp breath of surprise. Her reaction made it clear she recognized the blade they'd used in their blood bonding ceremony years ago.

"Tonight I intend to make you mine all over again," he said with soft determination. With a quick movement he flipped the blade and sliced open the old scar in the palm of his hand. "My life for your life."

"What are you doing?" Atia gasped and took a quick step forward to grab his hand. "We blood bonded a long time ago."

"But that bond wasn't strong enough, was it?" He handed her the blade, hilt first. "This time I want it to be unbreakable, because I'm never going to let you go again."

She didn't move for a long, quiet moment, and for several seconds he thought she would refuse. Slowly, Atia took the dagger from him and flinched as she cut into the scar on her palm.

"My heart for your heart," she whispered. "My blood for your blood."

As they clasped their bleeding hands together, Marcus bent his head and kissed her. "*I love you, Atia. I'll never stop loving you, carissima.*"

Beneath his mouth, her lips were soft and compliant as he deepened their kiss. A searing heat registered in his hand where their blood merged to become one. Their bond in the past had been strong, but as her energy wound its way through his blood, he knew their renewed commitment to each other was indestructible. With a tender bite against her lower lip, he made her open her mouth to him. In a split second, his tongue mated with hers as the sweet taste of her assaulted his senses. Desire surged through him, and he was hard in an instant. *Christus*, if the woman only knew what she did to him.

"*I do know.*" The soft whisper of her laughter echoed in his head, tugging a responding laugh from him as he lifted his head.

"You're far too confident, *mea amor*. I think it's time I show you how difficult it is for you to resist me."

"A challenge." Her voice was soft with a streak of mischief running through it.

"No, *carissima*. A promise." He smiled as he gently pulled her toward the bedroom. "We belong to each other, body, mind, and heart."

She went eagerly with him, and they were almost at her bedroom door when she drew up short. "*Cleo.*"

"What about her?"

"I need to tell her . . ."

"If you're worried she won't approve, don't be," he murmured as he trailed his forefinger down the side of her neck. "She's already said she does."

"She did?" The bemused note in Atia's voice made him grin.

"Yes, just a short while ago," he said patiently. Her eyes widened as she stared up at him. A moment later her gray eyes narrowed with a small amount of irritation.

"You're manipulating me again, Marcus Vorenus."

"*No one* has *ever* manipulated you, *dolce cuore*." For a moment it looked like she was going to argue with him. He quirked an eyebrow at her, and she laughed.

"You're impossible."

"Which is one of the reasons why you love me." Marcus raised their clasped hands to his mouth and kissed her fingertips. "Come, I have a present for you. Close your eyes."

Gently, he guided her to the bedroom door and opened it. "Look, *mea amor*."

The scent of roses filled the air as she obeyed his command. Her gasp of delight when she saw the room gave him the same immense pleasure it had more than thirty years ago when he'd surprised her in the same manner. This time it had been more difficult to keep her from discovering the surprise. But the expression of joy on her face as she stared at the deep red rose petals sprinkled across the floor and the bed made his efforts worth it.

"When?" she whispered.

"I made arrangements with one of the *Vigilavi*. Do you like it?" Marcus knew what her answer would be, but he wanted to hear her say it.

"It's . . . it's beautiful, *caro*. Thank you." Atia's gaze met his, and a sultry look darkened her gray eyes. It was a look he knew he would never be able to resist. He pulled her deeper into the bedroom, closing the door behind him.

"Then thank me properly," he said with a wicked grin.

She laughed then willingly obeyed the Sicari Lord's command.